PRAISE FOR

RUTHLESS

"Ruthless is a beautiful companion to Unbetrothed, giving us an exciting glimpse into the life of Beatriz's mother, Cottia. Yamnitz dazzles with immersive description, thrilling action, and a splash of romance. The story also carries a beautiful faith metaphor, reminding the reader that change is always within reach. This was an enchanting tale from beginning to end and I enjoyed another journey into the world of the Agata Sea."

~**Ashley Bustamante,** author of the Color Theory trilogy

"Fans of no-spice romance with a dash of darker themes will love this book about an assassin changed by the unlikely friendship of a prince who can see beyond a person's past. The banter, the one-horse moments, and the Latin vibes will keep you turning pages late into the night."

~**C. F. E. Black,** author of The Starlit Prince

UNBETROTHED

It is overall a fun read for readers who like their fantasy mixed with a bit of romance.

~**Kirkus Reviews**

Candice paints a colorful Latin fantasy in *Unbetrothed*. It's a journey of change for a giftless princess and an enemy prince who must overcome their shortfalls and secrets if their countries hope to have a future. A definite read for fans of fantasy.

~Morgan L. Busse

Award-winning author of the Ravenwood Saga and Skyworld series

Unbetrothed is an enchanting debut enriched with adventure, love, and a pinch of latin flair. From the start, Yamnitz creates an inviting, magical world that will easily draw readers in. With its poetic prose and engaging plot, *Unbetrothed* is sure to be a favorite for many readers to come.

~V. Romas Burton

Award-winning author of Heartmender

Magical. *Unbetrothed* is an action-packed gem with a cast of complex characters that kept me guessing, and the unique twist of Yamintz's world-building, tinted with a Latin flair, captured my heart. A blend of The Selection Series, Hunger Games intensity, and imagination of The Story Peddler, the story takes you on Princess Beatrice's quest for identity, purpose, and love—in a way you won't soon forget.

~Sandra Fernandez Rhoads

Award-winning author of Mortal Sight

Soli Deo Gloria

ASSASSINS RISE

CANDICE PEDRAZA YAMNITZ

CONCEPCIÓN PRESS

Edited by Lydia Craft, Amber Lambda, Sarah Everest, Claire Kohler

Cover and interior design by Candice Pedraza Yamnitz Illustrations by Candice Pedraza Yamnitz

Title: Assassins Rise / Candice Pedraza Yamnitz | Audience: Ages 13+. | Summary: Seventeen-year-old assassin Cottia is desperate to leave behind the work she's been forced into.
Her lord offers freedom in exchange for one last hit. The assignment is to start a war by killing a target during the Giddelian prince's betrothal selection ceremony.
When the prince uncovers her identity, he offers her a new opportunity. Will his invitation grant her freedom from the notorious underlord?

ISBN: 979-8-9997479-1-4 (paperback)

ISBN: 979-8-3303-4019-4 (hardcover)

Subjects: Young Adult -- Fiction. | Royalty -- Fiction. | Teen & Young Adult Fantasy Romance

MAP OF THE AGATA SEA REGION

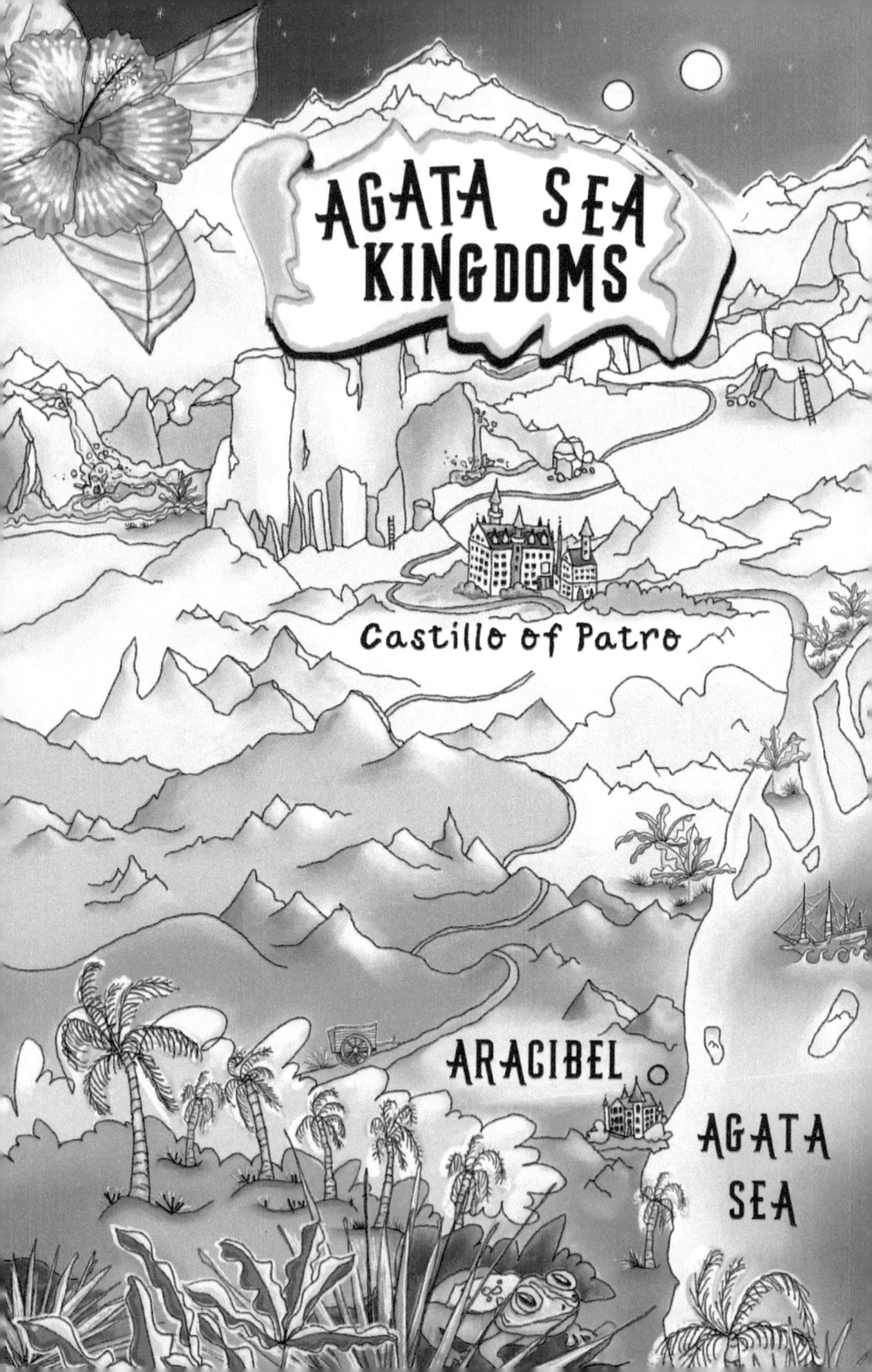

PART 1

RUTHLESS

CHAPTER I
COTTIA

THE SIGNAL WOULD COME shortly. Until then I hung in a dark tree outside a castle, searching for a getaway. But the lone horse and carriage bumping along the road below wouldn't be enough. I lived with invisible strings tethered to my heart and limbs like a puppet manipulated by a puppeteer, forced to complete my assignment no matter my thoughts on my master's bidding. My only consolation for a job well done would be to race back to the castillo—my prison.

Escape had been an idea in my mind since I turned seven years old. I rubbed at a puckered scar, along my wrist, from those young times when I hadn't yet grown into my ability to heal my own wounds with a touch. Back then I thought running away would be as simple as packing a sack and leaving. Hundreds of attempts later, Whyzer Patro made it evident that I could never disappear from his presence. He had burned his brand on my upper arm and could find me through our connection. Anytime he drew near, he could control my every move.

Now, at seventeen-years-old, I camped out in the tallest branches of a tree, spying on Señor Pascual. The whyzer's last collector was left for dead when Señor Pascual refused to pay the fee to be a part of the Black Knight's Brigade—a dignified name for the clandestine work the whyzer devised. To me that meant Señor Pascual decided to bow out of the cause or ... he grew a conscience.

Let him leave, I thought to myself, but Whyzer Patro's ego wouldn't abide such a slight. The last collector who came to pick up the dues still recovered from a beating supposedly administered by Pascual.

Whyzer Patro's words echoed through my mind, "The backers all understood that once in the brigade, there is no leaving unless death intervenes."

If death didn't intervene fast enough, I would become death itself. I tugged my black hood over my forehead, adjusted the leather vest over my torso, and hiked up my boots, making sure branches hadn't caught in my clothes. In order to do my job, I had to be like a cat on the prowl. Soon it would be time for me to drop from my perch.

The night kept me in shadow and only allowed me to see what the torchlight chose to grace. On the outer wall, a guard passed near me every hour. One other guard stood in a corner, keeping post. The front gate remained shut, but soon a messenger would arrive, allowing me access into the castle.

The tower where Señor Pascual slept remained dark, not from him sleeping. I'd been in the tree long enough for my feet to have lost blood circulation and to have seen the bald man in the courtyard prancing about his guests. He'd need a torch to return to his quarters.

The moon rose a fraction, cascading its pale light onto broad leaves, stone, and the forest floor. I caught a glint of light reflecting off a metal object to my left. It was the signal.

I pushed to my feet, caught a bough above to balance on the thin branch beneath me, and made my way toward the center of the tree. The climb proved easy enough. I dropped and landed in a crouch.

My boots flew me over the sparse grass, and my cape clung to me like a shadow. When I reached my associate, José, he flashed a shiny tooth and the rest of his malicious face remained in darkness. He was part of the Black Knight's squad from Himzo, the group with the least scruples. I kept my chin high, showing none of my cards. Any sign of weakness and this crook would exploit it.

"The man will take you in his cart." José's snake-like voice pricked the hairs on my neck.

"Any chance he'll betray us?" I asked.

Trembling, the man with the cart in the shadows smelled of sweat and all things cowardly.

José neared me, revealing his straight nose, thick lashes over beady eyes, and the thin mustache tracing full lips. "No." He broke into a wicked grin that complemented his features. "The man knows the stakes. The rest of the fellows are with our new friend's family." He clicked his tongue to add meaning to his statement.

A beat passed when I could have sliced José with my gaze.

Of course, José probably would have mistaken my stare for a flirtation. It wasn't. With efficient strides, I crossed to the man's cart and lifted the rough-spun blanket to find bread and wine spread across the bottom. The older man shook as he cleared up a sliver of space for me to fit. A yeasty aroma filled my nose as I squeezed in. The bread's heat bled through my cloak and caused sweat to form under my armpits and lower back. José took an extra loaf with full cheer. He bit off a hunk and chewed with smacking lips as I covered myself with the cloth.

"Make it quick," José whispered over me through my covering. "The Black Knight doesn't like when you play with your victims."

I rolled my eyes and kept my mouth firmly shut. What he referred to was an incident where I messed up. These jobs brought me no pleasure. I nearly got myself caught because of a horrid miscalculation. It took me days to speak again after being choked. Heat burned up my neck even remembering that day.

The cart rumbled and bumped through the forest. When we hit the stone road, the cart's rattle became deafening. We stopped while the older man chatted with the guard. Sweat slickened my back and my heart thumped with adrenaline. If the man decided to betray us, I'd be gutted before I could respond.

Rumbles continued, and I let out a blessed breath. We made it into Señor Pascual's castle. The moment we entered the building, light shone through the cracks along the edges of the wool blanket. I wouldn't risk sparking my ability until the old man unveiled the cart.

Though most of my gifting marks remained hidden beneath my clothes, the light from my knuckles would shine enough to give someone pause. Why would a glow come from a bread and wine cart? Everyone in the Agata Sea region understood that a strange glow meant a gifting was in play. A gifting could range from as useless as making music out of thin air to as useful as healing with a touch. I had the latter, except instead of healing I killed.

Minutes later, the man yanked the blanket off me. I got a good look into two fearful brown eyes.

The man's combed-over chestnut hair partially hid how it thinned, and the thickness of his mustache made his double chin more pronounced. "Please, *señorita*, don't hurt my family."

I nodded at him, not wanting the man to turn me in but also not willing to lie. José's fellows had a bad habit of leaving their wards a little battered. While I did jobs, his crew relished their work.

Taking in the scene, I peered at the shelves laden with food and jars. He'd brought us to a large storeroom where he replenished the drinks.

"Go left. The *señor* should be up on the second floor shortly." He kept his focus on his wine.

Tiptoeing, I slipped out and sneaked up a narrow stairwell to the second floor. Torches lit the passage above, revealing gilded portraits of refined people on chiseled stone walls. Red carpet lined the center of the corridor, muffling my steps as I explored. I opened one door to the right and got a glimpse of a wooden horse perfect for a small child to sit upon. My throat dried as an image of my childhood flashed in my mind when my sister and I pretended to be explorers.

Whyzer Patro hadn't told me that Señor Pascual had children. I exited and opened the double doors in the center of the passage. This time light reflected off a four-poster bed covered with curtains.

Beds made perfect hiding spots. They blocked my skin's glow, made it easy to relax while I waited, and allowed the victim to enter the room all the way before I did the deed.

I leapt onto the bed and sparked my gifting. Warmth tingled from my chest to my fingertips. Energy pulsed to whatever living thing stood within five arm spans, revealing no souls lurked anywhere nearby.

The golden halo emanating from my hands lit up brown covers, the lumps for pillows, and a small stuffed horse, a child's plaything similar to one I had growing up. My heart sank into my stomach. I couldn't breathe.

Footfalls stomped somewhere outside the quarters. Their heat radiated through my senses like sparks in the distance. Floorboards creaked outside the double doors, and so did playful laughter in high pitched cadences.

My palms slickened with sweat. I lifted my hands to the side of the bed, facing the doors. A gap in the curtains now threatened to give away my hiding spot, so I'd have to act fast.

The door opened. Instead of even footfalls, a stampede of choppy steps drew near.

Giggles danced in the air.

"Papá, do it again!" a tiny voice shouted.

Heavy footfalls stomped with a strange growling that sounded more playful than threatening.

Two sets of screeches pierced the air, and then came a tumble of easy giggles.

It reminded me of my little sister and I before death claimed our papá. Tears moistened my cheeks. I swiped them with my forearm, trying to keep my arm muscles from shaking.

The curtains ripped open.

A small face with a curly mop of brown hair stared up at me. "Who's that?"

I ducked on the other side of the bed. Four bodies pulsed in my senses, two of them very small.

"Go get the guard," said a deep male voice.

"Papá, she's gone."

"Why don't you wait for me in your room?"

"But Papá, I need to get Caballito."

"No buts."

All the people left but the large one. The door slammed shut and the latch clicked. I had but minutes to get the job done.

"Not in front of my family," the deep male voice said. This certainly was Señor Pascual.

I remained on the floor, skin aglow, my gift feeling the quickening pulse at the man's neck. Without hesitating, I squeezed at the vein with my gift, but my grip faltered.

"Will you tell Whyzer Patro that the Ancient One is real?"

The energy flowing from my body went out again like little fingers prodding, grappling with veins inside the man's body. At this short distance, I didn't need to see him to kill him.

"Your power tickles at my neck, but it won't work on me. Will you tell him that the Ancient One will administer justice for his wicked deeds ... and yours?"

I gulped. Sweat trickled along my temples. I stopped counting my kills long ago, though every face shone in my memory like ghosts.

"Is this Cottia?"

Señor Pascual knew my name. We'd seen each other but never chatted. Whyzer Patro didn't like to mingle his associates with his assassins.

"If it's you, you don't have to do this."

Boots clomped toward the room from the corridor.

"Turn the lock," I said and got to my feet, still hidden behind the bed curtain.

Metal clicked.

"Señor Pascual, are you in harm's way?" another male voice asked.

"Stay near," Señor Pascual said. "If I'm not out in five minutes, break open the door."

"But, Señor," said the man on the other side.

Señor Pascual sighed. "I have the Ancient One's bidding."

I fingered the hilt of a pocket dagger beneath my cloak and stepped out from behind the bed. "You're wrong, Señor Pascual."

The man mopped his bald head with a cloth from his pocket. His doublet and pantaloons screamed of wealth with all their silver stitching and heavy velvet. Yet something in the sheen of his brown eyes bespoke kindness. "Cottia, I know you've belonged to Whyzer Patro since childhood, but you can be free of your brand's bond."

A pitying look made me recoil, yet I wanted to hear what this man had to say. I let my hand drop from the hilt of the dagger. Now that I saw him, my gift easily kept hold of a thick vein in his neck. With one squeeze, I could accomplish my work. I pinched it with my invisible touch, but his flesh slipped from my grasp again.

"Cottia, I'm under the Ancient One's protection. Don't continue this evil." Señor Pascual held up his palms but dared not draw near. "Seek the Ancient One and you too can be forgiven and free."

Freedom and forgiveness were a faraway dream, but even so I listened. I never had my gifting fail even once and already I tried to slay him twice. His saying that I could be free of my bond stirred my tumultuous emotions, affirming that there was something more to be done.

How many times had I wondered what it would be like to be a maid or a regular townsperson?

"Who is this old man that you speak of?" I asked.

"The Ancient One?" Confusion squished on the bridge of his nose. He licked his lips and opened his mouth to speak.

"Papá!" shouted a tiny voice. "Papá."

An ache pierced my chest at the thought of taking her father who might not have attempted to kill the collector. Shouldn't Pascual be allowed to defend his case before we administer retribution?

"I'll let you live if you promise to lay low for several weeks and to never seek Whyzer Patro again." The words rolled off my tongue before I had the chance to think through my proposition. A beat passed, then two.

"Even if I make that promise," Señor Pascual put his hands on his hips like Papá used to do, "you will need to escape. Whyzer Patro will know."

The invisible shackles held by Whyzer Patro burned along the mark on my arm, and I resisted its pull. It begged me to obey my master.

But how could I take his life after seeing the child? Would she end up like me with her papá gone? The little girl must have been what threw off my gifting in the first place.

I spun on my heels and slipped out the window. With one last glance backward, I reached for my hook and rope, a strange sentiment careening within my soul. I jabbed the hook into the window ledge and propelled myself down the side of the castle. Letting Señor Pascual live would be my greatest mistake yet.

CHAPTER 2
COTTIA

THE PREVIOUS NIGHT HUNG over my head like a storm cloud that brewed and spewed its fury on all my steps through Whyzer Patro's castillo. The large country estate was run by each of his wards rather than a fleet of servants. My tasks entailed scrubbing all the bedrooms and the privy on my floor each Sunday, even if it was Noche del Éxodo—my favorite holiday. Missing the fun would be the least of my concerns if the whyzer found out about my failure.

By the time I finished with my tasks, the sun dipped into the horizon. I carried my broom, mop, and bucket down the back stairwell that spiraled from the fourth to first floor. It proved an excellent way to avoid Whyzer Patro and his other charges who might have returned for whatever reason from the festivities.

I slipped into my bedroom and passed the mirror, catching the guilty expression in my dark brown eyes. Anyone who wasn't blind and knew me would have questions. I removed my dirty apron and dumped it into a wicker basket. The ensemble for tonight would take time to fit onto my body and arrange in such a way to make myself presentable, giving the extra time I needed to come up with a cover story for Señor Pascual's beating pulse. If

Whyzer Patro or any of the other assassins found out, it would be best to have a good retort.

Once I finished putting myself together, I could pass as a most elegant panther. The mirror revealed my black mask glittering with obsidian beads and letting my full lips show beneath it. The dress's hood covered my head and cinched at my waist. The plain fishtail braid would be a good enough hairdo. A silvery brocade covered my front in patterns that matched leaves in a forest. It'd take a keen person to recognize me, and an even more observant one to read my expression.

I sped through the darkened corridor that opened up to a courtyard and down several flights of stairs. A remnant of those working the kitchen carried trays of empanadas, cuero de pernil, and spiced tamarindo. My mouth watered at the savory dishes, but I plucked the tamarindo into my mouth. An explosion of sweet and spicy coated my tongue and caused a reflexive hiss to push between my teeth.

The front doors remained swung open with guards lined across the castle courtyard.

"Is that you, Tia?" Roberto asked.

I pursed my lips, trying to think of a way to avoid this conversation.

"You know Whyzer Patro wants to see you?" Roberto was tall with dark, round eyes and cropped curls atop his head. His muscular form made most of the ladies swoon, but not me. Though he had the appeal of a candy, he lacked substance.

"Later," I said.

"But he's not going to be happy." Roberto's jaw shifted, a worried gesture.

"It's Noche del Éxodo." I walked backward to keep moving, yet maintain eye contact. "Should I not enjoy the festivities? Besides, when is the whyzer not upset?"

Roberto glanced at his companions, who shared no love for me and would betray me at a shake of the whyzer's staff. Whyzer Patro liked to use my abilities to inflict pain on the guards.

I spun around toward a torch-lit road leading to the town square. Musicians plucked their lutes, pressed their bows to their viols, and smacked palms on the drums. The rhythmic music pulsed through the air, setting in motion old women's hips and young dance partners.

In a flurry of masks and colorful dresses, the mass of humanity gathered under banners running from one pole to another. Where was Gema? She had declared weeks ago that she would be a fox and let her red curls flow down her back. No one in the crowd had her appearance, so it should have been an easy enough task to find my best friend.

Squishing between poofy brown dresses, red sparkling gowns, sleek green renditions of lizards, and spotted monstrosities, I suffocated. There was no chance Whyzer Patro stood among the peasants. At least I was safe for now. Yet even so, what would he do to me as a punishment?

The last assassin who failed him had been publicly whipped in the castillo courtyard and no one saw him since. I swallowed a lump of fear. Even being the whyzer's favorite wouldn't save me from consequences. Gema would surely know what to do about the matter. The girl was a genius. She had saved me from many lashings with sly maneuvering. Now, where was she?

Music shifted to a calmer melody meant for a partner dance.

A young man in a wolf mask cut in front of me. "Loba." He called to a young lady in a she-wolf mask and a dress that hugged her in all the right places, frilling out into a delicate A-line. "Will you do me the honor?"

I sidestepped the couple. Judging by the rosy color creeping up the girl's neck, she would say yes. I rolled my eyes. All this nonsensical partnering and romantic gestures, for what? To bring children into the world who would be trapped under the whyzer's tyranny? The greater mercy would be not to have children at all.

Even so, I was glad to have tried to allow Señor Pascual's girls to live a better life than mine.

"Tia! Tia," Gema shouted from somewhere to my right.

Does she have to be so loud?

Spinning to find her, I knocked into the hard chest of a man dressed like a panther.

He caught my wrist, steadying my faulty steps. His wide smile spread underneath the black mask that covered his nose and eyes. The perfect cut of a small beard covered a cleft chin of Cristobal, another assassin who liked to compete against me as if death were a game.

"It seems we're destined to dance." Cristobal's words came out in a sensuous purr.

"Does that line ever work for you?" I twisted my wrist from his grip and strode toward Gema, whose gifting marks ignited into flames along her arms.

She raced in my direction but didn't make it before he grabbed my waist and twisted me around. I slapped him across the cheek.

A collective gasp erupted. Drawing attention to myself would land me in Whyzer Patro's study quicker than news of Señor Pascual's breathing.

"I do love a challenge, Tia." Cristobal wiped his lip with his palm, letting me go.

"My name is Cottia to you."

Gema arrived with her gift alight for all to witness. Red flames emanated from her skin and burned the edges of her long orange sleeves. She patted out the fire on the velvet without dropping the grimace on her high cheekbones and full bow-shaped lips. Smoke drifted behind her, giving her the appearance of Hades on legs. "Take your hand off her."

Cristobal relinquished his hold, chuckling. "Caramba! I didn't realize asking my matching lady to dance would be such an ordeal." He gestured to his panther mask.

"Come on, Tia." Gema looped her arm through mine and pulled me toward the food stalls near the store fronts.

I glanced over my shoulder. The dancers pressed around Cristobal, who stood like a statue, crossing his arms. His attention remained on me and only me. A shiver shimmied between my shoulders.

"You know, Tia, I think he likes you." Gema reached beneath her dress fabric and retrieved a purse from where it was situated in her bosom. She waved the leather pouch in the air as if to dry it off and pulled out two coins. "Churros con chocolate?"

Resisting an eye roll, I nodded. Even if I said no to either statement, Gema had a theory about everything—one being that deep conversations must be discussed with fried dough in one hand and melted chocolate in the other.

She handed me my treat, stuffed her small purse away, and snatched her delicious prize. The conversation couldn't begin until we settled on the outskirts of the fiesta near a fountain farthest away from the castillo.

Like two content pigeons we devoured our midnight snack with efficiency because, as Gema says, full stomach, happy heart.

"So," Gema hedged. "Are you finally going to admit you like him?"

I lifted my mask so she could see my face clearly under the sparse torch light.

"Ay-caramba! It's worse." She squinted her eyes, their green color lost in the shadows. "You loathe the man for real, for real, and don't know how to get rid of him."

Pursing my lips, I clasped my hands. "What if I told you that my troubles have nothing to do with Cristobal?"

"Listening."

Pitching my voice low, I leaned closer to Gema. "Señor Pascual lives."

Her eyes flew wide, and a squeak escaped her throat.

"I need to get away."

"Impossible."

"Gema," I reprimanded her. "You're my idea machine. You can think of any way out of situations."

The flattery worked because she sighed and curled her mouth into her pondering expression. Quiet seconds passed with only prickles of nerves shimming up my spine.

"Any ideas?" I asked.

"You request a miracle and want it done instantly?" Indignation crackled in her tone, though a hint of a curl lifted the edges of her mouth.

The music continued to wail through the air and the mass of twirling dancers shifted an arm's throw away. Stray couples and groups of people speckled the long stone courtyard. A glow caught my attention to the left, and I peered at a romantic pair. The young man sparked his gifting, causing a blue glow to shine from his palm.

The girl gasped and reached for an object where the glow had been. "It's frozen. The rose is hard as a rock."

Though romance intrigued me, I never could understand how someone could pledge life and duty to another on purpose. A silly parlor trick had the girl snuggling close to the fellow. What of his ability to control his anger? What about his work ethic or how he cleans?

My mind wandered to Cristobal. He proved an excellent example of a young man who had a good appearance and vastly greater skills than this Pedro who could freeze objects with his hands. But Cristobal knew how all the ladies at the castillo looked at him. He strutted around, patting himself on the back because he was born with the power to take control of another person's body like the Prince of Giddel.

That's probably why he pursued me like a panther does its prey. Cristobal thought too much of himself and couldn't stand that I hadn't a speck of interest in him. He also hated how my lesser gift did better work than his greater powers. I could only feel the inner workings of a person's body and pinch and nudge people from the inside. Even with my small gifting, I was called on more by Whyzer Patro to do the hardest jobs.

Something stirred in the crowd. Soldiers with no masks pushed dancers out of their paths, and a familiar face caught my attention. I cursed under my breath.

"Ehhh … I see an old, bald man climbing the podium." Gema squinted. She didn't have the best vision and wouldn't admit it. "Tia, is that who I think it is?"

"Yes, that is Señor Pascual. I am dead."

"No, I'm pretty sure he is."

Whyzer Patro's personal guard in black and red livery appeared before us through shimmering air. "Whyzer Patro would like a word with you, Cottia."

Both Gema and I got to our feet. The guard pinned Gema with a glare that bespoke a vicious message through his stiff upper lip and narrowed steel-eyes.

Gema brushed the guard's pauldron. "Pedro, is it?"

"Luis," he countered.

Her joke didn't fly past me. Half the men in town were named Pedro.

He clutched my upper arm. "I'm ordered to bring Cottia to the master." He yanked away from her touch. "That's all."

"Pedro, baby." Gema had a glint of mischief arched in her eyebrow. "Couldn't I do your invisibility act with you?"

"Not if I want to keep my head." He dragged me alongside him through the outskirts of the festivities.

Gema worried her bottom lip as she waved from her spot near the water fountain.

CHAPTER 3
COTTIA

Continued sounds of music and merriment drifted from the courtyard and through the windows, but I stood in front of Whyzer Patro in his second-floor study. Shelves with ancient tomes lined the two side walls. Narrow windows with arched tops framed the cushioned armchair where the whyzer did his "negotiations," as he called it.

"You summoned me?" I bowed my head and clasped my hands behind my back in a non-threatening gesture. I'd made the mistake once of extending my hands out to him. I nursed broken fingers that night.

The slim man in his gray whyzer's cloak remained seated. He raked his long beard as if in thought like the true holy men were known for doing. What a sham. The old man had left his vows to be a bestower of the special giftings and decided to wield powers on his own terms. Some people in town treated him like a revered sovereign, but I knew better.

"It's come to my attention that Señor Pascual isn't as dead as you claimed him to be." His calm tone rattled my bones. It meant anything but good tidings.

"Yes, señor."

"This means you lied to me. Did you think I wouldn't find out?"

"Not so quickly, señor." The honest answer rolled off my tongue with painful ease. When caught, I'd learned to tell the truth even when it hurt. There was no digging myself out of this one when Señor Pascual marched to the podium like a fool.

"Why did you do it?" Whyzer Patro lifted his staff, sparking the powers within it. A glow emanated from the gnarled top of the piece of wood.

I glanced around to catch any hints of distorted light from Luis's eavesdropping. Could I admit to my master that my gifting had failed me on this job? Señor Pascual's notion about the Ancient One protecting him was merely superstition. There had to be more to my failure. When signs of Luis didn't appear, I cleared my throat. "He had children with him."

"Your soft spot."

Humiliation heated my cheeks. I had had enough experience to make me callous to my work, yet children could waylay my plans and set my nerves on edge. Why did I admit this to him? Did it even matter, since I was as good as dead?

When I lifted my head, Whyzer Patro met my gaze with a frigid expression that seemed to calculate and pull on the invisible strings he used to control me. My upper arm stung like a lump of coal had been set on my flesh. He combed his fingers through his beard, waiting for something.

My tongue burned. Unable to resist the urge to speak, I said, "Señor, I don't want to do this anymore." The words came out in a whisper.

He clutched the staff tighter.

The brand on my upper arm burned as if fire licked my skin again. I rolled my shoulders back and lifted my chin high with the posture expected of assassins.

"Good. I can't stand a groveling subject." Whyzer Patro laid his staff across his lap. "What exactly do you request? And speak up."

My mouth felt as if it were stuffed with ashes. Should I risk telling him the full truth? Gema's words about escape being impossible rang through my mind like a town bell gonging one too many times, but Señor Pascual had insisted there could be a way. He himself could not be touched by my gift, which proved he might have stumbled upon a revelation—though the Ancient One did seem absurd. What did I have to lose, when even Whyzer Patro's favor had its limits? I was a walking dead girl.

"Señor, is it possible to leave this line of work to live a townsperson's life?"

Whyzer Patro guffawed. The deep sound had a malicious note to it, more mocking than angry. That allowed the knot between my shoulders to loosen the slightest bit.

The whyzer's laughter settled. "You're serious, aren't you?"

I nodded.

"Hmm." The whyzer leaned back in his chair with a glint in his dark eyes. "You know that you are a most gifted killer?"

A coconut-sized lump filled my throat. I managed a choked, "Yes." I'd at least speak the truth before my end came.

"Look at me." Whyzer Patro lifted his staff again, sending a sharp pain through my body. "If this is what you desire, I have a proposition for you."

Flickers of longing swelled in my lungs. Might I get what I coveted most? I dared not breathe in case his next words retracted his first.

Images of gaunt, dead faces and lifeless bodies in dark corridors flashed through my mind. A queasy sensation roamed through my gut at all that I'd done in the name of fulfilling the whyzer's propositions. As a child, I enjoyed the whyzer's flattery and thought the people would revive. The day I understood that the victim on the tile floor wouldn't wake again, I cried myself sick. I learned to remain detached. One friend was all I allowed, and I distanced myself from my sister.

"A most dangerous proposition arrived that suits my greater ambitions to find the last relic."

My stomach shriveled at the mention of the relic. Whenever those ancient powers were part of the conversation, he acted without inhibition.

He steepled his fingers. "Have you heard about the death of the Giddelian prince's betrothed?"

I shook my head. The only news I ever heard from outside the castillo came from the words of desperate and dying men.

"There is a ball where any damsel like yourself may attend. You will get close to the prince, seduce him if you must. He's probably out of your reach since he's known to be particular. Find out which councilman would make the best fallout for a hit, maybe the prince himself. Your job will be to assassinate Señor Trucio, an important investor of Pedroz, in the Palace of Giddel. It also serves as a retribution that you failed to administer. Señor Pascual just made a deal with Señor Trucio, and Pascual's family will lose everything if the man ends up dead. The Kingdom of Pedroz won't take kindly to Trucio's murder and will start a war over it."

My palms grew sweaty. All his deal required was pretending to be a rich damsel, attending a ball, seducing the prince, getting the investor alone, and executing the hit. I could walk out the palace gates as if nothing transpired, with no one the wiser besides the prince, who will be implicated. There had to be a trick in his deal.

Whyzer Patro observed my every twitch. "You must make sure to do your job in such a way that the kingdom of Pedroz blames Giddel for the infraction. Though it almost would be better if you could become the little bird tweeting in their ears by wooing the prince. Our Giddelian spy has the perfect disguise for such a thing as that."

A long silence stretched as Whyzer Patro's gaze shifted in thought. He mumbled to himself, "Even you couldn't win a mourning prince who's known for his devotion to the Ancient One." He let out an airy laugh. "No, spark a war between the kingdoms. If Giddel no longer holds a place of power, the other kingdoms around the Agata Sea will scramble for control."

A slow exhale escaped. Pulses of energy vibrated with frightening strength on those chords that tethered him to me. I kept my expression as neutral as possible so as not to give away the panic and hope that grew too large for my chest.

"If you can cause a skirmish between Pedroz and Giddel, then you will be free to live your life as a ... townsperson." He laughed at the last word.

Ignoring the mockery, I lifted my chin. "Could I go wherever I like?"

"Yes, this is no ruse, and we'll seal it with an oath that even I cannot break."

A beat passed where I let his proposition sink into my soul. My tethering mark to the whyzer ached with his powers wrenching on my consciousness, pressing his will into the forefront of my mind. "Will you remove the bond?" I clutched my upper arm where he'd branded me.

"No, dear Cottia, I must have some assurance you won't kill me in my sleep."

Disappointment sunk at his words. He could make me a slave again if I ever drew near to him, but an oath could solve the problem. People had been known to keel over and die with the slightest veering away from their word under its protection.

"I accept your proposition, if you seal it with an oath."

He lit his golden markings that raced along his knuckles in swirling patterns and glowed in the shadow of his cloak. They traced his cheekbones and continued upward to brighten up his forehead. Most people only had markings on their hands. The powerful ones had them on their arms and maybe their backs. A quiver skipped up my spine at witnessing his immense gifting. Black veins then spread along his skin between the beautiful gold.

My breath hitched.

He remained seated with a slight upturn of his lips, unperturbed by the foreign, dark lines. When he opened his mouth, he spoke words in the ancient tongue.

A cool breeze swam through the room, bringing a chill that hadn't been there seconds before.

"I promise to free Señorita Cottia Luzelena Jaime Pacheco from my services if she assassinates Señor Trucio and starts political turmoil between Giddel and Pedroz. Should she not complete her duty before the two moons rise, Cottia will return to me as an oathbound slave, and Gema will be punished."

My stomach clenched with his final declaration.

His skin dimmed. The air in the room warmed to a comfortable temperature again.

Heart sinking into my stomach, I opened my mouth to speak, but my jaw snapped closed without my consent. The invisible strings puppeteering my every movement tugged and pulled at me. Why had I agreed to his deal before hearing the oath? Did I even have a choice in the matter?

"Good." He got to his feet, his extra height casting a shadow over my body. The top of his staff lit with vivid orange and yellow. "As for your punishment for disobedience, I will take a portion of your gift."

Energy swirled out from my body before me like flecks of sparkling dust. It suctioned into his staff and left me with an empty sensation between my ribs.

He quirked an eyebrow. "You leave tomorrow for Giddel. Now, I have an execution to attend." He strolled out of the study as if he'd won multiple battles in one stroke.

CHAPTER 4
COTTIA

THE MOMENT I CROSSED through the Giddelian gate the next day, a shadow tailed my every move. This hadn't been the first time I had to lose someone. I darted right through a busy lane with brightly painted shops.

A man in a black cloak and dark boots remained a stone's throw away. I dodged in front of a burly man, hoping his broad body would cover me. When a cart approached, I waited until just after it passed to duck and sneak behind it.

Someone grabbed my wrists. I inhaled sharply.

"What's your business?" the cloaked man asked.

Powers shot out my fingertips and clawed at his face.

He let go and grunted. I ran.

Dress swishing as I turned into a narrow alleyway, I risked a glance behind me.

People passed along the way, staring at the bent over man and then at me.

This job might be a disaster if I got caught before the work had even begun. Heart racing, I zigzagged between pedestrians. It could have been the king's guard assuming a lady in an all-black dress to be suspicious or a rivaling criminal group who sought retribution. Either way, I didn't want to find out.

"Over there!" a man shouted from down the lane.

I turned left between buildings and sprinted.

The main thoroughfare bustled with life. I went right and paused to make sure my tail was gone. Morning sunlight flashed on the curved turrets of the Palace of Giddel. Tonight, I'd enjoy its grandeur. Echoing footfalls approached from the alleyway.

A man in a cloak appeared from another passage a few stores ahead. I dodged into Don Armando's bakery. A long line of people waited in front of the counter and continued around the perimeter. The profile of the cloaked man with a crooked nose and prickly chin appeared close to the window outside the bakery.

I slipped behind a lady with a baby on each hip and two young children scrambling around her. She dropped her basket which gave the perfect excuse for me to crouch low.

Seconds passed with me in a squat. I peeked around her, catching the backside of the man stalking away.

"Can I get my basket back or is this a new form of robbery?" the mother asked.

I shoved the basket toward her and cut to the front of the line. "El Capitán wants a dozen bow ties."

"Hey, pretty lady, the end of the line is back there." An older man pointed to the mother with all the children.

"No, no, no, señor, El Capitán has a special order." Don Armando's smile pressed harder into his cheeks. He dragged his gaze from his wrinkle-faced customer to me. "At your service." He fumbled through a bread display, placing my order into a basket, and handed me the woven handle.

Heat radiated up to my hand along with a yeasty aroma. I crossed the road into a gangway beside an aqua blue snuff shop. The two-story buildings had enough large-leafed shrubbery to hide the narrow path and prevent curious pedestrians from wandering through. I peeked through the leaves, searching faces for the cloaked man so as not to give away the whyzer's spy. Nothing could get in the way of this oath.

Lifting my skirt to avoid stepping on fresh slop, I tiptoed to a back door. The man who lived there had the details of my new identity and the invites to the ceremonía. I rapped the wooden door twice and counted to five before striking it again.

"What do you want?" a gruff voice called from behind the door.

"I have the good pleasure of bringing you a dozen bow ties." I rolled my eyes at the thought of me toting puffed pastries to this dump.

There was a click. The door opened a crack, and I slid my way in. This place always reeked of booze and a stale smell I couldn't place. My eyes took a minute to adjust to the dim lighting. The stout, bald man slogged down the stairs grunting about who knew what. I had yet to ask his name, nor did I care to know it. He was no threat to me, though the darkness he lived in wearied my bones. Whyzer Patro always said I relied too much on my eyes instead of my gift.

I trudged behind him. "I presume you have my package. Whyzer Patro promises double the pay if everything goes smoothly."

The man crossed the dingy room and opened a cupboard. I stepped off the last creaky stair and into the man's dank apartment. A rodent scurried past a rocking chair to somewhere under the bed. I cringed.

"You're Señor Marden's sixteen-year-old daughter." The man tottered toward me with a bundle in one hand. He inspected me like a prized horse and wrapped his free arm about me. His breath reeked even worse in his embrace.

"She's considered a sickly creature. So, you might want to do something about that smug look on your face."

Pushing against his iron hold, I yanked the package from his grip.

He laughed, a malicious sound, and groped my behind. I couldn't be blamed for practicing my gifting for fun. Warmth coursed through my fingertips, extending like invisible tentacles into his knee. With my thoughts, I clutched a swollen spot on his knee cap. He buckled over onto his rocking chair.

"Enough of that. Whyzer won't take kindly to your meddling." He winced.

"Mind your manners because unlike me you are replaceable." I clutched the bundle at my chest and fled. Good riddance. This would be the last time I darkened this dungeon.

Whyzer Patro secured an apartment on the coastline where all the wealthy resided when they came to Giddel. A cooling sea breeze struck my cheeks. When colorful doublets and no black cloaks filled my vision, I yanked my hood back and straightened my spine to mesh better with my surroundings.

I turned a corner by a line of sandstone townhouses where José opened a mahogany door to usher me into the building.

Rushing up the polished steps, I sped past several courtiers who resided in the apartment across from me. They whispered to themselves about the ball tonight and lowered their voices further, asking each other who I was. I pulled my dark braid over my shoulder, side glancing in a way that added to the mystery. Little did they know that I wasn't a contestant.

Señor Trucio was my new job. I did some investigation and discovered the man made his riches swindling rich lords of their fortune, including my papá. He was the reason Papá lost everything. I would settle that score and start a war over his rotting flesh. Walking into the apartment, I hoped to avoid any conversation with my escorts. This hit would be so much more pleasant if I had Gema assigned as my maid, but Whyzer Patro wouldn't allow it.

"Did he come through for us this time?" Omar the Himzo crossed his arms while lounging on the couch.

"You should get ready. Señorita Luiza of the Marden Estate cannot be escorted by Himzo trash." I entered the bedroom door knowing how Omar seethed at the jab.

"One day, my country men will—"

I slammed the door shut before Omar could say another word. His muffled curses tickled that part inside that wanted everyone to be miserable along with me. I sat the bundle on my silky sheets and pulled on the strings to untie it. A sparkling blue material winked in the sunlight. Long silver gloves held an envelope with the royal seal that secured the flap shut. My invitation and ticket to freedom.

Now, to figure out a way to free Gema too. She didn't have the same bonds as me because of her gifting. Fire skin was unburnable and set aflame only at her command. Yet so long as I remained under the whyzer's binds, she wouldn't leave. I still hadn't shared Whyzer Patro's deal with her because she had been included as collateral should I fail. But even in my succeeding, the whyzer would never willingly allow her to depart as long as she was valuable to me. He used my friendship as a tool time and time again.

Not anymore. I would storm the castillo if needed. But first, I must prepare the kill of a lifetime.

CHAPTER 5
COTTIA

OMAR THE HIMZO CLEANED up well enough. His black hair pulled back into a small tail that sat on a navy suit jacket with golden thread embroidered into leaves on the neckline. I lifted my chin, hoping to appear unimpressed at the arched entrance stretching above my head. Omar handed a servant our invitation and we were escorted into the hall to be announced. Heads spun in my direction at the entrance of the mysterious Señorita Luiza of Marden Estate.

I feigned a slight limp as I curved my back to give a frail appearance and pushed away from Omar. He would stay behind with the other servants to get information from them. The purple coloring I had smothered on my bottom eyelid could be seen in reflective glass near the entrance.

An older woman gasped. "She's not that sickly."

"Oh, the Ancient One! That can't be her," another woman said.

Many of the younger ladies fanned themselves with tight lips and critical eyes, taking in the sparkling blue gown far too near the common shade for brides. After all, Prince Ezer of Giddel did need to find a new betrothed. I savored the heaviness of expensive jewels around my neck and being openly accepted into the palace, though I could do without the glares.

Unbidden thoughts poured in like a steaming cup of coffee, pleasant and appetizing. This should have been my life if Mamá hadn't squandered all our wealth. Tomorrow, I'd be long gone and forgotten if all fell into place. But the señoritas hadn't a clue they were sizing up someone who'd become a free and obscure nobody soon enough. My insides filled with satisfying warmth at the thought of blissful freedom. I let a familiar, cool expression slip over my face, the same one I used at every job. Failure wasn't an option.

"Señorita Luiza, how we longed to meet you," an older woman said. "We are eager for your company." Thick creams and powders gathered at the creases around her eyes. The silliness of all the latest trends allowed me an easy disguise.

I faked a cough. "Who do I have the good pleasure of meeting?" I intoned my voice like that of the upper class.

"Señora Anna of the Castillo Buena Luz." The older woman continued to introduce me to all her nieces and close acquaintances. They made my job easier by giving me a way to mingle in the crowd. Now it was a matter of finding Señor Trucio to give him his parting breath. How delicious would it be if I could manage to have a member of the royal family in close proximity. Such a feat would surely invoke a skirmish.

"The prince is to die for." Señora Anna clasped her hands as if describing the evening's dessert. "With your connections and those large eyes, you'll be top in the running." She bobbed her mantilla covered head, affirming her own words. "That I am sure. Look, they're getting ready to announce his entrance." She clapped with more excitement than the young ladies.

I flipped out a fan. "Sorry, I get dizzy spells."

The señora patted my hand like a doting grandmother. "Let me know if the excitement is too much for you."

A trumpet sounded as we held our breaths. Prince Ezer of Giddel meandered through the room in his forest green doublet embroidered with the city emblem over one side of his chest. He waved and the ladies swooned. If he hadn't had such a high title, I doubted their responses would be so ridiculous.

A sea of people chatted amongst themselves. I had memorized the drawings of the man with a strong chin and thick mustache who destroyed Papá.

While everyone focused on Prince Ezer, servants announced the entrance of Señora Trucio. Her white hair weaved high on her head, and she wore a snarl. The upturn of her nose and shift of her gaze bespoke that her disposition might have something to do with the modest entrance. After all, women who wore purple silk dresses with gems sewn into their hems did have a tendency to want others to notice them. It also could be that Señor Trucio did not escort her. I pretended to be wracked with coughs and groaned under my breath. My supposed illness would be a great excuse to retire to a different room and snoop around to find the man.

"Señora Trucio looks lovely, doesn't she?" Señora Anna pressed into my shoulder, waving a fan over her face. "They're new money, of course, but no one can stop talking about them. If Señora's daughters weren't all married women, Prince Ezer would surely choose one of them."

"Oh?" I asked in my most bored voice. "Do you know Señora Trucio?"

Señora Anna pursed her lips together. "Do I?" She grabbed my wrists and pulled me through the crowd toward the señora I longed to meet, but stopped suddenly.

I slammed into her back, knocking her into another señora. The other lady righted herself and curtsied while passing me a side-eyed glare.

"Sorry, weak ankles." I coughed, making a slow turn of my head toward the dance floor. The prince was watching me.

Prince Ezer closed the several paces between us. I peeked about at all the bowing women. Señora Anna dipped her head with color painting her cheeks, and the lady on the other side curtsied too low for comfort. He grinned, still staring at me with golden-green eyes. He had dark cropped hair, a caramel tan and full lips, the type of man any lady could fancy.

"Will you do me the honor?" His husky voice carried a hint of amusement.

I turned my head in case he spoke to someone behind me.

A deep chortle escaped his mouth, and he extended his hand to reach for mine.

Should I faint? That could get me out of this without having to embarrass the prince. But then I caught Señora Trucio greeting the queen with a bow and amicable conversation, solidifying Señora Anna's story about the families being close.

This was not going to help the mysterious identity I intended to keep, but how did one decline the prince's invitation to dance with so much attention on the request? I lifted a reluctant hand, and he pulled me from the throng to join him on the dance floor. All the world fell into my peripheral as I squared up to the prince. He placed a hand at the center of my back and lifted my other hand high. I studied the brown-and-gray flecks in his ever-changing eye color as his gaze drank me in like he enjoyed what he saw. Heat filled my cheeks.

"I've never seen you here before." He spun me around like the dance dictated. "What is your name?"

"Señorita Luiza of the Marden Estate." I looked away at the crowd, searching for my target's wife. Many ladies grimaced at the prince's choice of dance partners. Inside, I puffed with amusement at their prickled pride. But I reminded myself, *Keep it professional. This is just a job.*

"Señor Marden's daughter?" His pitch rose.

"Yes." I released a small portion of the gifting I had left; energy trickled along my arms to my fingertips. The pulse at his neck felt like a constant bu-bump, no extraordinary suspicion.

Stringed instruments started in a slow melody that set my feet into the common waltz. Thank Whyzer Patro for demanding I learn these silly dances. I had asked him why an assassin would need such trivial skills. It turned out that I'd only use them on the job of a lifetime.

Prince Ezer turned me about the room, guiding me into more challenging steps I had never attempted before. Somehow my legs moved on their own, knowing the exact place to land so that I spun with ease. My dress lifted off the floor, and my feet didn't click against the hard marble. Was I floating?

All the world blurred around me as the music crescendo led into a powerful part of the song. He released one hand and rotated me into his body. He dipped me low, keeping my torso pressed to his so as not to drop me. Looking up, I admired the mischievous grin with a well-placed birthmark over his upper lip. Applause abounded, marking the end of the dance. He set me upright, and I curtsied and caught my breath.

He wove my arm through his and escorted me across the floor. "I hope you don't mind me using my gift to help you along."

My eyes flicked wide, now understanding how I managed to do such skillful dance maneuvers with ease.

"Yes, I do mind," I said. My curiosity perked at how he did it without me noticing. Cristobal didn't have that useful skill. But even with my wonder it was better not to bother getting to know him unless necessary. The job would be done faster on my own.

"I'm sorry. I should have asked." He clutched my wrist before releasing me back into the crowd.

"It's forgiven." I swayed back and forth and breathed deeply for a hacking cough that scraped my throat. "I must retire a moment." My heels clicked as I fled.

An older woman cut between him and me with a pretty lady at her elbow. That should have kept him occupied while I remained focused on hunting for the older man. I exited the hall and plopped onto a small, cushioned bench in the passage just outside the hall's doorway.

Should I shed this gown and wear something more practical?

"Allow me to make it up to you." Prince Ezer strode from the hall.

Cielos! How do I get rid of this prince? I coughed and slouched my shoulders to maintain my ruse.

"Let me fetch someone to get you a drink." The sincerity in his offer gave me pause. He made a quick request from a passing male servant and sat beside me, brushing his leg against my dress skirt since there was barely enough room for another bottom. "I shouldn't have pushed you so hard through such a difficult dance. I'm so sorry. I won't use my gifting on you again without your permission."

"You're forgiven." I felt my face twitch in spite of my best attempt to conceal the heat rising up my neck.

He cocked his head to the side, showing off a heartwarming smile. "Now, how can I make it up to you?"

A servant in a tailored green jacket carried a white teacup with steam billowing out the top and gently pressed it into my grasp.

Sweat slickened my neck, and slow seconds ticked by with the prince's attention beseeching a response.

I took a sip of the sweet floral brew. The warmth soothed the dryness from all the coughing. "Thank you for your attention. You needn't—"

"No, you won't shrug off my favor that easily." His bottom lip pouted the slightest bit, strengthening his masculine chin and adding to his charm.

If he wouldn't let me go, I'd have to use him. "Then, will you not introduce me to your most esteemed guests?"

He nodded. "As you wish, my lady."

This attention may prove useful after all.

He hopped to his feet and offered me his strong forearm, as if oblivious to the giant room full of señoritas swooning for him to notice them. I hooked my arm through his, and we promenaded into the crowd.

Music continued to twirl about the room and couples filled the dance floor. Señora Trucio chatted with a couple beside us. I'd need to figure out how to steer him that direction without giving myself away.

We met guests dressed in the finest silks with the most ostentatious hair arrangements that reached a head length higher than natural. The men had gold embroidered coats that looked like paintings sewn onto their backs. It made me think more highly of the prince that he wore a simple yet refined jacket with only one small design on his chest.

Señora Trucio escaped to a solitary spot against the wall. Her gaze was blank as she heaved heavy sighs every now and then.

Prince Ezer led me to her and did all the formalities. "I notice that Señor Trucio does not accompany you."

She pouted. "He is up in our room feeling indisposed this evening."

Cielos! My simple plan unraveled into a frayed ribbon. I gritted my teeth, keeping a placid curve to my mouth. If I couldn't get to the wretched thief, I'd have to use his wife to draw near.

While she continued to speak about her stay in the palace, I released a ripple of power toward her, feeling the pump of her heart and the flow of her blood. She put a hand over her chest while furrowing her brow.

"Madam, is something the matter?" Prince Ezer noticed too many details. "Should I escort you to the infirmary?"

She clutched the ruffles of her dress for a second and trained her gaze toward me. "Your friend is a beauty. May I ask, what is your name?"

I coughed into my fist and gulped down the rest of the tea.

Before I could answer, Prince Ezer responded, "She is Señorita Luiza of Marden Estate."

The hairs on my arms prickled. Sweat beaded over my nose as I nodded.

Señora Trucio's dark eyes dug into my skin just as a palace servant ran up to the señora with a note on a silver tray. She turned her attention away and the thick pressure over my skin lightened. Was she also manipulating my body? I had never experienced such powerful and well-wielded gifts before. Whyzer Patro only warned me to make my work quick, but he didn't explain why. The servant took my cup and strolled away.

Prince Ezer tilted his head down in my direction. "You seem to have lost some of your vigor. Where are you staying?"

"At an apartment off the coastal road."

"You don't seem well. Perhaps you could stay in a guest room to rest." Another of my wracking-cough performances inspired a concerned line to deepen on his forehead.

"Yes," I said, "that would be lovely." Although this invitation gave me an easy way to complete my job, what were his intentions in keeping me so close?

Prince Ezer's easy smile showed no sign of suspecting anything amiss, though there was a twinkle in his gaze that kept me guarded.

Señora Trucio interrupted. "I can take Señorita Luiza to her room. Señor Trucio needs my assistance so it will be no trouble. You know I have a good command of the palace layout."

I clung tightly to the prince's arm trying to come up with an excuse to say *no* to her while keeping my *yes* to him. "You are all kindness."

"It's settled. Which room?" Señora Trucio fanned her face.

"The East Green Room," he said.

Señora Trucio sped toward the exit. When she looked back, her pout showed no patience for my lack of movement.

Prince Ezer kissed my knuckles. "Come back down when arrangements are settled. Thank you for the dance." He lifted his voice for the older woman to hear. "Thank you, Señora Trucio."

We stepped out into the wide atrium where Omar chatted with a line of other servants at the ready, should their wealthy benefactors need something. I lifted my hand.

"At your orders, señorita." Omar's tone held a hint of mockery though his manner would never alert someone who didn't know him.

"Retrieve my trunks. I will be staying the night at the palace as the prince's guest in the East Green Room." I lifted an eyebrow.

His face stilled for a beat, his nostrils flaring in annoyance. "Of course."

Señora Trucio continued her promenade to the main stairway, so elegant in the stonework all along the balustrades. We continued upward in amicable silence though something about her made me wary. I had learned to trust those hidden senses long ago. I sparked my powers. The swish of blood in her veins pounded with an emotion I couldn't place.

The moment my foot hit the second floor, she spun around. "Who are you? I know your type." She whipped her fan on my shoulder.

I stepped away from the stairs in case she plotted to push me down. "I didn't realize I was a type."

She curled her lips while looking down the flight of steps. "You're the assassin, aren't you?"

"What type of accusation is that?" My heart pounded against my ribs. "I don't have to take this treatment. I'm going back down to the ceremonía."

She grabbed my wrist and dragged me down the corridor. I reached through my thoughts for a vein near her heart. It raced with blood. One squeeze and she'd be gone, but she wasn't my target. Señora Trucio took a sharp left into a short hall, then a sharp right, and stopped in front of a set of doors with a window between them. Torches lit the corridor, but not another soul haunted the space. This would be the perfect location for a crime if the line of servants hadn't seen me trek up the stairs with the older woman, and if Prince Ezer didn't ask me to set up a room with her escort.

The moonlight shone in her dark eyes. "I was hoping the whyzer would choose someone good for the job. He always has a taste for pretty little things." She tapped my nose with her manicured fingernail.

Realization settled in with every quiet second that passed. She wanted to see me kill her husband. I never got details about who paid for the jobs, nor did I care to ask. But *this* had never occurred to me.

"Luiza!" A husky voice called from the short hall behind us. Shoes tapped along the hardwood.

Señora Trucio rolled her eyes before she stretched a smile across her face and spun to find Prince Ezer had followed us.

"I realized mid-dance that I preferred your company, Luiza. Will you have my conversation tonight?" Prince Ezer's eyes gleamed with delight and mischief.

"It seems imprudent to converse here." I released a steadying breath, unsure if he saved me from the señora or caused more trouble.

"Of course." He stared at Señora Trucio with a smug air. "We can speak in the gardens where all could see, but prying ears can't hear."

Something about his statement dug like a personal attack on Señora Trucio. Her nostrils flared wide, wiping away the dignified expression that made her appealing for her age. The doorknob to her room turned. A balding man with squinted eyes appeared. Señor Trucio.

A moment of indecision on whether or not to get business done right now crossed my mind. Surely, Señora Trucio would take my side, and the prince being in the same vicinity during the man's death would make for gossip.

Enough to start a war?

Señora Trucio darted glances between him and me. "I thought you were indisposed." She enunciated each word.

"Would you have me lie around all day? I'm not dead yet, dear wife." He stalked past us, allowing me to see the tapestry of colors woven in his suit jacket.

Señora sneered. I imagined she wished him dead by this time rather than having to accompany him downstairs. Somehow it didn't feel right to follow through with the hit at the moment. I also rather liked the idea of keeping Señora Trucio miserable for the next few hours. I smirked as they marched away.

Prince Ezer looked after them until their footfalls could not be heard. When he returned his attention to me, the torchlight caught a glint of something calculating in the angles of his cheeks. "Before we continue, I must know one thing. Who is your intended target?"

My shoulder muscles tensed, but I swayed like the sickly Luiza was about to faint. "Are you asking me who I intend to marry?"

He dipped his head in a single nod.

A fear about him catching me squirmed in my gut. He was far too attentive for a first meeting. So, it seemed, the handsome enough Prince Ezer would have to be dealt with. If I dispatched him now, I could beat him before he took control of my movements. Something about his steady gaze told me he wouldn't hesitate to do what he must. Yet he didn't know the power I wielded.

Releasing warm tendrils of energy, I reached into his chest and found a thick vein. I squeezed, but my grip slid.

I tipped my mouth to the side in a flirtatious grin changing my tactics. "None other than you. Who wouldn't want to be the new betrothed?"

He stretched a forced smile across his face.

"We could head into the quarters since we're here already." I lifted a suggestive brow. Desperation leaked out of my pores. Another failed attempt. I might have to use my dagger with this one.

"I'm no mind reader, but I have a feeling I won't be walking out of that room if I enter. Just so you are aware, the Luiza of Marden Estate is not half as lovely as you."

Swallowing hard, I tried again. His blood-filled vein throbbed against my touch, but I couldn't press into his artery. "Do you blame me for wanting to win your favor?" I bit my lip, trying harder to cut off his ducts, but my invisible touch slipped just like with Señor Pascual.

He groaned in a teasing sort of way while lifting a hand over his heart. "Don't toy with me. Your gifting feels like an enemy pat down. All my healers work gently with their gifting to keep their subjects calm." His flash of teeth almost seemed inviting.

Two times in such a short period? I squeezed again, but my grip failed. "Fine. You know what I am. Why the pretense?"

"I had a hunch." He took my hand and examined my skin, tracing my marks that indicated I was indeed very gifted. "I'm also good friends with Señorita Luiza's brother and I've met her once or twice. Don't agitate yourself. I'm curious. Who are you?"

I pinched my lips tight. My life and Gema's life depended on getting this job done and this prince couldn't thwart my plans. Whyzer Patro's words echoed in my mind: *Seduce him if you must. Be the bird tweeting in his ears. He's probably out of your reach.*

Prince Ezer drew near, a royal swagger in his step. He'd be my ticket to completing this job, even if it wasn't the quick one I'd hoped it to be. Servants scurried toward us with my plain black trunk between them. We must have looked like two fools enjoying a passionate moment. We stepped aside to let the servants enter the room unobstructed.

The servants fled as quickly as they came.

"I have it your way." Prince Ezer wove his fingers with mine. "Answer me this. Are you satisfied?"

"What do you mean?"

"The money. The lifestyle of an assassin. All of it."

My breath released in long, weighty intervals. What did he want?

Answering, I tipped my chin high, putting on a smile that seemed to win male favor at the castillo. "It's not as simple as you think."

"It never is." He let go of my hand. "Come tomorrow to the garden lunch. No mischief, you understand?"

I cocked my head to the side. "Seems like a trap."

"Or a simple invitation. No one will recognize you without the thick creams."

"How will you recognize me if I'm unrecognizable?"

"Those eyes." He stepped backward. "Plus, you'll be the only lady hiding in the background looking rather guilty."

A chuckle escaped my throat. "I can't just walk away from my life."

"We always have choices." He flashed a boyish grin that did something strange inside my stomach. Pushing open my guest room door, he said, "You're invited to stay." He strode the opposite direction, exuding confidence.

Long after the tip-tap of his shoes waned into the shadows, I remained like a statue in the passageway. Why did my gifting fail again? Prince Ezer must have some trick hidden beneath the fine stitching of his doublet.

I'll play the prince's little game and figure out why I couldn't kill him. My thoughts darkened with bitterness. *Prince Ezer out of reach? Whyzer Patro could burn his words and eat them.*

CHAPTER 6
COTTIA

THE NEXT MORNING, I awoke under the canopy of a four-poster bed surrounded by curtains the shade of a verdant forest and gold tassels along the edges. This was new and brought a thrilling shiver to my spine. If I could complete Whyzer Patro's deal, I might get freedom to sleep in a bed like this all the time if I really wanted to. I needed to break my bonds. Prince Ezer's talk about walking away fed the long-dead idealist hopes I once believed, along with the mystery of why my gifting had failed on him.

I hopped out of the bed, and it occurred to me that he thought I would cower in a corner while the other ladies vied for his hand. The assumption bristled the part of me that never backed down from a challenge. I'd show him.

A blaze of sunlight blasted through the windows as the sun pierced the horizon, reminding me to do my stretches. Afterwards my body had a limber feel, which meant it was time to move on to exercising my gift. The more I did the exercises, the more precision I had with my powers.

A hard knock shook the door.

"Señorita, señorita," called a female voice from outside the room. She rattled the knob, but I had jammed the lock with a sturdy chair. To think, these people didn't have double locks.

With a hard hip bump, I removed the chair and then cracked the door open, letting myself peek through less than a hand's breadth of a gap.

"Señorita, your servant requested your presence. He said he had a message for you but wouldn't entrust me with the missive. You see, he's not allowed to go upstairs as he's not in the king's service."

"Don't trouble yourself. Where is he?"

"He's in the atrium."

"I'll be down shortly."

I readied in a plain blue dress and rushed to the atrium, where Omar chatted with other male servants who shut their mouths at noticing me. But not Omar. He whispered to the short man beside him and sneered in my direction. The short man coughed, barely containing a twitch at the corners of his mouth.

"You called?" I drawled in a sophisticated accent typical for courtiers.

"Yes, a missive arrived at the apartment." He gestured with pointed lips toward the main entry, suggesting we needed privacy.

"Accompany me to the apartment." I took slow, deliberate steps out of the palace.

Once we were out of earshot, Omar pitched his growling voice low. "What in the blazes do you think you're doing? I'm not being paid for you to measure your prey before you devour it."

I maintained a passive expression but let a trickle of power escape. No other bodies approached in the space between the entrance and the long path to the gate. Omar's steady heartbeat pounded through his veins with an intensity typical of someone throbbing with anger.

"Well then." I smiled, flashing my teeth. "Do you have any pertinent information that can help me position the desired outcome?"

He grimaced at the jovial shift in my countenance. "The Trucios are the only family without an eligible daughter. They're staying for three weeks for who knows what reason. Well, we know. This should be an easy job for you. Patro said this would be a short one."

"Did he now?"

A swear dropped out Omar's mouth. "I'm not getting paid for you to pretend you're someone special."

"Did the *whyzer* not give you the other half of his plan? Because the *whyzer* wanted this one positioned in a specific way."

"You can drop this whyzer business because none of their type ever did anything for a Himzo like me." He stopped, peering over his shoulder at the guards ahead. "Second, what in the blazes are you talking about, 'positioned in a specific way'? What, does he have to be stretched out on the floor or something?"

The sincerity marked in Omar's furrowed brows and pent-up breath revealed he wasn't lying. Whyzer Patro didn't inform another soul about our deal nor his desired outcome for war. That would have made my escape too easy. I'd have to earn my freedom within the next three weeks before the Trucios planned to leave. As of now, I had no real way to leverage the rich man's death. Kingdoms didn't start wars over merchants.

"No, Omar, nothing like that." I crossed my arms and appraised the velvet gown that could pass as refined, but nothing extraordinary. "Accompany me while I go shopping."

Omar's beady eyes rolled to the sky. "So, you're going to torture me now?"

"Nothing of that nature. If I want to catch a prince, I have to look the part."

"You have to be –"

"None of those foul words. I just need your opinion."

Several hours later, I was starving and *ready for the plucking*, as Omar worded it. The vulgar Himzo served his purpose and returned to his post with the other servants. The garden party had already started, so I crossed the sun-speckled marble floors through the center of the palace to the glass doors out back.

Prince Ezer would help me with my mission, and he had given me a delectable challenge. Señor Pascual's children must have prevented me from giving the slaying blow, but I could make no such claim about Ezer. What did they have in common? The enigma twirled in my brain, ready to be solved. Then there was the matter of the prince believing me to be some greedy, spineless waif. Like I could just walk away with no repercussions.

See how he would respond once he had a look at the rouge gown that hugged my shape all the way to my hips. The ladies at the boutique even added coloring to brighten my eyes, cheeks, and lips and accentuated my attributes. Whyzer Patro would eat this up if he could see it. The bond to my soul tugged with his bidding: *seduce him if you must.*

Two servants broke open the doors to the terrace, and I meandered among the other ladies who chose modest day dresses. When one of the fathers did a double take, I grinned wide at his slackened jaw. He appraised his sweet-looking daughter, who had honey curls and a pink gown stitched with gold brocade that screamed wealth.

My eyebrow rose, and I slipped deeper into the mix of young ladies who hoped to make themselves into the princess of Giddel. Now where was the prince? He had to be surrounded by an entourage of hungry fortune hunters.

Under the white tent, Prince Ezer drank from a golden goblet, accompanied by a pretty little thing and an even more eager mamá. Strain marked his tan cheeks as he tried hard to look interested in the conversation. I marched to the tent and snatched a glass of some sort of fruit beverage. The heat from the mingling people was almost worse than the uninhibited scorch of the sun. I weaved between the crowd until I managed to station myself between the elegant mamá and Prince Ezer.

Hiding wouldn't be my strategy. I bumped the prince's elbow and grinned up into his hazel eyes, rimmed with thick lashes. Prince Ezer snapped his attention in my direction and his expression broke into a real smile. His gaze drank me in with unveiled admiration.

The mother wolf turned to her daughter, giving her a look. "Julieta and I would love to see more of the grounds. Would you give us a tour sometime?"

Prince Ezer hesitated for a moment, licked his lip, and answered the ladies. He settled on having the palace historian lead a group through the extensive gardens behind the palace. As he spoke to many attendants organizing the endeavor, he snatched glances in my direction. I remained near the food table, tasting the almond and sesame brittle. One bite into sweet goodness and I couldn't resist making my rounds around the long table. Gema would have devoured the mini churros with chocolate. All the treats were meant to satisfy the ravenous women, though I supposed their hunger resided more in the power they'd gain in securing the prince's favor.

Almost all the attendees crunched along the gravel trail in the long caravan. The prince had disappeared from view, leaving me alone with several older damsels in attendance, including Señora Trucio.

"Do you always make yourself so noticeable on the job?" Señora Trucio grabbed a floral-printed plate with gold lining the outer edge. She plucked a sausage from a platter and several mango slices.

"What do you mean?" I bit into my churro, sugar sprinkling my bottom lip.

"Let me guess, you've decided to vie for the prince's hand while abusing your new comforts." She chomped into her hunk of meat. "You waste your time, child. Once he figures out what type of lady you truly are, he won't hesitate to tie a noose around your neck." She squished her cheeks into a pitying expression.

Footfalls sped toward us, and lo and behold, Prince Ezer caught his breath beside me.

I snorted. Little did she know, he already knew my profession and for whatever strange reason hadn't killed me yet.

"Greetings, Señora Trucio." He inhaled deeply. "I trust all is well."

Señora Trucio flipped out her white fan in a conspiratorial fashion. "I leave in two weeks and I so look forward to getting to know you better."

Two weeks? Omar said three. Someone fed me lies. Would Omar have a good reason to want me to fail? Or was the señora who hired a hit on her own husband to blame for the incorrect information? My churro churned in my stomach. I supposed two weeks would still give me plenty of time to set up my game pieces and strike.

Prince Ezer adjusted his doublet. "I thought you both planned on staying longer this time around. Papá and Mamá always enjoy your time together."

I took a deep breath, relieved that Omar told the truth after all. Yet even so it didn't stop the churro from tossing or the job from feeling off.

The señora cackled to herself. "We do, but Señor Trucio has some relic business to attend to at home. I beg your leave. It's much too hot standing here with so many seats closer to the seashore." She strutted away before Prince Ezer formally dismissed her. The familiarity in their manner spiked curiosity at how I might use that as fuel to erupt a figurative fire.

"Now, Luiza, I'd love a private walk along the shore." Prince Ezer extended his elbow, inviting me to place my hand atop his forearm. "We can talk more freely without so many prying ears."

"Truly, it doesn't bother you that I'm here? You're supposed to be focused on a bride."

He chuckled. "Promise me one thing. No mischief in the palace or on palace grounds?"

"Doesn't showing up speak for itself?"

"Yes, but I'm not sure you understand the invitation includes some parameters."

"Does it now?" I dumped my plate on a passing servant's tray, aggravated that the prince played some game with me and was untouchable by my gift. "Pray tell, do you have some immoral plans to take me hostage or to make me part of your royal guard? I'd like to settle that I am not for sale."

He flinched and blinked several times. "Not at all. You are stunningly beautiful, but..." He seemed to turn the words in his mind, opening his mouth and shutting it again.

His declaration burned in my cheeks at the way he stated it like a truth acknowledged and not some form of manipulation.

"But I haven't a need to make you into anything besides a friend. You're the only young lady who isn't tripping over herself to settle a betrothal."

An airy chuckle escaped my throat. How I wished to share this delectable turn of events with Gema. "So what you're saying is that I am the only ineligible señorita, and you want to spend the day getting to know me anyway."

"Yes, but I'd still like your promise." He lifted his arm across his chest like a soldier making a pledge. "No mischief?"

Giggles poured out my mouth and sounded foreign to my ears. Nothing of such a frivolous nature had ever exited my lips since I lived at the castillo. "No mischief on palace grounds," I assured him, though I had no conviction behind the words.

To make matters worse, a small poisonous flower among the bramble piqued my attention, but I'd have to investigate some other time when Ezer wasn't so attentive.

He led me along a walkway, down several sets of stairs to the beach. Curiosity wriggled its way inside me like a worm. Was the protection from my gift some sort of ward in the palace? I sent a gust of power straight through his chest, into his heart. The initial blow would have taken down the burliest of men.

Prince Ezer laughed. "I thought you said no mischief. That tickles." He continued down the steps without me.

That tickles? My death blow tickled; the word swam through my mind, revolting and offensive. The amount of energy I poured into the maneuver left me winded as if I really were Luiza. I trudged down the rest of the stairs.

He leaned on a wooden post with wind-swept hair, completely undaunted by my attempts to murder him. Though I daresay now with so many spectators above I might have held back if my gift could touch him ... possibly.

I tried again. This time I worked with precision, hitting a spot in his brain that should have rendered him useless.

He sighed with exasperation. "Still tickles."

And again I reached for his aorta and squeezed. My grip slipped.

Prince Ezer rolled his eyes. "Tickles. Come on, let's walk before you make yourself faint from exhaustion."

I tossed my head back and grunted. What in all the Agata Sea was this? Though my ability failed, somehow a part of me liked my gift being something other than the executioner's noose. I plodded through the sand, too queasy from all my efforts.

"Are you coming or what?" He waited for me several body lengths down the white sand beach.

The rest of our walk was spent in trivial conversation about favorite colors, sea creatures, and the weather. The chatter remained lighthearted, most of the time. I found myself laughing with too much frequency until he mentioned the Ancient One. Turns out Ezer was not talking about an old man, but our creator and the one who gave us our gifts.

If the Ancient One exists, he must have hated me since my youth. But I kept that thought to myself.

CHAPTER 7
COTTIA

SITTING IN THE PARLOR the next day, I carried a book in hand, pretending to read *The Time Before the Fall*. Once all the pretty little schemers got to the practice yard, I'd go back to the beach because a little flower gave me an appetizing idea to carry out. Wouldn't it be a shame if Ezer's personal goblet were found in Trucio's quarters with a heavy helping of poison? A poison found only in the northern region of the Agata Sea.

As the puzzle danced through my mind in convoluting steps that resembled a paso doble, ladies and their mothers took to the trails outside the many windows in the parlor. They paraded on the gravel road, past the corner of the palace, and beyond a wooden stable to the guard's castle. The invitation to the exercise yard arrived at my door early in the morning. Joining the others to watch sparring matches between the prince and several soldiers would almost be alluring if the courtiers' absence didn't provide the ideal opportunity to execute my plan.

I leaned back in my armchair and tossed my feet onto a footstool, an unladylike posture that might earn me a whooping if Whyzer Patro ever found out. That brought a wicked grin to my face.

Footfalls approached. I righted myself just in time to find a caped fellow haunting the doorway. For a second, I believed Whyzer Patro had been summoned by my thoughts.

"You could have given me a hint." Prince Ezer pulled back his hood enough for me to get a good view of his face. "I spent the past hour trying to locate you."

"It only took you an hour?" I lifted the tome to cover my agitation.

He stepped closer and flipped the book over.

"Excuse me." The indignation in my tone struck all the right notes.

"You should at least have the book upright if you want anyone to believe you're reading it." He plopped into a verdant armchair across from me.

I pouted. This prince paid me far too much attention and would ruin my plans. "Is there a particular reason you aren't showing off your sparring technique for the ladies?"

"Yurde, my double, is at work showing off my muscles for me. I know you believe me to be quite generous, but I couldn't have an assassin prowling about."

"Prowling? That's lovely. I thought you said I can choose to free myself of my naughty deeds."

His mouth tipped up in the corners and a glimmer waltzed in his eyes. "You showed up, but I thought about our conversation and I'm not sure you actually promised to behave."

"I did too. Has anyone died?"

"When I couldn't find you this morning or Señor Trucio and Señora Trucio, I thought you might have been involved."

Slapping the book shut, I narrowed my gaze at him. "What does it matter to you what happens to the old couple?" I held my breath, hoping he'd give me the information I needed.

They had to have some familial connection to the Pedrozian King or some resource all the kingdoms wanted. Perhaps a deal was on the king's desk waiting for Señor Trucio to sign it for the sake of various territories.

"Señor Trucio is a friend. It would break Papá's heart, and we'd have to find another liaison to the northern territories of the kingdom of Pedroz."

"That's all?"

He flinched. "You admit that he's your target."

"No, I daresay it might be Julieta. She seems like a pretty thing."

"That's not funny."

"I'm a bit nervous to turn away from Julieta's mamá, lest I find a dagger in my back."

A deep chuckle tumbled out of him. "That might be true. Since I can't have you wandering the palace unguarded, would you like to take a walk with me through the town?" He tugged the hood down past his forehead.

He can't be serious, I thought. The earnest expression awaiting my answer proved otherwise. I asked, "Are you going to be dressed like a whyzer?"

"Of course not. I'm a townsperson. Don't you see the rough-spun clothing and the cloak goes a long way in hiding my face? Look, the ruse won't work if I'm spotted elsewhere."

"A young man who lives on the edge. Refreshing." I got to my feet and strode to the door, but he didn't follow. "I supposed you were coming on our walk."

"You didn't answer." He hopped out of the chair like an excitable child who was offered candy.

The quiet exit through the servant's door made a great way to escape Omar's notice. Prince Ezer confirmed my suspicions about Señor Trucio being of no consequence. If Señor Trucio meant more on a personal level than politically, I must conclude that Whyzer Patro gave me a false deal, one in which I could never win. Though it could be possible that the prince didn't know about all that transpired between the kingdoms.

Prince Ezer and I made it to a narrow gate. He tugged his hood slightly back in order to show the guards who he was. The gate flung open to a cobblestone road and fortress on the other side of it. Something about the windowless building gave me a chill.

We turned right toward the portion of town with all its shops tailored for the wealthy to have every luxury at their disposal. First Prince Ezer took me to his favorite bakery. Then to a dress shop where he allowed me to choose whatever material I liked.

"Are you sure I can choose *any* fabric?" I lifted an eyebrow.

"Of course, I much prefer you not select such a seductive red gown again."

I pursed my lips, contemplating.

He leaned over my shoulder. "You must have some bone of self-preservation? Julieta's mamá will sharpen her dagger."

"You're the one who said any fabric I want."

"I give up." He tossed up his hands and left several gold coins on the seamstress's counter. "I've got to check in with Yurde." He left.

An older woman with short graying hair brought over several colors of thick fabric. "Was that Prince Ezer?" She leaned close to me in a conspiratorial fashion. "Are you his chosen bride?"

"Bride?" An idea sparked in my mind that was too delicious not to execute. "What would you have me try on if I said yes?"

Wrinkles crinkled across her forehead, but she didn't prod any further. Instead, she lumbered through her store plucking a flurry of dresses for me to squeeze into and for her to appraise.

By the time I made it out of the shop, I thought I might have to walk to the palace alone. The heavens had shifted from a sky-blue shade to an orange hue.

"Luiza!" Prince Ezer waved from down the road, carrying a basket. He ran in his dreary robe toward me. When he arrived, he caught his breath. "Would a picnic on the dock sound pleasing?"

"Does it matter what I think?"

"Of course, it does."

"Good."

A horse-drawn carriage clomped by, and I crossed the road. "Did you find out how Yurde did at the match?"

"I even watched myself win one against a giant. I must say I am an excellent swordsman, though a little showy with my muscles. I might have to talk to Yurde about all the flexing."

My guffaw surprised me. "Prince Ezer, I'd be excellent myself if I fought like you."

He found a spot on the grass overlooking the galleons and the Agata Sea beyond. The waves reflected the evening sun and painted his face with golden light. From this angle, I almost understood why all the ladies swooned in his presence. The thought shook my insides as I glanced at the prince.

"You don't have to call me Prince Ezer. I much prefer Ezer."

With a nod, I dug through his basket of warm empanadas, ribs, and tostones. A jar of garlic dip had my stomach growling. We ate side by side, eyeing each other. I couldn't say this was the most comfortable meal I'd ever had, but it had more to do with the jarring warmth that tingled beneath my skin.

"Did you have servants pack the meal for you?" I asked.

"No, I had to sneak in the kitchen and steal from tonight's supper."

Trying to keep from smiling, I shoved another empanada in my mouth.

"What's one of your dreams?"

I pointed to my full mouth, still chewing.

He chuckled and stared out to sea. "Mine is to find the last relic and destroy it."

Swallowing a huge lump of goodness, I rushed to answer. "Why that of all things?"

"How many people have lost their souls trying to find the relic? If rumors are right, even if they get it, would we want people with no scruples living forever?" He glanced at me to gauge my response. "We could at least burn the maps so criminals and adventurers would stop their pursuits."

"Couldn't we forget about the relics altogether? Then we all can be content and live our lives."

"Is that your dream?"

"No, I want to be a laundry girl with Gema, my best friend. Live in a small town, make my wage, go home, and sleep. That's all. None of this other work."

He covered my hand with his, and my eaten empanada flipped over in my stomach. I yanked my hand back and stood, unsure why a prince would be endeared to a person who wants to be a laundry girl.

Movement caught in my peripheral. Several pedestrians walked along the road, but one man with a thin mustache caught my attention. Omar stared at me from across the cobblestones and leaned against a building as if he'd been there for a while.

My heart hammered against my breastbone, but why? I'd done exactly what Whyzer Patro asked and seduced the prince. Yet even in all my plans something inside me had shifted ever so slightly. I tipped my chin high and reminded myself to focus on the job. More than one life depended on it.

CHAPTER 8
COTTIA

THE BANQUET A COUPLE nights later proved another spectacle. I may have chosen a light blue gown, the exact shade used for weddings, and I may have twisted a white mantilla into my hairdo with lace along the edges. If there wasn't food involved at the banquet, I would have covered my face with a thin veil to give the ladies more of a fright. One walk on the beach with their prince obviously meant he formed a secret betrothal with me, according to the whispers I heard through the passages.

Señora Trucio knocked into my side as I strode through the atrium to the dining hall. "Careful, child, you play with fire."

"Whatever do you mean?" I turned to find Señor Trucio a step behind her.

The man wore an ostentatious doublet with puffed sleeves that kept all others handbreadths away. His bald head and curled mustache did nothing for his looks, but judging by the cocky lift of his chin, he didn't care three flips about what anyone thought, including his wife's good opinion.

I grinned at Señora Trucio as she assessed her husband with distaste scrunched on her nose.

When she caught me staring, the older woman spread open her black-and-red fan and cocked her chin high in the air. "Sit by us. I could use some entertainment tonight."

Servants in green livery stood guard outside the double doors into the banquet hall with faraway stares. We traversed the entrance in amicable silence. Upon entering, I observed the long table at the opposite end with the Giddelian king and queen already in their seats. They chatted with Prince Ezer beside them, but with such a large room I couldn't hear a word. Tables encircled the hall's perimeter in a U shape, and it seemed more than half of the other ladies had arrived early. Many of them ditched their drab outfits for red gowns in a similar shade to the one I had worn at the garden party.

Julieta's mother gasped at seeing me. "Have you ever seen such an uneducated..." She pitched her ranting lower and continued to complain to poor Julieta.

Hushed mumbling rippled through the room that gave the royals pause. Prince Ezer met my gaze and slapped his face in amusement. His smile crinkled his features in such a way that his eyes twinkled. I pressed my shoulders back and lifted my chin, enjoying entering a game of vying for the prince's attention where I had zero stakes.

Señora Trucio swatted my chest with her fan. "We're sitting over here."

I kept my focus on Prince Ezer for a second longer than necessary. I wouldn't allow myself to break into a bigger grin than the one already twitching the corners of my mouth. Finally, Prince Ezer tipped his head as if to say, "that's enough fun for now," and I followed Señora Trucio to a seat all the way at the end where the most esteemed guests ate. How delicious it felt to have so many angry pairs of eyes boring into my back.

From across the table, Señor Trucio flinched his beady eyes as if seeing me for the first time. "Did you know that you look like a bride in that gown?"

"Do I?" My intonation had a heavy layer of sarcasm.

The feast continued with platters coming and going far faster than I had a chance to taste. Soup, sausage, vegetables, fried plantain, bread, and so much more. Señora Trucio proved an excellent companion since she could spill dirty little secrets about each family.

The mother-daughter duo beside us had somewhat appealing faces, if it weren't for the unfavorable shape of their noses. According to Señora Trucio, their family lost their fortune to gambling debts.

Prince Ezer eventually made his way around the tables with all the eager ladies hoping for him to notice them. When he started at the opposite end of the large U from me, many haughty expressions turned in my direction. I dabbed my mouth with a cloth napkin and met their insult with a grin.

Though I truly didn't care for the prince to choose me, since that would be impossible, I couldn't help but glance at the way he walked with confidence. His strong jaw and tan skin had a rugged appeal that kept my eyes entranced.

"Stop staring," Señora Trucio whispered in my ear. "It's not befitting for someone like you to pine."

I glared at the older woman.

Her dark eyes danced with delight, and a self-satisfied smirk hitched up her cheeks as she leaned back in her chair.

"Are you now my mamá?"

"If I were her, I'd tell you to get up and find something else to do. I promise you'd be thrilled with the result." She sipped from a pewter goblet distinct from the royal family's and quirked her dark eyebrow upward like the conniving woman she was.

A war waged in my heart for the briefest of moments, like a storm that erupted out of nowhere. But I got to my feet. Her prompting would either cause me to humiliate myself if Prince Ezer didn't take notice, or it could cause a tasty stir to the mundane. My brief hesitation caught many gazes, but not the prince's. I excused myself with a slight bow and cough at my companion and the man I meant to kill. He grunted and tipped his goblet toward me. Then I strode around the U to the double doors at the apex of the tables.

I risked a peek backward and met Prince Ezer's eye. In the seconds we watched each other, a question furrowed in his expression.

Cielos, the conniving woman was right. I spun to exit. The small passage from the dining hall to the atrium echoed my clicking heels. When the atrium opened before me with its tall arched ceilings and lonely space, I panicked at having no aim.

A rush of footfalls sounded behind me. "Luiza," Prince Ezer called. He caught my wrist. "Where are you going?" The pressure from his touch, though welcome, allowed my gift to feel his heart pumping faster than normal.

Was he nervous I'd cause trouble, or was it something else?

"Prince Ezer, I'm honored you came racing out to meet me."

"You're going to miss the illusionist's show," he said.

"Is that such a tragedy? Don't they usually reverberate tales from the ancient tomes?"

"Yes, but I thought they might speak to you in a different way this time." His answer gave me pause.

Why did it matter what I thought about the tales of old?

"I had no plans on leaving, but I might need some help locating the privy. I suppose that might not be a task for a prince."

His chuckle tumbled out in a delightful cadence. "Here I was thinking you might be up to no good."

"You suppose much." I signaled to my wrist still firm in his grasp.

"Since I'm out here, allow me to lead the way."

I yanked myself from his grip, watching his jaw tighten with an emotion I couldn't quite place. "Does it matter so much what I'm doing out here when all the important people to you are in there?"

He backstepped and opened his palms in surrender. "I just didn't want you doing something you'd regret later." The melody of his words rang so sincerely that they caught a lump in my throat.

I tried to swallow around the strange bunch of emotion, but I found myself clearing my throat several times. The red gown and the blue wedding dress had all been done to disrupt his little competition, and here I was still playing games. To what end? To steal his goblet and pin the murder on him so when I finally executed Señor Trucio, it would cause a stir big enough to cause political retribution.

What I never accounted for was the kind man before me taking an interest in my conscience.

"Prince Ezer, your persistence has paid off. Lead the way to the privy."

The line of his mouth upturned. "I think this might make us friends. You can drop the formalities in private and just call me Ezer."

CHAPTER 9
COTTIA

THE NEXT MORNING, I brushed my hair in my guest suite without makeup or a sensuous gown. All that remained before me was a girl in a thin chemise and my naked face in the mirror. A feminine version of Papá's sloped nose and his full lips reminded me of when he was alive—and that there was a time when I used my gifting to heal. A scar ran under my chin from a knife wound; my exhaustion from fighting had drained my ability to heal it. Large, brown eyes that had seen death too many times stared back at me, asking if I could assassinate one last man for Gema's protection and my freedom.

My fingers brushed over the raised skin hidden in the shadow of my chin. Ever since then, I'd been quick to do my jobs ... besides the incident with Señor Pascual. I also learned that Whyzer Patro wasn't benevolent. His branding on my shoulder tugged and pulled at my skin when distance kept us apart, and I dreaded his control over my body when I stood in his presence.

Why was I hesitating after all these years? First, I decided not to assassinate Señor Pascual with his children present. Now I had second thoughts about Señor Trucio, who deserved punishment for what he did to Papá, yet I didn't have it in me to be ruthless. I simply wanted to be free.

As for Whyzer Patro, Señor Trucio's crime seemed to be an association with Señor Pascual and the perfect alignment for the whyzer's greater ambitions—something to do with a relic—more power. What were the whyzer's true intentions?

A knock rattled the door on the other side of the room. I placed the brush on the vanity and pushed out of my cushioned stool. I wrapped myself in a thick green robe just in case it wasn't one of the young maids.

With my gifting sparked, I turned the lock and cracked open the door. "Yes?"

"Señorita Luiza, your servant brought you a missive and package that arrived just today." The young girl held it on a silver platter, confirming her story.

Prodding the girl with my gift, I reached for her throat with the invisible fingers and felt the blood in her veins swooshing about at a normal pace. She told the truth.

"Thank you." I snatched the sealed letter and a rectangular parcel, slim and no longer than my forearm, and shut the door. My heart pounded against my breastbone with unusual ferocity. Prince Ezer, I mean Ezer, wouldn't send me a letter through Omar, and the seal had a tree shape like that of anyone in the castillo back home. The only possible senders would be Gema and Whyzer Patro. But the whyzer would never risk his name being exposed in such a location as this unless he put a spell on the letter.

I ripped open the wax and drank in the sight of Whyzer Patro's handwriting. I should have known. He had placed what he called a ward over the words themselves, which was a signature ability he enjoyed flaunting. Even before reading his message, I could sense the sick joy he managed to instill in the strokes of his letters. The pulse of power trickled off the document like tiny spiders marching toward my tongue to keep me from disclosing its contents. It was a good thing I had no one to tell.

Young Luiza from your whyzer,

Omar sent word that you have garnered the prince's favor. Bravo, my dear. I didn't think you had it in you. I'm sure you figured out that the prince is untouchable by your gifting. That detail might have slipped my mind. Continue to fulfill our original deal and then pursue the crown. You will gain more than freedom with this addition to our bargain.

Once you are princess, you must kill the king. I've delivered a dagger glazed with the oils from a flower found only in Pedroz. Tensions will be high, but I think you can manage such an affair. Your extra reward will be me granting Gema's freedom as well as leaving you to be Queen of Power. You'll get all the independence you desire.

There is the small matter of our oath being sealed with words of power. So, you must put an end to Señor Trucio in no more than three days to show your agreement with the new deal.

Should you fail, Gema will die, and a more competent assassin will be sent.

From your favorite person

The letter grew heavy in my hands. I had three days to start a war with the death of a nobody. Señor Trucio had swindled Papá, but I couldn't resuscitate Papá by killing the man who ruined us.

My head spun with thoughts about how I'd been duped into believing freedom was in reach. Whyzer Patro also had to have known my Luiza identity wouldn't hold for long. Ezer's words came whispering to mind like the chirping of insistent coquí frogs at night. Could I simply *walk away* like he suggested?

Of course, there was Gema to consider. What if I retrieved Gema? The whyzer would never expect that, and I'd still have time to kill Señor Trucio if I couldn't come up with a better plan while traveling to the castillo.

Sneaking through the palace in my thick robe, brown trousers, and a simple green tunic, I tiptoed through a servant's stairwell descending to the main floor. Many maids chattered below, but I escaped the stairwell before they realized who snuck about.

The stable had to be somewhere on the far side of the palace. I had the choice to walk straight through the corridors and risk running into Omar or exit out back.

Once I arrived on the main floor, I turned left and kept my head low. Servants passed me with curious expressions, but there was no change in their heart rates. Since over a dozen strange girls and their mothers stayed in the palace, I had a chance at escaping without alerting a soul.

A new passageway opened to my right. Sunlight poured in through a wall of windows beyond a room with double doors to my left. One of the doors remained cracked open, which of course spurred some curiosity, but not enough to thwart my plan to exit the back of the palace.

Just as I raced forward, Julieta crossed into the corridor. Her mamá's voice echoed from a stone's throw away, and I spun on my heels. The double doors offered refuge from being seen. I slipped into the mystery room and met an enormous space with shelves of books covering three of the four walls. In the center, tables and chairs were sprinkled throughout with one person sitting at the table.

The man turned his head slowly from his tome. Sunlight from tall windows caught in his gaze, making Ezer's tawny-green eyes shine like honey.

"Luiza?" Ezer got to his feet. Not a single hair twisted out of place, nor a wrinkle marred his simple yet refined doublet.

Sweat droplets sprung from the back of my neck. I searched the far corners of the library, but my only escape remained behind me. "Yes, Ezer. Buenos Días!"

"Would you like to join me in my studies of the ancient tomes?"

"No, I was just curious about where the doors led. Now I've seen, and I must be off."

He furrowed his eyebrows, giving my body a once-over from afar. "Are you wearing trousers?"

"Where I come from, they're all the rage." I clutched my robe tighter, realizing the strap around my waist had loosened enough to reveal my less than appropriate attire.

"Please join me." A pleading note marked Ezer's voice. "I've been wanting to show you this."

I pursed my lips and considered all the excuses I could make to flee, but I might run into a wall of women upon exiting. "At your orders." My boots tapped the distance between him and me with only the slightest of sounds.

Ezer offered his chair, and when I sat, he pushed it in for me. He quickly filled the spot beside me with something like boyish excitement tipped on the corners of his mouth.

"What is it you want to show me?" I asked in a deadpan voice.

My mood didn't disturb his jovial one. "Remember how I said you could always walk away from your profession?"

Keeping my spine upright, I resisted an eye roll. My plans to escape were going to the wolf of death as we spoke.

"Well," he continued, "I wanted to show you that the ancient tomes say that you can be forgiven. All who come to the Ancient One will be heard if you seek him with all your heart."

Ezer's words were written in fancy ink on the page before me. This prince really tried my patience and my ability to hold in a good eye roll. Heat flared up my neck with a confusing stir of anger roiling through my insides.

"Look, Ezer, if the Ancient One exists, he abandoned me long ago."

"How can you say that?"

"You're a prince who has had a silver spoon dangling from your mouth since you were a baby. What do you know about hardship?"

A muscle in his jaw ticked. His intense stare unnerved me with the twinkle of passion behind his gaze. "You're right. I don't know your story or why you dress like you're about to commit a crime. I just know what I've seen."

"And what exactly have you seen?"

"He comforted me when Maria died."

"Your former betrothed?" I asked.

"Yes. I don't like to speak about it much, but it's hard to want to fill her place. She'd been a friend growing up. She went out one day for a ride on her horse, something so common and normal, but she fell off and hit her head. I guess you never know when your time might end."

"Sounds like a powerful god, indeed." The moment the words slipped out my mouth, I bit my lips at my callous response.

He blinked the sheen over his eyes and continued in a much more business-like tone. "I've seen prayers answered. Heard the whispers of things I do not know. Your gifting fails to subdue me every time. I've seen the spark in your eye when I said you could walk away from your current life."

Knees bobbing, I gnawed my lip. How much should I tell him? I opened my mouth, and my voice came out in a whisper. "What if I told you that that is exactly what I am doing? But I need to ride out to get my friend. If I don't retrieve her, she'll get the punishment for me walking away."

His slight hunch straightened. "Can I go with you?"

"No."

"You can't go on your own and my gifting would be useful."

"No."

"Do you even know where to find the stable or which horse to choose?"

I sighed. "I have an idea."

"Let me show you." He pushed his chair back and got to his feet. In an exaggerated motion, he offered his arm for me to take. "I'm here to serve you."

"Don't you have a squad of women to attend to?"

His gaze drifted to the windows and then back to me. "They're boring, and I've got the Ancient One's work to do. That is who guards me from your tainted gifting, after all."

Now, that got an arching eye roll from me. *Tainted gifting? Cielos! There's no way in all the Agata Sea that this Ancient One is protecting him. There has to be something else.*

"You and this Ancient One. Couldn't you take control of some other girl's dance moves?"

He guided me to the doors and peeked out into the passageway. "I much prefer to use my gifting to free you from the clutches of crime."

"I've heard the rumors and danced a waltz without knowing the steps, but I'd like to hear it from you." I crossed my arms. "What exactly can you do?"

"I can take over any person's or animal's movements within my view. I'm not sure how many people at a time since I've yet to be tested. I'm not sure of my limits." He slipped his hand in mine like he had the day we walked through town. A swirl of warmth twirled through my stomach, and I pacified myself by figuring that this was his way of making sure I followed him.

Hand in hand, we ran along the back corridor as co-conspirators.

CHAPTER 10
COTTIA

EZER AND I RAN through the wide passageways in the palace like school children being told they had extra time to play. We burst through a side door and passed guards who gave each other looks. If I had to guess, they thought we were enamored with each other.

"Come around this way," Ezer said. The wide, perfect grin on his masculine face drew my eyes to him one too many times.

We crossed a grassy area to a tidy stable with three workers tending the horses.

"Prince Ezer, at your orders," a stableman called with a quick bow. The older fellow had wide shoulders, a brown apron, and a thick, graying mustache.

"Actually," Ezer pointed toward the palace, "I'd like a moment alone with Señorita Luiza."

"Of course, Your Majesty." The man whistled for his companions to follow him away from the stables.

The three of them marched out, peeking over at me and whispering to themselves as they left. Grins covered their faces, and I even heard a whisper of the words, "She's the chosen girl."

If only they knew. I could never be chosen. Prince Ezer merely offered to help me escape, which in itself was quite remarkable. Ezer slipped his fingers between mine and squeezed. The warmth in his touch suddenly felt more personal than him directing me to the right location. Pleasant tingles swarmed up my arm and settled in my chest.

Ezer stopped in front of a white horse with speckles of gray and light brown in its mane. The creature had a muscular body with a royal air about it.

"His name is Fuego." Ezer petted his side, and the horse nudged the prince's shoulder. "Not today, good man. Will you take the señorita to her destination?"

Fuego snorted in response.

"Alright, fellow, I'll get you some carrots."

Ezer marched out the stables, his silhouette displaying his masculine gait and broad shoulders. Fuego also peered at his master with a twinkle of excitement behind thick black lashes. When Ezer returned, he gave the horse a giant carrot and smiled at me with a boyish glee that melted my insides to butter.

"Thank you." I fanned myself with the collar of my wool robe. The heat must have been from wearing so many thick layers of clothes.

"You are welcome." Ezer squared up to me and ran his fingers along my jawline. "I hope we can make it back and forth before nightfall."

A trail of delightful warmth remained under his touch, muddling my thoughts. What did he mean by we?

I pushed away his hand. "Ezer, you aren't coming with me."

He cocked his head to the side and furrowed his brows. "I won't let him hurt you." He reached for me again, but I batted him away. Disappearing into the next stall, he prepared the other horse for riding.

His kindness and intuition would make him a suitable match for someone, but not for me.

"No, I'm going to disappear. Gema and I have talked about traveling the wilderness together away from all this. Just let me go."

The prince peeked his head from the other stall, and his expression darkened. I couldn't read the emotion flitting in the quirk of his mouth or the slight bob of his Adam's apple. "You'll still need me to join you for part of the trip. The guards won't open the palace gate for you to exit nor the guards at the city's wall. You'll be on royal steeds with no royals."

"But after that you must turn back. If you are caught, I can't promise you protection."

Ezer saddled Fuego. His silence didn't give me any confidence in him understanding the plan.

I pursed my lips, trying to find the right concoction of words that would keep him in Giddel. "As a prince with so many beautiful guests, I'm sure you are needed in the palace and, Pat—" my upper arm throbbed from almost saying the whyzer's name, "I doubt yours and my gifts together would be formidable opposition for what's to come."

The prince offered his arm and motioned with his head for me to mount Fuego. "Do you work for a corrupt whyzer?"

My breath caught in my throat, and I swallowed around the lump. "You're cute when you're concerned." I climbed into the saddle.

His face was now beside my knee with a searching gaze and a firm line at his mouth. "I assume you know how to ride?"

"Yes," I answered. A strange impulse to muss his cropped hair itched in my fingertips. Would he finally leave me alone if I did something so odd? Or maybe the urge had more to do with his gentle touch from earlier. Instead, I let my powers trickle along my arms.

He shoved the reigns in my hands and mounted the stallion beside Fuego. We were off before Ezer acknowledged my plea for him not to follow me. With my ability, I could break a ligament in the horse with a thought, but with such a stubborn man, that might not be enough to change his mind. The idea of hurting an animal fell like a boulder in my belly, and so did the consequences of this rash outing. Whyzer Patro would do worse than kill me, especially if Ezer found out the whyzer's identity and location. But what else could I do but try and save Gema? I let my invisible touch drift to Ezer's unharmable body as I led Fuego behind him on the gravel road to the gate.

The iron bars flung open. Ezer maintained a steady pulse with only the slightest hint of adrenaline seeping into his system, despite us marching through the cobblestone roads with far too many people swarming the walkways.

Many people bowed before their prince and pointed at me. The questions about if I was the new bride whispered on the breeze. Ezer had to have heard the people. The king and queen would learn about Ezer taking a ride with the girl who wore a bridal gown to the supper.

A strange squeeze gripped my chest at that thought. Did I care what Ezer and his parents thought about me? I waved it off. The sensation must have to do with all the nerves over the punishment waiting, should I get caught stealing Gema.

The outer wall of the city came into view between the buildings. The arched door of the city had several guards atop the wall and several on the ground. A line of country folk with mules lugging carts, barrels of produce, and baskets lined up to enter Giddel.

When our horses clomped to the gate, the guards parted the way for us. One soldier in a decorated doublet approached Prince Ezer with a bow. He asked something about whether his highness needed more guards. I pleaded with my eyes for Ezer to refuse more intruders on my trip.

Prince Ezer twisted around to peer at me. "No, that won't be necessary."

I let out a long breath.

Thank you, Prince Ezer, for not ruining my plans again.

We continued down the long path to the main road. Once we arrived at the crossroad, Prince Ezer stopped, and I pulled up next to him.

He rolled his shoulders back with an impeccable posture befitting someone of his station. "Where are we going?"

"You're going home." I spurred Fuego onward to the western road.

But the prince continued behind me with an unreadable expression.

Dozens of arm spans later, I shouted behind me. "Thank you for letting me borrow your horse and helping me leave Giddel. You are no longer required."

He guided his horse to speed up, then slowed the horse's gait as he caught up with me. "I can't very well be seen leaving Giddel with one of the potential brides and returning without her."

I glared at him with the fury of a storm. *Fine. Let him gamble with his life. That's his business.*

He quirked a grin and bobbed his eyebrows playfully as if my desperate plans for freedom were some joke. As if Whyzer Patro wouldn't use one of the other assassins to gut me when he realized I stepped out of line. Worst of all, the whyzer might manipulate me into harming myself, which I'd seen many times over again.

Prince Ezer had no idea what danger he willingly galloped into.

CHAPTER II
COTTIA

"I can't believe you followed me all the way here."

Ezer shrugged while he tied up his horse to a tree beside Fuego. "Are you under his control?"

"What do you mean?" I couldn't meet his gaze and found refuge in staring at the forest floor, between the dense foliage, and at the petals of a small white flower only found in this region. A fire lit in my cheeks at how vulnerable I was.

"These are Whyzer Patro's lands. I twisted scenarios in my head, and the only conclusion I could draw is that you are under his power. I've heard of such things while studying the dark arts."

My binding was the last thing I wanted to think about right now. We had a long walk ahead into town where Gema should have been doing chores for Patro Castle or working the orchard. Though Gema was a living fireball, she tended to be left out of jobs unless absolutely necessary.

"Like I said before, I can't return home without you." He crossed the space between us and shrugged. "Everyone saw us leave together. People would make up some interesting rumors."

Relieved that he changed the discourse to future plans, I responded, "Say you took me home. I'm of a sickly constitution, remember? I'm Luiza of Marden Estate." I started walking.

The chuckle rolling out his mouth made me want to slap him. Though that had been his go-to response since I met him, I wished he'd take my warning about us needing to part ways with some level of caution.

He kept close to my side, his shadow towering over my small form. "I can say that, but those other señoritas wouldn't believe it."

"Fine. Say someone stabbed me in my sleep to get rid of the competition." My clipped tone did too much to give away my turbulent emotions about Ezer.

He grabbed my elbow, stopping my next step. "Truly, do you want to do this by yourself?" He bent to meet me at eye level, his gaze fixed on my face, drinking me in with his hazel eyes, made browner by his dark tunic. "What's your real name?" He swallowed.

"Cottia."

"It's nice to officially meet you, Cottia." The breathy way he said my name flipped my stomach like a tortilla. "Look, I should have turned you in the moment I recognized you weren't Luiza. No one else in my family would have known since Luiza's a recluse. I see something good in you. Like one day you can choose the Ancient One's ways and ask for forgiveness."

"You make change sound so easy." I pushed him away from me, headache throbbing in my skull.

He caught my wrists. "It is that simple. I read you that part of the Ancient Tome. All who seek the Ancient One find him. Stop murdering and ask the Ancient One for forgiveness. It's only complicated because you think you're stuck."

"What do you mean? I am stuck." I got louder. "What do you know about being marked by—" My throat constricted, and the unpalatable name stuck to my tongue.

"Whyzer Patro," he offered.

"Yes. What do you know about being in his guild, where the only way out is death or by contract? If I simply walk away, I will be hunted and tortured. So, forgive me for thinking I'm trapped."

Ezer's face pinched around his mouth while compassion grew in the way he looked at me.

"Now do you understand why I can't have you following me? I am getting Gema and fleeing as fast as these legs will take us."

"All things are possible with the Ancient One." Ezer maintained a firm jaw and stance with no hint of backing down.

I grunted. "You are insane." My boots smacked the ground as I stomped forward through the forest around town.

My ears pulsed with an anger I didn't quite understand. The mystery of why I failed to kill him with my gifting couldn't possibly be the Ancient One. It could have to do with Whyzer Patro taking half my powers, but of course the same happened with Señor Pascual. Why was Ezer's faith in this Ancient One so annoying? Yet there had to be something to his claim. Was it more powerful than my master? Could it free me from bondage?

Footfalls sounded beside me. Ezer kept close, too jovial for a person headed for his possible torture and death. Whyzer Patro would eat Ezer alive and feed the bones to his dogs. No, better yet, the whyzer would get the war he desired. I could get what I wanted after all by turning in this lunk.

But a hole burned in my heart, considering I'd have to betray Ezer who gave me a chance when anyone else would have put me in shackles. Now that the whyzer believed I was Ezer's chosen betrothed, he would puppeteer my moves, therefore controlling the throne through me. Whyzer Patro would never let me go even if he didn't dictate my day-to-day living.

We crossed into the valley where buildings covered both sides of the mountains. The river flowed at the bottom and the castle stood like a beacon at the highest point in town. Faraway figures crossed the roads and walked about like miniature living dolls. I squinted to search the orchard's many lanes. Even from afar, Gema's hair could be seen if she were there. No pile of orange-red hair glittered in the sunlight, but she could be in a tree. She had to be there. Every other location required we breach the castle's or the town's walls.

Silence marked the long walk through the shadows of the forest. Whether Ezer understood the gravity of our situation or not, he followed my lead. The blazing sun made for brilliant cuts of light we needed to avoid. Guards always watched for intruders along the town's wall.

I prayed under my breath. "Ezer's Ancient One, if you are there, please let Gema be in the orchard. Let that be a sign that you're real."

An extra bounce marked my step, satisfied with the bargain I made. If the Ancient One pulled through, it would be a double win for Ezer and me. If Ezer's God wasn't real, then I'd let Ezer know he'd been wasting his time with all this Ancient One talk.

Ezer grinned as if he'd heard my thoughts. I felt my facial muscles contort into something that might have been a scowl, but in reality my insides flipped with the boyish tip of his lips. His effect on me exposed my weaknesses more than I would have liked. I scanned the empty forest and risked another glance at Ezer. He was so different than Cristobal or even Roberto, who always treated me with an extra dose of kindness.

The prince wagged his eyebrows at me, catching me staring.

Inwardly, I groaned. A twig cracked somewhere in the distance. I yanked Ezer's sleeve and scrambled up a trunk to the crook of giant branches. Ezer leapt up soon beside me, his body pressed against my side—far too close for comfort. More footfalls sounded in the distance. The heavy stomp had to have been from someone who never had to hide their presence, which meant it couldn't have been another assassin like Cristobal. Ezer's breath mingled with mine. I tipped my head to the side and puckered my lips to point to a higher branch where we'd be less exposed.

He nodded and led the way. I climbed and veered to the branch next to his so we wouldn't put too much weight on a single bough.

Minutes later, Omar appeared, red-faced and breathing hard. "Patro couldn't pay me enough to work with that girl. Leaving the job like that. If I don't get paid..." He continued mumbling his tirade.

Some part of me understood Omar's anger since Whyzer Patro didn't pay for failed jobs. Had Omar been following us though? Panic rose in my throat. So much could go wrong if Whyzer Patro believed Omar about me deserting my duty. I had told the whyzer my desire for freedom. Omar's tale would be believable.

I reached with my hand, releasing energy flowing through my arm. Omar's blood pulsed through his veins, agitation evident in his raised adrenaline. I pinched a vessel with my invisible touch. Omar dropped to his knees.

"Cottia?" Ezer gripped my shoulder. "What are you doing?"

Without removing my focus from Omar, I continued to squeeze. Omar slapped his chest, moaning.

"Stop, Cottia. This isn't you." Ezer pleaded.

I glared at him. "And who is he to you?"

"A person."

"Do you know how many people he's killed?"

"Then he deserves a trial, for the law to condemn him. Not you." Ezer's fingers bit into my arm.

I let go. A tingle of energy returned to my fingertips and danced along the markings over my skin. I heaved heavy breaths and dropped from the branch, landing like a cat.

Omar tipped forward; face planting in the underbrush.

Ezer climbed out of the tree and raced to stand beside me. "Is he dead?"

"Sadly, no." I glared at him for stopping me and for reminding me of how easy it was to slay a man simply because I wanted to save my behind. "This will cost me."

"Should we get a healer?" Ezer lingered over Omar's limp body stretched across the dirt.

"I am a healer." I continued through the trees, my boots swishing through the brush and grass. A growing distance formed between Ezer and me as I moved toward the castle orchard.

"Then come back and help the man." Ezer wouldn't budge.

With him shouting, he'd get us caught. The guards wouldn't hesitate to use him for their gain.

"Shhhh." I rushed to shut Ezer's mouth. "Are you trying to get us caught?"

He stretched his arms out to Omar. "Whatever you did to him, he's not getting up. We can't just leave him here."

"You can't be serious."

"It would be murder to leave him like this." Ezer rolled Omar over. "If you can heal him, it'd be the right thing to do. It says in the Ancient Tomes—"

"Enough of the Ancient Tomes. I'll try to heal him." I slapped my hand over Omar's chest, already regretting that I said I'd help. Healing would require more energy than I was willing to expend. Heat flowed like a river pouring out my fingertips.

Omar's insides didn't quite feel right. Though I understood a little about anatomy, I didn't know enough to fix the parts that I'd snapped out of synchrony. I set my hand over Omar's chest and let the outpouring flow with no direction in mind. The energy diverted on its own to different body parts. An ache formed, and I leaned in with more of my power. It tapped into my muscles, exerting them as if I'd run up a steep hill.

"His color returned." Excitement touched Ezer's words.

A sprig of joy peeked within my soul at having used my gifting to heal rather than destroy. But Omar heaved a breath and realization came pouring in.

"He's going to kill me once he wakes up." I lifted my hand off Omar's chest and marched off.

Ezer ran to catch up to me. "If it means anything to you, I think you did the right thing by helping him." The sincere way he spoke and the earnestness in his expression did something inside of me, like heavy rocks falling from my pockets, leaving me light on my toes.

The orchard opened up before us with trees laden with plums. "Gema has red hair. The sooner we get out of here, the safer we'll both be."

We trudged through the shadows, scanning between the boughs. The closer we got to the wall, the more my heart panicked. We made it to the last tree in the first lane and dodged into the next row. Several aisles later, I planned my entrance into the castillo. Ezer's good-natured smile vanished and was replaced with a worry line on his forehead. He continued a few paces ahead of me, eager to find my friend who might not be out here doing her normal task.

I was about to call to Ezer to tell him our next moves when a hand clasped over my mouth.

CHAPTER 12
COTTIA

THE PERSON BEHIND ME yanked at my elbow, spinning me around.

"What in all Agata are you doing here?" Gema threw her arms around me, swallowing me in one of her back-breaking hugs. "Please tell me that stud is the one you plan to elope with, and you just couldn't get married without your Gema." She laughed at her own joke.

Heart pounding, I tried to catch my breath, a scream still lodged in my throat.

"You haven't gone soft?" She pitched her voice low. "Introduce me. If you're not going to go after that hunk, I'm looking for someone to fly me away from here."

A nervous laugh quivered between my lips. "Well, I brought horses and I wanted to free you."

Gema's smile sobered. "Are you joking?"

I shook my head.

"Did you at least do the deed?" She leaned closer. "Like how quickly is Whyzer Patro's wrath going to come down on us?"

"If we go now, we have two days."

"So, what you're saying is, I can get my bow and arrow, a few daggers, and a change of clothes before I let you steal me away?"

"No, what I mean is, I need you to come with me now. Omar followed us and *this hunk*, as you say, made me revive him."

"What, did Omar get hurt?"

"I may have done some damage when I saw him, and..."

"Señoritas," Ezer cut in between us, "can we have this conversation while we're walking back to the horses?"

Gema sidestepped around Ezer. "Wait, so this," she pursed her lips, pointing at Ezer, "got you to use your healing? Like you stopped mid-slaying?" At my nod, her eyebrows shot halfway up her forehead.

If my glare could speak, I shouted at her to stop being so obviously shocked when the fellow was mere breaths from us.

"I'll take that as a yes." Ezer pressed his palm into the small of my back and judging by Gema's forward movement, he did the same to her.

We stumbled out of the orchard and into the forest area where Omar should have been. No trace of the man remained, which brought goosebumps to my arms. Though Omar had been born to a race of people who didn't normally receive gifting powers, the man had grown up in the countryside of Giddel. A whyzer gave him the gift of speed in his legs. He could run farther and faster than most people I knew. He got tired like regular folks, but he could be a formidable enemy.

Crossing the forest became an eerily quiet affair. The sound of our boots had me on edge. Once we got to the horses, we had to decide who rode with who.

"Why don't you both ride on Fuego and I'll go on Encanto?" Ezer untied Fuego and placed the reins in my palm.

Gema snatched the cords. "I don't think so. You two go together. We're going to need reinforcements. They won't bargain with me if I bring an assassin and a strange man."

"No, Gema," my words escaped before I could think better.

She leapt onto the horse's back. "Where should I meet up with you two lovebirds?"

Heat shot up to my cheeks along with a heavy helping of rage. Was she trying to make me furious at her? Because it worked. "No, you can't go off by yourself."

Ezer answered, "The Palace of Giddel then?"

"No, the inn at the Fantasmas." I kept my focus on Gema, who sat on Fuego. A quirk of my eyebrow and glance at Ezer bespoke that we needed to shed the prince. We were a danger to him.

She nodded in understanding. "The plan." We'd daydreamed countless times about meeting up at this inn at the edge of Giddelian soil, to a world beyond the whyzer's control.

"That works." I reached for Fuego, but Fuego pulled away.

Gema clicked her tongue. "Like I said, meet you at the inn. If I'm not there in two days, go without me." She tucked her hair under a scarf. A fire burned in her blue eyes, real flames licking up her eyelashes.

Fuego sped off with Gema atop it until she became a speck on the mountain side and disappeared behind a bend.

"How long does it take to get to the inn?" Prince Ezer asked.

"Two days, riding at a good clip." Part of my heart sank to my toes at me simply letting her slip away without an argument. The other, pricklier part of me glared at Ezer. If he weren't here, it would be simple to join Gema at a fortress of criminals and call in a favor. If it also weren't for him, I wouldn't have a chance of outrunning Whyzer Patro with this beauty of a horse.

I jabbed a finger at his chest. "Your Ancient One brought Gema to me." The words hadn't been planned or thought out, but it's what I felt, and it shocked me. I inhaled to steady the emotions swaying inside my chest. "Can the Ancient One truly free me from the oath contract I made with the whyzer?"

"Yes." He worked his jaw, pensive. "I'm not sure what oath Patro made. I can't imagine someone so wicked sealing it with a true oath from the Tomes. Surely if you believe and pray to the Ancient One with all your heart and change your ways, it can be done."

"A few stray words and the bond is gone?" I exhaled, defeated by the burning on my arm and the invisible cords, tugging within my chest for me to go back to Giddel to finish my job. The whyzer still worked like a puppeteer though he couldn't control my movements from so far away.

Ezer undid the saddle and threw it up in a tree, trying to hide the evidence of the ornate piece that screamed wealth. "Take me up on my word and see what happens." His offer warmed a part of me with its sincerity evident in every contour of his face and round eyes.

He held out his hand in a gesture asking if I needed his assistance. "Allow me to take you to the inn and I'll find another horse to ride back to Giddel."

I stared at his calluses between his thumb and his index finger along with the ones running up and down his palm, evidence of time spent with the sword. Perhaps he didn't always use a body double for his duels, and he could prove useful. I boosted myself onto Encanto with his help.

He climbed on after me. His warm torso pressed against my back, which did nothing for the queasy sensation overtaking my stomach. "Lead the way, Cottia." The husky way he said my name ignited a shiver between my shoulders.

Two days on the back of this beast with the prince? I fanned my face.

CHAPTER 13
COTTIA

WEARY FROM TRAVEL, WE set up camp on the mountainside far off the main road. It would take us a couple hours longer because of the detour up the mountain, but what else could we do?

Ezer tied Encanto to a tree in a grassy area. I picked up branches and fumbled through my boot. A small dagger resided in each of my tall leather boots, but the blade I kept in the left one was my favorite. I sliced off the tiny shoots to make a cozy shelter from the rain and the cool breeze. The green robe I stole from the palace would have to work as a blanket for the both of us.

Ezer's strong form could best be appreciated from afar, I decided as I watched him pet Encanto and offer him some of the fruits we'd picked up earlier on the road. He turned in my direction, offering me a heartwarming smile. I spun around at such thoughts and lopped off the twigs as if the motion could sever my treacherous musings.

Strong form? Best appreciated? What was happening to me?

Though we'd been together on the back of the beast all day, we hadn't spoken much about anything. In fact, he whispered under his breath in prayer to the Ancient One. Snatches of words caught my attention, ones like: Cottia, freedom, and bride.

He couldn't have meant for me to be his bride. The idea was ludicrous. Instead, I'd take a shot in the dark. I said my own prayers about a future. A place where I could live with food, simple work, and hope. If I could get away, I would believe in Ezer's Ancient One. The whole Gema being in the garden could have been coincidence, but me being free could never happen without a miracle.

"Do you need help with that?" Ezer swiped a long branch from the ground and produced his own dagger.

We formed a small lean-to in companionable silence while the skies lit up with two moons and the stars.

"Perhaps I should sleep outside the shelter." Ezer stood with hands on hips, observing the heavens.

"Don't be silly." I spread my cape out like a blanket. "It's a cool night and there's no way we can share the robe that way."

"No robe sharing." He continued to star-gaze.

"Why?"

He took the wide cape and cut it in half. A beat passed where he opened his mouth as if to speak. Then he pinned me down with a look that softened his features. "I like you too much to sleep next to you."

Heat bloomed on my cheeks. "Enjoy the open air, then." My snide tone was an easy way to dismiss him saying he liked me. He could only have meant he appreciated my company or thought me pretty. Now that was possible.

His grin tipped the corners of his mouth, and moonlight caught a fierce look in his eyes. "Cottia, I'm not just helping because I have altruistic motives."

A cool breeze brushed against my skin, sending goosebumps down my legs.

"What does that mean?" I wrapped my half of the cape around my shoulders.

"I think you're beautiful and interesting." He stepped closer and glanced at my lips. "Now, I would much prefer to make this declaration in the palace, but this is also part of who you are."

The closer Ezer got, the more my heart throbbed with his speech. He cupped my cheek with his sword-calloused palms, warm and inviting. He leaned down and met my eyes as if requesting permission.

My chin quivered and the air stalled in my lungs. The pale light from the moons brushed his forehead and nose and made his eyes glow with earnestness. I wanted him to press his lips to mine, but what would I do when he came to his senses? He and I could never be anything more than a stolen night, and that wouldn't do for me.

I pushed Ezer's shoulders. "Go to sleep. You're merely entranced by a little excitement." I raced under the lean-to and covered my torso and head with the robe. My body trembled with a desire to run back out and wrap my arms around the prince, but I couldn't tease myself like that.

Footfalls and rustling sounded outside the little shelter, but Ezer eventually settled. My thoughts overwhelmed my mind before I fell asleep. Did Ezer truly like me? Could Gema and I run away from Whyzer Patro? What happened to Omar? He had to have known I escaped the palace. I should have left him to die, but if I had, I'd be the same Cottia as I always had been. I didn't want to be the assassin anymore. I wanted to wipe the blood from my hands and use my gift to heal.

The next morning, ominous clouds covered the sky, promising we'd face a storm soon. We made preparations to leave and then hopped on Encanto's back. This time, I insisted that he travel in front of me, as I detested how Ezer's touch inspired dreams about him holding me close. Of course, now I wrapped my arms around Ezer's torso which had all the awkwardness of feeling someone's abdomen.

We swayed with Encanto's heavy footfalls on the decline of the mountain. The jungle around us echoed with bird chirps and buzzed with insect life. Though no sun poured out its rays, thick heat swallowed us and produced pools of sweat under my armpits and at the small of my back. Clomping sounded somewhere below, which snaked an edge of fear into my gut. This road had other people on it.

A hawk swooped to the ground and left with a prize in its claws. The omen couldn't be good.

"Did you see that?" Ezer looked over his shoulder.

An arrow whistled over his head. I spun to glimpse behind me and swore under my breath.

Omar and several other men in brown-and-black attire approached, bows and arrows at the ready. "Oh, Cottia, you made this too easy," Omar said.

All of Omar's men moved impossibly fast toward us.

I turned back around to meet Ezer's eye. The muscles under his tunic grew taut as if ready to fight. His jaw ticked with an unspoken threat to Omar and his four companions.

Ezer lifted his arms in seeming surrender, but a glint of mischief shone in the tilt of his lips. With a nod, he slipped off the horse, and I followed suit.

Omar laughed. "You know, we don't really need you for much of anything, Cottia. With him, we can get our riches." He paused, unnaturally stiff in his stance. "Let go of me and it might go better for Gema."

Instinctually, I swallowed hard. Did he know about Gema escaping?

"Cristobal will gut her." Omar's neck muscles strained under some unknown pressure. "You keep me alive, and I can bargain for you."

Ezer had said he could control people's movements, like he had at the ball with his gentle coaxing during our dance. But judging by the stillness of the four men, Ezer's powers far exceeded my expectations.

My eyes popped wide open, taking in the scene. Ezer wasn't merely a swordsman, and Omar couldn't bargain with the lowliest guard for anyone's sake. His twisted brain had never tried to help another soul.

"What's going on, Ezer?" I called to the other side of the horse.

"Well, Cottia, I have the men restrained, but I can't quite figure out what we should do with them," Ezer answered from the other side of the beast.

I leaned my head to see around the flicking peppered tail. Encanto decided to relieve himself in that exact instant, giant plops of ick way too close for comfort.

Ezer strolled around the horse to stand in front of me. His knuckles and fingers glowed with warm light. "You were saying?"

"Would the Ancient One approve of me dispatching them? Or is protecting yourself some sort of infraction?"

"Can't you knock them out?" he asked. "You don't have to kill them."

"I'm sorry if my training didn't include gentle resolutions."

Horses raced from behind us, blocking our exit. Omar's smirk confirmed it was his men. Ezer's mouth pressed into a flat line.

I lifted my eyebrow at him in question.

When the four horses barreling toward us got to be only a stone's throw away, Ezer lifted one arm and froze the steeds mid-stride. The beasts toppled over like statues, sending their riders flying through the air. The sickening crunch of bone rang through the forest.

"Why don't you merely knock them out?" I mocked.

"Not funny. Can you heal them?"

"No, it's a miracle I could revive Omar when I knew his injury."

"Fine." Sweat trickled down Ezer's hairline. "I'm going to grow exhausted, and we'll still have to figure out what to do with these men. I need a little help."

"Prince, you have to do better training with your gift if a few minutes gets you this tired." I released the energy quaking to escape. Warmth poured out my fingertips, forming invisible appendages that felt all the bodies within view. Two horsemen already raced toward death, judging by their pulses. The other two needed some assistance passing out, so I squeezed—but for a shorter period of time. Then, I worked on our four restrained friends.

"What are you doing?" Ezer asked.

"Making this easier. You can let go."

Ezer lowered his arms and panted from the exertion. The four bodies dropped at once with a sickening thud from the work I had done with my gift. So much for changing my ways. Ezer climbed onto Encanto's back with sorrow painted over his countenance as he grabbed my arm to help me up. I refused to look back at what I'd done and leapt onto Encanto.

A whistle pierced the air, and pain throbbed throughout my shoulder. A cry escaped my throat, and I caught sight of the not-quite-dead horseman.

"What was that?" Ezer asked.

"I'm hit."

My powers shot out toward the horseman at such a speed that they killed the man on contact. This time, I was certain he died.

CHAPTER 14
COTTIA

ENCANTO GALLOPED THE REST of the day with only short breaks. We managed to remove the arrow and bandage the wound with a section of the robe. How many purposes could the blasted cape have?

"There's said to be a library out here with the oldest version of the Tome." Ezer turned his head, which shifted my body.

My shoulder was on fire. I grunted and rested my cheek against his back.

"Then, I will have to take you another time." Ezer clicked his tongue, spurring Encanto to go faster. "To the inn."

The sun set over the mountains as we rode to the meeting point. Short houses and thatched roofs peeked over the horizon, indicating we approached civilization. Stretching before our descent was a seemingly never-ending cobblestone road. The tallest building happened to be the inn at the end of the main road with its yellow walls and arched entrance.

Ezer slipped off of Encanto. Worry creased his forehead. I must have looked like I knocked on death's door. My right shoulder throbbed. A headache pounded through every section of my skull. My powers swirled somewhere in my chest, but I couldn't summon them.

"Swing your leg around." Ezer lifted me by the waist so I wouldn't fall, but my body didn't want to cooperate.

I knocked him on the head. He tipped to the side and adjusted himself. The apology in my throat couldn't make it off my tongue.

He set me on the ground. "Can you walk?"

I swayed on my feet, dizzy, but I managed to stay upright. "Yes."

Though I affirmed my ability to use my legs, Ezer slung an arm around my waist. I leaned heavily into his body, and he swooped me into his arms. The movement touched my shoulder, and a groan escaped my throat. I snapped my mouth shut, firming my jaw. I could handle this. Though I'd never been struck with an arrow before, I'd been cut, punched, and beaten. A tear slipped along my cheek, and I curled into Ezer.

He kissed my forehead and whispered against my skin, "You're such a fighter. You're doing great."

I looked up into his lamplit eyes. In that instant, I knew I was a goner. With his strong arms keeping me aloft and the warmth of his kiss lingering on my forehead, he had my heart. The dizziness and pain also could have been influencing my nonsensical thoughts. I could pound angry fists into his chest if I had any strength left. Why did he have to tease me with his affection? Why did I let myself be attracted to someone I could never have?

"Let's see if Gema made it." His whisper came out far huskier than any man should ever speak. He shifted me in his arms as he swaggered into the yellow light of the inn.

A chunky man about our age waited at a wooden desk. "How can I help you?"

"We're wondering if a Gema arrived." Ezer shook a bit but kept a tight grip on me.

The attendant checked his records. "No, señor. But would you and," he checked my hand for a ring, "the señorita like two rooms?"

"No, one room will do." Ezer set me gently on my feet and pulled out several coins. "Only let Gema know where we stay."

I flicked a confused gaze at Ezer, but he merely responded with a pressed-lip smile.

"Of course." The man's thick fingers traced the edge of the extra gold coins.

The attendant turned to a cabinet and handed us a key chained to a piece of wood with a thirteen etched into the surface. "The kitchen is only open for another hour. The rooms are up those stairs." He pointed past the dining room to a wooden staircase that twisted about halfway up to the next floor.

Ezer swooped me into his arms, and I bit hard on my bottom lip to keep a whimper from betraying just how hurt I was. We crossed the cozy dining room full of travelers. One table in the corner had men far too focused on Ezer and me, but I couldn't quite place their faces. A muddled flash of people I knew appeared in my mind's eye: assassins, associates, Himzos, Giddelians, country folks. Nothing about these men strained through my block of a brain.

We made it upstairs to the first door on the left. Ezer opened it to a bedroom with a single floral-printed bed in the center. A dresser stretched across a wall, and a desk lined the other side. That was it. There was no way Ezer and I could share a bed. No way.

He set me down on the bed, and I turned on my good side, sinking into the soft material. A mouthwatering garlic aroma drifted up the stairs, giving the perfect excuse to send Ezer away. "Ezer, could you get me something to eat?"

"Yes. Anything else?" He opened the door.

"Some water and another bed."

"Got it."

"And Ezer? Find out who those men in the corner are. I think I know them. They might be dangerous."

He tipped his head in agreement and closed the door behind him.

Left alone to sink into my pain, I closed my eyes and prayed we'd survive and that Gema would arrive soon. I asked the Ancient One to let my gifting return in spite of no energy left in me. Then I'd believe, and my powers would be used for healing and not destruction. Even in my desperation, I saw the irony of praying to someone who didn't exist in my mind. It was almost like I already had some belief.

CHAPTER 15
COTTIA

"Get up! You have to go." Ezer shook my side.

I startled awake, disoriented by the bed beneath my body and the darkness surrounding me. Ezer hadn't returned before I fell asleep.

"You were right about those men." Ezer leaned down and brushed hair from my cheek. "I heard them speak about waiting for the redhead to show up. I think they're supposed to bring you and Gema back to the whyzer."

Mind spinning, head throbbing, and shoulder screaming, I flipped my head over to meet Ezer's achingly handsome face right above mine. His stubbled cheeks measured our time together. The whisper of wrinkles on his forehead and the lines bracketing his mouth showed his concern.

He said, "I'll distract them, and you find a fresh horse out front. Encanto will be too worn from all the travels."

I captured his hand in mine. "What about Gema?"

A smile crept from his mouth up to those two beautiful, wide eyes. "Let me take you to the hidden library. The whyzer who runs it might be able to free you from your oath. You'd be safe there while I wait for Gema. Then all of us can go back to Giddel together."

"And you trust this whyzer?" A heavy dollop of skepticism coated my tongue.

"Yes. Not all the whyzers are corrupt." He brushed a stray hair from my cheek.

"Wasn't me staying at the palace your intention all along?" A bitter edge laced my tone, though the words lacked power with my body broken and achy.

He traced my jaw with his thumb. "Not if you don't want to come back." Sadness skipped down his face.

I lifted my head, drawing even closer to the prince. He inhaled, parting his lips. This might be the last time I saw him if we got caught. I turned toward his cheek and planted a kiss there. "Thank you." I pushed myself up.

"For what?" He moved to the side.

"For not getting in my way. For helping me. For not imprisoning me the moment you saw through my lie."

He grabbed a small bag and rope and cracked open the door. "You can thank me later when you're safe."

With that, he waved me to his side, and we took a left turn down the long passageway. Was there another way to escape? Were the men still downstairs waiting for me? I tiptoed behind Ezer, putting my full trust in him. I would have laughed at myself for putting confidence in another person if the vibrations from the laughter wouldn't have caused searing pain in my shoulder.

We dodged through a door without a number. A dark stairwell with a halo of light at the bottom filled our view. This hadn't the lacquer on the wood panels or on the railing like the other stairway. Ezer slipped his fingers between mine, and we raced down. A laundry room stretched before us with floral sheets hanging from cords attached to the walls. Not a soul stirred, which was most important. Surely someone would come back to put out the lamp soon.

Adrenaline surged through my bloodstream, giving me a boost in energy I hadn't felt moments before. Only one exit opened to us at the far end of the room. But a window let in a light breeze that billowed against thin curtains.

Ezer took two strides to our right to inspect the small window. "Metal bars." He crossed to the doorway and peeked into the corridor outside the room.

I ducked under the hanging material and joined Ezer. It seemed we'd have to hope for another back door where we didn't need to cross into the dining area or the main entrance.

We darted into the darkness to the left. Several wooden doors lined that hallway, but none would budge at the turn of the knob. The last one at the end had several locks barring what I assumed was the exit because of the thick plank set across the door. Ezer lifted the plank and propped it against the wall.

Someone entered the far end of the passage behind us that led to a room full of firelight, possibly the kitchen. Ezer slid two bolt locks and pulled, making a creaking noise. The door wouldn't move any further. He had missed a sliding chain latch.

"Did you hear that?" a man asked.

Hip bumping Ezer, I pushed the door shut again and slid the last lock with no heed to where the chained bolt landed. Metal clanged against the wall as it swung.

Footfalls approached along with a halo of candlelight. A tall man appeared in a kitchen apron. "Thieves!"

Ezer pushed my lower back, coaxing me into the night's darkness. We bolted left to the front of the establishment where a line of horses and carriages parked outside the inn. Ezer sped ahead and chopped a leather cord tethering a brown horse to a pole. He leapt on its back. As I clasped Ezer's arm to climb up, five men busted through the inn's front entrance.

"Those are the thieves." The tall cook pointed.

I kicked the sides of the horse. We were off down the hill with unnatural speed. By the time we made it two stone's throws away, the men pursued us on horseback.

"Hold tight." Ezer leaned forward.

Despite the jarring pain breaking open my wound, I wrapped both arms around Ezer's abdomen and leaned my cheek on his back. Without a proper saddle, I felt like I might fall.

The hooves of several horses echoed behind us, but the beast beneath us didn't relent. Wind whipping my face, fear striking my heart, I tried to summon any semblance of power to my skin. Heat encircled my wound and wouldn't let go.

One horseman came into view, speeding up enough for me to make out his thick beard and the Himzo crest.

"Ezer, they're coming." My panicked heart raced.

"Hold tight." Ezer twisted his head around and stretched out his palm.

The horse's knees buckled, sending the rider crashing into the darkened jungle. I wrapped my hands with a vicelike grip on Ezer's doublet as he swung back around. For hours, hooves stomped in the distance behind us, but we continued south on the main road to Giddel. It was the straightest shot to Giddel and the most dangerous one for any traveler hoping to stay inconspicuous.

Ezer turned off the main road onto a dark path and lit his skin with his gifting. "Don't worry, I'm going to drop you off at the library and go back for Gema."

Sometime later, we turned up a rockier path. Ezer's skin glowed brighter, shining on the smooth bark of thick trees and catching on two nocturnal eyes on the forest floor. I kept my cheek against Ezer's back, in too much pain to care about the sweat stain I left on his tunic. The ache in my body pulled every limb into tight knots, and Ezer's ability to control muscles did the rest of the work to keep me upright.

"We're almost there," he said.

I could barely hear him over the thump of the horse's hooves. A chill shuddered through my bones. My spine slumped to the side, giving me a dizzying view of where I'd land if I fell.

"Stay with me, Cottia," he coaxed.

Warmth seeped like tiny pinpricks jabbing into my skin. He must have been exerting himself.

A small stone fortress appeared out of nowhere, where a thin, older man in a white robe waited for us. A lamp hovered in the air and remained levitated close behind the bearded man as he approached.

"I thought you might come." The man's voice sounded too cheery for the night sky, yet held a hint of concern in its weathered timbre.

The horse slowed. I let my muscles relax, yet I didn't fall. Darkness overtook my vision.

"I have her," said the weathered voice.

The pin pricks subsided and were replaced by a warm breeze pushing up against my skin. If the older man turned out to be a whyzer like Patro, I'd at least be too drowsy and worn to feel the pain he inflicted.

Someone placed me in a bed. Though my eyelids kept shut, the scent of coconut and lime bathed my senses. The bedding had enough cushion for me to sink into its embrace.

Rough fingers undid my bandage. "I think her wound is open." Ezer continued to prod at my achy shoulder. "Is there anything we can do?"

The older man said, "I see her walking by your side on the palace beach, though I dare not say I am certain when this transpired."

"What color dress did she wear?" Ezer asked.

"Blue." The older man touched my wrist with his cold fingers. "Interesting ... she's a healer."

I cracked my eyes open. "I wore red."

Ezer let out an airy laugh and drew near, concern folded into the squeeze of his eyebrows. "You're right, but Whyzer Aimar can sometimes see snatches of the future. You're going to live, and when you do, I'm going to marry you." He kissed my forehead with a gentle press of his warm lips. "I must depart to retrieve Gema."

My mind screamed for him not to go. For him not to leave me with a whyzer. But what of Gema? Her only crime had been being a good friend to me. Ezer hesitated but left through a darkened doorway across the room.

The whyzer faced me, and though a smile peeked beneath a white mustache, I quivered at what he might do to me in such a vulnerable state.

"Be at peace, dear child." His skin glowed like firelight lived within him. "I'll share the little I have to help you heal."

Warmth flowed from his touch into my veins and raced through my chest. My gifting revived. The skin on my shoulder knitted together. What had been a sharp burning turned into the dull ache of a bruise.

"What did you do?"

"I shared my power with you so that your gifting would work." He let go of my wrist with an extra bounce in his movements and pushed his stool back.

"Why would you do that for me? You must know I am bound to another whyzer."

"Bound? That shouldn't be."

"Isn't that what all you whyzers do? You give gifts and bind them to your own powers."

"Oh dear, we neither give abilities nor take them as our own."

I stared at the plain white ceiling reflecting the flame from his lamp. "Ezer said that if I came to—what is this place?"

"My home and a library."

"Then you might be able to free me from an oath spoken by—" My tongue stilled with the name I could not pronounce.

He plopped back in the stool. "Do you mind if I pray for you? There is no incantation that can free you, but only the will of the Ancient One to break the bonds of our past."

I nodded. "Go ahead. If I could take back all that I've done, I would. If only these invisible cords that tie me to my master were gone." Tears gathered at the corners of my eyes, trailed along my temples, and soaked into my hair.

The man bowed his head and spoke into the darkness with simple words requesting my freedom. Though nothing in the room changed, the tug on my heart loosened. No longer did a voice murmur for me to seduce Ezer, nor did a pull to obey my master churn between my ribs. The tension between my shoulders broke until all that remained was the exhaustion from the day. My eyelids grew heavy, and I fell into a deep slumber unbothered by the ghosts who liked to taunt me in my dreams.

"Wake up!" Someone stood above me.

I awoke to find flames in the eyes of my friend. "We've got to go. We're being followed."

"Gema? Is that you? Where's Ezer?" I pushed myself out of bed.

"He's here." She pointed behind her. "We tried to lose them but you-know-who sent more."

The older man was gone. My pains and utter exhaustion had disappeared as well. Though my body still ached from overuse, I leapt behind Gema. We followed Ezer out the bedroom door and into a room full of books on every wall. The shelves climbed two stories high. I must have been in a daze not to notice this.

"Cottia, come on." Gema growled.

Ezer took my hand, and I slipped my fingers between his, remembering how he said he wanted to marry me.

"Are you able to hold on if you ride with me?" he asked as he tugged me out the front door.

"Yes." I clomped down the two stone steps and waved at Whyzer Aimar as I passed him. So many questions about this man and what he'd done remained between us.

Whyzer Aimar tipped a quick bow and held a glowing staff between his palms. "I'll hold them off for as long as I can."

"Who?" I turned toward Ezer.

The prince mounted a black stallion and reached down to help me up. "Patro's people are coming after us."

I mounted with only a little help from Ezer. The horse sped away, leaving the little old man on the steps in the distance. Gema and several strangers rode on horses behind us. Gema kept a fire lit on her curls to act as a torch through the dense forest. My heart beat like a hammer hitting an anvil.

When we arrived at the main road, Gema cut off her flames, leaving small plumes of smoke evaporating into the night air. We slowed to make the first turn and take stock of our surroundings. Ezer looked over his shoulder, and I followed his gaze.

Orange flames glowed deep in the forest where we had come from. Only Whyzer Aimar stood guard against Whyzer Patro's forces. What would happen to the kind old man? Part of me already knew that if his beautiful library burnt, we'd never see him again.

Ezer clicked his tongue and spurred the horse to pick up its pace. Danger came barreling toward us.

CHAPTER 16
COTTIA

HOURS LATER, LAMPS ATOP Giddel's great wall shone below us as beacons of hope in utter darkness. I clutched like a barnacle around Ezer's waist as we descended a mountain toward the coastal city. Gema and her three companions remained close behind us, and clomping from pursuers in the distance remained an ever-present threat.

Yet, hope lodged itself in my heart at each passing minute when I couldn't sense Whyzer Patro's sway and his invisible strings. Tears rolled down my cheeks at the freedom I hadn't experienced in so many years.

The walls of Giddel grew taller at our approach. The darkness became more ominous.

"Stay quiet." Ezer rubbed my knuckles to comfort me. "This might not go smoothly without the royal horses."

Flames danced on the watchmen's torches as they ran across the top of the wall. The silhouette of bows and arrows could be seen at the ready.

Ezer slowed the horse's gait and lifted a kerchief from his front pocket, waving it like a white flag signaling peace.

"It's Prince Ezer," a guard shouted.

"Open the gate," said a baritone voice.

With slow, methodical steps, the horse marched through the main entrance. Several torches were held up from burly guards inspecting Prince Ezer's face.

"Are they with you?" A middle-aged man gestured to Gema and the others with her.

"These four are with me." Ezer's voice took on a royal cadence he didn't use with me. "Allow no one else into the city for the night."

"Yes, Your Highness." The man bowed his head.

The guards lowered their light, letting us in without further questions. I let out a slow breath.

Still, we needed to cross through the city roads and get into the palace. And surely this horse needed rest, water, and some food. The quiet houses looked like sleeping faces with all their window shutters snapped closed for the night. Quiet encircled us with an eerie quality that should have brought comfort. The night appeared normal with nothing but the stirring of a stray black cat trotting alongside the road.

The palace entrance emerged at the end of a courtyard with beautiful iron gates and an arched entrance. Several palace guards lit up their giftings, arms aglow with power.

Prince Ezer declared his name and said a strange utterance that put the guards at ease. It must have been a password of some sort. The gate swung open with the whine of iron rubbing against iron.

We strode through on the back of the exhausted horse. Two guards ran ahead of us to the main entrance of the palace building, but we veered right to settle the beast. Finally, I could breathe despite the ache that filled me once the tension left my muscles.

A stableman came running out as we dismounted before the small building. All so orderly, without a threat or attack to worry about.

I looked over my shoulder at Gema, her helpers, and the quiet of the night. Trees swayed between us and the guard house, and a wall kept all others out.

Without the bindings, within the palace walls, and with Omar dead out in the Giddelian mountainside, I truly might have a chance at escaping Whyzer Patro for good.

"Thank you." Ezer patted the stableman's back. "Anything exciting happen since I've been gone?"

As I walked, my boots flipped up the hay sprinkling the ground and scuffed against smooth stone floor. A mixture of wood, a hint of manure, and a dank scent permeated the cozy space.

The older man led the horse into a stall. "No, Prince Ezer, His Majesties were worried about your sudden departure, but since we mentioned how you left peaceably with the señorita, they were giving it a few more days before they went to search for you. Some of the other señoritas left and even the Trucios decided to return to their estate."

My heart perked at his comment. If the Trucios left, Whyzer Patro would send another assassin into the countryside rather than the palace. Gema wasn't in any immediate danger now, and Whyzer Patro wouldn't dare attack Giddel head on. We had time to protect ourselves. I could send word to my sister to stay hidden. Ezer would help when Whyzer Patro came for me. My old master would not let any slight go unpunished, but we'd be ready for him.

A tall shadow of a man with a walking stick, sharp angles on his face, and a black beard appeared from the dark opening across from me. In that instant, I could have thrown up. He came to finish the job himself.

I turned to Gema, who remained far behind, and motioned for her to stop.

Gema signaled to her helpers, and they dodged out of sight. My time had run out. The poor stableman and the prince would be caught up in my fight.

"Ezer?" I whispered.

He spun around. "Yes?" His gaze shifted to something in the distance outside the stable. He'd seen the whyzer too.

"Please," I begged. "Leave with the stableman. This is my problem, not yours."

The stableman checked with Ezer. At the tip of Ezer's head, he ran into the night and away from trouble, but Ezer stepped between the whyzer and me.

"Whyzer Patro." Ezer stood tall and kept his voice steady and strong. "I know of your plan to murder Señor Trucio. We have enough evidence to convict you of that and much more."

"Really, Ezer, you should head into the palace." I tried to project more confidence than I felt.

Ezer kept his focus trained on the whyzer who strode into the lamplight with all the cocky malice of an old man who believed himself king.

"Convict me of what? Do enlighten me." Whyzer Patro's deep voice lilted with restrained rage.

"Murder. Human trafficking. Bindings. Use of dark magic. Need I go on?"

"No—" My throat constricted. The brand on my arm burned from use. I wrestled with thoughts invading my skull.

Kill the prince.

No.

Kill him.

No, you have no hold on me.

"Oh?" The whyzer stroked his dark beard with feigned innocence. "Did you finish the job? Omar seemed to believe you went back to the castillo to get Gema. Surely, Gema will be there when I return."

I glanced at Ezer for a boost of confidence, but Ezer never turned toward me. "I have no intent—" My tongue stiffened, but I pushed past the whyzer's invisible grip. "By the Ancient One, let go of me." The whyzer's hold slackened and left me free to speak.

Whyzer Patro clicked his tongue. "You make me out to be heartless."

"I have no intention of becoming your pawn queen. I will die before using Ezer to do your bidding."

Ezer flinched at that revelation.

Shame shriveled in my gut. "Ezer, I'm sorry. I truly wanted you to stay home and safe and far removed from the oath."

The whyzer swung his staff and lifted me off the ground. Pain encumbered my shoulder at his rough levitation. The branding mark burned on my arm, pain slithering into my chest.

I screeched. Ezer flung his arms up, taking control of the whyzer's ability to move. But the whyzer didn't need his staff or arms. I slammed to the ground.

"Finccio," Whyzer Patro shouted in the ancient tongue.

Ezer remained unmoved, but I went flying against the stable and the wooden side cracked from such a hard hit. Bones rattling from impact, I watched sweat trickle along Ezer's hairline from the effort of taking control of the whyzer.

"You can't hold me forever." Whyzer Patro remained like a statue with his staff glowing in the air. "If you don't let go, I will destroy Cottia."

Ezer let out a soft grunt. He couldn't give Whyzer Patro the final blow without risking my life. Yet even so, why didn't the whyzer attack Ezer? Did the esteemed whyzer have no grip on Ezer either?

"Enough of the games." Whyzer Patro wriggled as if trying to free himself from Ezer's ability. "You understand that the girl must be punished for such treachery."

Footfalls approached from somewhere behind the whyzer. He managed to jerk his head around with glee dancing in his gaze. When an arrow struck the whyzer through the leg, his sick joy transformed to rage. Another three arrows flew in quick succession, but he flung his staff around, sending the arrows away from his body.

With the distraction, Ezer scooped me off the ground, holding me close to his chest, and ran in the opposite direction. Another three arrows released, but they whistled through the stable and struck Ezer's shoulder, arm, and chest, nicking my side.

We tumbled forward. Our bodies thumped against the ground.

Ezer's chest moved with shallow breaths. I searched the dark stalls for something to rip off to stop the bleeding. But I only had pants and my own bloody tunic to work with.

Whyzer Patro continued sweeping his staff through the air, deflecting the onslaught of arrows until one sliced through his hand. The staff dropped. Blood oozed from his wounds, and he let out a guttural growl.

A voice from behind us said, "Get out." Gema dropped her cape, bow, and arrows into my grip and stomped toward Whyzer Patro. Enormous flames floated off her body with a strong sea breeze, making her look ready to explode.

Gema's fellows continued attacking Whyzer Patro. It brought an extra rush of adrenaline through my bloodstream and hope into my achy steps. But I needed to get Ezer far away from here and alert the guards before Ezer slipped away from us. Gema would do some real damage, quicker than I could heal him. I pulled on his vest, dragging him out with every fiber of my being.

I yanked Ezer farther out the building and started up the gravel path.

Whyzer Patro looked in my direction. He didn't dare stop me with Gema aflame and his staff on the ground. I couldn't sit back now when our adversary was weakened.

Finally one last yank got Ezer out of harm's way, onto the grassy front lawn of the palace. My sleeve took a bit of effort to slice, but I severed it, yanked the arrow out of Ezer's shoulder, and wrapped the cloth around where he bled out. I ripped a part of Gema's cloak, and another. My fingers moved quickly to wrap the wounds. I pressed his chest.

Prickles of heat drained from my body into his, healing the worst of the injuries—at least I hoped. The speed in which I worked wouldn't completely knit his wounds, but it should give him a chance at surviving. I leaned close to his face. A wheeze of breath met my ears. Now to free the horses and help Gema—if I could do much damage with a half gifting that had been wrung out several times over.

My boots crunched along the gravel way, and I marched into the stable.

Gema shot flames from her fingertips, scorching the whyzer's robe. I swung open a stable door and then another. Flames burned wayward hairs as the whyzer and Gema continued to spar, but her flames dwindled. My fireball of a friend needed to recharge.

Three cloaked men approached Whyzer Patro with swords at the ready. The very gifted never used weapons. Defeat whispered through my bones. The whyzer dodged weak flames and waved an arm, flinging the three men like rag dolls through the air. Gema dove for the whyzer's staff, but he flipped Gema over onto her head. She curled up into a ball on the ground.

So, I prayed fervently. *Ancient One, please free us from Whyzer Patro. I'm ready to change my ways and want a chance for freedom to do your will with my gift of healing.*

This plea warmed my insides with a sort of peace I couldn't explain. A whisper of agreement danced on the wind as a breeze rushed through the stables. The marking that bound me to the whyzer went cold on my upper arm.

Gema flew backwards like a shooting star and her body thumped against the wooden wall. Her flames burst and caught on the rooftop. Wood crackled like logs in a fire which wouldn't bode well for anyone below the roof should it collapse.

I sprinted toward her, but I couldn't help with her skin still aflame. How could I do anything to defeat Whyzer Patro with my spent power and injuries?

Whyzer Patro's mouth curled in victory. He lifted his arms, and a pressure snaked around my body, tingling against my skin. His smile flipped into a snarl as if something had gone awry. At that moment, I realized our connection had been completely severed. The wound did not burn nor did his invisible talons do more than tickle my limbs.

Fear caught in Whyzer Patro's gaped stare.

Part of the roof collapsed behind me.

Ash plumed, and I covered my eyes with my hands. I lost sight of the whyzer, blinded for a long moment. I needed to get back to Gema beneath the rubble and Ezer who still suffered from his injuries. My vision came back into focus in time to catch Whyzer Patro's shadow snatching his gnarled staff from the floor. He escaped between the guards who ran toward us.

CHAPTER 17
COTTIA

GEMA GASPED AS I dragged her out from beneath a beam. Her skin was now pale and her body lifeless. Blood pooled at the back of her head where she struck the wall from the whyzer's thrashing. I placed my hand on her cool arm.

Pin pricks of power careened from my fingertips, doing something inside her. I could feel the sticky sensation of wounds coming together while my own wounds on my stomach and head bled out. But Gema's healing was worth my powers transferring to her.

"Cottia," Gema whispered.

"Yes, it's me." I gave her a gentle squeeze on her hand. "You survived."

A quaver of air puffed out her mouth, a laugh of sorts. "He's going to come back."

"But not tonight." I lifted the corners of my mouth to attempt a smile. "I prayed, and he couldn't use me anymore."

Even limp and hurt, Gema's eyes widened at that.

"Señorita, señorita, do you need help?" An older man called out to me. He passed his bucket of water to the man beside him. "This is no place for two ladies. The flames still burn hot." He lifted Gema as if she were a life-sized porcelain doll.

"Can you take her to my guest room?" I asked.

"Of course."

As I followed the servant who carried Gema, I scanned where I had left Ezer, but he was gone. I comforted myself with the thought that another servant or guard could have helped him already. My maid servant recognized me at the palace entrance and directed the man to my old guest room. By the time he placed Gema on one side of the bed, I felt my powers knitting together my own wounds. Gema smiled though pain-marked lines on her face. Both of us needed rest.

"Are you sure you don't want to leave her with the palace's healer?" The young girl asked.

"No, we stay together." I slumped beside my friend, bed shifting beneath my weight.

The girl bobbed her head, not completely convinced she should accept my response. "She can almost bring back the dead. You should have seen how fast she had Ezer hopping on his toes."

"Ezer's alright?" I asked in sudden concern.

"He was looking for you, but the healer sent him to his room. He got mighty good bruises where I could see." She passed me a small candle, sped to the door, took one last peek at me, and left.

In the candlelight, I caught Gema staring at nothing particular overhead. A sheen of unshed tears threatened to fall. Was she also thinking about how we'd made an enemy out of Whyzer Patro? Did she wonder when we'd be kicked out of the palace of Giddel?

Even with those questions burning in my consciousness, I massaged my wrists with no invisible strings linking to someone in the distance. No heart tug yanked at my emotions and thoughts. A simple prayer had shrugged off my burden, proving the Ancient One to be real and even more powerful than Whyzer Patro himself.

I took care of my needs in the privy and returned, candle in hand. Gema's eyes shone with curiosity in the lamplight, but she didn't say a word. I set the candle by the bedside and changed into a nightgown, shedding the pants and tunic that had traveled with me to the castillo, the inn, and back. The ratty things smelled of sweat and animal and didn't deserve the folding I gave them.

Though the future remained unknown and even murkier than before, I smiled. Tomorrow I wouldn't need to get a job done.

A knock pounded. "Cottia," Ezer called.

I flung open the door.

Ezer stood on the other side with one hand leaning against the doorframe. Candlelight caught a glint of relief in his tawny-green eyes. He pushed in without invitation. We kept close, breaths mingling, emotion like electricity cracking between us.

"You're alive," I said.

"Jacinta told me she situated you here."

"Jacinta?"

"The maid." He wrapped his arms around me, placing one hand on the small of my back and the other around my shoulders.

The air in my lungs stilled.

"You can stay here as long as you like. You know that?" His achingly handsome face drew nearer, setting my pulse into a riot.

I nodded.

"My papá knows that I decided."

"What do you mean?"

"Tomorrow all the other señoritas will be sent away."

"No, you shouldn't. You don't even know me. It's been only a couple weeks, if even."

He cupped my cheek. "Then, we'll get to know each other. I'll give you as long as you want to decide. We'll put up a ward to keep the whyzer out of Giddel so you can be safe."

Shifting noises sounded to my right, reminding me that Gema watched all of this interlude.

"Look, Ezer." I gently moved his hand off my cheek though his warmth remained on the spot he'd touched. "The past several days have been a dream come true. But people like me don't end up with princes. I've done things I could never admit to you. I know that the Ancient One heard me because this is a miracle, fighting off the whyzer and earning my freedom."

"You believe?" An earnestness settled into his posture.

"Sort of." Heat puddled in my cheeks at such a strange admonition, so I added, "I'm confused and would like to know more."

He bit his bottom lip and nodded.

Gema sighed. "So, are you going to kiss the girl?"

I glared at her. She clapped a hand over her mouth, giving her sorry-but-not-so-sorry shrug.

Ezer let out a deep chuckle. The laugh lines bracketing his mouth buckled my knees a bit. "No kiss until you give me the word. Wait until you know what you want. Until then, you and your friend are under my protection. The entire city of Giddel will have a ward around it tomorrow." He pressed a kiss to my forehead and left.

The moment the door latch clicked shut, Gema squealed. "Cielos, Cottia! A prince?"

"It's never going to happen." I hopped into bed next to Gema, avoiding her mischievous stare.

"You actually like him too. Just admit it." She poked my side.

"Aren't you supposed to be resting?" I slipped under the petal-soft covers, desperate for sleep even if my mind thrummed with the memory of every interaction with Prince Ezer.

Gema's grin hung ear-to-ear with so much meaning behind it.

"No. Not going to happen."

Her expression didn't falter.

I closed my eyes, but the candle still burned on Gema's bedside, giving the back of my eyelids an orange hue. "Can you put out the light?"

"Cottia?" Gema's voice had a strange quality to it.

Flipping over to meet Gema's eye, I caught a tear rolling down the side of her nose. "What's wrong?"

"We're free."

My eyes pricked also. "We *are* free."

Gema snuffed out the candle flame. For the first time in forever, I looked forward to waking up the next day.

PART 2
RESTLESS

CHAPTER 18
COTTIA

PRINCE EZER WOVE HIS hand with mine as we took our early morning walk through the cobblestone streets of Giddel, my new home. His warmth and firmness stretched a blanket of protection over me that I had never experienced before. We strolled through the kingdom, enjoying the yeasty aroma from a nearby bakery and each other's company like we had every morning this last month. The sun rose behind the Palace of Giddel, an enormous sandstone building with extensive grounds atop a cliff, but I wanted to get this one conversation off my chest before we returned.

"Should we go to the docks?" Ezer stopped at an intersection where we could still view his palace ahead or turn down a narrow walkway between buildings that led toward the cerulean shore.

"To the Agata Sea, of course." I smiled at him, a smile that came without effort or pretense.

We turned the corner and headed on our way without constant worry or danger lurking around every corner. I never thought someone like me would get to enjoy such a day in her lifetime.

Movement caught my attention to the right. A lady with a hood pulled over her head crept away from us. She was likely spying on our sweet moment because Ezer was supposed to be deciding which of the dozen ladies waiting eagerly in the palace would make him a suitable bride.

With head lifted high, I kept my composure at such an intrusion. He had chosen his bride a month ago, but every time Ezer had told me he would declare me as his choice, fear had struck my heart.

But not anymore.

Today I would declare that I was ready for him to announce his decision, to name me his betrothed. To think, only a month ago, I'd been a slave to a wicked whyzer, forced to murder for the twisted lord. But the Ancient One and Ezer had changed all that, the Ancient One with his tomes and undeniable power and Ezer with his kindness.

Each footfall down the stone steps brought us closer to our forever future. Vines hung on every small terrace above, giving the path a magical sensation like all of this was meant to be. But part of me inwardly clenched, waiting for Ezer to wake up and realize I wasn't a fit choice for a prince.

When we returned to the Palace of Giddel, I would rush to find Gema, the only other person who could understand how I felt because she had been a slave to Whyzer Patro too. She had been my best friend for the past five years, save a couple of weeks when someone else had held the honor.

We reached the shoreline road and crossed to the other side. This would be the day and the place where I admitted how much I adored the prince despite the fear clawing in my chest alongside my special gifting. Perhaps I should use my ability to check Ezer's heart rate and breathing to assure myself that he was experiencing the same wily bodily symptoms I had flowing through me.

He tugged me down the stairway to the docks, where galleons flowed with ship workers. I yanked him back to a short stone wall that caught the yellow haze of the morning light just right. This spot had the best view of the turquoise sea, making it ideal for a declaration of such importance.

More people moved along the road than I'd daydreamed about the entire walk, but that was my fault. I should have moved us along before the town awakened and the guards opened the gates into Giddel.

"Ezer?" My voice came out far too high-pitched for my liking.

"Cottia?" he returned. His hazel eyes gazed intently at me over the most heart-melting grin. Everything about his masculine jaw and the way he held himself drew me into his embrace.

"I have something to tell you."

He held my waist as if he were hanging on my every word.

"We've gotten to know each other, and I've told you everything about Papá dying, our poverty, Mamá sending me off to Whyzer Patro, and what happened there. Do you fully understand who I was and what I did?"

"I do." His Adam's apple bobbed.

"You know about my sister and how much your title scares me." My thoughts screamed at me, *Get on with it, Cottia. Now you're just stalling.*

"I want you to choose today."

"You do?" His quick response and wide grin bespoke his excitement.

"Yes, and I have to tell you how much—"

"Excuse me, *señorita*," said a short man beside us. The man held out a missive closed with a red wax seal. The emblem was the one Isabelia, my fifteen-year-old sister, used when she had an important message that required a cipher to read.

"*Gracias.*" I snatched the paper from his grasp and broke open the seal. The unique handwriting was Isabelia's, and the date suggested she'd sent this two weeks ago. A weight pressed against my breastbone. The messenger I'd sent to tell her of my new residence hadn't been able to find her. She should have sent something like this to Castillo Patro.

"That was odd." Ezer followed the man with his stare. "What is the message? Who is it from?"

"My sister."

"Was that her courier?"

"No."

We both looked after the short man walking away in a rough spun jacket. He turned his head backward to meet our eye with what could only be described as a sneer of delight. The face morphed ever so slightly into a pointy nose and twisted lips that would forever be chiseled into my memory. This fellow had a weak illusionist ability that allowed him to change his own features ever so slightly. In all my nerves over accepting Ezer's proposal, I'd missed the signs of a gifting in use, and I didn't recognize the man behind the illusion. I couldn't breathe.

"What's wrong?" Ezer's eyebrows pressed together in concern.

"We must go back to the palace."

"Why?"

"Whyzer Patro is after me."

CHAPTER 19
COTTIA

THE MESSAGE WAS CLEAR. I would never be out of Whyzer Patro's reach so long as he lived.

Gema and I searched the grove behind the palace garden for poisonous, white petals sprinkled atop the cliffs beside the Agata Sea. Midday light dappled my fine blue gown and added a sheen to Gema's hair, the fiery color of the flesh within a mamey sapote fruit.

"Do you think he'll send an assassin?" Gema stuffed the petals into her basket beneath a pile of orchids and roses.

I cringed at how she handled the flowers and mixed them with the roses I had planned to brew into tea. "Not sure. Try not to—"

She passed me a withering look, telling me to back off from correcting her.

Perhaps I had been particular all morning concerning our preparations for battle. But I would never apologize for taking extra precautions when it came to Whyzer Patro.

"Have it your way." I rubbed at my sleeve where I'd tucked my sister's missive. She'd encoded a name amidst her rambling sentences: Benito.

Gema ripped off her boots to let her toes sink into the lush foliage, truly carefree and wild, like her unruly curls. "Why do you look like you swallowed a sour berry?"

"It's nothing important." It was my first lie since I'd read not to lie in the Ancient Tome.

From the moment we'd settled in Giddel, my friend had acted as if all our binds had disappeared, as if we were free. I understood the sentiment more than she did, since the whyzer had turned me into his puppet by burning a binding mark on my upper arm.

"Today, Prince Ezer plans to make his selection announcement." Her much-too-perky tone matched her confidence.

And here was the conversation I'd hoped to avoid. Sweat slicked my palms with a new obstacle I wasn't used to handling. I could work with assassins all day long. Love interests? Not so much.

Gema's expectant gaze prodded the words from my mouth.

"Prince Ezer made a mistake." I uprooted a precious flower and set it in my basket for safekeeping.

"But he has chosen you."

"He barely knows me." I adjusted my puffy skirt.

"I know just what you need."

"Don't say it."

"But I must—"

"Gema, you're my best friend. We've known each other since we were young girls ripped away from our families. Spare me your silly notions and place your feet on the ground."

"As I see it, my feet are more on the ground than yours." She stuck out her tongue and wiggled her toes.

"Even if Ezer can look past our old lives under Whyzer Patro's tutelage, his parents won't. His kingdom won't. To them, I will always be . . ." The words stuck to the roof of my mouth.

"Say it. We're alone. There's no reason to hold back the truth in private."

I pitched my voice low. "A murderer."

"There. Was it so hard to admit the truth to yourself? You needn't worry so much. The prince is starstruck by you, and every lady vying for his hand knows it. They're all jealous. Now, let's see if the cook has any churros on hand. Ehh?" She led the way back toward the palace.

Though the churros should have added a fire of anticipation to my steps, the idea of being named the princess-to-be shriveled my stomach into a walnut. On the walk back through the forest and palace gardens, I couldn't speak. I couldn't even pray to the Ancient One.

Why couldn't my apologies shred the guilt lodged in my heart? It affirmed that no level of sorrow on my part would ever make up for all the lives I'd stolen. Surely, the prince of Giddel would one day wake up in regret when other people found out about me.

We walked in through the servants' entrance, and the scent of yeast from baking bread and fried dough curled through the kitchens as if it were a palpable force guiding Gema to the counter.

"Ask and you shall be rewarded." Gema spun to the plate of churros and chocolate waiting for her.

The cook, an older woman with a stout form and pursed lips, watched us with a dark stare that could have burned a hole through my head if she'd had the gifting. Gema savored the pastry with animated pleasure. Though the cook did not know how to smile, the evidence of satisfaction twinkled in her brown eyes in response to Gema's savoring. It had only taken a few days for Gema to win Cook's heart.

"*Señora*, you outdid yourself again." Gema scooped up the dessert-laden dishes and leaned over to me in a conspiratorial fashion. "Let's go up to our quarters so I can convince you why you're being a fool."

I rolled my eyes but followed Gema. We made it up the service stairs and had just cracked open the door into the main corridor when we heard two familiar voices. Gema backstepped, jostling the chocolate on the plate and knocking her flower basket into my face.

"She will ruin him."

"Mamá, I know. You speak of nothing else."

"If you don't work fast, we will have a commoner as a princess, and you will be the reject."

"What do you suppose I can do? The prince already told me his plans to announce her as his chosen. There was no convincing him otherwise. The only reason I could speak to him in such a fashion was all our years of friendship."

"You cannot let that mosquito win. I will speak to the queen. I've sent word to an associate to look into her past."

Gema glanced at me with her lips firmed and fire burning in her gaze, literal flames licked over her green irises. She whipped the door open, almost smacking me with it in her fervor.

Julieta and her mamá, Señora Virginia, stood against the wall with eyes flashed wide. Señora Virginia recovered her expression by whipping out a fan. Julieta averted her tawny eyes to the floor, not willing to apologize despite the words her mamá had flung like daggers into my soul.

"Good day, ladies." Gema's voice purred with a sickly-sweet candor. "Aren't you excited about Prince Ezer's announcement today?"

Señora Virginia waved her lacy fan as if she had a dagger hidden inside. I tensed my muscles, power rolling through my body at the potential danger. The hatred crinkled into her glower promised she wouldn't leave me in peace.

My heart ached. Julieta's mamá would find out about my past, and the embarrassment and public punishment would be worse than bowing out. I tightened my grip on the flower basket and headed up the stairs, my boots scuffing the gray marble.

At the landing, Gema turned left, but I spun to the right. I had to speak to Ezer before I ruined both of our lives.

"Cottia?"

"I'll be right back."

"Don't let those *chupalmas* get to you." Her comparison to the soul-sucking ghosts in *Valle de los Fantasmas* would have produced a chuckle if my life and heart weren't at risk. Gema pursed her lips, pointing down the stairs where the panic-stricken, mother-daughter pair sped out of view. "We won't let them win."

"This isn't a competition." I gestured, flower basket swinging on my forearm. "This is my life."

CHAPTER 20
GEMA

THIS WASN'T MERELY *HER* life. Cottia blazed from the stairway around the railing overlooking a mezzanine, her chin lifted in the air like she was always meant to be queen. Of course, she was enslaved to the idea that assassins would always be assassins.

With a plate full of churros in one hand and no one to share them with, I spun on my heel and twirled to the back stairwell. The flower basket dangling from my elbow would have to wait for my attention since a plan was stacking in my mind like the most elaborate domino arrangement. This one detour would be the first domino piece to set the others in motion.

I would never let Cottia self-sabotage if I could help it. My shoes clicked down the back stairwell, and so did the voices of two of her competitors.

"It's her again," a lady even paler than me said from below.

The other girl with the perfectly sloped nose and rich brown skin didn't bother hiding the wrinkle of disdain on her lips as I descended. "More proof that even pigs can fly."

They giggled, but I continued forward with a smirk painted on my face. It was much more satisfying to stay quiet when I already had the upper hand though they didn't know it. I had Prince Ulyses's ear while they couldn't get a single prince to notice them.

Sunlight poured in through the windows, warming my skin as I took the marble hallway to the library. Both princes had a penchant for reading the Ancient Tomes, and Ulyses had a new obsession with traveling to historical lands now haunted by chupalmas.

I pushed open the library doors to find Ulyses at the back of the large, book-laden room. The curtains had been pulled back from the wall of windows to the right, and rectangular tables filled the majority of the space, with stacks of books covering several tabletops.

"You know, you don't have to be so predictable." I strutted down the middle of the room, now all too aware of the sweaty scent I'd earned from picking flowers.

He spun his head around. Brown hair fell to his temple and framed his masculine face. The stubble on his chin had grown since I'd arrived, and I liked it very much. The way his lips upturned at the ends when he saw me set my heart aflame.

"Did you come back to chastise me?" His deep, silky voice kindled my emotions.

"Of course. Valle de los Fantasmas is known for making expert killers disappear only to be found months later, dead." I stopped several arm spans away. The musty scent I carried filled my nose with a warning not to get too close.

"This is different." He yanked an old book with yellowed edges from its spot.

"How about this—"

"Is my Gema going to make a deal with me?" He placed the book on a table and opened it up to the table of contents.

My Gema? The phrase stoked warm tendrils up my spine. "I will assist you in plotting your expedition if you help me with Cottia."

His finger stilled from grazing the page. "Why would she need help? My brother offers her his full devotion." He continued until he reached a line and flipped through the pages in the book.

"You aren't understanding." I drew nearer and plopped the plate of churros and chocolate beside his books. I set the basket of flowers on a separate table—we wouldn't want our poisons mixing with our treats. I crossed my arms but then pinned them to my sides, attempting to prevent my odor from escaping. "She goes to your brother right now to tell him that she will not marry him."

He shook his head. "No. Ezer is too taken with her to let Cottia escape that easily."

"Perhaps you haven't heard what the other ladies say among themselves." I cocked my head to the side, forcing him to give me his attention.

He stopped his search and met my gaze. Those hazel eyes of his twinkled at me either in admiration or just because he was too friendly with everyone. "Cottia is like a sister to you?"

"Now, you're understanding."

He chuckled. "And you say you will help me map out my expedition?"

I snatched a churro and dunked it into the smooth liquid chocolate. "Yes, but I expect you to talk to your brother to make sure his affections are sincere. Cottia was upset by a letter she received from her sister."

"I'd be happy to talk to my brother, but I'm not sure how doing that will change Cottia's mind about severing ties with him. And what does the letter have to do with anything?"

"Churro?" I gestured and took a bite. A sweet flavor exploded in my mouth, easing the fears that poisoned my soul.

"You do know that you shouldn't eat these every day?" He took a bite of the sweet dough despite his statement.

"Don't hassle me about chocolate, especially when you look forward to eating it with me." My cheeks flushed at such a forward comment to a prince, no less.

He shook his head, but his joy didn't falter from his cheeks.

"And as for the answer to your question, the letter means that Whyzer Patro found a way to get to Cottia. He's not the type to allow anyone to insult him without retribution."

Prince Ulyses groaned as he swallowed his treat. "Does that mean Ezer's in danger?" His tone suggested he didn't need me to answer.

"And I was hoping you would investigate with me to see if anyone has infiltrated the palace. It's odd that a letter would arrive through one of Whyzer Patro's men. You know, the whyzer has no qualms about using disguises to achieve his goals." I bit my bottom lip.

His eyes dropped. The books in front of him would have to wait until the risk had passed. He bowed his head and sighed. "We'll start our investigation at the gates."

I shouldn't have felt pure bliss running through my blood at the thought of investigating Whyzer Patro's movements in Giddel, but I was over the two moons. It meant time to make Ulyses realize he loved me just as much as I loved him. Never in my life had I met someone so sincere. I could wrap my arms around him and hug him forever.

CHAPTER 21
COTTIA

Traveling the passage to Prince Ezer's room with its polished hardwood floors and brightly painted walls should have been a joyous privilege. None of the other ladies who stayed in the guest quarters were welcomed to this portion of the palace. None of them could stride past the guards in green doublets without a man blocking their way.

For me, this marked the end of beautiful, unattainable possibilities.

Prince Ezer's simple but elegant polished door stood before me like an exquisite invitation to an event for someone else. I lifted a fist to pound on the wood but stopped. Almost a month ago, I had traveled through the countryside with him and he'd saved my life as many times as I'd saved his. The awe captured in his hazel eyes at witnessing my prowess remained locked in my chest along with his devastating smile. Then he'd almost died, and that had made something inside me want to break. Even with all that had transpired, I couldn't pretend he wasn't a prince. Dragging out the inevitable would be selfish.

A prince could never marry a señorita like me.

My fist landed like a hammer, striking with self-inflicted conviction.

Aged wooden floors on the other side of the door groaned with footfalls. Ezer's tan face appeared, eyebrows pinched with curiosity. Then his expression arched into delight. His smile cocked into the very one that melted my insides like malleable wax.

He brushed a rough knuckle along my cheek. "Are you ready?" The excitement dancing in his eyes crumpled part of my resolve.

My breath hitched. "That's what I came to speak to you—"

"There's no one but you." His words poured out with profound emotion. "Please don't force me to wait another day to make the announcement"—his eyes squinted as if he could read my thoughts—"or suggest I entertain anyone but you."

"How can you know that? This past month and our trip were . . ." I opened my mouth, searching for the exact word to encapsulate the thrill and emotion woven into the fabric of our time together.

"Extraordinary?" he suggested.

"Ezer, there's no way you could know that no other señorita could be a good match for you."

He covered my hand with his own. The touch sent a shiver up my spine. "When I saw you that day at my *ceremonia*, I prayed and prayed for clarity. I am not the type of person who says I hear the Ancient One speaking, but it was like a whisper on the wind. *Her.* I promise you, after I found out you were an imposter I no longer trusted the voice I had heard."

My heart hammered, remembering that day. I hadn't noticed the prince drawing nearer to my side of the ballroom or the lady who had stopped in front of me to curtsy to her prince. A blush crept up my cheeks at his attention. His golden-green eyes drank me in now as they had that night.

All conviction withered in my ribs as I resisted the urge to scoop him into a hug.

He continued, "Then you showed up to the garden party right after I prayed for you and begged for another word."

Breathless, I shook my head. "You invited me. Of course, I would show up. Couldn't it have been coincidence?"

"Or providence." He kissed my knuckles with a gentle peck. Ripples of warmth radiated from his touch, not the magical sort, but nonetheless thrilling.

"Ezer, you've changed my life." A sheen of tears gathered, but I blinked them away.

"What's changed since this morning?"

Every part of me longed to throw my arms around his neck and allow him to sweep me up in his strong embrace. Yet, we didn't live in a fictional world where ex-assassins fell in love with princes and lived happily evermore. Instead of telling the truth, I said, "Have you told your parents who I am?"

His smile sobered. "They'll understand once they get to know you."

"You haven't told them." I slipped my hand from his grip and adjusted my flower basket hiding poisonous flowers at the bottom. "You must be truthful to yourself. I will always be a risk to your rule. Consider the letter that arrived. Even if Whyzer Patro can't step through the Giddelian walls, someone who works for him can."

He leaned closer. "Don't."

Though my skin pricked with delightful goosebumps, I shook off the romantic notions. Why let this daydream linger when all that lay at the other end was heartbreak?

He leaned close enough for our breaths to mingle and lifted my chin with the gentle tip of his finger. His eyes requested a kiss as he glanced at my lips.

I rolled out of his grasp and took a step backward. We shouldn't act like we would be together forever when no promises had been made. In fact, I'd already declared many times over that we'd fooled ourselves into believing this could work. Señora Virginia's voice flashed through my conscience: *I've sent word to an associate to look into her past.*

Even the enamored prince before me might be revolted if he knew more about me. It was one thing to be told my profession and another to hear stories from those who had witnessed what I had done.

"Ezer, please. I'm tainted."

He stepped forward, but I maintained our distance. "You've got to forgive yourself."

A queasy sensation swarmed my stomach. I lifted my chin higher. "If you only knew what I've done."

"If the Ancient One who sees all has forgiven you, why would you continue to hold onto such things?"

A beat passed as Ezer's declaration filled the space between us. Footfalls of someone passing through a distant passage broke the spell and echoed like a reminder that my past would always ring through the corridors of my life.

"Please, Prince Ezer, let me go quietly." I backstepped farther away from him.

He leaned against the doorframe, working his jaw. The intensity in his furrowed brow bespoke rebellion at my gentle statement. "I promised you and Gema protection. Whyzer Patro is still alive. Am I correct?"

My knee buckled slightly, and I lost my balance for a second. A constant threat still had a hold over my life. The bond on my arm couldn't turn me into a puppet again so long as I called on the Ancient One, but would I ever be safe from the effects of Whyzer Patro's malice?

"Let me help." Ezer's intensity and conviction stirred my heart more than they should.

His effect on me might prove a greater liability if the whyzer found out just how deep our mutual affections ran. My chest throbbed, unprotected from the pain love might inflict.

How could I let another person in when I'd done an excellent job keeping my mother and sister at arm's length? My affection for Gema had nearly cost her everything. How could I allow another person to expose himself to the danger that came with being near me?

An aching silence stretched between us like a taut rope where one of us would topple if they pulled hard enough. I snapped my mouth shut. I couldn't give into his plea to name me his betrothed. Opposition would arise, with Señora Virginia as a prime example of someone who would not be satisfied until I disappeared.

Ezer sighed in defeat. "I'll see you downstairs."

With a curtsy, I fled. A dam of tears broke over my eyelashes. He had finally given in to my request. Every step back to my quarters pounded nails into my soul. This was what I wanted, yet it hurt more than the many injuries I'd endured before.

Tears didn't stop until a knock at my door rang through my room. No one spun the knob, so it couldn't be a maid. I removed a bolt and cracked open the door to find Gema's pinched forehead and a tray with two churros left and plenty of chocolate for dipping in a small bowl.

"What? Are you serving rooms now?"

She rolled her eyes. "Would you want the maid and all the other ladies to see you like this? Let me in."

I opened the door just wide enough for her to enter and replaced the bolt. At least my room could be protected when I was inside the four elegant walls.

"You look like Julieta whipped your tail end. The ceremony starts in less than an hour, and I can't have you going downstairs like that."

"Fine. Do whatever you like. I should probably slip out during the ceremonia."

"If you were a wimp, I'd agree." She set her tray on a desk. "But my friend, wherever she is, has never backed down from a fight, and she doesn't lose. We need cold water." The tap of Gema's heels echoed on the wooden floor.

After splashing my face, pinching my cheeks, and demanding my hair submit to her torture, I might have passed as presentable enough to make my way downstairs. I snatched the last of the churros and dunked them in the chocolate sauce.

"I hate to break up your moment, even if it's with my special cuisine, but it's time." Gema unlatched the door, peeking at another señorita tapping through the corridor.

Gema and I marched out the door, down the stairs, and over marble floors into the full hall. Pretentious ladies and their mothers murmured in low tones around a platform with the four empty thrones facing us. The plush green seats with all their polished wood and gold embellishments shouted that the royal family would arrive soon and confirmed the dreaded announcement.

Many wealthy courtiers ringed the edges of the lattice floors, keeping away from the ladies as if they were spectators betting on horses at a race. I sidled closer to Gema and upturned my chin at the whole tradition. Midmorning sunlight poured through tall windows on each side of the room, heating the space to an intolerable temperature. This is when I truly wished to be a laundress who wouldn't have to wear a stiff bodice and so many extra layers of adornment.

Whispers ensued wherever we walked.

"I heard he's to dismiss us because of her." A tall lady with a pointy nose and black hair glared at me.

Many others had the decency to drop their voices. Julieta and her mamá simply stared as Gema and I found an empty space at the back of the crowd.

Gema gestured with her hand toward my chin.

I furrowed my brow. "What is it?"

"Chocolate?"

The chocolate dip I'd swallowed upon exiting was stuck to my skin. I wiped it away with one swift motion, hoping beyond hope that the offending treat hadn't added to the gossip.

Raising a hand to her lips, Gema whispered, "It's gone."

Ladies snickered from somewhere to my left, and a bitter urge to cause them pain swelled on my fingertips. The gifting marks on my skin lit up as power surged from my chest to my fingertips. I reached out with my invisible touch, sensing the inner workings of the laughing lady.

"Enough, my dear friend." Gema took hold of my hand, stifling my wayward plan to make the girl suffer.

This was why I didn't deserve Prince Ezer. I let the prickling power ebb from my touch and coiled the energy into my poisoned soul.

A trumpet sounded, and all the guests bowed as the king, queen, Prince Ulyses, and Prince Ezer took their places on their thrones. A thin male servant stood off the platform below Prince Ezer and flared his gifting, which sparked electrical tendrils in his palm.

Prince Ezer spoke over the man's glow, voice amplified. "Ladies, family, and friends, I'm so thankful you joined me for this ceremonia. As you know, I lost my betrothed in a tragic accident and didn't have any idea whom I should choose next. Now, I have narrowed down my selection." His gaze drifted across the crowd, landing on me.

My heart hammered. Sweat slicked my palms at such attention.

Prince Ezer retrieved a small parchment from his doublet pocket. "The ladies who will be staying are as follows: Señorita Julieta Carrasquillo Colón . . ."

A part of my heart sank, but this would be for the best. Gema and I could figure out what job might suit us in town, and we'd still be safe.

"Margarita Antonia Torres Del Campo, Saray Noelia Sastre Alcalde, Cecillia Maria Lopez Gallardo, Estefania Ynes Gil Molina, and . . ." Ezer licked his bottom lip and folded the paper in his hands.

I clasped Gema's arm for support. He'd listened to my plea to not be chosen so far and seemed to be at the end of his list of names. I was nearly in the clear.

"Señorita Cottia Luzelena Jaime Pacheco." Ezer met my stare with a slight tip of a smile.

The mass of people around me blurred into an arrangement of colors. He knew my full name, yet I'd never told him. He should have said Señorita Cottia Jaime de Castillo. When had he done his research? How much had he found out? My thrumming heartbeat rushed through my ears, dulling the sound of angry murmurs.

If he'd discovered more about my past, why hadn't he thrown me out like the rotten apple I was? My pleading had at least forced him to keep more ladies in the running, but he still hadn't let me go.

I had to find another tactic to push him away and guard both our hearts. After that, I could investigate what my sister had meant in her last letter.

CHAPTER 22
COTTIA

Supper that night proved a musical affair, full of dancing and families celebrating the ladies who remained. The dining hall had tables set in a semicircle around the outer edges of the room. Chandeliers shone warm light on the platters of food covering the polished tables. The king, queen, and two princes perched at their high table overlooking the families who danced to the tunes strummed and plucked by musicians in the corner.

Gema leaned closer. "Who do you think Prince Ezer will choose to dance with first?"

My back went rigid. The roasted pig and *tostones* in my stomach swam in twisted circles. "Not me. He knows better."

"But does he?" Gema dabbed her lips with her cloth napkin. "Prince Ezer and Prince Ulyses have not stopped peeking in this direction all night long. The brothers are quite striking."

I narrowed my eyes.

Her cheeks flushed, making her freckles more prominent. "Was I not supposed to look?"

"We're trying to disassociate from them. What would happen if Julieta and her mother *did* find out more about us? How might the king respond when he discovered his son was smitten with someone like me? Now imagine if his other son had similar taste. Ehh?"

Someone cleared their throat beside us. Gema and I whipped our heads around. The golden stitching of a royal doublet filled my vision. We craned our necks upward to meet Ulyses's broad shoulders, thin mustache, and large hazel eyes dancing above a knowing grin. Had he overheard our conversation?

"Your Majesty," Gema and I said at the same time.

Prince Ulyses stood awkwardly between us. "I was wondering if I could—"

"You do know how to get a señorita to say yes." Gema giggled in her sultry voice. "I'd love to join you for a *danza*."

His cheeks flushed, but he extended his hand to Gema, whose eyes flickered with golden flames. Prince Ulyses glanced over at his family's table while Gema led him to the busy dance floor in the center of the room.

The whine of the violin suggested the next melody would be a couple's waltz rather than one done as a group. Gema wore her flirty expression I'd seen so many times in the *castillo* when she'd attempted to conquer the affections of a cute guard. Prince Ulyses contrasted her exuberant smile with a stern set to his jaw, but the admiration painted in his gaze couldn't be hidden. Why did Gema have to play with Ezer's brother? Even though she enjoyed the whole flirting game and never gave away her heart, this could be a recipe for disaster.

I got to my feet and crossed onto the dance floor, ready to break up my friend from the prince. Any excuse would do. Every movement forward solidified my decision to keep Gema and me apart from the royals.

A hand caught my wrist. Another snaked around my back. I snapped into the too-close-for-comfort partner dance position with a dark and handsome assassin, Cristobal.

What was *he,* of all people, doing here? He should have never gotten past the wards since he worked for Whyzer Patro.

Pulling away, I found my fingers tingling with the urge to slap him.

"Don't make a scene, Cottia." Cristobal leaned close to my ear. His cedarwood scent tickled my nose in delight though I never would have admitted that to him. "I'm here for a job."

"Let me guess." I stared into his dark eyes, lined with lashes any lady would die to attain. "You're here to retrieve me for your master. Patro must be writhing on his throne at having lost a subject."

We moved to the music, feet knowing their places without a thought. A guttural chuckle escaped his throat. This man had enticed many ladies in Whyzer Patro's castillo, but never me. What did it matter if Cristobal had a perfectly straight nose, full lips, and a square jaw? The man lacked any real substance. He strutted around, thinking of himself more than others because he possessed the same ability as Prince Ezer. Yet, Cristobal was no prince. He could take control of another person's movements but couldn't make a single move against Whyzer Patro, nor would he.

Cristobal spun me around and brought me back into a side-by-side position as the dance prescribed. We walked in a large circle, following the many couples in their promenade. I glanced up at Prince Ezer, who locked stares with me from the royal dining table beside his parents. His hardened expression and palms on the table warned that he might pounce on Cristobal any minute.

"Listen to me." Cristobal's breath grazed the skin on my neck. "You have nothing to worry about from me, but it's your sister, Isabelia."

My head snapped in his direction, our noses almost touching. "How dare you come here and threaten my sister."

A muscle ticked on Cristobal's cheek. "It's not a threat."

"Why are you here?"

"I think you know why." He ground the words out with an emotion on the hard edges of his jaw that I couldn't place.

"Enlighten me."

Cristobal searched my face as if attempting to discover a secret hidden on my skin. "You think I come to royal dinners to merely dance with the prince's preferred partner?"

We pulled away, spun, returned to each other.

"You're here to snuff me out."

"We have a wealthy donor who'd like you gone, but Whyzer Patro would prefer to keep you."

"Then why are you threatening my sister?"

"She's not as safe as you think she is. You upset a powerful man."

I swallowed a lump of fear attempting to claw its way from my stomach. "Are you going to do your job?"

He glanced away and then back at me. Everyone in Castillo Patro understood Cristobal's one weakness was me. "You know I won't, but I do have another job. If you help me with it, you'll get rid of me faster."

"Is *that* a threat?"

"No, it's a request." His mouth lifted into one of his wolfish smiles.

Maintaining my deadpan expression, I wouldn't let him discover that I wasn't completely oblivious to his appeal. "I'll think about it. How long does my sister have?"

"A week."

Prince Ezer tapped Cristobal's shoulder. "I'll have the next dance."

Cristobal bowed out. The contrast between the two men was evident. The assassin had darker hair but lighter skin. The prince had darker skin and lighter everything else. Cristobal had an even darker past than mine, while Prince Ezer had devoted himself to the Ancient One and followed a moral code that would condemn a murderer like me.

Prince Ezer took his place, palm pressing against my back and holding my other hand high. The music began, and we went through the motions.

"Are you mad at me for naming you?" Prince Ezer's words cut into my swirling thoughts.

"No. I mean, I'd hoped you would let me go. We'll only hurt each other."

"Does our time together mean nothing to you?"

Guilt pounded in my chest at the thought of every moment I'd let myself slip into a fantasy. All those days lying on the beach, listening to Ezer read psalms that bespoke of the Ancient One who knew me, loved me, and wanted my devotion if I would come in all humbleness and honest appeal. Ezer had almost gotten me to believe. So many tranquil days had passed with no hint of Whyzer Patro, until my sister's letter had arrived.

"There's something else on your mind." Ezer turned me into the side of his body so we fit together like puzzle pieces walking hip to hip. The clean lemon scent wafting from his skin drew me closer to him to smell it one last time. His gentle touch and warm presence did more to draw me in than the wild allure of Cristobal's provocative gaze. "Cottia, please speak to me."

I tugged Prince Ezer from the dance floor, breaking all societal rules. The message to all would be clear, and Prince Ezer's humiliation would be enough for him not to follow.

Yet, he did pursue me back to the table with concerned lines etched between his eyebrows.

Looking over my shoulder, I spotted Gema laughing with Prince Ulyses and decided to head to my chamber without her.

Prince Ezer blocked my way, demanding a response.

"It's my sister." I sidestepped around him and marched out of the banquet hall.

"Prince Ezer," a feminine voice called for him.

He sighed under his breath and spun to meet whoever had called him because that was what societal norms dictated. Good. Let him do the expected and leave me to my affairs.

I continued up the stairs. Isabelia was gifted in disappearing but always returned to Mamá. In the time Isabelia didn't appear, Mamá would send me letters complaining about it, which I'd learned to ignore. Sometimes Mamá would lose my sister for days. What if Isabelia hadn't merely made herself invisible but had been taken this time?

I stepped onto the second floor and turned left to my quarters. Something moved in the darkness to my right. A person waited for me in an inky-black corner of the passageway.

My muscles tensed.

Catching movement in the passage's shadows, I sparked my gifting. The warm tendrils of energy spread like vines from my chest and tumbled down to my fingers. I reached toward the person, whose bones seemed too skinny to be Cristobal's yet whose heart remained even like the best assassin's. It had to be Cristobal. Who else would wait for me?

"You're coming across a bit too desperate for someone of your caliber." I strode past Cristobal in the shadows, turning toward my chamber.

"Who's a bit too desperate?" asked a feminine voice.

I spun around. A name rolled to the tip of my tongue. "Julieta?"

Sure enough, Julieta stepped out from the shadows in a black cape and a puffy navy-blue gown. Something about the quirk of her eyebrow felt off, as if she'd suddenly taken on a more malevolent persona that she'd been hiding all this time. "What will it take for you to leave Prince Ezer alone?"

"You have nothing I want." I curled my fingers into my palms. "If I leave, it will be because I want to go."

"That's a beautiful thought." Julieta tittered in a high-pitched note as if I'd said something to amuse her. "But truly, after hearing your full name, Mamá and I will retrieve so much more information to relay to the king and queen."

"Go ahead." My insides quivered at the thought, but I lifted my chin high.

"I'm glad we understand each other, Cottia." Julieta's normally angelic face twisted with something sinister, making her look more like Señora Virginia than herself. I prodded with my gift again, sensing the correct size of her body structure, but I was still not convinced what I felt was right. She strode around the corner where her heels clapped down the stairs. The waning sound of her flight stirred up a furnace in my core.

What was that about?

CHAPTER 23
GEMA

With so much music, dancing, and chatter, the wide dining room spilled with joy as bright as the candlelight shining from the chandeliers. My pinched toes required rest, and Ulyses happily escorted me back to my spot at the dining table. I collapsed into the seat, feeling instant relief in my feet, but not yet in my mind while I searched the dancers for my friend.

Cottia twirled in Ezer's arms in a stiff manner, possibly from him naming her rather than letting her escape. Thank the stars for his stubbornness. The girl would self-sabotage any chance she got with love.

"How did you meet Cottia?" Ulyses took the place beside me, interrupting my thoughts, and leaned his elbow on the table. "You two seem very close."

At his targeted attentions, I could have squealed, but I placated the fire bursting in my soul and answered, "She found me sneaking pastries from the kitchen and told me that she wouldn't tell the whyzer as long as I shared." My gaze followed Cottia as she went through the prescribed motions on the dance floor. "I knew we'd be best friends for life."

Julieta stood off to the side glowering at Cottia and Ezer, and Cristobal drew near—I gasped. What was he doing here? This couldn't be good. Cristobal was one of Whyzer Patro's favorite toys who had his own team of miscreants and enjoyed his work. Cristobal glanced over his shoulder and sped out of the exit. I stood, unable to see past the dining hall doors.

Ulyses's eyebrows knitted closer with concern. "Is something wrong?" He followed my line of sight.

Several beats later, Cottia darted out. Prince Ezer chased after her, but Julieta wrapped her talons around his arm, stopping him from pursuing my friend.

The chupalma literally dragged him to the dance floor while he kept spinning his head around toward the door. Dumb protocols. He should be chasing after Cottia and not trying to be polite. I jumped out of my seat.

"Does Cottia need your attention?" Ulyses stood.

The jolt of him crossing in front of me sent my thoughts spinning. "An *old* friend is here."

He got to his feet. "Can I meet her?"

"It's a *him*. And no." My terse tone couldn't be helped. "You do understand what this means?"

"I'm not a fool, Gema." He gave my hand a gentle squeeze. "You asked me to help you investigate, and I fully anticipate you're going to help me map out my expedition. Don't think this is free."

A grin curled up my lips, and I giggled, the girlish sound I made any time I liked a boy. "Follow my lead then."

I sped around the table, and Ulyses kept one step behind me. By the time I made it to the hall entrance, Ezer spun Julieta while meeting my eye. He had the decency to look downtrodden. She, on the other hand, couldn't be more enamored, with her innocent baby doll appeal.

Ulyses drew nearer. "Do you still see your old friend?"

"No, but I should check on Cottia."

"Is she in danger?"

In a panic, I rushed out the door.

"I'm going with you." Ulyses quickened his pace as I turned toward the main stairwell.

Footfalls echoed above, and Cristobal descended the stairs. A cocky tilt of his head marked his demeanor like he was head rooster over this domain.

"What in all the Agata Sea are you doing up there?" I must have shouted because Ulyses gestured to a passing servant and popped his eyes wide with a don't-be-so-loud look.

The several minutes it took for Cristobal to descend the second half of the staircase had me cracking my knuckles, ready to combust.

"Gema, my dear." Cristobal reached the landing and gave Ulyses a once over. "Nice company." His words dripped with sarcasm meant to insult, and I hated it.

"Don't you think you should at least attempt some civility with the prince?" I yanked at Cristobal's puffy sleeve, trying to get him to face me.

Ulyses cut in front of Cristobal. The hard set of his jaw and the cold, steel-like manner in which he measured Cristobal ignited a different fire in my heart, the type that sat with fresh churros, chocolate, and *café con leche*—a very high position in my books.

"So, now you're going to sic a prince on me?" Cristobal asked in a mocking tone that sounded more like his friends than him.

"Why are you here, and what were you doing upstairs?" The questions poured out so fast I didn't get a chance to consider how to best extract the information from him. "And don't tell me you just came by to visit."

Cristobal shifted a predatory glare on me. "You know why I'm here, and you know why I won't end your friend."

Warning bells sounded in my mind that something was off. Though Cristobal didn't coat his words with sugar like he did for Cottia, he also didn't hate me.

My mouth went dry as my brain scrambled for purchase in this conversation. "Do you have anything to do with the letter she received?"

"I have everything to do with the letter, and if she's smart, she'll forget about her family." Cristobal started walking back toward the dining hall.

Tripping over the hem of my dress, I wobbled, trying to keep balance—not my smoothest moment. Ulyses caught my waist and set me on my feet. Unease slithered from Cristobal's snarl.

"What are you trying to say?" I rushed to overtake Cristobal and jabbed his chest with an index finger.

Cristobal looked down at my small finger, suggesting I back off, but no way would I let the creep go until he'd answered my questions. "I was hired to make sure Cottia was distracted and left. But you know who's waiting for her once she steps out of Giddel."

"That's great, but what's your real plan?" My finger tingled with fire, threatening to light. "We've never lied to each other before."

"If you take your paws off me, I might be a little more apt to talk. And you might want to get your guard dog to back off." He pouted his lips, pointing to Ulyses.

I pressed my palm over Ulyses's chest, assuring him that I wouldn't be hurt if he gave me some room.

Ulyses nodded but only backed off a couple of arm spans.

"Good." Cristobal bent down and drew closer to my ear. "I'm going to finally woo your friend and find a way for us to escape." The cool scent of mint coated his every breath like he'd just chewed on a peppermint leaf.

"You barely had a chance before." I lifted my eyebrow. "I doubt you'll have a chance now."

He chuckled. "We'll see about that." He swaggered away with a confidence I could respect in a fellow.

But when I twisted toward Ulyses, instead of anger, his eyes widened in shock.

"What is it?" I asked.

"He lied to you." The words came off the prince's lips in a whisper.

"How would you know that?"

"I don't know."

"Not to be rude, but what *is* your gifting?"

"I can talk to birds."

At that, I laughed.

He let out a mirthless chuckle. "It's true, but I know that something he said was a lie. Let's go to the library. I must look for a book." He slipped his fingers between mine, and his gentle squeeze had me forgetting everything besides our shared touch.

"I didn't think even princes had two gifts."

"We don't," he said with a severe tone, bespeaking the fear I read in his expression.

Cristobal had been in love with Cottia forever, so it couldn't be a lie that he sought Cottia's affection. So, we were safe for now. We had time to explore the answers Ulyses needed.

CHAPTER 24
COTTIA

EVERY STOMP BACK TO my room vibrated up my legs with rage at Ezer for revealing my true name in front of all Giddel and at Julieta for threatening me. With blood throbbing in my ears, I flung my door wide open.

I didn't quite feel the buzz of energy through my quarters until the door slammed shut. My body froze midstride as an unnatural force took over my limbs. I twisted my neck around to find a shadow approaching.

Skin heating, I released pent-up energy. My powers leapt off my fingertips and raced within his body. Sticky organs. Veins like trees stretched to his heart. I grappled for a thick vein.

My knees buckled, slamming me onto the hardwood.

"Let go," Cristobal hissed.

I pinched his vein harder, unrelenting in this power struggle.

"A proposition." His words came out strangled. Cristobal collapsed; a resounding thud vibrated when his body connected with the floor. He was unconscious.

My muscles recovered their ability to move. I sank onto my haunches and released my hold on Cristobal. Dimming, the markings on my hands retreated under my skin. My blood tingled with the sensation of an army of ants marching to my chest. The energy in the room settled like dissipating ripples in a pond, and Cristobal was the rock drowning at the bottom.

Though murder might have been the wiser course of action, I would let Cristobal recover and slip away from my quarters. I pushed onto my feet, knees aching from the effects of his abilities. Warmth pooled in my legs, healing the hurt Cristobal had caused when he'd taken control and smashed them on the floor. I tiptoed closer to my assailant.

In the darkness, his limp form could be anyone, a stranger. What if he didn't recover? I could walk away and still not be guilty of a crime. He attacked me first. But somehow that didn't seem right.

I prayed under my breath. *Ancient One, what would you have me do?*

The answer came like a whisper on a breeze.

Heal him.

My fingers curled into my palms. The answer had tickled at the corners of my mind, but the idea of offering Cristobal anything more curdled the rich meal in my belly.

Heal him. Another breeze carried the whisper again.

I checked the far windows to see if the air could be from the sea, but they were closed. Beyond the glass, there was nothing to see besides dim torchlight haloed from the grand entrance below and dispersing into the night sky.

This whole Ancient One business was a new thing for me. Prince Ezer believed in a higher being, and I'd promised loyalty to the Ancient One if I gained my freedom, which I had. No longer did I have to skulk around homes to dispatch Whyzer Patro's latest prey. The whyzer should have been a purveyor of gifts for the benefit of society, but instead he extorted the people and used the abilities he granted for his own benefit. Cursed was the man.

By some miracle, I'd been able to defeat the whyzer, and all of it while praying to the Ancient One. The thought of angering this force that I couldn't see or touch compelled me to kneel beside Cristobal and place my palm on his chest. My markings lit up over my knuckles in an instant response. A burnt-orange glow formed under my fingers and shot out more force than I was accustomed to wielding.

This had to be the Ancient One.

In an instant, my powers zipped through sinew and bone, prodding along the veins, and patching up the damage I'd done. Blood coursed through his veins again without a single detour. I attempted to pull away, but my palm remained firm on his jacket. The shiver of power roamed throughout his body, vibrating with life, and doing something of its own accord. Cristobal's pain overwhelmed my heart; his headache throbbed at the base of my skull.

I hadn't healed others often before I'd met Prince Ezer, but when I had, this deep understanding and sharing of pain had never happened before.

Cristobal's lips parted. He gasped awake. His brown eyes flicked open, illuminated by the glow of my palm. In that moment, I could see myself through his eyes, and I was beautiful.

The pulse at his neck beat with yearning, but not simply the type one could find at any brothel. His affections had been sincere all these years. Memories of slapping him at the festival and baiting him when he'd approached me in the castillo tore through my mind's eye.

How was I supposed to have discerned that he'd meant every word about getting to know me better?

The light on my skin dimmed, and my powers rushed back into my hand. Pinpricks raced along my forearm and dove into their home in my chest. I pulled away, dumbfounded by what had transpired and unable to replicate it.

"I thought I was dead." Cristobal pushed up to a sitting position and ran his fingers through his hair.

My eyes adjusted to the darkness as we remained in companionable silence. He didn't see me as another one of his conquests like I had always perceived. Confusion hammered through my skull with so many instances in the past uncovered and set in a new light, one that made the previous interpretations of my memories unrecognizable. Gema had prodded me about him since he'd sought my attention on a regular basis, but I had assumed it was her romantic fancies running away with her.

"I didn't mean to scare you." The tenor in Cristobal's voice was gentle.

"But you did."

He let out an exasperated breath. "I came to ask you a favor."

A simper escaped my throat. "Didn't I just do you a favor?"

"Saving my life after you tried to kill me isn't what I had in mind."

"Well, I'm not sure what you expected after skulking into my room with—"

He pressed a finger to my lips. "Yah, yah, yah. I'm asking you to help free me." His palms shone, revealing his serious expression. The glint of light reflecting off the sheen of his eyes betrayed tears gathering along his long bottom lashes. When he spoke again, his voice came out hoarse. "Help me fake my death. Your escape inspired me."

His Adam's apple bobbed with the emotion working its way through his face. I hadn't considered how my freedom could inspire others. Cristobal had always seemed to love the hunt and even had his own team of miscreants, but I also understood wearing a mask to cope with life. This teary-eyed Cristobal had never existed in my mind.

I cleared my throat. "What's your plan?"

"There's the matter of your sister."

My teeth clenched. Isabelia remained so far out of reach from the palace, and even sending a missive might prove her demise with Whyzer Patro out for vengeance. Then again, if I did nothing, the whyzer might find her anyway. That might be why she'd sent such a strange word hidden in her last message.

"Don't worry." Cristobal tipped my chin up with a fingertip. "Never let your chin fall. Sorry." He flinched back, leaving warmth in the spot he had touched. "The girl you met out in the passage wasn't Julieta."

Tipping my head to the side, I asked, "What do you mean?"

A wolfish grin curled along his cheeks. "That person is part of my team and our key to retrieving Isabelia."

Heart pounding with hope and fear, I edged closer to Cristobal.

CHAPTER 25
COTTIA

CRISTOBAL SCOOTED UP TO a relaxed seated position on the hardwood floor of my chamber. His wrists rested on his pulled-up knees, reminding me of our childhood days when we'd considered ourselves friends.

"Who is she?" I asked.

"An illusion."

I swore. "Don't play with me."

His mouth curled up the sides as if he enjoyed dangling half-truths in front of my face. "This is no game. That person out there changes how you see him."

"It's a fellow?"

"It's a disguise. If you had stuck around a little longer, he would have had to drop the ruse. He can't hold it too long when the person is so different, but he's quite good at knowing when to slip out of a room and reset. Male illusions are much easier for him to maintain."

"But I sensed a female bone structure and felt the typical veins. He can't be that good."

"Oh, but he is. He's not able to disguise himself. He's an illusionist. He dulls the senses and replaces them with something other. Someone who can merely change a face can be revealed with a touch."

One of my eyebrows rose with disbelief at how he could trust someone like that, especially one who worked with crooks like him. "How do you know he's not always lying to you? I mean, come on. What if you have never known his real face?"

"You make a valid point." Cristobal scooted beside me. "But he's got an oath bond and needs permission to use any disguise or else he falls dead."

I shook my head at the cocky way he tipped his head back. Somehow it made me want to wring his neck and drew my eyes to look at him all the more. Guilt wriggled in my gut at feeling any allure toward the assassin. I wouldn't be the young lady flip-flopping like a tortilla with my affections. Prince Ezer had already won me over with his patience and kindness when he'd fought for my freedom from Whyzer Patro. Even the memory of his gentle smile stirred warmth in my chest. No, Cristobal couldn't change the part of me already attached to another—even if that other person could never be mine.

"Cottia"—Cristobal pushed up to his feet—"do you know where we can find a map?"

"The library," I suggested. "I still don't trust him and don't understand how you plan to weave your ideas all together."

He reached out a hand to offer me assistance to stand. "Ahhh, yes, the plan. I'd love if you could knock me out in front of Whyzer Patro's cronies. I'll get my freedom, and you'll get to save your sister like the hero you are. If it were anyone else, I wouldn't think they could pull it off."

His compliment was like a well-placed two-punch combination.

I grabbed his strong hand and pulled up close to him. For the split second that we stood squared up to each other, the memory of seeing myself through his eyes lured me closer. All this time, his stern jaw set and his crinkled gaze had registered to me as cocky. Yet, he had backstabbed me once upon a time. His declaration about never hurting me only applied to physical injury. Would he fail me again?

"Stay close." I spun toward the door. "The servants' stairwell should be clear for now."

"Got it." Cristobal stepped behind me as I crept out of my quarters into the passage.

"You also need to explain how you'll keep your illusionist in line," I whispered over my shoulder.

He didn't say anything as we slunk through the darkness and took a narrow stairwell to the first floor. Footfalls echoed for a minute.

Gema's voice carried. "So, you're sure that only whyzers get multiple gifts?"

Ulyses responded, "That's what the Ancient Tomes said."

A note of unbelief marked Gema's tone. "No, no, but you couldn't be—"

"Hush," Ulyses whispered, "it might have been a one-off phenomenon."

The passage went silent of footfalls and chatter. I'd never considered what made a whyzer a purveyor of gifts. Though the strange conversation between Gema and Ulyses needed investigation, I hadn't the mind space to think too deeply on the full implications when Cristobal and I had his faux death to plan.

I turned into a passageway where the party's music echoed from across the palace, but not a single person could be seen. We raced into the double doors of the library, and I tapped the door shut and twisted the lock. My heart rate remained even.

Moonlight shone through the tall windows along one wall into the large room with tables in the middle and shelves lining the three other walls. I sparked my gifting, letting the heat roll down my arms and brighten the vine-like marks that glowed along my skin.

Cristobal kept a calm demeanor that matched his even heartbeat. He remained by my side. "I think you've lost your touch. Private conversations in an open passage?" He tsked.

I rolled my eyes. "My assassin days are over. Need I remind you?" Before he could answer, I strode to the large book of maps in the corner, grabbed it, and dumped it on the first table. "Where's my sister?"

"You know that's an impossible question to answer." Cristobal sidled up to my elbow.

"Then explain to me why I should help you if you have nothing to offer me. She's not in danger if no one can find her."

"There's a crew waiting for her to show up at Monte Verde." Cristobal opened the maps and flipped to the one where Mamá and Isabelia lived. "I can point out the key houses that will be staked and the friends who might lure your family to come out of hiding. Need I say more?"

Someone jiggled the library door. I cut the flow of power. My arms dimmed.

"I thought I saw something in here," a male voice shouted through the corridor. "Do you have the key?"

"No, but it's just the library," said another deeper voice in response. "Let Cesar get to it in the next round."

Footfalls clomped away, and silence followed for several long seconds. Cristobal's round eyes reflected the white light of the moon as he watched me with an unreadable expression. The temptation to stick my tongue out to mock him nearly got the sensible part of me. Old habits seemed to cling to my behavior.

"*Mira*, look, Cristobal, I'm willing to do you this favor—"

"It's an exchange." The husky tenor of his voice assured me he meant every word.

"If you can do one other thing for me . . ."

He pressed his lips together.

"Pretend to be my betrothed in front of Prince Ezer."

His eyebrows shot up with amusement and he covered his mouth.

"Is that a yes?"

"Will I be a dead man tomorrow?"

"It might take a couple more days than that."

"A couple? Seriously, I saw the way he interrupted our dance." Cristobal shifted his hips and arched his chin high, mocking the aristocrats.

"He's not that type of person."

"He's a *prince*." Cristobal's voice intoned with meaning.

"That's exactly why I need you to do this." I stretched out my hand for us to shake this deal into existence.

His Adam's apple bobbed, and he clasped my hand with his. "It's a deal, beloved bride-to-be."

I flicked his ear as if he were a young boy who needed a good reprimanding. "Only in front of Prince Ezer."

"As you wish, Señorita Cottia."

CHAPTER 26
COTTIA

THAT NIGHT, I COULDN'T sleep. Cristobal and I had conjured a plan where he'd be dead in Whyzer Patro's eye, I'd warn my sister about Whyzer Patro's threat, and Prince Ezer would stop with the delusion that an assassin and a prince could ever be together. Our hearts were too precious to allow such games.

I reached for the cold side of the large bed. Why had Ezer insisted Gema get her own room? Having another breathing soul so nearby for the first couple of weeks had made this place cozy like a home. But now, the giant space with a four-post bed, desk, dresser, vanity table, and chest felt hollow. No number of objects could stop my heart from squeezing with worry at the plan Cristobal and I were set to enact.

Today, Cristobal and I would fake a betrothal. Why hadn't we worked out more details before I let him escort me back up here? How would we share this information with Ezer in a way that wouldn't break his heart—if that were possible?

The day marched on when a maid helped me get dressed in a fine white gown for the henpecking, as I liked to call it, or breakfast with the prince's potential brides. I knocked on Gema's door, and she promptly answered.

She stepped out of the room in a fine black gown with sleeves that matched her fiery hair. "You missed all the fun last night."

"What, like you flirting with Prince Ezer's brother?" I lifted a playful eyebrow.

"There was a little of that, but Prince Ezer refused to dance with any of the other ladies when I got back to the hall. It made for an entertaining night. Well, after my run-in with Cristobal. You must have noticed him."

My breath caught in my throat, but I had to give her an answer. "I did. We came to an agreement."

Gema looped her arm through mine as if she hadn't made today ten times harder for me with her account about last night and her interaction with Cristobal. "An agreement? As in, he won't slay us in our sleep if we play nice?"

I kept us moving toward the stairs so I wouldn't make eye contact with her. "He's a little more on our side than that. You've always said that he was attracted to me." Even she couldn't know about the plan if we wanted to make our betrothal look real.

We made it to the stairs before Gema stopped our promenade. She pulled against my arm with her own. "Please tell me you aren't going to do something daft."

With the most serious expression I could muster, I set my gaze on Gema.

My friend crinkled her nose and lips as if she perceived my response. "Cottia, what did you do?"

"I'm glad you had a pleasant night. Cristobal won't be a problem. I made sure of it." I dragged a complaining Gema down to the dining hall.

Right as we approached the entrance, she tilted her chin high and spoke out the side of her mouth. "This conversation is *not* over."

Prince Ezer stood outside the dining hall and stilled upon catching my approach. His clear preference must end and mine also, but no other man had ever worn a simple navy-blue doublet and transformed it into a masterpiece like he did. Something in the way he pressed his shoulders back and held his breath scrambled my thoughts. His happy appraisal tracking my every move stole some of my resolve to destroy this dream.

"*Buenos días,* Señorita Gema and Señorita Cottia." Prince Ezer dipped his head as if he saluted equals.

"Buenos días," Gema and I chorused.

Gema continued walking on, but Ezer held my elbow, preventing me from entering. The sudden stop yanked Gema back. She spun around and smiled at Ezer's attentions. "I'll wait for you inside." She released my arm.

"Please." Ezer leaned closer. "My mind is already made to court you. I've done my research, as I'm sure you deduced already." His tender gaze searched my face and pleaded for a favorable answer.

My stomach squeezed into a tangled ball of yarn. Everything I should have said stuck to the roof of my mouth. Instead, I asked, "Do your parents know what you found out about me in your investigation?"

"No."

I pressed my lips together and swallowed the words I'd never be able to take back. "Then, I am right about their soon-to-be lack of approval?"

"We haven't tested your theory."

"An old friend came into town." I leveled my gaze at him, not willing to flinch. "He offered a proposal, and I accepted."

Ezer's jaw firmed, and his eyes rounded. "Do you love him?"

"He's a better match." I ripped my arm from Ezer's loosened grip. "You need a princess, not me." My vision blurred with the sheen of unbidden tears I would never shed. The tumult in my heart pacified at having to walk to my seat at the long breakfast table. All the other girls had already found their places.

Julieta's stare fixed on me over a strained pout. Jealousy sprouted from her like a palpable thing, slithering over her shoulders and consuming the girl.

Was this the Julieta impersonator or the real one?

The fact that I couldn't decipher the difference sent a chill down my back and inspired a more erect posture. I looked toward Gema, who sat alone at the head of the table, a place of distinct honor from Ezer, and she waved me over. We hadn't formed any alliances like the other ladies, nor did we care to participate in the game. I took my seat across from Gema, who couldn't beg any louder with her eyebrows arched so high they reached halfway up to her hairline. I shook my head. This wasn't the place to explain what had happened with Cristobal.

Prince Ezer marched into the room. All the ladies shifted in my peripheral vision, but I refused to watch him, to pine for him. He pulled out the seat between Gema and me at the head of the table, which earned a tell-tale eyebrow wag from Gema. I rolled my eyes at her glee. She wouldn't be so delighted if she understood the plan.

Then, Prince Ulyses snuck into the spot beside Gema, and I couldn't get her to look in my direction. The two spoke in hushed tones, laughing and chatting about who knew what. She flirted like she always had, yet a quickening heart rate rattled through my senses. Ulyses might mean more to her than a distraction or a rich husband—not that she was concerned about being wealthy.

Servants dumped trays of food on the table and slipped a meal in front of me. The steam snaked to my nose with a mouth-watering aroma that knocked on my stomach.

"Ezer, why do you take delight in torturing these other señoritas with your attentions to me?"

He cut into his hunk of meat. "Torturing? That's a bit severe." He chewed on his morsel, gesturing like he was thinking over his words. "They can leave for all I'm concerned. Just say you'll give us a chance and they're gone."

I leaned over my plate and twisted toward him so no one else would hear. It was one thing to reject him and another to humiliate the prince. "Betrothed, remember?"

Prince Ezer craned over his plate too, as if he also had a secret to share. "I don't believe you." The smirk creeping up to his eyes nudged at me to admit the truth. A second skipped with our gazes fixed on each other and our heads lowered over our meals. His eyes drifted downward toward my lips.

Warmth blossomed on my cheeks.

Perhaps he was waiting for my confession? I pushed my chair back, scraping the floor before I could think better of making a scene. "I'll be in the gardens with . . ." I mouthed *my betrothed*.

His nose flared, and he squinted. Gema's eyes flashed with suspicion, possibly because she understood my inaudible words. We'd had plenty of practice reading each other's lips. Yet even so, she dared not budge with so much food to be eaten and with Ezer's brother at her side. She had a tendency for wooing unattainable dreams.

My shoes clicked along the marble floors, signaling the nine other ladies to glance in my direction. The señoritas liked to pretend I didn't exist but couldn't wipe off their grins whenever they thought I'd lost.

Keeping my stride even, I pressed my shoulders back, not giving them a hint at the dismay nestled between my ribs. My boot tip crossed the threshold into the atrium.

Cristobal leaned against the wall on the far side of the passageway. His rogue expression and handsome appeal would do the trick if Ezer were watching.

I turned right toward the back door. He sidled up and rushed to open the metal handle before one of the palace servants could catch the door. The humidity from outside smacked me in the face with its sticky fingers and oppressive thickness. A gentle sea breeze tried to dance through the terrace but couldn't even tousle the stray hairs on my hairline.

"Did you tell him?" Cristobal broke the silence as our feet reached the last step of the terrace and our shoes stretched for the gravel path.

"Yes." I let my footfall crunch onto the trail. "But he didn't believe me." I snuck a glance at Cristobal.

A wolfish smile curled on his lips, emphasized by the thin mustache and stubble over his chin. "We might just have to make it more convincing."

"We might." The rose garden with all the red buds in bloom came into view. A floral scent hung heavy at the entrance, enticing me to dive into its embrace.

"Then may I hold your hand?" Cristobal reached for me.

I dodged Cristobal's touch and continued along the path, skipping the section I intended to peruse. "I don't want to embarrass Ezer too badly." The hibiscus garden caught my attention ahead. "Did you send the note to my sister?"

"Yes." The way he hedged gave me pause.

"What aren't you telling me?" I met his stare.

He pointed with his lips at a grassy trail into the hibiscus section.

I gazed around. An older man was watching us from the terrace. His long beard and unforgiving frown indicated judgment of some sort. We didn't know his gifting, and if it entailed an ability to hear from long distances or if he could read lips, we'd be exposed to whomever he served.

We disappeared among the foliage and spoke in code.

"My favorite hibiscus understands the rules." I touched an orange-yellow flower and sniffed the perfume it released.

"That's not it. I believe that the root would love nothing better than to stomp on the flower that fell from its reach." Cristobal yanked a white-and-magenta flower and tucked it behind my ear. His fingertips grazed the top of my ear.

"What are you trying to say? And does he suspect we would ever be . . . friends?"

The last word flew out like a dart at Crisobal. He hunched in response, hurt in a way I couldn't understand by such a casual question.

"I don't know." Cristobal leaned closer and closer until his lips almost touched my ear. He obviously wanted to share details without prying ears, but the proximity did stir conflicting sensations in my belly. "Cottia, if I could pass through Prince Ezer's wards, who else might be working for Whyzer Patro? All the whyzer had to do was loosen my bindings and make hefty promises so I would return to him."

Cristobal didn't have to explain the task once more. Whyzer Patro wanted me dead. I met Cristobal's eyes, understanding why warning my sister might be harder from within Giddel's boundaries. Who could I trust?

An emotion tiptoed on Cristobal's face, causing a muscle to leap at his jawline. "This whole job feels like a test. He wants to see if I can complete my task." The intensity in Cristobal's dark stare revealed more than he said.

"Do you think we're being watched?" I asked.

Seconds passed.

He dipped a single nod. "We should leave sooner than the next dual full moon. My illusionist will cover for our absence."

"Not yet." I shook my head, loosening the flower he'd placed. "Ezer isn't convinced of our betrothal."

Cristobal adjusted the drooping hibiscus and left his hand on the back of my neck. "Let's go before lunch."

Rustling drew my attention to the garden entrance.

Prince Ezer stood by himself. His shoulders stiffened, and his normal jovial expression shifted into something more menacing at the snap of a finger.

Cristobal smirked and traced my chin with a finger. He winked at me.

I shriveled inside. This had been the plan. Cristobal's affectionate touch should not upset me, but it did.

"Who is this?" Prince Ezer asked.

For a blink, the real answer slipped along my tongue, but Cristobal entwined his hand with mine.

"She's my betrothed. We're to wed as soon as we get to Cottia's family."

"Her family? Hmm?" Ezer swaggered closer with a deep wrinkle of curiosity pressed between his eyebrows.

Please, Cristobal, don't invent a story. I couldn't recall what I'd told Cristobal or Ezer, but both had done some research. Who knew what information they'd uncovered?

"Yes, her family." Cristobal lifted my knuckles to his lips and kissed the back of my hand. "Families typically are involved in such affairs."

My insides squirmed.

Ezer lifted his chin and appraised me as if he were dealing with a merchant trying to scam him at a market. When he spoke, his voice came out low. "Tell me you want nothing to do with me, and I'll go away."

I opened my mouth, but the lie tasted of sour milk on my tongue. A proverb raced into my mind: *A liar will not go unpunished.* Instead, I swallowed and looked to the side.

What was wrong with me? It should have been easy to shoo him away with a simple answer. Now, the proverb had me regretting the first lie about me being betrothed to Cristobal.

"That's what I thought." Ezer squared up to Cristobal, lips curled at the ends. "Where are we going?"

CHAPTER 27
GEMA

"Do you think they're returning?" Ulyses drank from his coffee cup and glanced over at the dining hall entrance.

"I don't know. I should talk to her." The moment I stood, Ulyses covered my hand with his.

"No, you'll make more of a spectacle chasing them."

The ladies around the other end of the table whispered amongst themselves and watched me. "I suppose you have a point." As calm as I could conjure my demeanor, I took my place again.

"You might want to smile or laugh at one of my hilarious jokes," Ulyses coaxed with a toothy grin, which earned a snarky chuckle from me.

"This faking perfection act isn't what I do." I stabbed a hunk of meat with my fork and stuffed it into my mouth.

"Emotions are high with those two. I'm sure it will blow over soon."

I swallowed my half-chewed morsel to get a word in. "Am I to assume you and your brother always have a new young lady linked to your elbows?"

A smirk tugged at his cheek, and he peeked at me with a side-eye that could only be labeled as mischievous. "Why? Are you jealous?"

With my fork, I flicked his forearm.

He flinched away and chuckled. "I'm sorry, I couldn't help myself. We're sitting around a table of ladies desperate to get Ezer's attention. Ezer has made it quite clear he's willing to die for Cottia. And not one of those ladies has even bothered to notice my presence besides you." The warm affection in his gaze tingled along my skin just as much as my gifting did when sparked.

Why was I so easily affected by Ulyses's attentions? He hadn't declared his undying love like Ezer had to Cottia, yet I longed for it. Why shouldn't I dream about a kind and handsome prince too?

"Prince Ulyses," said a deep voice.

We spun our heads around to find the skinny majordomo standing just behind us.

His mustache emphasized the grim line of his mouth. "Your father requests a word in the back room." A strange note touched his voice, and he gave me a poignant look that chased away any illusions of myself being an acceptable match.

"Of course." Ulyses's playful expression sobered, and he extended a hand as if to help me stand.

I lifted my eyebrow in question.

"Come on, Gema. Do you want to stay here by yourself . . . and with your best friends?" He tipped his head, pointing at the rest of the table.

"You make a valid point." I slipped my fingers into his warm palm as if I needed his help. His touch continued to spur on the fluttering in my stomach, especially when we kept holding hands the entire length of the dining hall and through a back door.

Ulyses clenched my hand upon seeing his parents in the far end of the room. Whatever daydream had woven itself in my subconscious evaporated as if a cold bucket of water had been thrown on the both of us. The king and queen perched on chairs with gold armrests in a giant room with couches, a fireplace, and huge windows that overlooked the garrison grounds and the woodworkers rebuilding the stable. The luxurious private parlor would have been the fanciest room in Whyzer Patro's castillo, but in the Giddelian Palace, it was simply a private back room.

The king, a more severe version of Ulyses, had a stern expression that made me want to go skipping back to the pretentious ladies at the table. I bobbed a curtsy, trying not to be impolite.

"Why is *she* here?" The queen's austere tone could have sliced me open with its sharpness. "We requested your company to get you away from her, but I suppose she might need to hear what we're about to say."

"No. Let me escort Señorita Gema to Señorita Cottia."

The queen shook her head, the crown she wore catching the sunshine from the windows. "Son"—the queen's single word jolted me—"your papá and I need you and your brother to stop chasing after women of questionable repute. You are a sensible person and understand that we serve the Ancient One and Giddel. You are required to marry someone who will benefit all of our kingdom."

Ulyses clutched my hand tighter. "We can continue this discussion later."

"No," the king barked. "You chose to bring her into our private parlor, and she will hear the truth spoken frankly. This is a consequence. We've already told you and your brother our expectations, and we will not be ignored. We've arranged for the princess of Pedroz to arrive in a month. Your official betrothal will be announced during the visit. Do I make myself clear?"

"Yes, Papá."

"Good." The king shifted back in his seat. "Now, you can remind your brother that he is to marry a lady of Giddel with parents who haven't fallen out of society's good graces."

My chin quivered at the smart look in the king's golden-brown eyes.

Ulyses's thumb rubbed against my knuckles as if he meant to comfort me. "I will not, Papá."

"How dare you speak to your king in that way!" The queen huffed. "This isn't like you. I know she has something to do with this." She wagged a finger in my direction.

"No, Mamá, the Ancient Tome speaks of us loving our neighbor, and you gave Ezer the directive to marry a lady of Giddel of his choosing. I will not convince my brother to go against his heart when it aligns with your instructions." Ulyses firmed his jaw. A muscle leapt in his cheek with an emotion I wanted to understand. Was it anger, disappointment, or something else?

The king shifted forward in his seat. "Ask this commoner about her past and see if the señorita in question makes a suitable queen to take your mamá's place."

"Pap—"

"Do your investigations before speaking back to me, son." The king gestured in dismissal toward the door.

In a daze, I kept my shaky hand in Ulyses's as we exited through another fancy door in the far end of the parlor and into the back passage. My boots tapped along the long marble corridor, though it sounded muffled with my heart pounding in my ears.

"Gema"—Ulyses pitched his voice low—"I'm sorry you had to hear that. I should have anticipated it."

Rolling my shoulders back, I tried to carry myself with some crumb of dignity. Why had I let myself have feelings for Ulyses? Like I could somehow make him fall so in love with me that he wouldn't care about my past. Cottia was right about princes not ending up with people like us. What had I been thinking? I opened my mouth, but snapped it shut.

Ulyses drew me into a hug, pressing my face against his chest. From so close, I got a whiff of his lemon soap. Warm tears gathered in my eyes before they dripped onto my skin and evaporated.

Finally, Ulyses tipped up my chin. His face now was but a breath away from mine which wasn't good. Everything in me begged for him to lean down and kiss me.

"I think some churros with chocolate might be good right now." That wasn't what I'd meant to say. The real words clung to the lump of emotion clogged at the back of my throat as if I were some sort of owl that needed to hock up a pellet.

For one long moment, his gaze traced from my forehead to my eyes and down to my lips. I inhaled and didn't let go of the breath. He glanced away far too soon for my liking, but here I was again, grasping for someone who could never be mine. I exhaled.

"That is a fabulous idea." He pulled away, fidgeting with his hands. "Then we can plot out how I'm going to dodge the Pedrozian princess and make my way to Valle de los Fantasmas."

We walked side by side in the general direction of the kitchen.

Keeping step with Ulyses's long strides, I forced some semblance of joy into my cadence. "Or maybe you can find yourself an illusionist who's skilled in disguise so he can be you while you can do whatever you want."

He chuckled. "That would almost be a good idea except for the fact that illusionists of that caliber are scarce, and they might try to kill my whole family for the crown." He cocked his head to the side and followed up his dreadful statement with a toothy grin.

A maid passed by, and Ulyses ordered a batch of churros to be brought over to the library. Though we didn't talk about his parents or their cruel assessment of Cottia and me, their statements hung between us and made the easy stroll to the library feel like wading through a bog.

By the time we got our treat and sat in the empty library with churros and a bowl of warm chocolate dip, I could have sobbed. Sobbed because his parents were right. Screamed because Ezer's and Ulyses's Ancient One couldn't save us from other people's judgment.

"Did the churros work?" Ulyses dabbed a cloth napkin on his lips, though a drip of chocolate remained on the tip of his nose.

I laughed.

"What?"

"You've got chocolate." I rubbed at the tip of my nose.

He dunked a new churro in the chocolate and spread it on his cheek. "Does this look better?"

I smashed my lips together but couldn't hold back a guffaw. In that instant, I was turned upside down and inside out with love for this offbeat prince. He wasn't as self-assured as Ezer or as presumptuous as the many gifted assassins I'd met.

"It's good to see I got a real smile out of you." He leaned back in his chair and let his shoulders droop.

"Ulyses, I . . ." What was I going to say? I love you? I wish you could marry me? "I think we should look up why you have two gifts."

"Now you believe me?"

"When did I not?"

"When I told you that your friend lied to you about something, as I recall."

"Well, everyone knows that only whyzers have multiple gifts, and strapping young fellows aren't supposed to be whyzers."

He bowed his head with a cheek twitching, evidence that I could trip up a prince. "That's what I was afraid of."

"What? That you're a whyzer in the making?"

"That . . . and well, that you might like me."

Our eyes locked for a long breath that I did not take. He knew, and I wanted to make it obvious, but after hearing his parents and the betrothal plans, I couldn't spill my heart to him.

Ulyses's expression sobered even more, if that were possible. "Please tell me something. You've been helping me go through the Ancient Tome and commentaries, but I have yet to hear you speak of your relationship with the Ancient One."

Without thinking, I answered, "Is this topic truly that important?"

"It's of the utmost significance. We spend a lot of time in each other's company, and you heard my parents' thoughts about seeing us together. I need to know if we are merely friends."

I curled the edges of my mouth and forced merriment into my voice. "You think too much of yourself." I fluttered my fingers in a dismissive gesture. "Now go get a book."

And he did get several books about the topic of giftings and whyzers. I wanted to hate him for being so kind, but mostly, I wanted him to be mine.

CHAPTER 28
COTTIA

"You're betrothed to Cristobal?" Gema's nose scrunched above her crinkled upper lip. "I don't believe you. When have you wanted anything but to slap the cocky little grin off his ridiculously handsome face?"

We turned backward to stare at the man in question where he stood purchasing fruit bowls from street vendors. One street vendor's fingertips lit up as he mixed the fruit into a cream, and the other sculpted it into a frozen mountain peak using his glowing palm.

Before Cristobal joined us again, I hurried to say, "We *are* betrothed, and he is a much better fit than Prince Ezer. Don't you forget that Ezer and Ulyses will never be a real option for us."

Gema narrowed her green eyes at me and scrunched her lips. I'd struck the mark, and it had nothing to do with me. She had been encouraging me to pursue Ezer so she could feel at liberty to chase after Ulyses.

"Don't think I haven't noticed how you seek Ulyses's attentions or the way you flirt. He's not one of the guards at the castillo."

"I know that," she shot back with enough venom to burn a hole through me.

"Good."

Cristobal walked up with three full bowls of sculpted fruit with small wooden spoons sticking out of the sides. He gave Gema her treat first, and she snatched the bowl like she meant to throw it at me. Fire burned along her lashes with anger ready to explode from her skin. She must have had more than a small liking for Prince Ulyses to get so riled by my reminder.

"I got you frozen *limber de coco* and *limber de parcha* since you didn't share your preference." Cristobal placed the cold brown *dita* bowl in my palms where I could admire the way the vendor had sculpted the coconut cream and frozen passion fruit into a half-white-and-half-orange galleon. "Is Gema upset with me?"

She stomped on ahead along the coastal road where the rich had apartments overlooking the Agata Sea. Her blue dress fluttered in a warm breeze. The promise of a coming storm lingered in the humid air almost as much as Prince Ezer's promise to see me tonight. I'd been saved by his parents' summons before we'd left for our walk through town. That would have been something. Us taking a stroll with Gema in her current state, Cristobal—the fake betrothed—and Prince Ezer.

"Does she know why I'm here?" Cristobal cut off my view of Gema and leaned down like he meant to keep our conversation private.

"No." I scooped a heaping spoonful of coco into my mouth. The sweetened coconut melted on my tongue, chasing away the distress of lying to Gema and Ezer for a moment. I should have told her the complete truth, but she was stuck on the idea that I truly could marry the prince of Giddel.

"She knows I wouldn't hurt you?" He clasped a hand over my shoulder.

I rolled from his touch. "Sorry, I don't like lying to her about us."

"Then tell her the truth." He quirked his cheek like all of this had a simple solution.

"Do we want this to be believable for Whyzer Patro, or do you want the old crew to sniff out our lies before you escape?"

The intensity in his dark gaze sparked a fear looming in his soul. He and I knew that we had to make this betrothal believable, and we needed our running away to go without a single hitch. I had to make him pass out in front of Whyzer Patro's crew, and we needed my sister to make us disappear long enough that anyone following us would lose our trail.

We didn't have room for Gema to let on that this was, indeed, an act. We didn't have the flexibility of more than a few days to convince Prince Ezer not to pursue me.

Cristobal's gaze flicked over my shoulder with a snarl lifting one side of his lips.

I spun around to find Prince Ezer with two guards behind him, marching in our direction. If I weren't me and he weren't a prince, I would run over and wrap my arms around him. Prince Ezer was far too smitten with me and I with him.

My ability to put on a good show would be tested to its limits.

CHAPTER 29
GEMA

Was Cottia out of her mind? How could she trust Cristobal? Even if he'd been on his best behavior yesterday, he still managed a crew of assassins for Whyzer Patro. She could marry the prince of Giddel, who was devoted to the Ancient One and lived out his conviction, yet she'd chosen Cristobal? Though I wasn't certain about this Ancient One business, even I could see how someone with scruples, who had saved her life, was better than a murderer who enjoyed the kill.

A day had passed since she'd told me about her decision on our little walk, and I'd never felt so lonely. This entire enormous palace with all the maids, ladies, and servants could never replace Cottia. I could strut to her room and knock on her door and try to hear her out. But she was wrong. So, obviously, that meant we were walking side by side as if everything was all right, but refusing to talk, because that was the sensible thing to do.

Unfortunately, Ulyses did not join us for breakfast to bring some relief to our dead conversation. Then, in the parlor, we played card games without saying a word. The other ladies stared and whispered behind their fans because they still had to hate Cottia.

"Are you sticking with your story?" I asked her as we marched outside to the archery competition.

"You mean the truth?" She cut in front of me to choose a longbow on the table laid out before us. Some of the other ladies had their own equipment which didn't seem fair.

"Just admit it," I hissed. Drawing closer to her and dropping my voice even more, I let my guard fall. "You're in love with the prince and don't want to take a chance that he rejects you. He must have done research to know your full, real name. What are you so scared of that you're willing to attach yourself to someone like Cristobal? You aren't that person anymore."

"What if Cristobal has changed? And you have to admit that he's quite the attractive catch." She avoided meeting my eye while she tried out a bow by getting in her shooting stance and tugging on the string.

I crossed my arms, helpless to change her mind or to stop Ulyses and Ezer from approaching us without my heart sinking into my swaying stomach.

"Ladies, please line up before me so I may explain the rules." A man in a white outfit stood before the targets lined up against a set of tall trees.

Cottia and I shared a severe look, which I understood as *don't court unrealistic dreams*. If she only knew how aware I was that Ulyses lay out of reach, then she might not hassle me. Instead, she might even tell me the truth about this whole Cristobal business because it had to be a giant lie.

Ulyses stopped by my side, and Ezer continued to Cottia's. Though I didn't bother making eye contact with the rest of the ladies, their grimaces were as evident as the storm on the horizon. We had but an hour to get this competition done before the coming clouds soaked us.

"Are you mad at me?" Ulyses kept his voice low.

"Why would I be?"

"You seemed upset yesterday after the incident with my parents." He shifted his jaw.

I had to look away. Quick tears burned along my lashes and formed a mist before my vision. Ugh, why couldn't I cry like a normal human? That was when Cristobal snuck into the crowd to whisper a word with Julieta's mamá. Señora Virginia spoke in a cordial way to Cristobal and even offered him one of her rare smiles. Something wasn't right about that scenario at all.

"Here are the rules," the man in white proclaimed. "We will start with a game of accuracy and end with the flags in the field beyond. The ladies must stay behind the marked lines or points will be deducted. The lady with the most points wins alone time with our fair Prince Ezer." He gestured to the prince.

Ezer waved to the small crowd though his proximity to Cottia sent a clear message about his favored competitor. Where were the king and queen? This little contest had to be their doing.

The man continued, "The top three scores will stay for the remainder of the competition for Prince Ezer's betrothal. The three lowest scores will be sent away tonight."

Cottia turned her head to the side, enough for me to see a calculating shift of her mouth. I shook my head at her, wishing I could beg her not to throw the competition. She wasn't as skilled an archer as some of the others at the castillo, but she wasn't bad. Everyone there had constantly trained for worst case scenarios.

Nerves bundled in my stomach when I caught a glow dance on Ezer's knuckles as he adjusted a glove on his hand. Was he going to use his gift to rig the game and choose who stayed and who went?

A hard lump formed in my throat, and I glanced at Ulyses to see if he had come to the same conclusion as me.

When he bit on his bottom lip and met my gaze, I nodded at him.

He leaned down to my ear. "I think Ezer is going to rig the competition."

I leaned close to his ear. "Cottia's going to try to throw the game."

His eyebrows drew together in confusion. "Why?"

"I don't know."

Ulyses and I stood to the side as helpless spectators while Cottia and Ezer tried to force the hand of fate in their favor, or possibly to their detriment.

CHAPTER 30
COTTIA

Five of Ezer's other chosen señoritas stood behind the line with long bows in their left hands and determination in their eyes. They fought for a crown while Prince Ezer nudged my side and leaned close to my ear. "I love you and don't want anyone else."

His words wrapped around me like the tenderest of hugs. I fought the urge to meet his gaze and instead flicked a glance at Cristobal in the crowd. The assassin stood a head taller than all the insufferable mothers around him. More courtiers had gathered to watch the competition, solidifying the results in my mind.

I had to lose miserably to get away from Ezer. How could he run a kingdom with me weighing him down? Whyzer Patro and my soiled reputation would be a constant threat to the future king's good name.

Prince Ezer paced between the other señoritas, offering them greetings of best wishes, yet retrieving gloves from the satchel at his belt. No one wore gloves on a sweltering day unless they planned to hide their gifting. This was no real match. He would sway the competition in his favor.

I bit back the chuckle in my mouth. I had to outsmart him to fail, but not so miserably that he knew I was doing it.

"Our first contestant, Señorita Julieta," said the tall announcer. He stepped off to the side, placing one arm atop his paunchy stomach and the other behind his back. The dead stare he administered to the contestants gave no clue to his preference in winners.

Julieta nocked back her arrow and aimed at the target attached to the tree several arm spans away. She managed to appear serene in her white-and-gold dress without a hint of nerves. When Prince Ezer slipped on his leather gloves, I smirked. How could I not? If there was anyone who should fail, it would be her.

She let loose her arrow and hit the second ring on the target. I glared at Ezer.

You could have diverted her arrow a little more.

He passed me a tiny shrug, not even attempting to hide how he'd manipulated the game.

Margarita, with her curly bunch of hair mounted beneath the veil of her tall *mantilla*, expertly lined up and nocked back her arrow. The confidence in her stance ensured a bull's eye. But just beyond her, Prince Ezer crossed his arms and fidgeted with his fingers.

The señorita flinched right before letting loose the arrow. She lowered her gaze and flared her nostrils. The arrow sunk into the tree, missing the target altogether.

Saray positioned herself behind the line while wearing a haughty smirk, almost teasing Margarita for her failure. But then she flinched at the wrong moment, and her arrow soared. It even missed the tree and skittered over the grass. A señora in the crowd let out a tiny cry as if the sight pained her.

After the two other ladies managed to hit the outermost ring, it was my turn. I picked up my longbow and nocked back my arrow. I aimed, holding my muscles taut in the perfect position, a little too perfect. I risked a peek at Ezer, who lifted an eyebrow and offered the smallest of waves.

I'd test him all right. I let loose the arrow, and it went flying to the bullseye.

The gasps in the crowd proved I would never be a favorite contestant, which didn't bother me as much as being manipulated did.

I marched to Ezer's side. "You said that you would never take over my movements without my permission after our dance. Did you forget?"

"That's funny. I don't remember that." The smug tip of his lips suggested otherwise. He slipped past me to Julieta's side.

My fists wrapped around my bow as I wished to slap him over his head with it. Two could stomp in the *canario* dance, and I would be louder.

With sleeves only to my elbows, I wrapped my forearms with the elegant hanging sleeves that went down to my knees. "There's a welt on my forearm," I said far too loudly with no particular listener in mind. "I can't have the string snap against my skin."

Julieta rolled her eyes and glanced back at her mamá. I followed her line of sight but stopped when Cristobal crinkled his nose and lifted his thick eyebrows into two confused slants. Even from our five arm spans of distance, he hadn't a clue I was about to light up my gifting. No one had stated this was against the rules, but competitions in the refined world never included giftings—that much I knew.

The next round went faster. Julieta missed the bullseye by a handbreadth. Margarita grazed the edge of the target. The other three didn't bother with the showy stances or sly looks over their shoulders and managed to hit the outer rings of the target. Just before stepping up into position, I released the heat from my gift and let the warm tingle rush to my fingertips. It flew into Prince Ezer's body and traveled the sticky passages to this one spot in the neck.

Ezer yelped in pain.

It was my turn, and I didn't wait for a signal. I let loose the arrow and sunk it into the bark beneath the mark.

"Should we get a healer?" suggested the tall announcer leading the games.

Prince Ezer massaged his neck and grimaced. All five of the other señoritas approached with concern. He lifted his head, leveling me with two dinner plates for eyes. I pressed my lips together into a line to prevent myself from releasing the smug smile that naturally wanted to twist up my face.

He calmed his expression. "It must have been a pulled muscle from all the excitement. No healer is required."

The last round was more of the same until it reached my turn. Prince Ezer came up behind me as I picked up the next arrow and dropped his voice. "Do you truly hate me so much that you'd injure me so you can lose?"

I glanced over my shoulder, almost knocking my forehead on his. The intensity in his gaze broke a well of emotion inside of me that wanted to wrap my arms around his neck and protect him. "No, but you've given me no other choice."

His jaw ticked, and a flicker of something desperate sparked in the green of his eyes. A fat raindrop landed on my nose, bringing me back to the task at hand.

"Prince Ezer, can I get a little room to finish the round?"

He shifted his hips to let me pass to the line. I lifted my bow and nocked back the arrow, measuring what it would take to hit the bullseye, and then shifted upward to miss. Just as I was about to let go, my front arm swung down before I could think of why I had moved.

The arrow sliced through the rainy air and hit the target right in the center.

I spun around. Fat rain droplets slid down my nose and soaked into my dress.

Ezer stood there, one arm crossed over his chest and the other hand cradling his chin. Unapologetic guilt marked his playful shrug. "That was impressive."

A deluge fell. Our viewing party ran toward the palace of Giddel. Señora Virginia tripped over herself trying to run in her rain-soaked dress, but Cristobal helped the older woman. Gema stood off with Prince Ulyses by her side, deep in conversation and unaffected by the interruption.

"Are we going to let a little rain postpone the competition?" I let a playful candor slip into my tone.

"Señor Alfredo, continue the game," Ezer shouted over his shoulder to the announcer. "A little rain never hurt anyone."

The little rain he spoke of made it nearly impossible to see the targets and formed streams over the paths and grass. Julieta, Margarita, and the other three señoritas stopped in their tracks with utter shock trickling from their gaping mouths. An unspoken question buzzed through the air with more force than a bolt of lightning. What would they *not* do to attain a crown?

"Let's continue to the field." Señor Alfredo's lumbering form crossed onto the grass and waved us over. "This will be the last round unless our prince chooses otherwise."

"One more will do," Prince Ezer shouted over his shoulder and returned his hands to his hips in a far too jovial stance.

I wanted to leap the arm span away and strangle him with my bare hands, but mostly I wanted to run into his arms and tell him we could be together forever. Instead, I closed the gap between us, blinking the rain from my eyelashes.

"We can end this whole charade even sooner. Just say the word and I am yours." Prince Ezer scooped me closer with one arm, only the long bow keeping a slight distance between us.

With my heart hammering and my tongue sticking to the roof of my mouth, I swallowed inhibition. "Prince Ezer, whether or not you and I end up together is in the Ancient One's control."

"I could say the same to you as well."

"And . . . for such a devoted follower of the Ancient One, I would expect an attempt at keeping His precepts."

"Yes, I couldn't agree more," he said.

"Then where in the Ancient Tome does it condone lying and cheating?"

He slackened his hold on me, and I didn't wait for a response.

With waterlogged boots, I marched through the rain to the row of weary señoritas following Señor Alfredo onto a mostly empty field. He stopped at a white flag and pointed to a red flag off in the distance. I had to squint to make out its location.

"The one to get their arrow closest to the flag is the winner, and the one to land the farthest loses. At present, Señorita Julieta is in the lead, followed by Señorita Cottia and Señorita Margarita. For the sake of warmth and dryness, can those three ladies approach me?"

Julieta jolted forward, hair matted to the sides of her face and the back of her neck.

"Are you ready?" Señor Alfredo asked.

She nocked her arrow back and let loose. The arrow arched high in the air like its only mission was to catch the flag. The arrow speared the ground but one foot from its target, making my job easier.

Señor Alfredo nodded. "If Señorita Cottia can land an arrow the same distance or closer, she will win."

I spun around. Prince Ezer removed his glove, revealing natural tan skin unaffected by a gift.

"Señorita Cottia?" Señor Alfredo called.

Even though I had decided what must be done, my next move felt like a hammer to my chest. I put the arrow in place and pulled the waxy string back. A cut of sunlight pierced the clouds above, yet it brought no relief or hope. I let go.

The arrow soared and crashed far beyond the red flag.

"This gives even Señorita Saray a chance to take the top three position." Señor Alfredo leveled Prince Ezer with an unspoken question ticking in his graying eyebrow. Then, the older man spoke to the two señoritas closest to my score. "If, by some miracle, you can land closer than Julieta's, you will be in the top three."

The pale Saray stepped up to the white flag and nocked back her arrow. The rain slowed to a drizzle. She let loose her cord. The arrow cut through the air with a perfect arch and nearly speared the red flag.

That still left me in the top three half.

Margarita took off the mantilla and handed it to Señor Alfredo. She measured her angle with slow deliberate movements. After a moment, she let go of her string. The whistle of the arrow sliced through the sky as I arched my eyes to follow the movements until it landed beside Julieta's arrow, closer to the flag. The señorita twisted a mocking look in my direction.

I'd gotten what I wanted. I'd lost.

Ezer gave a single nod. "The three winners may stay, and all the others are expected to leave in the morning."

As I fled the empty garden, Ezer's squeaking footfalls remained only a pace behind me. We crossed into the palace, where a horde of soaked onlookers, including Gema, and a crowd of servants stood around with towels.

Where was Cristobal?

I had to tell him that we must expedite the plan. I must disappear and warn my sister about the danger following her. But what about Gema? With her crush and false sense of security, she wouldn't want to leave.

No, Gema should stay. I could come back for her eventually when Prince Ulyses proved unattainable. Then, she'd disappear with me for a quiet life in the country cleaning laundry, like we'd always daydreamed about. The throb in my chest was unbearable.

I slipped between the mass of people, feeling their skirts and elbows pressing in on me. This farce couldn't go on a day longer.

Cristobal stood off by himself, leaning against the wall.

Like a dart, I flew toward him. "We're leaving tonight, and you'll be dead tomorrow," I said. "Get dressed, and meet me at my room."

But Cristobal looked over my shoulder at Ezer, who stood slack-jawed and only a pace behind me. Our plans could be ruined.

CHAPTER 31
COTTIA

MARCHING DEEPER INTO THE palace, past all the guests drying off, I stormed ahead with one goal in mind: *Get out of here.*

"Cottia," Ezer shouted through the passages, drenched from the rain and devoid of regal dignity.

A flustered male servant holding out a towel as if it were a life-saving elixir tailed Ezer. Many heads turned, but we continued into an empty atrium.

"Why can't you just let me go?" I kept marching up the stairs, clinging to the railing and lifting my soaked dress skirt in the other hand.

"Because I think you're running for the wrong reasons." Ezer grabbed the towel.

I whipped around, a flare of hot rage shooting through my veins. "Have you told your parents who I am?"

He wiped his face with the towel while racing up the stairs. As he reached the step below me, I evenly met his gaze. My eyes caught on the constellations of golden specks surrounding his green irises. Steaming breath pushed between my lips with anger, confusion, and a desperation to give in to Ezer's sweet plea.

His stare rounded, and a tender line creased his forehead. He touched my hand, and I jerked back from him but slipped on the hem of my dress.

On instinct, he scooped me in his arm and prevented me from hitting the hard marble stairs. "Cottia, you're correct that I have not spoken to my parents and that they would not approve."

My hands pushed against his chest, but when he lost balance, I regretted the rash motion. The flustered servant at his elbow grabbed Ezer's arm to keep us from tumbling.

"That was a close one." Ezer's mirthless chuckle danced on his breath. "I love you, and my parents will keep their word no matter my choice."

I pursed my lips and let out a shiver of gifting off my fingertips, instantly traversing the map of veins through his body until I reached within his chest. His steady heartbeat indicated that every breath he spoke was true. But even with Ezer's best intentions, I understood how power poisoned everything. Whyzer Patro was an excellent example of that. Though my knees threatened to buckle in the prince's embrace, I couldn't be delusional.

"Please, Cottia, I am willing to tell everyone how your past has nothing to do with the future the Ancient One has in store for you." He grazed his knuckle against my cheek, almost making me believe a future together was possible.

"Your Highness, should I get you a change of clothes?" The flustered servant again almost rested his head in the crook of Ezer's elbow.

The peace in Ezer's declaration broke when he turned to his servant. "Yes, bring the change of clothes to Señorita Cottia's chamber."

"Ezer," I reprimanded.

"You have some other burden on your mind." He brushed matted hair off my cheek. "And it started with that letter you received."

Why did he have to pay far too much attention? How I liked and hated it all at once. "You are correct. Others besides Gema and I are at risk, and they may not know it. This is why you must let me go."

"I understand, and I'm more than willing to help." He gestured to the man still hovering near his elbow.

With all swiftness, the servant departed.

Ezer continued, "Please allow me to escort you to your chambers. I'd hate to see you trip again."

Though I should have said no, I nodded and took hold of his bicep. We marched up and onward in silence. A yearning to express how much he meant to me swelled along my tongue, but a nagging thought wouldn't let me out of its clutches.

What if he grew to despise me when judgment came? What if Whyzer Patro killed him because of me? Either of those scenarios threatened an entire kingdom and my heart.

We arrived at the door to my quarters.

Ezer squared up to me and held my hands. "I'm sorry if my pursuit was unwelcome. When we came back from saving Gema, we lived a month of ease."

"You forget all the hiding from the other señoritas and señoras."

He cocked his head to the side with a wry smile overtaking his face. "There was a lot of that. But we also explored secret caves and daydreamed about the future. I would have let every other señorita go, and you know it."

I felt my head bob. Whenever he had mentioned announcing his choice, I'd begged him to give the others a chance.

"Tell me the truth. Did you ever share my sentiment?" His eyes shone with unshed tears.

Heart thumping behind my breastbone, I prayed in my head. *Ancient One, what should I do? What I want and what's practical and possible don't line up.*

The moment stretched into a tight cord where he neither spoke nor moved. A quiet settled around us, and I ached to fill it with the lie about my betrothal to Cristobal.

My mouth fell open. "I'm—I'm . . ."

Tell him the truth, a still small voice whispered to me, yet not a soul lurked in any corner.

Heat rushed up my neck, suffocating. "I'm not betrothed. Cristobal is just someone from Whyzer Patro's castillo. He knows Whyzer Patro's plans for my sister." A weight fell from my shoulders.

Ezer continued to watch me while an impassive expression settled into the tight line over his mouth. He cocked his head as if he wanted me to say more.

"I deeply, ardently care about you, and it scares me." The words came out choked and missing the actual statement I wanted to say. Why was *I love you* so hard? I couldn't meet his eyes, so I turned my gaze to the floor. Tears slid in hot trails along my nose.

He lifted my chin and leaned forward, but footfalls rushed toward us. The flustered servant caught up to us with a tidy stack of folded clothes in one hand and boots in the other. Ezer grabbed the items from the servant and dismissed him.

I crossed my arms and lifted an eyebrow. "What do you plan to do now? Disrobe in the passage?"

"There is a guest room across the way. Promise me we can finally discuss the real issues plaguing you." The sincerity in the arch of his eyebrows and slight tilt of his head warmed my insides, though my soaked dress cooled my skin.

He stepped away, leaving behind a disquiet about where our relationship would lead. I still had to warn my sister . . . and even Mamá.

I couldn't pretend she didn't exist anymore. The truth hurt, but living in a lie was torture.

Sets of footfalls approached while Ezer changed. Cristobal turned the corner with Julieta at his side. I let my gifting flare to life. Cristobal's form had all the bones and muscles expected.

Cristobal gestured to my wet dress with a smirk painted in place. "You put on quite the show. I didn't think archery was your better quality."

Julieta stood off to the side, hands on her hips and with a hint of a smirk. Everything from her doll-like eyes to her pointed chin looked like her, yet the fine line that marked a crooked smile didn't fit her normal demeanor.

"Is that . . . ?"

Cristobal stepped closer. "I assume you're free to do as you please now. You did lose the competition."

"Yes, but you didn't answer my question." My fingers pressed into my arms on instinct, covering the front of my dress that now pulled down at my chest from all the weight on the fabric.

"This is indeed Pascual and not Señorita Julieta." He gestured behind him. "You said we could leave soon?"

"We must expedite our plans and"—I shifted my gaze toward the guest room door where Ezer was changing—"Prince Ezer's not convinced about us, and . . ." I bit my lip. Why did I hedge instead of saying that I'd told Ezer everything?

Cristobal wrapped his hands around my waist and pulled me closer. "Should I try a little harder to convince him?"

"That's not what I was about to say." I pounded my fists against his chest.

The door clicked open from across the passage. After finally telling Ezer the truth, this wouldn't look good with Cristobal playacting.

Cristobal leaned closer to my ear. A minty scent met my nose. "You should laugh like I told a joke."

Letting out a sound that could be construed as a ragged breath or laughter, I pitched my voice low. "Ezer knows about us."

The jovial lines around Cristobal's eyes smoothed out in an instant. He let go of me. "This puts me in more danger."

I gnawed on my bottom lip, unsure what to say since he was right. Yet, I wouldn't take back finally telling Ezer the truth. "I should get out of this dress. You two can talk it out." I slipped through the door and slammed it shut behind me.

Voices carried on the other side: Cristobal, Ezer, Julieta. How would Cristobal and I escape now? My sister lay outside these walls, and I'd made a promise to Cristobal to help him disappear. I had to return for Gema, but would Ezer want me back after I left? My heart could have been a hammer on an anvil.

And why had Cristobal brought his illusionist?

Shuffling sounded outside the room. I sped to a trunk, needing to change before the two out there wrestled each other to the ground.

CHAPTER 32
GEMA

WHERE WAS COTTIA? THE corridor was stuffed with servants and all the courtiers still soaked from head to boots. The two other señoritas who'd lost were crying in their mothers' arms. Julieta strolled through the passage with chin high and shoulders pushed back like a parading pigeon beside her equally showy mamá. The courtiers toasted to her clear victory.

Servants dashed over to refill their pewter mugs, indifferent to the wailing losers. One maid slipped, spilled a tray of mugs that went clanging across the marble floors, and landed on her rump. While Julieta's party looked down with incredulous lifts of their eyebrows, Ulyses rushed from my side to help the maid.

Did he have to be so kind? It would have been easier to move on to more practical suitors if Ulyses had ignored the girl and acted like others were beneath him. Instead, he righted the girl and whispered in her ear. The mousy maid laughed while Ulyses collected the dropped pewter mugs for her. When he turned back toward me, he stilled.

I took several paces in his direction, concerned at what could jolt him. That was when I overheard Señora Virginia's speech to her small audience.

"We toast to the demise of an undeserving competitor meeting her end in this quest for the crown. I tell you, instead of giving her a crown, we should place her in shackles."

An alto voiced lady responded, "Shackles? Virginia, competing against your daughter is no crime unless you have some other accusation against her."

Señora Virginia dropped her voice and murmured something to the woman.

The lady gasped. "*Caramba*, Virginia! Why haven't you made this known to the queen?"

Ulyses strode to me and swept an arm behind my back, though I tensed, wanting to stay in place to hear what the ladies knew about Cottia. And me, for that matter.

"Gema, let's go." There was a husky quality in his voice that melted my resolve. He steered me away from the drying crowd, deeper into the palace.

What if she knew of our association with Whyzer Patro? What if she'd found out we had committed crimes for our master? I had to know. I had to get to Cottia to see if Prince Ezer would allow the competition to stand and if we were in danger here in the palace. Panic burned in my gut as I realized the implications of Señora Virginia's discovery. I spun back toward the crowd, but Ulyses kept a firm grip on my midsection.

He shuffled me away until we arrived at the library doors. "Did you hear Señora Virginia?"

"Yes." I met his gaze and turned to the floor. Though Prince Ezer knew about Cottia's and my past, did Ulyses? I doubted he would condemn us, but I couldn't handle him thinking ill of me.

"We should get out of the corridor." He opened the library door and gestured for me to enter.

Flames licked at my skin with the worry coursing through my blood.

"You do know that books are made of paper?" Ulyses flicked a meaningful glance at my arms.

I laughed nervously and extinguished the fire. Energy tingled beneath my skin, building a heat inside my blood that couldn't be put out so easily. I entered the grand room in a daze. Cottia had been right to worry about what could be exposed. All my dreams came crashing atop me in that moment, and a spring of emotions erupted from my eyes and formed a haze in front of my face. Unbidden sparks leapt from my skin and bounced along the floors. I kept close to the doors, ready to escape if the heat inside of me burst into full-out flames.

"Ezer told me." Ulyses's steady voice broke my sobs. "I've always known about you and Cottia. You are safe with us."

My heart stopped.

He closed the space between us and backstepped a particularly large spark flying from my eye.

"Sorry. They're hard to control when I'm like this." I shut my left eye to contain the inferno threatening to char him.

"You are safe with Ezer and me." He touched my shoulder and immediately loosened his grip. "And you are hot."

A small chuckle released from my throat. "I know." The words came out as a cry.

"The real questions are how Señora Virginia found out and what she intends to do with the information."

Tears evaporated the moment they reached my eyelids and puffed out as steam, blocking my vision.

"Are you crying?"

"Yes."

"Does that always happen?"

"Most of the time."

He placed his fingers on the edges of my steam. "I also know that she's lying about something."

"It happened again?"

"Yes. I must find a way to touch her skin. The tome we read said skin contact is necessary for truth finders."

"So, you are a whyzer?"

"I don't know, but that doesn't matter right now." He swallowed and dropped his hand. "We have to make sure you and Cottia are safe from Señora Virginia. Go get Cottia. I'll find my brother."

CHAPTER 33
COTTIA

WEARING A SIMPLE DARK dress and leaving my wet clothes dripping on top of the open wardrobe, I flung wide the chamber door. "Ready."

Ezer leaned against the door frame on one side, and Cristobal leaned against the wall on the other. The scathing looks exchanged confirmed the waiting hadn't involved friendly banter.

"Perhaps we should continue this conversation out of earshot. Where's . . . Julieta?"

Cristobal strode into my chamber. "She went to attend to something."

"How do you know Julieta?" An accusing tone marked Ezer's voice. "It occurred to me that I overheard a clip of your conversation that didn't settle right."

"Would you believe me if I said we were old friends?" Cristobal sunk onto a bench with stretched-out legs and arms crossed. One of his wolfish smiles curled the edges of his mouth like it always did when he was up to no good.

"Do you take me for a fool?" Ezer crossed into my chamber but remained near the door and rubbed his palms on his trousers in clear discomfort. "How does a respectable señorita come to have a friend of such ill repute?"

"I could ask the same of you—no offense, Cottia."

Though the barb was fitting, I slammed the door to end the childish bickering.

My pack, with the meagerest of clothing for the trip we would make through the mountains, lay on the bed. I slid a couple more blades into the small compartment in my favorite boots. "We have to go tonight."

Ezer leaned back against the wall. "Who has to go?"

I stood in the middle of the two men as a person torn between her old life and new, unable to sever ties with either. I didn't see the heartfelt desire in Cristobal to change, but I couldn't deny him an opportunity to be free. "Cristobal and I made a deal, and I must find my sister."

"Let me help you." Ezer drew near, cutting off my view from Cristobal. "I need only a few days to smooth things over. I can't draw out this selection any longer."

Cristobal shifted onto an arm, leaning closer. "Don't mind me. I'm only the fake betrothed while you all get your coconuts lined up."

"Please." Ezer slipped his hands into mine. "Today, I'm going to tell my parents everything and let the other señoritas go."

"That's a great plan." Cristobal was almost flippant. "Because I really had hoped to do a dying act tonight."

Ezer's eyebrows nearly collided.

Shifting my jaw, I kept my emotions at bay. Half of me wanted to wrap my arms around him in triumph, but the other half couldn't work past the fear snapped around my wrists like iron chains. "Whyzer Patro took off Cristobal's bond to get past the barrier, and he wants me to make a show of ending the assassin Cristobal in front of Whyzer Patro's men. In exchange, he'll help me warn my sister and tell me Whyzer Patro's plans. He also agreed to play the part of my betrothed."

Ezer let his gaze drop as the truth settled over him.

A beat passed, then two. Cristobal shifted back on his elbows against my bed, letting out a rustling noise to fill the silence.

The hardwood groaned from the passageway. Before I could head over, Cristobal cracked the door open and peeked through a hairline space.

"Who is it?" I whispered.

Cristobal sighed. "Pascual."

Ezer and I glanced at each other with hesitation evident in the purse of Ezer's lips.

My maid with her slight frame and pulled-back hair hunched through the door under Cristobal's extended arm, propping open the door. Her thin nose was scrunched instead of smooth in her typical, carefree smile. Her gaze bounced between Cristobal and Ezer, but she remained silent.

"Don't worry." I patted her bony shoulder, which ignited my gifting. A waterfall of energy poured from my chest to my fingertips and kindled heat that sprouted droplets of sweat along my arms. The powers infiltrated my maid's body like tiny invisible tentacles digging their way under her skin. It dragged back nonsensical information.

The bones were thick, and her muscles bulged with extra weight that couldn't possibly come from such a small form. Something about her heartbeat pumped in a foreign rhythm to the one I'd grown accustomed to prodding.

"He's either not as good as you say or not hiding." I directed my statement at Cristobal.

Cristobal's mustache twitched with a hint of a smile crease forming on his cheek. "My ward."

The person beside me grew into a pudgy young man with a round nose and small eyes. He couldn't have been too much older than me and hadn't any feature to draw my attention besides the smug set of his jaw.

Cristobal peeked out the door and shut it again. "Sorry, I thought I heard something. He is bound to me, and he will be covering for us when we're gone."

Ezer smoothed a hand over his crumpled expression as if he was trying to massage out his reservations. "I don't think so. Not with him gaining access to so many high positions."

"Then you can stay." Cristobal cut in between the strange man and me and put his arms around us both. "My ward is bound to me, so we are tethered through chupalma magic."

"Chupalma magic?" Ezer cocked his head to the side. "That sounds like something outside the Ancient One's giftings."

"It works," Cristobal countered.

Ezer sighed and raked his hair. "I much prefer an oath. Bindings are sanctioned in the Ancient Tomes, though they too are not recommended."

Cristobal stiffened at such a request. Oaths had deep consequences if broken, and who knew what might happen to Cristobal if his ward didn't keep his word. Whyzer Patro had taught all his subjects to never say an oath if possible. Even Whyzer Patro's oath with me over a month ago had put all the responsibility on me rather than him. A binding was much less dangerous. Why was Ezer hesitant to use the burnt binding?

"Go on." Cristobal snapped at the young man. "Give the prince some assurance."

The ward shifted his jaw, but when he opened his mouth, golden lines shone all over his flesh. He spoke thunderous words in the ancient tongue, forgotten by most. The dust in the room suspended. My heart squeezed. An overwhelming power pushed into the chamber and left Cristobal and Ezer with their jaws dropped.

"Should Prince Ezer of Giddel give permission, I promise to only use Prince Ezer of Giddel's identity or another of the royal Giddelian line these three days. Should Prince Ezer not return before sunset on the third day to the Giddelian palace, the promise shall be void. Do you accept the terms?"

Ezer's Adam's apple bobbed with the weight of such a deal. Wards didn't allow those with illusionist abilities to impersonate royal family or even advisors. If Ezer gave Pascual permission, Pascual could impersonate Ezer and anyone in the Giddelian household. Ezer fixed his attention on me and just as I saw him fix his mouth into a no, he said, "Yes, I give you permission and accept the terms."

The ward's skin dimmed into the young man's natural olive tone, now seemingly dull and lifeless.

I cursed under my breath at such a tight schedule and for not asking him the exact wording of the promise beforehand.

Several raps against the door cut through the moment.

The four of us stood dumbstruck as if we'd forgotten what the sound meant.

Someone knocked again.

"I'll get it." My feet swooped across the floor like a seagull who'd found food. I cracked the door open to find Gema's face a handbreadth from mine.

We both gasped.

Holding the door with a vice grip, I caught my breath. "Where's your prince?"

She laughed and drew closer. "What are you hiding?"

"Isabelia is in danger. Cristobal told me that you-know-who is searching for her to get to me."

"Is Cristobal in there?" She rocked onto her toes to peer around me. "Is that why you're blocking me out?"

I nodded.

She dropped her voice. "He might be tricking you, even if he doesn't know it." Gema's green irises shifted into flames. "Whyzer Patro would do anything to put you at the end of a noose, and he surely has a vendetta against Prince Ezer."

"Don't you think I know that?"

"Yes, but—"

"But what?"

"You're still planning on retrieving your sister, aren't you?" Gema bit her bottom lip. "That's why you lost?"

"Yes."

"There's something more." She looked over her shoulder at a maid passing by. "Let me in. I think I can handle seeing Cristobal again."

Tensing my muscles against her push, I grappled for a good enough excuse to keep her out. "No, he's changing."

Her nose flared. "Then my chamber?"

I shook my head. If we had a more personal conversation, I might say too much about the plan, and we needed to keep a small group to protect Cristobal. "Don't worry about me."

"This isn't like you. This is wrong. You said that you'd never give your heart to another assassin." Gema's tone grew desperate. "Cristobal is nice enough—I guess—but . . . Cottia, Prince Ezer adores you, and you should give him more attention. You're not thinking right."

"Stop already." I flashed a glance over my shoulder at Ezer's stoic expression. Heat consumed my cheeks at what I'd just insinuated about myself and Cristobal. The one little lie about me being betrothed had caught fire and turned into something I couldn't control. I returned to meet Gema shaking her head. If I let this go on any longer, she might burn down the door and pull Cristobal out by his tunic. "I am betrothed to Cristobal, and he is going to help me recover my sister."

"You can stop saying that stupid line. You're not fooling me." Gema stepped back; a pink hue tinted her skin. "But Prince Ezer . . ."

"Cover for me."

"But—"

I tapped the door shut. The back of my head slapped against the wooden door with a dull thud. I glanced at Ezer, who flitted looks between Cristobal and me. The rest of the words caged in my throat grew bitter as they slithered into my stomach: *I just lied again to my best friend. This better not be a trick.*

Cristobal whispered, "You did well. I promise this will all turn out."

I shot him a glare. "You'd better be right."

CHAPTER 34
COTTIA

THE DARKNESS OF THE night sky blanketed the palace gardens, providing us with the perfect conditions for our escape. Ezer, Cristobal, and I treaded close to the stone wall that encircled the palace grounds. Pascual took the shape and garb of a palace guard scheduled to be lookout—my eyes took in the taller fellow, somewhat fit, and his styled, thick mustache.

The imposter's face now held all the same angles as the guard's did, but the real fellow lay alone in bed from a stomach bug induced by a potion whipped up by Cristobal. I may have had a hand in picking the offending herbs, and Prince Ezer may have distracted the young guard with a kind word.

A sliver of guilt nestled in my stomach, and I reminded myself why we were risking our lives.

My sister is being hunted because of me. Cristobal won't be able to escape Whyzer Patro's clutches unless he is presumed dead. What's the point of life if I let those around me drown when I could have done something?

Ezer drew close and pitched his voice so low I grappled to understand his words. "Are you sure you want to escape this way?"

I glanced at him and nodded.

His bottom lip firmed into a frown, but he continued to trek along the wall. Earlier in the day, he'd mentioned a secret passage we could use for escape, but we would have to separate from Cristobal and reunite outside Giddel. I wouldn't chance us losing each other, so we chose the more dangerous route.

Our boots scuffed as we kept to the wall's shadow. No moon graced the sky, which had its own perils and perks. Cristobal held my hand, guiding me to the northern guard tower farthest from the turrets and grandeur of the palace across the expansive grounds. Ezer caught my eye. A hint of emotion quirked along the lines of his face. But Cristobal drew me into the tower before I could think too deeply about Ezer's trepidations.

The low reflection of a flame painted the top of a stairwell.

"Hide under the stairs," Pascual intoned.

The three of us obeyed. We crouched on our haunches, hidden by inky darkness in a dank corner. Footfalls scraped up the stone steps until all we heard were low murmurs above.

"This is disheartening," Ezer voice came out in a whisper.

"What is?" I asked.

Ezer's elbow bumped into mine. "That a portion of the wall will be left unguarded so easily because of a custard and a compliment."

A chuckle escaped Cristobal's throat. "If only you knew how easy it is to breach a wall. At least this fool believes his friend takes his place."

Ezer shook his head. "Still—"

"Shhh." Cristobal's gaze rounded into a wordless reprimand.

Ezer exhaled loudly in protest. I supposed a prince wouldn't be accustomed to such terse manners, but he had the foresight to forego his ego for the sake of my mission.

Boots scraped in quick steps toward us. We caught the back side of a broad-shouldered man ready for a break from his duties. A whistle pierced the quiet tower, signaling for us to go up. Cristobal led the caravan.

We made it to the top floor, which was a small room with a wall of weapons on one side. The other side contained a square table with chairs and a lamp to light the stairwell. By the time we crossed the simple space, Cristobal had the hook and rope ready to throw over the side.

Our impersonator stood at the ledge with a grim set to his lips typical of the guards, but something about his eyes danced with an emotion I couldn't read. It reminded me more of the chubby man behind the face. My powers ignited again without me calling them. A tingle zipped along my skin, sending out my invisible reach.

Cristobal worked efficiently to dig the metal hook into a groove sturdy enough to hold our combined body weight. He tossed the knotted rope over the ledge and started to rappel down.

Ezer watched the impersonator like I had. A pulse shot like rapid fire through his veins, proving the oath wasn't enough to settle his apprehension about our plan. That detail comforted me that someone remained disturbed by disorder. The other two fellows had the steady beat of well-worn criminals, unperturbed by danger or anyone else's opinions.

Ancient One, please protect Ezer on this trip. This man would make a just ruler who knows what he wants.

"Cottia, Cottia?" Cristobal called from the side of the wall.

I gripped the rope and slid my foot onto the first knot. The inky ground stretched far below, inviting anyone to fall into nothingness. My hands worked of their own accord in the rhythmic motion I'd done so many times before.

Ezer climbed over the ledge and wavered for the slightest of moments. Below me, Cristobal hit the ground and flattened himself against the wall.

The silhouette of a guard tower could be seen to the right and left, but the distance between them provided some level of protection.

The impersonator leaned over the ledge, looking down at us with the same grimness that had captured my attention earlier. Ezer missed a knot. He grunted and slipped down a fraction. Once the rope calmed from the jerky sway, I let my gaze travel back to the impersonator, who now inclined his head near the hook. Would he cut the rope? Would he help Ezer, should he get stuck?

Now, with the full light behind the man, his face remained hidden in shadow, though I could sense a shift in his tense muscles and the uptick of his heartrate.

My boot hit the ground, and I continued to crane my neck back just in case the impersonator and Cristobal had arranged to do away with Ezer without telling me.

Cristobal stood against the wall with ease, so my notion seemed unfounded. According to him, the impersonator was under his control, so I shouldn't worry. But what if the magical binding between Cristobal and the impersonator had been broken when the whyzer released them to infiltrate Giddel's wards? I needed to get my hands on a text that explained such bindings. Whyzer Patro had only discussed and demonstrated his ability to take over my body with a thought.

Thank the Ancient One for breaking that bond.

Ezer missed another knot that wriggled from his foot. I grabbed the rope, steadying it. He sped down faster and hopped to the ground, landing a handbreadth from my side. Healthy male sweat met my nose. His breath came out in pants. Though I could only make out his dark form, I could feel his perusal.

"Thank you," Ezer said.

A whistle cut through the air. My muscles jerked back. The metal hook landed with a clunk to the ground, along with the thick rope. Our compadre might have dented our skulls with how carelessly he'd released the rope.

Cristobal swooped to retrieve the cord and wrapped it around his arm. "We've got to go."

We didn't have time to waste. Threats could come from the palace if another guard caught us, and from the forest beyond. Cristobal led the way. My gaze scanned the forest, skimming along the edges of the darkness. I let my powers stretch out from my body, prodding for life ahead and around us. It lit the markings along my arms and let out a small glow from the cuffs of my dark tunic. The invisible tendrils of gifting naturally stopped about a stone's throw away, but I reached farther to access our path.

Just when we crossed into the forest, an arrow whistled past my head. I dipped lower without breaking stride.

Several more flew over my head and behind me.

"Run," Cristobal yelled.

Ezer grunted.

CHAPTER 35
GEMA

"Did you find your brother?" I closed the library door behind me.

"No." Ulyses pulled stacks of books from the shelves and laid them out on a table. "What about you?"

"I found Cottia, all right." I crossed the long room, boots echoing with each clomp forward. "But caramba, she wanted nothing to do with me. If she'd had a broom, she would have swept me out of her doorway like a *cucaracha*."

Ulyses peeled his gaze from the page and lifted a heart-igniting smile. "She's hiding something?"

Calm yourself, Gema. Flames threatened to burst from my cheeks with how flustered he made me with a single look. I flipped back an errant curl and fanned myself with my hand. *Try not to act so taken by him. Stand straight, but not rigid. Say something, anything.* My thoughts screamed at me.

"Certainly."

Ulyses gazed at the text and shut the book. "What if I told you that we could spy on Cottia?"

"Could we spy on Señora Virginia and Julieta too?"

His cheek quirked. "I'm not too sure the Ancient One would be on board with that one."

My eyes threatened to roll at the mention of the Ancient One, but I closed my eyelids before I insulted him. "So, it's wrong for me to see if the señora plans to make a formal accusation?"

"How about this . . . you tell me a truth and a lie to see if I can figure out which is which?" Ulyses reached for my hands like he wanted to hold them.

I didn't miss a beat. The feeling of our palms pressed together was just like any other touch, yet my heart swayed as if it were floating on a river. "Let's see." I thought for a moment. "I've never been on a ship, and I love mangos. Which is the lie?"

His eyebrows drew downward. "How can you hate mangos?"

A burst of laughter pushed out of my throat. "They're stringy and get stuck in your teeth. Gross. How did you know? Did I make a face?"

"No." He shook his head with a grin so wide it might as well have hung off his ears. "Tell me another truth and lie."

"You're getting a bit demanding, Prince Ulyses. I'm thinking you might have to order a batch of churros to make this up."

"I'll get you something better."

"Fine, fine." I sighed. "Though, I can't imagine anything better than churros."

"Struggling to think of something?"

"Ehh . . . you caught me. It's not easy to think so quickly and on demand." My brain churned with memories, some too gruesome to want to recall and others so mundane I might fall asleep.

"Gema, anything."

"All right, I once kissed a frog because Cottia dared me to do it, and Cristobal used to be Cottia's best friend."

He pulled back, releasing his hold on me. "Well, I'm glad you've never kissed a frog. Were they truly best friends? You said Cottia hated Cristobal."

"That's a little creepy how you can know that so quickly. You really do have a truth-telling power."

"It's a gift." Ulyses raked his fingers through his hair and exhaled. "It's like the Ancient One whispers in my ear 'truth and lie.'"

"So, the creator of all Agata takes the time to hear you and whisper something no one else can hear in your ear?" The deadpan tone revealed my lack of faith more than my words.

"Did I not know which of your statements was the lie?"

"You did, but . . ."

"But?" His eyebrows rose in question.

"What's this about? You talked about spying and then promised something better than churros, which I highly doubt is possible, but I'm curious what you think is better than the best."

He wagged his eyebrows much too playfully and waved me over to a bookshelf.

I pressed my lips together, unsure how he could think a book would spy on my friend and be better than deep-fried dough.

His fingers reached behind a book, and a click sounded. He glanced at me but focused again on pushing the shelf inward. The furniture gave way to a dark tunnel with walls of rough stone. "You promise me to never enter without me or unless you're in mortal danger."

My breath stilled in my lungs at such a request. I couldn't lie to him, and I understood that this invitation wasn't something he offered to just anyone. We might never marry, but we had become friends.

"I promise."

With a gentle nod, he led me into the darkness and flared his gift. "Let's see what Cottia is up to."

CHAPTER 36
COTTIA

My legs continued to pound forward through the mountainous forest. Brambles tripped my toes. Branches clawed at my shoulders and dragged their fingernails across my nose.

Cristobal's markings lit up around his neckline and along his knuckles. Mine gave a dim glow as I worked within Ezer's body to slow the gush of blood as he tried to keep up behind us. Someone at the wall had caught sight of our movement. Did they know they'd hit someone? They would come to find out and stop our plan.

"Keep going." Ezer waved us forward with his pale hand, the glow of his gift barely visible. "Don't mind me." His heartbeat faltered from lost blood, and his life flow clogged at the spot on his arm where the arrow remained lodged.

"Take the wretched thing out," I called to him as I continued to jog.

"No, I'll bleed out." Ezer's breaths now dragged out of his lungs in audible heaves.

"Let me fix it."

Ezer stopped, hands on his knees. Dark rivulets of blood snaked down his knuckles. He couldn't go on much farther with the arduous climb ahead.

"Cristobal?" The question in those three syllables was all I needed to communicate.

As an assassin who'd worked enough jobs, Cristobal had to know my meaning. He strode to my side and motioned with his hand in a yanking motion. Ezer lifted his good arm and yanked the arrow from his own flesh with Cristobal's power controlling his movements.

"No!" Ezer shouted, but he couldn't stop Cristobal from taking over his muscles with his own gift so weak. Blood drizzled out of his wound. His pulse slowed at a rapid rate.

Before my invisible tentacles could find the spot that I needed to press, I watched as his body landed with a thunk on the forest floor. He'd passed out.

I grabbed a cloth from my satchel and drove my knees to the ground beside him. Good old-fashioned pressure would have to do while my gifting churned to life. My fingers worked quicker than my gifting, exhausted from keeping on high alert for the past hour. Worries poured into my consciousness. What if I couldn't save him? It would be my fault if the prince died.

Heat trickled through my fingertips and careened through his body, far too dry and sluggish. Sweat sprouted on my nose as I tried to force my powers through him. The most it could do was clot the blood in his wound. Panic stomped through my chest. Why wasn't this working?

"We've got to go." Cristobal hovered over me. The glow of his hands gave me enough light to catch the slight grimace on Ezer's pained face.

"Not yet. He can't even move." My words came out clipped.

"Allow me." Cristobal nudged me to the side and lifted the prince. "We can't stop here, but I do know of a cave up ahead."

"He's not doing well. He needs healing." The desperation in my voice surprised me. I inhaled a ragged breath, which settled my quavering muscles.

Cristobal looked over his shoulder. "You can't heal him if you've exhausted yourself."

"But he'll die. I can help." I caught up to Cristobal's side.

"You're not going to help anyone if you drain yourself completely." He continued to climb the steep path.

For what could have been an eternity, we tramped through the dank forest. All conversation had turned to heavy breathing.

Ancient One, I am so undeserving, but Ezer loves you and should live. The prayers sauntered through my brain and sometimes escaped in whispers.

Cristobal stole glances in my direction, yet he didn't ask about my murmuring. He even bolstered my step with his gift when he caught me faltering up a rocky slope. His intuitiveness made his features that much more handsome. He gritted his teeth but did not complain as he climbed a steep section of the path with a limp Prince Ezer in his arms. Ezer wasn't a small man either.

The temptation to release my gifting assailed me, but Cristobal was right. I kept my gifting tight to my chest where the powers ruminated in their home, gathering strength. Sleeping would be the best remedy.

I couldn't save Ezer if I depleted my gifting. My lips grew raw from my teeth biting into them, gnawing on the chapped portion of skin.

"How much farther?" I tripped over an unsteady rock and landed with a huff on the damp ground. With only dappled starlight bleeding to the forest floor and Cristobal's dimmed arm aglow, it was difficult to find the right footing.

"You're not hurt?" Cristobal asked.

"No." I pushed off the moist ground, dirt caked between my fingers.

"We're less than a hundred arm spans away."

By the time we found the cave hidden behind a hedge of bushes, I was desperate to lay my palms on Ezer despite my exhaustion. A little more healing might make a difference.

Cristobal lowered the unconscious Ezer to the cave floor. "I'll go collect some firewood."

I nodded and dove beside Ezer. I flipped his cape from around his wound. My gifting sputtered to life despite my exhaustion, tracing hot tracks within my skin. I pressed my palm to the uninjured portion of his arm. Ezer remained weak and depleted.

Come on, Ancient One, what can you do with the little I have? I prayed. Nothing spectacular happened. The trickle of energy continued to flow like a current of seawater beneath his flesh, working slowly on who knew what. I hadn't a clue how to heal. The few times I'd done it, the gifting had acted on its own.

A warm hand clasped my shoulder. I jerked away but calmed down when I caught sight of Cristobal's face; the pinch of concern darkened over his eyebrows. His hand lit up as his powers pressed through my skin like electrical fingers, spurring my limp healing touch forward.

Ezer's wound knit together on its own, a deep bruise left in its place.

"Let go." Cristobal squeezed my shoulder.

"No, it needs more." I gripped Ezer's forearm tighter.

"You're spent. Let go."

"I can do this."

Cristobal lifted me up by my waist and threw me over his shoulder.

"You put me down right now." I kicked Cristobal's stomach and pounded my fists against his back, but he carried me across the cave and dropped me to the ground.

I shot up on my achy legs.

"Let the prince sleep." Cristobal pinned me against the cave wall. His skin was still lit from using his gift. He craned his head down and tilted my chin up to meet his dark eyes. "You love him?"

The fight left my muscles. I wouldn't avert my gaze and show weakness even if the question caught me off guard. Earlier in the day, I'd basically admitted the truth to Ezer even though it had left me vulnerable. There was no way I'd give Cristobal the same courtesy. "What type of question is that? I've only known the fellow a month."

Cristobal continued to analyze every shift of my face. Normally, I would prod his physical responses, but my splayed palm over his chest did nothing for me.

His mouth twisted into his wolfish grin as if he knew something more but wasn't saying. He released his hold and stepped back a handbreadth.

"Enough of your suppositions." I tucked my hair behind my ears, bedraggled from the rain, the climb, and the long march. "He wasn't even supposed to be here. *Cielos*, he's the crowned prince."

The way Cristobal shrugged with a smirk firmly in place told me he still believed I loved the prince.

"I had you pretend to be my betrothed, remember?"

His gifting marks dimmed until only darkness filled the space between us. "I do. Get some rest. I'll take the night patrol." The sound of his boots hitting the cave floor confirmed that he'd fled.

I lay on the ground, small rocks poking beneath my bottom. After several adjustments, my body relaxed, but my mind kept going. Though Ezer's breathing was the only sound, I couldn't sleep from wanting to make sure he didn't die on me. Why had we continued to travel despite his injury? I should have healed him right away. I should have . . .

Flipping to face the cave wall, I hid the tears streaking across the bridge of my nose. Cristobal would certainly think I loved Ezer if he caught me weeping, and that type of vulnerability could lead to more danger.

CHAPTER 37
COTTIA

THE NEXT MORNING, WE picked ripe mangos, chewed on herbs, and marched on through the thick forest. Ezer's pace slowed us down so much, I begged the Ancient One that my sister would not be caught by the time we got to her.

"Go on ahead." Ezer waved Cristobal and me forward.

So, we kept walking ahead. I wanted to give Cristobal a spattering of foul words should he betray me, yet I bit my tongue. The handsome man beside me wore his usual irritating smirk while checking to make sure Ezer didn't trail too far behind us. How could he show kindness while still maintaining the proper continence every assassin needed to thrive? I wanted to smack him and hug him all at the same time.

"Why do you stare?" Cristobal didn't look in my direction.

The crunch of boots filled our silence.

"Are you certain Whyzer Patro didn't send you here to trick me?"

He flitted a dark glance in my direction. "I promise everything I say is true."

"The whyzer knew you wouldn't kill me."

"You're right." He studied farther ahead and behind us again, maintaining constant awareness of our surroundings.

"I never told anyone about Isabelia." The thought stung. Somehow it felt like a betrayal to have kept my family hidden for the past seven years, yet it had helped keep competing assassins away from her. Whyzer Patro had known about her, so the secrecy hadn't saved her from his wrath.

"No, you didn't," Cristobal said. His irksome short responses vibrated through my weak bones.

"Speak now. I haven't all day to tear out the information from your throat."

He finally met my gaze with a slow blink, showing off his ridiculously long lashes. "The whyzer sent out another crew, and I had them followed. When I did my research, and maybe a little prodding through the whyzer's records, I learned about your sister."

"No." I shook my head, still not believing the whyzer would be so easily tricked.

"No?" Cristobal snorted, which endeared him to me a little more than I liked. The carefree sound didn't come from coldhearted murderers weaving together plans.

"Look, the whyzer let you find out about Isabelia and then sent you to Giddel to test your loyalty in the one spot everyone knew you were weak." I averted my gaze to the trail I'd set for myself. Though nothing marked where we should walk, I pictured the easiest route.

"You are my weakness, and I'm not ashamed to admit it." His admission stirred a yearning inside me that wanted someone to understand me and love me.

I glanced over my shoulder to find Ezer, who had fallen out of sight. Yes, Ezer loved me, but would he ever understand? Did he need to? Guilt traced its cold fingers down my back. "We should take a short break to let him keep up."

"As you wish." Cristobal rubbed his legs and perched atop a rock on the side of a hill. His broad shoulders slumped in a way that was foreign to him.

It reminded me of when I was a silly fourteen-year-old and we'd first met while doing a job. He had taken the branch I'd hoped to use as a hiding spot. His voice had cracked when he'd invited me to take the branch beside him, and I had. After that incident, Gema and I had sat beside him and his crew in the dining hall. At that time, I'd thought I could trust him and even called him a friend.

After climbing the steep hill, I sank beside him, our elbows touching. "Thank you for sharing your power last night. The whyzer would have turned a fiery rage on you for exposing yourself like that."

Cristobal let out an airy chuckle. "If he ever finds out, he'll call me an idiot before publicly whipping my back."

I patted his hand without thinking, and he clasped it.

He met my eye. All the lighthearted smile lines dissipated into something serious. "You know I never meant to hurt you."

"What do you mean?"

"When I stole your job and gave you false information."

My throat constricted at the memory. The beating that had followed would have put most people in the grave. It had taken me months to recover and made me the laughingstock of all those in the castillo. Old pain licked my spine and ached along the rib that had been broken.

"Gascon had set up a trap for you, and I didn't know how else to help you without exposing myself." Cristobal sandwiched my hand with his. "Looking back, I see how the whyzer pitted the assassins against each other. Whyzer Patro gave Gascon the go ahead and knew I'd overheard it. I was being tested. He saw our friendship and was threatened by it. I won't fail you this time."

Ezer crested the slope, and I slipped from Cristobal's grip. The tension between us gripped my heart—not in an explosive way whenever I let the memory surface—but in a manner that brought closure. I'd spent much of the last couple of years despising Cristobal when he had actually been trying to protect me in the only way the fourteen-year-old Cristobal could conjure.

I turned toward my old friend, finally letting myself see the boy he used to be through his now-square jaw and prickly chin. "You're forgiven. I've also done things I'm not proud of. That's the reason I wanted help to set the prince free from me." I flicked a look over to Ezer as he approached.

Cristobal's rueful smile held a sincerity rarely present in any of Whyzer Patro's people. "Don't sell yourself short. You've always had a good heart, better than those highborn ladies. If you love"—he pointed down toward Ezer with a pout of his lips—"then go for it. You deserve all the Agata Seas and beyond. But if you don't, escape with me."

My cheeks flamed at his compliment.

Ezer stood below us, waiting for our descent from the higher perch on a rock above the path.

Before I could hop down, Cristobal caught my wrist. A gleam of unshed tears coated his eyes. "You moved your sister, didn't you?"

"What do you mean?" I shied away.

"The whyzer couldn't find her last I heard."

This time, it was my turn to curl up my lips in coy pleasure. "I'm not a fool, but neither is our adversary."

"Then where are we headed?"

"I won't know until we get there."

Cristobal squinted and folded his arms.

My eyebrow rose. I wasn't lying. Isabelia and I had painstakingly come up with a code to discern if we should flee for where to find each other. It normally took me a week to deliver one message.

Since staying at Giddel, I had risked one letter, and the guard had not returned it, which proved Cristobal's story had merit. Whyzer Patro had either put an end to the messenger or paid him off.

Now, it was a matter of finding my sister before Whyzer Patro did.

CHAPTER 38
GEMA

Loneliness clung to me more tightly than my pink corset as I tried to eat the breakfast meal at the dining table. Note, I would never trust a maid's flattery again; the knots holding this restricting contraption together left no room for extra pastries.

Cottia devoured her stew in front of me without saying a word. Prince Ezer was nowhere to be found, so Ulyses decided to do some investigations of his own. That left me alone with this husk of a person who hid more than any best friend should. She hadn't been in her room last night nor had her favorite trousers and cape, always a sign that she was up to something. I would ask about it, but she wasn't supposed to know about my spying.

"So, why did you boot me out of your chamber yesterday?" I put my spoon down and rested my chin on my hands to prop my head up.

Cottia coughed like the question startled her. "Cristobal was changing."

"Let me rephrase the question. When did you abandon your sense of propriety?"

Her eyebrow lifted almost in a suggestive way. "He is my betrothed."

"Enough with that lie. We both know that you aren't the type of señorita who would let a man into your chamber to change out of his wet clothes when he could have gone to his. You wouldn't even enter Prince Ezer's chamber alone . . . and we all know how you feel about him."

"Tell me, dear friend, how do I feel about the prince?" She lifted the spoon to her lips with giant black saucers focused on me.

Everything about Cottia, from the shape of her eyes to her slender arms, looked and moved like her. But Cottia hadn't called me *"dear friend"* in a sassy voice even before she'd left Whyzer Patro.

"Tell me, *dear friend*, why you've let Señora Virginia's words possess you."

She smirked. "Possess? That's an interesting word."

"Ever since we arrived here, you've been different, in a good way. All this Ancient One talk has led you to be more open and not so caustic."

"So, we've turned to insults?" She lifted a spoon to her mocking grin.

"Maybe I've been spending too much time with Ulyses, and you feel like I haven't given you the attention you need. I'm sorry. You just haven't been the same since we overheard Señora Virginia say she would expose you." Desperation burned through my veins to break through to my friend. What was wrong with her?

"I have plans with Cristobal later today. Details with the nuptials. Nothing that would interest you." Cottia got to her feet and adjusted her red dress, the color of blood.

"Of course I want to help." A sudden realization of just how alone I'd be pounced over my heart. "Are you going to stay in Giddel?"

She glanced at the far end of the table to all the other señoritas who laughed among themselves and leaned over the table. "Cristobal and I will be leaving Giddel within the week, and we prefer to keep our plans secret. You understand?"

Steamy tears evaporated before I could stop myself. I fled the room, unable to breathe. I headed right and then left through the back corridor. Sunlight poured in through the line of windows, firing up my already-tumultuous emotions. Cottia didn't care about what happened to me or just how alone she'd leave me. What had changed in the last few days? Before, I had always been in her plans and worth consideration.

Just as I turned to go into the library, someone grabbed me from the side and pulled me into a hidden passage and shut the door.

I flared my flames.

"Caramba! Gema! It's me." Ulyses jerked back.

Air heaved from my lungs as I tried to catch my breath. "You could have just called my name."

"Shh . . . someone is in the library."

I let my fire return into my skin, but my flesh remained aglow from the sudden onset. "Who?"

"Señora Virginia." He blew on the red burns on his palms.

"I'm so sorry. I didn't mean to hurt you." Guilt slid over me like the shadows in this hidden tunnel.

"Don't worry about me." He drew closer again, opened his mouth, and snapped it closed. Something about his not-so-perfect posture unsettled me even more. "I still can't find Ezer, and I think Señora Virginia might be behind his disappearance."

CHAPTER 39
COTTIA

By the time we arrived at Valle de San Pedro, a sleepy village with nothing to endear it to travelers, I found myself unable to stop peeking at Cristobal. The stubble on his chin and the sway of his swagger now drew my attention more than the smell of the bakery. He'd been guarding me all those years ago. Now, he was scanning around a building corner, protecting me again.

Ezer still followed at a sluggish pace. He grimaced with his head bowed low, focused on his foot placement. Though pale, he drew close behind me, every so often meeting my gaze with a question lingering in the stiff set of his jaw. I longed to touch his skin and heal the wounds left inside his body, but I had to be practical. If Whyzer Patro's associates attacked, I needed to recover enough strength to take them down efficiently. I was sure Ezer regretted his decision to follow me from the palace now. His notion about the Ancient One choosing me for him had surely diminished after such an injury. It wasn't like last month when we were alone.

When I turned the corner behind Cristobal, Benito's Bakery painted atop the small stone building stopped me in my tracks. Our plan to tramp through town to find a sign of Isabelia had worked. Cristobal turned around and met my eye. I signaled for us to cross the road to the wooden shop door.

The two men split up. Ezer stayed out front. Perfect, since no one would recognize him in this quiet village where no one traveled farther than the next town over. Cristobal crept to the back like a panther in the shadows. I opened the bakery door, setting off a bell that rang far too loudly for my liking. The yeasty aroma set off rivers in my mouth.

"Buenos días, Señor." I dipped my head at the man behind the counter, whose waist spoke of him tasting his treats as much as he sold them, always a good sign. "Could I get—ooo—four pestiño cookies, six *trufas de chocolate*, and three *empanadas*?"

The baker lifted his bushy gray eyebrow at me. "I assume you brought a basket?" The rough texture of his voice made it sound like he was gargling marbles in his throat.

"No, but I can pay for one." I took out several coins from my satchel.

His gray eyes grew two sizes before he slid his glower back in place. "I take it you're visiting one of the lords in the hills?" He bent over his display, shoveling the deep-fried cookies into a small white cloth, the chocolate truffles into another cloth, and wrapping the meaty turnovers.

"Not exactly. A friend of sorts. A Benito." I enunciated the word, keeping my focus trained on him to gauge his response.

The baker stilled. Had the code word been for the location alone and not for more information? Springs of sweat formed on his nose. "Never heard of another Benito."

I glanced out the window, catching Ezer as he stepped across the storefront. The way this old man moved, we might not even get a snack before Whyzer Patro's people found us.

"You look familiar." The baker drew my attention to him again. He wrapped the empanadas in another cloth and shuffled to the end of the display. "You wouldn't happen to know Señora Lucia?"

It was my turn to break into a sweat. Growing up, Mamá had introduced me as her twin. "Do you have something else for me?"

He plopped the small wicker basket on the countertop, mopped his forehead, and bent low to where I could only see his back half in the air. When he came back up, he slid me a missive marked with a red wax seal.

I touched the raised edges of the rose imprinted on the wax, signaling I had asked the right baker and would need the cipher to read it. "Another coin for your troubles." I slid the metal to him, grabbed the basket, and fled out the door.

The jingling bell rang again, setting my nerves on fire. Something was off. The front cobblestones glimmered with sunlight, but there was no Ezer. I turned the corner.

Cristobal should have been at the back end of the bakery. Instead, I found old women in worn dresses with giant baskets walking toward me.

This couldn't be happening. We'd remained on the edge of town, careful to stay in the shadows. Panic consumed my chest, but I reminded myself to stay calm, to not give myself away. Two old men played dominoes at a small café across the way. They gave me a cursory glance and continued their game. Nothing extraordinary had happened yet, so the fellows must have followed suspects.

My stomach churned, and I plucked an empanada from the cloth. I might need some energy for a fight should it come. Vomiting might also be another possibility, but I wasn't about to ring a warning alarm just yet. I bit into the savory meat-filled pastry.

We had another meetup spot should anything go wrong, and I still had one more stop to make. I kept moving down toward the river where a cipher remained hidden in the notch of an old tree. My basket swung on my arm as I marched up the hilly road. An old lady across the way did a double take after laying eyes on me. The exaggerated way she scanned my body with a disapproving downturn of her lips showed her shock at my appearance. Ladies didn't wear pants.

I smiled at her and stuffed the rest of an empanada into my mouth. Crumbs fell from between my lips. Gema would have scolded me for unnecessarily making myself a spectacle. But the grimace that crinkled on the old woman's face made my lack of manners worthwhile. I stomped off, needing to find the cipher before Whyzer Patro's thugs found me.

Chickens clucked outside a small, thatched house, stealing my attention from the glaring woman. A black-haired fellow with gray streaks and smart eyes watched me from the front of another thatched house. The quality of his doublet suggested fat coin, yet the house might belong to someone who worked in the fields. I continued striding but kept spying on the verdant surroundings.

Footfalls followed.

The energy in my chest leapt, begging to be released.

Not yet. I whispered to myself.

He picked up his pace and would catch up to me in less than three arm spans.

A path opened up to the left in two arm spans. I could make it.

"Señorita," he called to me.

I marched, not peeking backward.

Power raced to my fingertips. Tendrils of invisible energy careened toward the man. Like a reflex, it shot through his skin, gripping an artery.

He gasped. I spun around.

The man pinched a missive with the red wax seal between his index finger and thumb. He clutched his heart with his other hand. I let go.

A choking sound escaped his throat as he folded over. I snatched the missive and ran down the path. Had I been wrong about the man? Was I turning back into Whyzer Patro's monster?

My feet didn't stop moving until I arrived at the thick tree as tall as a cathedral. The river flowed just below the small knoll. I left my basket beside the tree, praying to the Ancient One that an animal wouldn't get to it before me.

The trick to get to the hidden notch in the tree was to climb up a small tree on the opposite end of the path. Upon reaching the halfway point, I hopped onto a thick branch on another tree, which provided the right height and leverage to get to the giant tree's lowest bough. I clung to a branch above while I balanced on the thick branch that led to the trunk with the notch.

The dark hole had twigs at the end, which might prove another problem altogether. I ripped off the twigs and poked inside the hole. Whatever lived or had lived there was gone. The rough edge of an object met my touch, and I pulled it out. A rough sack dangled before me.

Within the bag, a brass sheet with holes punched along the material caught a stream of gleaming sunlight. I broke the seal of my letter and skipped reading the contents. The form of the letters matched Isabelia's hand, and the signature couldn't have belonged to anyone else. She had even drawn her telltale rose in the upper right-hand corner, which meant she didn't need help yet.

When I placed the cipher over the letter, the message told a different story.

The highlighted word read: Nana Farm.

Isabelia had retreated to an old friend's farmhouse, which meant Whyzer Patro's men must have discovered all the other hideouts. This valley had to be crawling with unscrupulous men who'd do anything to grow their coffers. I stuffed the note in my pocket and stowed the cipher back in its hole.

The climb down took just as much effort as the climb up, but it had all proven worthwhile now that I knew Isabelia's location.

My feet landed in the grass. I picked up my basket, and thick arms wrapped around my neck and torso. I tried to scream, kick, and elbow. But the man behind me had muscles like stone.

Power ignited in my chest, but I couldn't breathe. Flecks of darkness circled my vision. My body shut down. Instead of reaching out, my energy remained locked away, saving my own life.

The verdant path ahead of me offered no hope.

No one came to save me.

CHAPTER 40
COTTIA

I LAY ON MY back with my eyes closed and skin cold though clothes covered me from neck to toe. I cracked my eyelids open to a ceiling supported by solid wood beams. Sky and branches should have been above me, not wooden beams. Where was I? What happened to Prince Ezer and Cristobal?

Aches consumed every part of my body. When I felt for my gifting, it was like I was standing at the precipice of a well where one could neither see the bottom nor hear the plink of coins drowning. An emptiness resided in my chest where the warm licks of power had always existed.

"Cottia Luzelena Jaime Pacheco," Whyzer Patro's deep voice cut through my thoughts.

Cold sweat sprouted from the pores on my back. It sent a shiver up my spine that throbbed along my quivering muscles. I blinked away tears. The last month had been for nothing. I was a slave again.

"You did play a good game." Whyzer Patro chuckled from a seat beside the bed I lay atop. "But you forgot the first rule."

Cielos. Tears dribbled out the sides of my eyes, and I couldn't do a thing to stop them. "What rule is that?"

"Never show your hand, my dear." He leaned forward. His bony fingers patted my arm.

Someone else stood off in a corner like a shadow. Power emanated, not from the whyzer but from the other person.

I resisted flinching away. This man had been my master since childhood and could read my expressions, so I swallowed down the hot emotions and used my deadpan voice. "My sister was a low fruit for you."

"So why wouldn't I grab it?" He sneered and leaned back in his chair. "Cristobal was a nice touch, don't you think?"

A quivering inhale vibrated through my bones. I'd truly believed that Cristobal cared for me, that his apology had meant something. I cast my gaze toward the closed window with shades pushed open as if the whyzer had no one to fear. Would Cristobal hurt Ezer? My vision blurred into light golden-brown hues and shades of gray.

"Hush now, child." The whyzer's condescending tone did anything but comfort. "Did you come to grow attached to Cristobal? He does make a handsome, predictable tool."

At the whyzer's final word, I stilled. *Predictable? Tool?* Those descriptions weren't words to describe a co-conspirator, but, rather, someone used for his connection. Even in my vulnerable state, a sweep of hope rushed through me.

"Where's my gift?" I sniffed back the effects of the springs in my eyes.

"I took it. You didn't think I'd let you keep it after betraying me?" He laughed, the sound of a man who believed himself the victor.

"You got what you wanted. Why don't you just kill me now?"

He jerked my chin toward him, hurting my neck. I bit back a yelp.

"You will die. No one who betrays me lives." The cold edge to his voice sliced through me. "But I also have another insect to catch, and you make an excellent lure."

My fists clenched, and I tried to push myself up from the narrow bed. I tightened my muscles. The effort left my head swimming, so I was only able to raise my head slightly. I managed to turn onto my side.

The whyzer pushed out his chair and stared at me with callous, dark eyes, his narrow features twisted into sadistic pleasure.

I flopped out of the bed and landed on my belly, face to the hardwood. My legs didn't cooperate. He'd poisoned me or had a strange gift at play.

"The drink we administered did excellent work." The hem of the whyzer's gray robes swished as he crossed the room toward a door. "Try not to hurt yourself before we've made good use of you. Eduardo, come with me." He exited with the shadow of a lanky man behind him and slammed the door in his wake.

The oppressive weight on my chest fled, bringing a hint of warmth back into my bones. This time, I did nothing to stop the free flow of thick tears from seeping out. They dropped onto the hardwood, wetting my cheeks. How could the Ancient One let this happen to me?

Desperation swam through my blood. There was nothing left for me to do. Unable to move my deadened limbs and unable to heal myself, I resorted to the one thing left.

Ancient One, could you save me again? Please, help Ezer and Cristobal find me. Protect my sister and . . .

Light footfalls groaned outside the room.

I shifted from side to side, trying to crane my neck.

Another click sounded.

It would be just like the whyzer to torture his victim.

The door flew open and revealed the last person I expected.

CHAPTER 41
COTTIA

THE OLDER WOMAN'S DRESS skirt swished as it grazed the bedroom floor. She had the same large brown gaze as me and a perfectly sloped nose. The only thing that had changed about her appearance were the small creases at the edges of her eyes. She carried the whyzer's staff—the place where he stored his stolen gifts. She tapped the door shut. Of all the people who could have returned for me, it was my mamá.

She whispered in a hushed tone. "*Corazón*, we're going to get you out of here." She placed a gentle touch on my neck, sending tingles under my skin. Feeling returned to my toes and fingertips with painful pricks that made me bite down on my bottom lip.

More and more energy poured through my blood and plunged into my chest. I pushed up from the floor.

"I'm not done yet," Mamá whispered. She held tightly to my neck, concern etched between her eyebrows.

A spattering of questions readied to launch at her, but we remained in this prison of a room.

She finally stood and offered her hand to help me up. I took it, still dumbfounded that she would rebel against the whyzer. She, of all people, the one who had sold me to him.

We skipped hugs and kisses and fled through the window. I made sure to close it though the effort might prove futile. One of Whyzer Patro's guards stood at the corner of the stone building only ten paces away. Roberto—combed-back black hair, boyish face, and friendly eyes. He had always shown me kindness when I'd lived at the castillo. Now, I mouthed *thank you* to him as he averted his gaze and dipped his head in recognition.

I followed Mamá through the forest. Branches and leaves whipped at our faces and grabbed at my cape. We left a trail any mildly skilled tracker could follow, yet we didn't dare slow down. This was madness.

Whatever compass steered Mamá guided her toward a stream where the well-dressed, older man with black hair and gray streaks waited for us. He grabbed at his chest as if remembering what I had done to him on the road. I slowed, but Mamá grabbed my wrist.

"He's my friend," Mamá said. "He will help us disappear."

Mind muddled, I continued to move at Mamá's pace. So, the older man hadn't been with Whyzer Patro? Where were Ezer and Cristobal? Where was my sister?

The older man clasped Mamá's hand. He and she blinked out of view, though I heard their footfalls in the stream.

Something warm clamped onto my hand, and Mamá and the man blinked back into view. The forest grew hazy, as if a glass barrier had been erected around us.

"What is this?" I asked.

The man yanked me into the stream. My boots and hem soaked with cold water.

"Cottia," Mamá reprimanded. "Follow along. We'll explain once we arrive."

"Arrive where?" I couldn't help myself. Rebellion flowed through my veins even though I knew I was being ridiculous. Mamá had saved me and even stolen the whyzer's staff.

Her lips pressed into a line. Emotion quivered up her face and settled into a dagger-sharp stare. "Do you want to die or worse?"

With that, all three of us followed the stream, which twisted and turned like a snake between the uneven banks. Keeping my mouth shut proved a difficult task, but Mamá shushed me like a child interrupting an adult conversation.

Footfalls echoed from somewhere behind us, fanning her harshness. Bitterness coated the inside of my mouth with a spout of curses I wanted to say aloud. *You did this to me. You sold me.*

But a still small voice whispered: *Forgive her as you have been forgiven.*

I'd read those words in the Ancient Tome with Prince Ezer, and they had stirred an ache in my soul. *How could you let her get away with exchanging her daughter for gold coin?*

My childhood flashed in my mind's eye as we continued to jog in the stream. The days after Papá had died had been filled with unending tears and Mamá holding my sister and me. We'd lived in a beautiful mansion but hadn't had enough food to fill our bellies. The fields had been ravaged by disease, the servants had needed payment for their work, and the house had required repairs. We'd fed ourselves on dreams and cuddles.

The splash of our boots in the stream settled into a rhythm. Mamá glanced over her shoulder, reminding me that she had just freed me from a man with enough power to kill us all with the sweep of his staff. She'd even brought the staff along.

In the midst of all this fleeing, where were Prince Ezer, Cristobal, and Isabelia? Were they safe, hidden, or in more danger than ever before?

Finally, the gray-haired man turned onto land, and Mamá hopped to his side.

"Where are we going?" I climbed out of the stream to a rock just to the side of them.

Mamá answered, "To Señor Lozcano's estate." She gestured to the man beside her.

"But Isabelia is out there."

"She's a clever girl and will know where to find us." Mamá's even tone brought some reassurance.

"But what of Prince Ezer and Cristobal?"

Mamá and Señor Lozcano shared a look. He nodded, but Mamá shook her head vehemently. Their silent conversation continued for another several seconds until finally Mamá grunted.

She turned toward me. "Did you have a meeting place where we might find them? I assume"—she lifted her eyebrow up at Señor Lozcano—"it will require drawing nearer to town again."

I nodded.

"And I assume Whyzer Patro might know about your two friends?"

I bit my cracked lip.

"What else aren't you saying?"

"The whyzer stole my gift. Could you get it from the staff?"

"My healing might have restored your gifting." Mamá tipped her head down and gestured with her hand as if asking me to try to use my gift.

The mellow heat beneath my breastbone churned, but my gifting marks didn't glow along my arms. My powers tingled. Fear threatened to suffocate me as I realized energy didn't pour down my arms like it always had before.

Mamá's shoulders slumped, and her cheeks grew taut. "Let me see if I understand correctly. You want to go back into danger with no gift in reach—because the Ancient One knows I need more time to figure out this staff. Then you want Señor Lozcano and me, a healer not a fighter, to save your friends who are being followed by a malicious whyzer and his very gifted team of assassins who are out for your head?"

Water gurgled along the stream. Rustling leaves and tweeting birds met my ears. Mamá begged with two wild, brown moons for eyes for me to trust her, but how could I? Señor Lozcano breached the distance between us and opened his mouth to speak.

I kept my gaze fixed on Mamá and cut off whatever he was going to say. "No, you two don't have to come with me. Just tell me which direction is south of the town."

Not a soul could convince me of a different plan when three out of the four people I called friends remained in danger's way because of me. And Prince Ezer still had time to get back to the palace before the imposter's oath lost its protection.

CHAPTER 42
GEMA

"THESE ARE NOT COOK'S churros." I bit again into the sweet dough and nearly lost a tooth with the way the hard bread rubbed against my gums.

In the dim glow emanating from Ulyses's skin, I caught an amused twinkle in his eye.

"I never said Cook made them." He swung the peephole cover to the side and peered inside Ezer's bedroom. "I said, 'I brought you churros. Try them.'"

Once the dough softened in my mouth, it still had the sweet flavor I loved rolling over my tongue. I placed the rest of the treat back on the plate and searched the darkness for a place to set it down. No table or chair offered its top in the cobweb-filled space, so I bent to set it down on the floor.

"Don't."

"So, I have to hold these rocks the rest of our wait?"

He chuckled. "Yes, unless you want to invite the rats."

"Then why did we bring this with us?" A whine marked my voice. We could be standing here for hours waiting for Ezer to return to his room.

"The last two nights, we've had to leave our posts for a snack. I would like to point out that Julieta was sleeping by the time we spied on her, so we missed all of her possible interactions." He swung the peephole closed.

"Fine, you make sense." I lifted the plate in front of me and rocked on my feet. Nervous energy threatened to spark my flames. "For the record, we did get a good spy on Cottia. She never goes to sleep without brushing her teeth and hair."

"I hardly call that good spy work. Everyone skips a day every so often."

"Not Cottia. And don't tell me you didn't sense a lie when we got to her peephole."

"I did, but—"

"But you know I'm right."

Shuffling sounded beyond the wall. Ulyses's and my eyes popped wide open. He slid the cover off and stared intently. I bit my bottom lip, rubbing the skin with my teeth. Something was very wrong with how we never saw Cottia and Ezer together anymore. Though Cottia had vowed to marry Cristobal, she was no wimp. She would face Ezer, even though she was likely to swoon like she did every time she neared him. She thought she kept her reactions hidden, but I could read her telltale inhales.

Unable to resist, I slipped into the narrow space between Ulyses and the wall. "What do you see?" I murmured.

His breath brushed the back of my neck. "Excuse me for blocking your way." His sarcastic tone didn't waltz past me, but I didn't care.

I rolled onto my tiptoes. The small hole showed me Ezer removing his jacket, tunic still underneath. He looked over his shoulder in our direction and smiled. He couldn't possibly know we were watching him. Then, he drew near, slipping the jacket off his arms, and looked into the hole.

I gasped.

CHAPTER 43
COTTIA

"WHY DON'T YOU LET Señor Lozcano retrieve the boys?" Mamá hiked beside me, letting the older man fall behind.

Head spinning from whatever poisons and giftings the whyzer had used against me, I lost my footing and caught myself with a steadying arm.

"See, you aren't well. I'm sure you have a password we could use to gain their trust. Let Señor Lozcano bring them back to us." Her presumptuous tone jabbed at my thinning patience.

"He obviously did a spectacular job at retrieving me."

She huffed. "We broke you out of that room, did we not?" Her stern bottom lip told me she wouldn't back down. A fight would brew because I had so many objections to working with her as well. Just because she'd brought me into this world did not mean she cared the way a mother ought.

"Who is this Señor Lozcano?" My voice rose loud enough for the man himself to hear, but I didn't care.

"You're quite careless." She scanned the forest. "I'm certain even his invisibility couldn't cover your tantrum."

I let my gaze drift up the hill we'd tackled and through the brush. The tentative dirt path ahead only revealed uneven terrain to threaten our way. "Fine. But you didn't answer the question. Who is he?"

"Do you remember the invitation I sent you?"

"So, he's your husband? My stepdad?" I spun my head around to get a better look. The man didn't have Papá's charm, and his nose, crooked at the bridge, stole from what might have been a somewhat decent face. When I spun around, I couldn't help the discordant notes flying off my tongue. "Are you embarrassed of him? Is that why you don't call him your husband?"

She breathed deeply, her nose flaring. "I can't win with you."

"I think you lost that privilege long ago."

"You're right. I'm sorry." She yanked her dress from a shrub that grabbed at her long skirt. "I wish I could turn back time and tell myself not to trust the whyzer. I wish I could have seen through his invitation to a school for the gifted. I wish I would have kept you nearby or visited more often." A tremor marked the cadence of her words like she'd rehearsed them but couldn't keep emotion from wrestling the speech away from her.

"You truly didn't know what Whyzer Patro was?"

The forest sounds and scraping boots pounded with the tumult inside my soul. I longed to snap a bowstring loaded with nasty words at Mamá, the ones I always practiced in the bath when no one else could hear.

"Cottia, I was barely living, barely understanding why your papá had died, confused at all our debt, and with two little girls to feed. The whyzer should have been good. People I trusted recommended his school."

"And you trusted him." The bitterness in my own voice could burn. Ezer had told me to forgive. I'd read it in the Ancient Tomes, but it was one thing to ponder and another to do.

CHAPTER 44
COTTIA

DURING THE HOUR THAT followed, Mamá, Señor Lozcano, and I tramped through the verdant forest, taking the longest way to get to the meetup spot—that I could tell. The staff proved only useful for steadying Mamá's faulty steps. She did everything to delay our arrival, claiming she needed a break or she'd found another bruise on my flesh that needed healing.

But to her dismay, the tall walnut tree hidden south of the valley still came into view when we made our way around a small hill. Señor Lozcano reignited the invisibility field now that our destination was nearing. Though no human could be seen lurking in the trees' shadows, I didn't believe for a second that we were alone.

I shifted my gaze from left to right, spotting a red bird, a mango tree laden with fruit, and a creature who shuffled around a tree at our presence. Though we remained invisible, the animals sensed us.

Chills scurried up my spine. We descended the hill. Our boots stomped louder than they should.

"Your gift doesn't muffle our sound?" I asked Señor Lozcano.

"It does." He kept his focus ahead.

"We're walking into a trap." Mamá squeezed my shoulder as if to comfort me despite her statement.

I jerked away. "Then don't come with me." I tapped on Señor Lozcano's elbow and pointed to the right.

We must avoid the clearing. Heading south and circling north might be the more prudent trek. He seemed to understand and followed a more southeasterly path.

Mamá rolled her eyes, reminding me of myself—though I'd never admit it to her aloud.

The nearer we drew to the meetup spot, the more my insides squeezed. Green leaves framed my view of the tall tree with rough bark and bunches of green walnuts. I caught movement in its skeletal boughs and stilled.

Who hid among the branches?

The person continued to shift, giving me only glimpses of a dark tunic and pants. Tan skin peeked between the leaves and so did a dark head of hair. Still, that meant little when most of those in this countryside town had those features.

"Something is off." I sniffed the air; it was poisoned with a scent I couldn't quite place.

"He's nearby," Mamá said in a matter-of-fact tone.

"Who?" I asked.

Mamá met my eye. "Whyzer Patro."

My head whipped toward the staff, glowing with life. A tingle itched up my skin and traced the markings on my arms. I reached for the staff.

Boom!

An explosion sent wood flying toward us. I threw my hands over my eyes. Señor Lozcano's invisibility bubble flickered. We dropped to the ground. Arrows whistled through the air, and male grunts erupted.

I massaged the debris from my vision, grit scratching under my eyelids. When my eyesight came into focus, Señor Lozcano lay on the ground, bleeding from a piece of wood lodged in his cheek. Mamá reached for the staff, but someone else scooped it into their hands.

It was Prince Ezer. His gaze drifted toward mine but averted to something behind me. He lifted a hand and flicked it.

A man grunted in pain.

My head spun around to find a burly man with a familiar face. Sweat trickled along his dark sideburns, and his white knuckled grip stayed on the hilt of his sword.

"Come on, Prince, you can't leave things unfinished." Cristobal burst from behind a tree trunk and flicked his wrist.

The man pulled out his sword and held it up. Strain marked the lines on the man's bearded face.

Cristobal flicked his wrist again.

I yelped and squeezed my eyes shut, knowing full well that Cristobal wouldn't hesitate to do what must be done.

The sickening sound of metal in flesh slurped. Liquid gushed, and a grunt followed. Metal rang through the air. More warriors in black attire moved through the forest.

Mamá rushed to my side, her powers washing through me like she meant to heal me again.

"Don't waste your energy." I pushed her hand toward Señor Lozcano.

She yanked the wood from his cheek and touched the wound. A glow warmed her fingertips. Señor Lozcano gasped with life. An instant sheen bubbled around us.

Cristobal held his hands up, taking over his adversaries' movements. One cloaked warrior moved with unnaturally quick speed. Another blended into the coloring of the forest with only the edge of his body visible.

Within a blink, the cloaked men stilled. I didn't turn away in time and saw their own swords plunge into their bodies as Cristobal controlled their movements. Prince Ezer carried the staff in one hand and slayed the rest of the group with his gift. Cristobal and Ezer fighting in tandem invoked awe.

The fight was done with me huddling on the grassy floor like a whimpering pup, hiding in her mom's shadow. As much as the disgrace chafed against my sensibilities, I admired the two ruddy men who had fought.

Cristobal with his rogue appeal and his thick lashes. Prince Ezer with his tall, stately presence and the memory of every word he had once said about choosing me.

Ezer swaggered in my direction, catching his breath. His handsome face and caring gaze drew my attention. But instead of him stopping when he reached us, he tripped over my leg and crashed to the ground beside me.

Señor Lozcano let the invisibility dissolve.

"Are you hurt?" I asked.

Cristobal let out a guffaw. "Sorry, I should have stopped him."

Ezer rolled over and pushed himself into a seated position beside me. He let out a self-deprecating chuckle. When he met my gaze, an emotion tiptoed along his forehead. "I'm sorry we lost you. I was worried."

Cristobal came closer, still searching the periphery like someone else might strike. "This idiot followed the whyzer's bait." He lifted the staff that had fallen with Ezer's tumble. The knobby top lit with life within it, reflecting off Cristobal's hungry gaze.

Prince Ezer dipped his chin to his chest. The sincere sentiment had my hand lifting to his cheek.

My fingers met his scruffy jaw. "I thought you two had exploded with the tree," I admitted to Ezer.

The edge of Ezer's mouth curled with mischief. "We caught Patro's men in their own trap." He looked over at Mamá and Señor Lozcano. "I thought you had a younger sister?"

"Did you hear that compliment?" Señor Lozcano helped Mamá to her feet.

Mamá brushed off her brown skirt and scooped stray hair behind her ear. "I'm her mother, and this was too easy."

"She makes a good assertion." Señor Lozcano got to his feet. "You two boys will never be a match for the whyzer unless you learn to stretch your gifts like a blanket rather than pick off your opponents." The older man offered Mamá his arm as if they meant to go for a casual walk.

A tender look crossed between the older couple.

Mamá slipped her arm around her husband. "Whyzer Patro must be nearby searching for his staff. We should go back to Señor Lozcano's estate now. Isabelia is an apparitionist who will not be so easily caught even by one so powerful."

"Papá died, and he had the same gift." I crossed my arms, disgusted with her lack of concern.

Mamá stepped into dappled light that had snuck between the leaves above. Her narrowed glare fixed on me like an archer nocking back an arrow and aiming at her target. "He, like you, played with danger."

"We will find Isabelia." I stood and offered Prince Ezer a hand. "I know where she's hiding."

Ezer smiled up at me, his warmth deepening at my gesture.

"Don't ignore me, Cottia." Mamá's tone sharpened. "Tell them about how you lost your gift. How the whyzer stole it."

Ezer's and Cristobal's heads whipped in my direction.

"The only reason I came all this way up here was to retrieve Isabelia." My teeth ground together with anger I couldn't quite dampen.

"Listen to me." Mamá used the same cadence she'd used when I was a child in need of a reprimand. "Your bitterness will kill you if you don't get a grip on it."

"Then so be it." I strode around Mamá.

One last stop before returning to Giddel. Mamá might give an amazing oration of the virtues of forgiveness, yet she could never understand and make up for the damage she'd left in her selfish wake.

The whole party continued behind me without question. Only Ezer chose to draw near, though he remained silent, and the rustle of leaves above sounded muffled.

My main goal remained out of reach and incomplete without Isabelia. I tried to shift the warmth in my chest down my arms, but my gifting didn't respond like normal. The markings over my knuckles appeared faint.

"Is it true?" Ezer pitched his voice low. "Is the whyzer able to steal gifts?"

"He can." I steadied my gaze over the next knoll, avoiding the regret and shame nestled against my heart. Prince Ezer shouldn't have been here, in danger. I should be willing to at least offer Mamá a civil word. After all, she'd rescued me this time and might have been another of Whyzer Patro's victims.

"I couldn't help noticing how you never mentioned your mamá before." Ezer maintained my brisk pace and his close proximity.

"She's the one who caused all of my pain." I glared over my shoulder while she dropped back to heal a wound on Cristobal's forearm.

"Sorry to hear that." A note marked Ezer's tone that assured me he meant what he said, but he continued to speak. "I hope that you, who have received the Ancient One's forgiveness, will also extend the same gift to her."

Anger lurched in my soul. "What do you know about this situation and the hurt she has caused?"

Ezer didn't shy away from me though I had spewed my question. "You're right. I don't know. I am mere flesh and blood, born yesterday and dead tomorrow. What do I know except what the Ancient One has revealed?"

"Exactly, what do you know?"

"Yet even with that, the creator bestows his attentions on someone imperfect like me. I'm nervous that the kingdom will judge my every move as harshly as you have hers."

I stopped. I could have grappled with a vein and squeezed it—wait, I couldn't. He would be untouchable if I tried to harm him.

Somewhere deep in my bones, I wanted him to agree with me and to substantiate my claims of vengeance toward her. Yet, nothing would be enough for what I thought she deserved. The more I considered the punishment, the hollower I felt inside.

"Cottia." Mamá caught up to me. "We're heading back to the estate. You're welcome to join us. Isabelia knows where we stay." She kept her gaze trained on me.

"Goodbye. We must return to Giddel before nightfall."

Her nostrils narrowed as she said, "Goodbye, Cottia."

CHAPTER 45
COTTIA

EZER'S TIME LIMIT CLOSED in around us. The oath would soon break, leaving the imposter free from the binding. I set a quick pace. We should have headed straight to the palace, but I refused to let Ezer's wounds be for nothing, and Isabelia would only have sent word if it was truly important.

"Remember our deal?" Cristobal nudged my side as we tramped through the grassy knolls.

I nodded and whipped my head around to check if Ezer had overheard the conversation from two paces behind us.

"Is your gift truly gone?" Cristobal leaned closer to me with the whyzer's staff in hand.

"It's here." I tapped my breastbone. "But I can't reach it."

"How far are we from your mother? With you unable to keep the bargain . . ."

Anger flashed through my body. "We can figure out a different plan."

Cristobal's jaw ticked. Our plan for me to fake his death wouldn't be happening today. His chance at freedom had been stolen from him. His pace slowed until he matched Ezer's stride.

Ezer and Cristobal followed close behind as we traced the east side of the mountain. Isabelia's hiding place crept up on us with its plain wooden house in a solitary spot on the side of the mountain. Many other thatched roof houses sprinkled this part of the mountain, an easy distance from work on the plantations and a short walk into town. If we retrieved Isabelia without incident, we could cover some ground today and make it to Giddel before nightfall tomorrow.

The sun set, painting the sky in hues of orange and purple. The trees up the mountain remained still as if holding their breath. Grasses below swayed in the suffocating heat. One swinging glance provided me with enough confidence to knock on the door.

"Something is off." Cristobal held tight to Whyzer Patro's staff, narrowing his gaze as he stared into the distance. The top of the stick glowed with life in Cristobal's hold yet grew dull in Ezer's. Perhaps Cristobal gained power with it.

"What is it?" I followed Cristobal's every step, peeking my head around the side when he traversed the breadth of the cabin.

Ezer blocked my way, shoulders rolled back like a guard's, but devastatingly prince-like in his stance. He cocked a grin and spared me a look, hazel eyes twinkling as if his time weren't running out.

It set off my insides like dominoes lined up in a row from my stomach all throughout my body.

"We should leave." Cristobal snuck to a window and peeked into the building.

"What do you see?" Ezer ignited his gifting, light tracing beneath his knuckles. He placed a protective hand on my forearm, unwilling for me to face the darkened forest on the west side of us.

"Nothing. Just a bed, table. Normal things. Are you sure she's—" Cristobal grunted.

"Get down." Ezer yanked my arm.

I crouched and checked around the building. My head nearly knocked into Cristobal's.

"You're shot," I stated the obvious.

An arrow pierced the wooden wall, and Cristobal's tunic soaked with blood. "It grazed my arm."

"We should go." Ezer gestured for us to take a downward path away from the cabin.

He was right. Isabelia wouldn't stay in such a spot and had the means to escape, but I couldn't leave without her.

Turning the knob, I pushed into the small cabin. Two narrow beds, a table, and a cabinet greeted us. A small missive with a red rose wax seal caught my attention.

"We've got to go now." Ezer brooked no opposition.

I snatched the missive and exited. Arrows whizzed through the air and plunged into the wood inches above my head.

Cristobal stood and swung his arm through the air. Ezer did the same, using his gift to command the arms and legs of people I hadn't seen. The grunts through the forest assured me that the fellows had succeeded.

Blood dripped from Cristobal's fingertips. He met my gaze, which must have given away my concern because he said, "I'll survive."

The coolness in my limbs left me feeling hollow. With no accessible gift to heal a wound and no way to protect myself, other than the daggers in my boots, I followed Ezer's lead, and Cristobal guarded the rear.

Ezer stopped. I knocked into his back.

Whyzer Patro stood before us with a knife to Isabelia's throat. Now that I could see him in my undazed state, I noticed how his black beard had more gray streaks than I remembered from a month ago, his wrinkles more pronounced. The skin on his face tightened with an angry smile that flared at his nose. "You will come with me, and you"—he pointed at Cristobal—"will die." The whyzer motioned with his hand, calling his staff to himself.

The staff flew through the air toward his grasp.

In a blink, Isabelia evaporated into smoke. The staff fell to the ground, and Mamá and Señor Lozcano appeared before us.

Mamá grabbed Ezer. "Fly straight." She flung a dagger at Whyzer Patro.

The blade flew giftedly fast.

Yet even so, Whyzer Patro dodged, whipped out his own dagger, and flung it at Ezer.

Mamá leapt in front of a wide-eyed Ezer. The dagger landed with a thunk. The sickening sound of blade meeting flesh resounded in the air. She landed in a heap at Ezer's feet.

Cristobal grabbed onto Ezer's shoulder, keeping him standing. His skin flared to life. He worked his hands.

Whyzer Patro reached for the staff on the ground, but he jerked and shook with the attempt, clearly restrained by a force outside himself.

Isabelia flashed atop the staff, plumes of smoke encircling her. Her thick, dark braid spilled over one shoulder and her doll eyes—so much like mine—narrowed. She threw the staff in my direction and disappeared. A cloud of smoke was left in her wake.

The whyzer broke through the fellows' control, his powers far stronger than the most gifted of individuals.

Señor Lozcano flashed behind the whyzer, but the whyzer struck him with a single blow.

Mamá lay on the ground, feeding the soil with her blood.

"Look around." Whyzer Patro pointed up and around where we stood.

A half dozen men I'd seen around the castillo, including Roberto, emerged from the trees. Many had powers of strength, speed, and to incapacitate their victims. We couldn't beat Whyzer Patro's most elite with only two exhausted fellows, a giftless runt, an injured healer, and a missing invisiblist. Where had Isabelia gone?

CHAPTER 46
COTTIA

SWEAT TRICKLED ALONG MY hairline. The air tasted tangy like the metallic scent of spilled blood. Queasy regret flooded my throat with the bitter taste of herbs.

Humid air clung to my skin. Judging by the sheen on Roberto's forehead and that of five of the whyzer's other loyal guards, they felt it too. The staff lay limp several paces behind me, but any sudden movement might set off the man with the bow and arrows at the edge of the wood. His target—my heart.

The back sides of Ezer and Cristobal revealed only taut shoulders and the glow of their skin reflecting off the edges of their bodies.

Mamá lay on the ground like a corpse. Señor Lozcano vanished in a blink. He must have been exhausted and could only cover himself with his gift.

I awakened the gifting in my chest, but the heat did not spread. It recoiled and left my limbs cold as I stood on the precipice of this slaughter.

Signs of Isabelia's smoke caught in my peripheral vision.

A groan escaped someone's throat. Smoke dispersed behind the dying guard with the bow and arrows. The five others with Whyzer Patro struggled beneath Ezer's and Cristobal's twin gift. Whyzer Patro pushed through their hold, and all fighting broke loose. Swords slid from their scabbards, punches flew, and a chaos of giftings sparked to life.

What could I do?

Someone let out a sharp whistle behind me.

I twisted around.

The staff flew to my face. I had just enough time to catch it. Warmth met and warmed my palms.

Light lit the markings on my skin. The sky darkened. Hues of purple, elderberry blue, and a kiss of gold from the setting sun.

My old master raced toward me with hands outstretched and fury in the angles of his slender face. His staff wriggled in my palms, responding to the call of its master. I tightened my grip and swiped at the man. He yanked his staff and kicked my stomach.

Attempting to flare my limp gifting, I extended it at his body. Tendrils of my invisible touch penetrated his skin. He lifted his palm toward Cristobal and yanked at his old subject with invisible strings.

Ancient One, protect me from him, I shot out a prayer. *Make this weak gifting work even for a moment.*

A guard sliced Cristobal's midsection.

Panic soared through my blood, but with his staff, the whyzer had control over Cristobal's body.

"Stop!" I screamed and threw up my arms. I gripped a thick vein with my invisible touch. The cold fingers before me glowed with life and feeling, though only weak heat slogged beneath my skin.

"Let go, and I will spare him." Whyzer Patro's voice quavered.

Another guard poked his knife at Cristobal's throat but stopped before reaching it. Ezer's hands splayed wide as he held his arms high in the air. He shook with the effort of taking control of his opponents' movements.

Cristobal flicked a look in my direction and leapt at Ezer. They tumbled and punched, kicked and twisted. Ezer had lost control of the other opponents now that Cristobal had been forced to turn on us.

Whyzer Patro smirked. My old binding burned on my flesh, but he couldn't control me.

How did I ever escape from such a foe? I yanked a dagger from my boot, having only one option left.

"You won't enjoy so easy a death, Cottia." Whyzer Patro's cadence rung with malice. "Every day in my dungeons, you will regret leaving my castillo. Neither your prince nor family will come from this unstained."

My invisible gifting reached into Whyzer Patro, who was escaping to the outskirts and fleeing like a coward. Muscle and bone stretched and contracted, full of blood and adrenaline. His warmth met my touch. His veins pounded with life.

I pinched a thick artery with a flow of power not my own as the energy grew weaker by the second. I jerked my arm, motioning to put the whyzer out like the assassin I was. He needed to die. The whyzer fell to his knees, clutching a hand over his heart. He deserved this.

Cristobal and Ezer stilled, swiveling their attentions in my direction. Whyzer Patro must have lost control over Cristobal.

But with my fleeing energy, I could heal also instead of kill. Hot tears welled over my vision, and Mamá's pale face lifted in the grass beside Whyzer Patro.

My iron grip over his body loosened, and I raced to get to Mamá.

Señor Lozcano appeared beside her and shouted toward the fellows. "Use your gift like a blanket."

Mamá jabbed a dagger at the whyzer's neck, but he blocked her easily. Smoke appeared behind her. Power from the staff shot like a bolt of lightning, cutting to where Mamá had once stood.

The valley went silent.

Only lightning bugs and gifted skin shone under the cover of night.

The whyzer looked about and fled, leaving his contingent of guards in Ezer's and Cristobal's power. Somehow, all the whyzer's fellows appeared like breathing statues. Their bulging muscles alight with caged abilities.

The sight of Isabelia bent over gripped my soul. I sped back toward Mamá, feeling only a remnant of energy still on my fingertips.

Too much blood had seeped from her wound. The crimson stain coating her dress seemed too much for any person to lose. She'd saved Ezer instead of trying to save herself. I fell to my knees and looked into her heavy-lidded eyes. I had but seconds to lay out my heart before the person I most loathed and loved. The dichotomy of the sentiments wrestled on the tip of my tongue.

"I forgive you." I touched her arm, pushing the supernatural dust of the gifting left on my skin.

She flicked a drowsy look in my direction and inhaled a quivering breath. Her gaze stilled off in the distance.

"Mamá?" I called to her. Tears spilled. "Mamá."

Isabelia held Mamá's hand and wept.

My lips curled. Heaviness pushed over my shoulders, my heart, my head, and my soul. Did she hear my last words? Did it matter? Mamá was gone, and I'd never get another chance to let her know that I'd let go of all the hurt between us.

CHAPTER 47
COTTIA

We stayed the night in Señor Lozcano's hidden estate. Isabelia clung to my arm, speechless in the wake of Mamá's passing. Cristobal required more healing than I could give since my full gifting had not returned. Prince Ezer remained sober and quiet after insisting that we bury Mamá and say goodbye, though it might come at a steep cost to him. We could never return on time to Giddel and must pray that Cristobal's fellow wouldn't abuse his power.

It turned out that Señor Lozcano lived in a sandstone mansion with rooms equivalent to those of the palace in Giddel. The estate remained obscured from view because he'd infused his powers into the wards placed on the substantial rocks on the grounds.

"It's my fault." Isabelia wept as we buried Mamá.

Again, Isabelia wept as we ate breakfast and said, "She'd still be alive if I'd stayed home."

Yet, I did not prod my sister about why she blamed herself for Whyzer Patro slaying Mamá. Instead, I scooped meat and beans from my breakfast bowl. The taste diluted the despair gathered in my mouth. The gray slab of light stretched across the sky outside the window made for the perfect solemn weather to mope about how I should have forgiven her sooner.

After breakfast, the horses were prepared to take us to Giddel posthaste. Señor Lozcano would go with us to keep us hidden from Whyzer Patro and other bandits and then return the horses to his estate.

Isabelia climbed onto a white steed speckled with gray freckles all over his rump.

Cristobal mounted in front of Isabelia and flashed me a look with those dark-lashed eyes of his. They beseeched me to trust him.

I swept the black skirt I'd borrowed from Isabelia to the side as I mounted astride. Breaking my neck wasn't an option, and speed required I be stable on my mount.

Ezer watched me with more than fine eyes to recommend him. "May I ride with you?" He had the bearing of a king, but the humble question reflected his kindness of heart and soul. The hint of a smile played on his cheeks, though I couldn't perceive what joy he could find on this day.

We were going to arrive late, which would open us up to an illusionist's whims.

The hours of riding left me sore, but we had to make it before the sun dipped below the mountain horizon. Ezer must take his place as the prince of Giddel before the oath's protection ran out of time.

Giddel appeared around a bend. A burnt orange sunset kissed the long sandstone walls, protecting the city within its embrace. My heart leapt at the sight of a place that felt more like a home than I had experienced all the years in the castillo. Gema was there. My bed was there. The promise of comfort shone in the gleam of the sandstone walls. Ezer and I would remedy our woes.

A steady echo of hooves set the rhythm of my heartbeat. We descended, the rump of the beast shifting my weight left and right. When we got to the gate, the city guards exchanged furrowed looks with each other and hesitated to let us pass. One tall guard with gold stitching around his collar and a Giddelian hibiscus sewn to his lapel called over more men to clear a way for Prince Ezer.

Of course, they hadn't seen us leave the city property since we'd snuck out at night, which inspired unease to tumble through my insides. The last time we had arrived in the city like this, Whyzer Patro had been waiting to attack us too.

The front gate swung open as only the afterglow of the sun traced the mountains in the west. Undulating stars glimmered in the east as if to tease us about our late arrival.

I dismounted first and ran to embrace Isabelia. "Everything will be better from here on out."

She leapt off the horse and squeezed me in return. Her thin form was much stronger than her lithe appearance suggested. When we parted, Prince Ezer had dismounted. He met my gaze with a tilt to his lips, reaching up to his hazel eyes. Cristobal sidled up to me and placed his arm around my shoulders.

The heaviness from his weight and the boulder over my heart weakened my knees. I slipped out of Cristobal's grasp, not meeting his eyes. I crossed several paces to Prince Ezer to make a request.

Isabelia and Cristobal remained behind me, whether in shock or confusion, I couldn't say.

"Prince Ezer," I said, now out of breath.

"Always Ezer for you." He craned his neck down and spoke in low tones. "What's wrong?"

"Could we not help—"

"Arrest him." A deep voice rang through the entrance. Another Ezer in a fine doublet and golden tassels over his chest arched his chin high.

Two guards seized the real Ezer's arms.

"No, he's an imposter. Check his story. Bring out the truth seers." Ezer stilled the guards' muscles with his own gift and crossed to the imposter in swift strides.

But again, the guards overtook the real Ezer. This time, a swift buzz cut through the tumult and Ezer went limp. Several more guards helped carry him from the palace grounds to who knew where.

The king appeared beside the imposter Ezer and gripped his shoulder. "Good work, *hijo*, son. I'm glad you have finally taken to your role with diligence and caution."

"As is my duty." The imposter flashed a devilish grin far too similar to the handsome one the real Ezer wore.

I spun toward Cristobal, ready to rip out his throat if he didn't fix the problem. "Say something. I thought he was your ward, under your control."

Cristobal pointed at the imposter. "He isn't the real Ezer."

The guards, king, and imposter stared unamused at Cristobal.

"And who are you?" The king sneered. Though he was half a handbreadth shorter than Ezer, his demeanor gave him the aura of a giant.

More of the ladies under consideration for Ezer's hand stood in the shadows inside the atrium. Señora Virginia and Señorita Julieta dared to approach, dresses swishing over the marble floors. A twinkle of pleasure crossed their expressions. They could vouch for Cristobal since they had hired him. They could also condemn him.

"I am Señora Virginia's friend and neighbor." Cristobal pointed to the cocky older woman.

Julieta's mamá cocked a smirk that made my heart thunder. Before she said the words, I perceived her next move.

"He's a neighbor, all right. A thief. I caught him days ago on the palace grounds and thought to give him grace. I see I was wrong."

Cristobal's nose flared.

"No, Cristobal." I warned.

But the murderous glare in his eye raged, and I didn't blame him.

A guard handed Cristobal a dagger, clearly straining against Cristobal's control. Cristobal arched his arm back, dagger aimed in Señora Virginia's direction. Just when he released the dagger, Isabelia grabbed Cristobal's side. Smoke billowed where Cristobal had stood. He and my sister were gone.

Julieta cried. Those around her gasped.

Señora Virginia lay in a pool of blood on the ground, bleeding out from where a dagger stuck out of her throat.

"Find that thief and bring him here," the imposter shouted at the guards behind him. "He will pay. He will hang for this."

My mouth fell open at the sudden turn of events. I flared my limp gift, which moved sluggishly through my veins. By the time the invisible gift extended from my fingertips, the horses had disappeared, along with Señor Lozcano. Not a trace of the older man remained.

I let my gift slip beneath the imposter Ezer's skin. His heart purred in a different rhythm than Ezer's, which I had grown to know so well. The slow pulse of thick blood and the pattern of vessels beneath his flesh mapped out a completely different person than the one I watched with my eyes. The discordance between my vision and the truth revealed by my gift wrestled in my mind. The imposter must have been tired to allow such information to slip out, but he held the ruse all the same.

The imposter drew near and pitched his voice low. "If the whyzer hadn't made me promise to keep you alive, I'd kill you now. But don't think you're free. I need you to feed me information so that I can blend in better without raising suspicions about my identity. Any foul play and I will make your prince suffer. Got it?" He squinted down at me with what should have been an endearing expression, yet I flinched.

I could kill him right now, yet I wouldn't break my vow to never murder again. What if I was caught? Who would free the real Ezer?

"Where's Gema?" I asked.

A gleam caught in the too-green color of his eyes. "She's in the dining hall with my brother."

"You won't get away with this. And when you're caught, you will be flayed."

"I believe I've already won." He let out a low chuckle. "And you aren't my chosen peach."

"You're right. I'm your screaming peach." I strode around him, determined to find out what I'd missed in my absence. Would Gema believe my story or be too spiteful to help?

The sconces lit a path through the main corridor to the familiar dining hall with its long table and raised royal spots in the back. The chandeliers let out a gentle glow over a few stray señoritas who listened to the rumors of Señora Virginia's death.

Gema and Ulyses hunched together at the end of the room, deep in conversation. Though they could appear as a couple enjoying privacy or two people conspiring.

I pulled the chair across from them and melted into the seat, weary in heart and bone. "Help me free Ezer."

Ulyses smirked. "It's you again."

Gema's gaze narrowed as she placed her unrelenting glare on me. "Why did you lie? It was that night in the room, wasn't it?"

"Yes, how did you know?"

"We've been spying, but we didn't know for sure until Ulyses sensed the lie." Gema flicked a warm glance at him.

"I thought he could speak to animals."

"That's what I thought too." Ulyses smoothed the small patch of beard over his chin.

Gema dunked a churro into a small bowl of liquid chocolate in a desperate attempt to find solace for her agitation. "Why did you do it?" Her words came out mumbled from having to speak around her treat.

"To retrieve my sister. Now, I don't even have her or Cristobal or Ezer."

Prince Ezer strode into the dining area with Julieta hanging off his neck. Her tears rang through the hall as they strode to a door at the opposite end of the hall.

Gema said, "So, the rumor is true?"

I nodded.

Ulyses lifted an eyebrow. "He chose her?"

"No. That's not Ezer." I slammed my fist on the table. The vision of Ezer going limp in a jailer's arms screamed at me. Why had I let him go so easily? Why hadn't I fought? Then again, what could I have done with my weak gifting?

The king entered the room, and we stood. With a stern look, he scanned the room and focused on Prince Ulyses.

As Prince Ulyses stepped away from us, he whispered, "I'll make this right."

But even watching Ezer's brother stride up to his father, I could collapse.

Gema linked her arm with mine. "So, what were you trying to do?"

"Get my sister."

"Where is she?" Gema craned her neck around searching.

"She disappeared with Cristobal. Cristobal is a wanted criminal. Mamá is dead, and I'm a complete failure." I smashed my lips together and dove into my disparaging thoughts. I had become this imposter's puppet, one who'd be thrown to my old master or worse if I didn't comply.

Gema hugged my shoulder, silent for once. Who could argue with my assertion?

Trust me. A whisper echoed in my mind.

I must be going mad.

Trust me.

Who knew if even the Ancient One could fix the mess I'd made. I would do anything to save Ezer and tell him everything on my heart.

PART 3
RECKLESS

CHAPTER 48
COTTIA

SEA-WATER ROARED IN THIS crevice of the cliff almost as loudly as my anxious heart. Sunlight tarried to soften the harsh edges of our new home, now only the kiss of moonlight traced the rock edges above.

Gema pulled at my wrist to divert me to a stairway chiseled into the wall of rock. "Where's your sister?"

"She said she'd meet us at the garden's edge." I swallowed the doubts and fears that had been stirring since we'd set a date to free Prince Ezer.

"I hate when she does that." Gema flipped her mass of curly red hair over her shoulder, allowing me to see her slender, freckly face where it caught an angle of the pale moonlight. Gema was more than just my best friend. She had become like a sister to me since I was taken to Whyzer Patro's fort as a child.

Few words bounced between us as we traveled to the top of the cliff where the royal gardens were cultivated. We caught our breaths from the steep climb and from extra vigilance. Gardeners, palace guards, or even guests could tramp through the tree garden on the Giddelian Palace estate and prevent us from making it to the prison.

Through the slender trees, I could only make out deep shadows in every direction. "She'll be here," I managed to say between steadying breaths. "Isabelia left with Cristobal to scout a good hiding spot for him."

Gema gave a throaty laugh. "Is that what the señoritas call it these days?"

"Call what?" Heat built up in my chest, but my lackluster gifting didn't flow down my arms as it had before Whyzer Patro stole a portion of my powers. The lack of response in my body stirred my doubts about being able to help anyone.

"Come on, Cottia," she said much too loudly. Then she stepped closer and pitched her voice low. "Don't act like you can't see how Isabelia bats her lashes at Cristobal. Just because you're not interested in the fellow doesn't mean your sister isn't."

"He hasn't changed. He lashed out and killed Señora Virginia, but that's not the point." My fingers curled into fists. "Isabelia is sneaking us into a prison today and our lives are at stake. She has a right to be extra cautious when the usurper prince is in love with his noose and is acting as regent since the king grew ill. I think our romantic notions can be put on hold for a while."

"Señora Virginia wasn't exactly innocent." Gema crossed her arms, readying to argue with me if I put up a fight. "She's the one who hired Cristobal and what's-his-name—I don't know, the impostor—to take you out."

I flashed Gema a narrowed gaze. We'd discussed this before, making our rounds over the same debate that had led to Cristobal staying in our cave hideaway, though I didn't fully trust him.

The darkness under the canopy of trees swallowed our voices, and the sea breeze rushing against the foliage muffled the hint of footfalls. We turned right, heading along the cliff edge where a line of trees hid our trajectory to our meet-up spot.

Within the secluded gazebo, we stopped and waited. It offered us a view of the beach below and of the flower garden, yet kept us hidden from the palace. A hint of red light cracked the horizon. Gema kept her gaze trained on the other side where the haze covering the flower garden revealed no one in sight.

Gema bumped my shoulder with her own. "Isn't it funny how it's our romantic notions that keep us here instead of enjoying our freedom?"

I cut a glare in her direction. She kept her green eyes trained ahead but couldn't hide the curl on her lips that revealed her smug attitude. She probably thought herself so clever.

"Go ahead. Pat yourself on your back. You forget that Prince Ezer is jailed because of me and that all of Giddel will be subject to the usurper who follows orders from Whyzer Patro."

"That's why we're breaking him loose."

"It will be by the grace of the Ancient One if this works." I prayed under my breath. *Please, Ancient One, open a path where there is none.*

Gema rolled her eyes. "I'm certain Isabelia's invisibility will do that, and so will Cristobal's gift of taking over bodily movement."

"You forget that jailers are picked because they can counteract strong giftings, and I can barely manipulate my powers these days."

She touched my hand and quirked her lips to the side in the pitying expression she'd been giving me this last month.

"If the Ancient One could protect me from Whyzer Patro, I think He can make things right again in Giddel."

With the roll of her eyes, Gema pointed at two shadows across the garden. "They're here."

The two figures disappeared into the trees. The manicured bushes and flower beds now lay as witnesses to our goings and comings. I glimpsed the palace doors a hundred arm spans away and caught the shadow of a guard on duty. The palace would awaken soon, and any chance of our plan happening today would be gone.

I turned toward my friend, unwilling to let her romantic notions question pass me by. "For someone who is here for the *romantic notions*, you do a terrible job at sharing your feelings with the one person who needs to hear them."

She stiffened her bottom lip and shifted away. "I've got to go to the kitchen."

"Fine. Go act the servant and do your spy work to drown the truth from existence."

Shadows approached. The male shadow had the cocky smoothness that marked Cristobal's gait, and the female one scurried in Isabelia's nervous fashion.

Gema opened her mouth and snapped it closed again. Isabelia and Cristobal entered the gazebo. Isabelia wore a rough-spun, brown dress, a long braid woven down her back, and fierceness in the set of her dark brown eyes. Cristobal lowered his hood, allowing us to glimpse the handsome face Isabelia gawked at even in a moment like this.

The haughty lift of Gema's eyebrow screamed she was right without having to vocalize a word.

"Thank you for keeping me company," I said to Gema as an apology for the harsh truths I'd thrown at her.

"That's what friends do. I'm off to work." She slipped out of the gazebo to maintain the ruse of faithful kitchen maid so we could know the coming and goings inside the palace. "I'll meet you at the caves."

I swallowed hard. By the time I saw Gema again, we'd either have what was left of Prince Ezer after his stay behind bars, or we'd be dead.

CHAPTER 49
GEMA

THE SUN ROSE ALONG the eastern horizon as I made my way back home. Cook didn't need the extra help this morning, and my nerves spun like wool on a drop spindle. I should walk the other way, toward the prison fortress. But what would I do, burn a hole through the side of the hold and let the whole kingdom know what we'd done?

No, I kept to the beach on the edge of the palace grounds. The cliffs stretched skyward to my right, and the vast sea rushed up to my feet to the left. I drew near to the inlet where a hidden door was sealed with a ward. Cottia, Isabelia, Cristobal, and I have made it our home since Prince Ezer was imprisoned. Prince Ulyses introduced us to the hidden coves, and only he knew our little secret.

I climbed the stairs that led to a path along the cliff. At the very end, I placed my hand on a particular mark with a small crease at the end. I lit my gifting. The cold stone warmed at my touch. A wheeze of air released and then a click sounded. The door slid open to a cavernous room with a boulder sitting in the center. A path snaked to the left and right of the rock that led to a tunnel with wooden doors on both sides of the man-made passage. Once my shoes hit a certain shadow of the path, the main door slid shut, sealing me inside.

"Anyone here?" I called.

No one answered. They weren't back yet, and Prince Ulyses hadn't arrived to check in on us. I marched on to Cottia, Isabelia, and my room, finally letting myself feel the impact of Cottia's words about me not sharing my romantic notions with Prince Ulyses. My stomach grew fierce at the prospect. Prince Ulyses had to know I was in love with him.

I lit my skin into gentle flames while tidying up the room with rounded asymmetrical cavern edges, shapeless walls enclosing me inside the tomb. Cottia and Isabelia left their beds in a mess of blankets knotted atop their cots. I touched the wick of a lamp to provide me with light so I could turn off my glowing skin. A chill raced along my flesh, lifting an army of goose pimples over my arms. Was this a premonition?

"Gema, are you there?" Ulyses's velvety voice cut through my fears.

With a lamp in hand, I exited our makeshift room to meet the kind face of the man I adored. He strode through the darkened path with a lamp held high, and the glow of his gifting flared alive. His jovial manner contrasted with the gloom of our situation.

"Have you heard any news?" I looked over my shoulder at the fellow's cove that opened up across from the girl's side. Cristobal's section of the cave remained shrouded in darkness. I could flirt without his obnoxious commentaries.

Ulyses gestured to the cave door several body lengths to my right, and I nodded. Darkness had a way of seeping into my bones and darkening my every thought. I slid my fingers into the crook of his elbow, absorbing his warmth through his green tunic. The crease of a smile formed at the edge of his shaped mustache, and he proceeded to guide me along the short path to the exit wall.

I cut in front of Ulyses, letting what Cristobal called a coy smile slip over my lips. Thank the gods, no one else was here. I would have thanked the Ancient One, but I could never imagine one all-knowing God letting someone like Whyzer Patro exist.

"It won't work unless you light your gift." Ulyses leaned close to my ear, and I whipped my head in his direction.

His breath and mine mingled. I could lean ever so slightly and touch my lips to his. His gaze almost appeared longing with the light of the lamp in his hand reflecting off the plains of his face and the touch of beard on his chin. Yet, I stopped myself from rocking onto my toes, and he held himself from craning the last breath forward.

Warmth tingled in my veins, and I let it burn to my skin on one side of my body. Small licks of flame fired on my cheeks. It had been like this between us for the past month, and yet I couldn't motivate myself to push past how Ulyses's parents had reprimanded him in front of me for our time together before they fell ill.

Ulyses straightened his posture and recalibrated his expression into a sad grin. The stone slid open with a dull grind. Whoever created this doorway had been blessed with a gift that had probably seemed stupid in its time and was our lifesaver now. The roar of waves crashing against the cliffs below ended the quiet and added to the chaos pounding through my mind.

I inhaled and stepped forward. The cliffside filled the edges of our vision. Morning sunlight speared the sea at the end of the cliff.

"We need to talk." Ulyses left the lamp within the cave and closed the door. His hand grazed mine as he led me onto the path.

My heart slammed against my breastbone, lighting up a wave of hope that had crashed and burned when his parents had declared that I wasn't a fit match for their son. Did he mean to clarify this dance between us that had grown and shifted into something bigger than anything I'd ever felt before? I followed him out into the sunlight and onto a boulder along the beach.

I should have been nervous about the jailbreak, but somehow it didn't seem as important as this moment.

Elbow to elbow, we kept our attention out at sea where a galleon approached along the horizon. My senses drank in the orange and yellow halo of light. Seagulls cried overhead as they glided down and soared up.

"I've been thinking about you." Ulyses moved his hand to his lap, stealing my secret hope that he'd hold my hand.

Now, these words meant nothing good.

His Adam's apple bobbed, and a muscle in his jaw leapt. "We've continued to spend more time together, and I've deluded myself into thinking that we could just be friends but . . ."

"But?" I leaned forward, craning my neck to make him look at me.

"I think you know how I feel about you." His words tumbled out, and he finally turned his gaze on me. The sorrow pressed along his eyebrow ruined what could have been a romantic moment.

"No, actually, I don't." I swallowed the rest of my thoughts that wanted to thunder out but caught on the lump of emotion forming in my throat.

A rueful smile twisted over his lips. "I love spending time with you, and you're beautiful. But I don't think your view of life and mine line up, and in spending so much time together, we might actually be setting ourselves up for heartbreak."

His last statement swung like a hammer over my chest.

"Gema, I still have to find out why I have two gifts, and this call to visit my whyzer in Valle de los Fantasmas nags at me. It's unfair for you to wait for my parents to get well and then wait for me to return from this trip when you don't share my same convictions. What if I'm not allowed to marry you?"

I leaned back on my hands and focused on the horizon. Cerulean seas with no end spread before me. The secret dreams in my heart were crushed to pieces.

Tears spilled to my lash line and hissed into steam. I stood. Blubbering like a fool in front of the person who'd crushed my heart wasn't an option.

"Gema, please, don't cry like that." He got to his feet.

Dodging from his touch, I managed to get several strides from him.

"Prince Ulyses," a male voice said.

Both he and I spun around to see one of the new servants that the impostor prince had brought in. The stout man grimaced from beneath a thin mustache. How had he snuck up on us?

"Yes," Ulyses responded.

"You are needed in the royal hall. Something of great consequence has transpired."

Ulyses and I shared a look. "Let me accompany Señorita Gema to her house."

"No time for that." The man's grave voice brooked no argument. "Guards must be executed, and you're the acting justice."

I waved Ulyses off, and the two men stormed up the beach toward the palace. It took all the willpower in my body to stay still while I remained in view. I needed to get back to the cave to see if Cottia and the others had returned with the true crowned prince of Giddel, Prince Ezer.

CHAPTER 50
COTTIA

Tiptoeing through the prison, Isabelia and I crossed a fellow slumped in the corner of the cell. He flitted a look in my direction, and I whipped my head back around to catch the sullen shape of cheeks I recognized, the bow shape of lips set in a severe frown, and hazel eyes that had stolen my breath time and time again.

I gasped. My sister dug her iron claws into my arm to quiet my reaction, and we pressed our backs into the stone wall as if we could melt into it. Though Isabelia had the gift of invisibility, it didn't dampen the noise we made.

Prince Ezer continued to stare at me, but his rounded eyes remained unfocused, showing that Isabelia's gift kept us hidden. We had to be patient and wait in the shadows. I prayed to the Ancient One that the jailor wouldn't run into us and that the head jailor hadn't changed the schedule we'd bought from a guard at the garrison. Some of the jailers had been called to a meeting with the fake prince, leaving the prison with half the usual staff.

A bolt unlocked. My heart hammered loudly enough to drown out the scrape of slothful boots scuffling in the passage. A round fellow entered this small section with a tray and a cup of water. Light from somewhere behind the door reflected off his bald head and absorbed into his dark green uniform. It took everything in me to keep from trying to flare my gifting and squeeze a vein, but I wasn't sure that was possible. I had sworn off murder anyway. We had a set of jail keys—also purchased from our favorite guard, Yurde—and a plan we'd been whipping up for the last month.

A glowing light flared over Ezer's arms, a sign that he was attempting to unleash his gift. The pulse of his ability floated through the air like a breeze that snaked from a hidden vent. Hairs on my arm rose, chilled by the gentle touch. In my peripheral, Isabelia's enormous brown eyes turned in my direction, but I didn't peel my gaze from Ezer.

The bulky jailer placed the tray on a slit between the bars on the floor and laughed, the sound like a low rumble. "You still trying that stunt with me, huh?" The water tipped over, spilling into the gruel served on the tray. "Thought the *prince* would be smart enough to figure out my gift is to be untouchable." He grabbed the door's edge, keeping his attention on Ezer, and wagged his head. "*Buen provecho*, dig in, idiot." He slammed the metal door shut, leaving my ears ringing.

Isabelia leaned her head forward, curling one of her smug smiles up her cheek. She'd betted on the jailer not noticing and had won.

But when we stepped forward, my ankles stilled. "Let Ezer see us." The pressure snaked up my legs until movement was impossible.

"Who's there?" Ezer got to his feet, revealing his stature and emaciated body.

My heart sunk at how the prince had been treated, though I understood the jailers believed him to be a traitor. The only reason the usurper hadn't beheaded Ezer was because the prince's brother had convinced the king and queen to keep him alive.

Pressure mounted around the core of my body and pinned down my arms. "Isabelia, drop the invisibility."

"I have." Her gentle voice came out airy.

An intensity flamed in Ezer's stare, reflecting the orange glow from the gift markings on his neck and forearms where his dirty, cream tunic did not cover. The closer he got, the more pronounced his cheek bones and the less I saw of the gentle fellow I'd first met. A hot tear threatened to roll out from my bottom eyelid. This was my fault. This never would have happened if he hadn't come with me to find Isabelia.

"Ezer, it's me, Cottia." My voice hitched with a well of emotions.

His eyes widened, and his mouth dropped open. He worked his jaw like he meant to say something.

"We don't have much time." I fumbled with the keys, clinking the metal together as I searched for the right one. "Isabelia will hide us until the jailer returns." My shaky hand stuck the first key into the hole. The key didn't turn.

A grunt and noise came from the room beyond the door.

Isabelia leaned into my shoulder. "Hurry up."

I chose the next key that might fit and stabbed it into the hole. This was the one part of the plan we couldn't practice. We had to trust that the head jailer would keep Ezer's key with the rest and that we could find it in time.

Sweat built up over my top lip. I flipped to the next key that seemed an adequate fit for the lock, but all the dozens of keys together in a ring sent palpitations galloping through my chest. I tried another and another.

Isabelia snapped her attention to the main door like someone might burst through at any moment.

I inserted the next key and couldn't turn it. Metal clinked against the lock.

"Shhh." Isabelia nudged my side and lit her skin, setting off a vine-like pattern of glowing lines filled with power. "Someone's coming."

We stilled, straining to hear, and were met with lumbering footfalls on the other side of the door. Just as a head crossed over a small rectangular hole cut at the top of the door, Isabelia clung to my arm, sending prickles of energy shooting through my body, and blinked us from existence.

The jailer's bald head and dark eyes crossed through the hole. "Quiet down in there."

Ezer grabbed the rail closest to my hand, allowing me to feel his heat. I wished to breach the mere hair lengths from him but refused to give ourselves away by connecting him to Isabelia's invisibility. Ezer kept a stoic expression that didn't relent under the jailer's fierce glare.

Finally, the jailer trudged away. I exhaled the breath I had held up like a dam while the jailer was nearby.

Isabelia released hold of her invisibility, allowing a moment of rest between bouts of using her powers. She'd said she could hold her invisibility on her own for hours at a time, but she could only maintain invisibility with other people in it for ten minutes or so. We couldn't risk her getting exhausted before we tried to make our break.

I continued to stick keys in the keyhole. By the twelfth key, I barely resisted screaming.

Ezer reached through the bars and caressed my hand, wasting time. "Calm down. There're still more cell keys to go."

How in all Agata could he get me to want to simultaneously smack him and hug him? I nodded and slowed my harried pace.

The next key still didn't turn. Isabelia whipped her head around at the sound of metal inserted into the lock of the outer door.

I shoved another key into the hole and turned.

The bald jailer entered the passage, deep shadows cutting across his snarling thick lips.

Ezer swung his cell door open, almost hitting me before I had a chance to dodge out the way.

Isabelia gasped, snapping my attention to my sister. The jailer held Isabelia by her long braid with a smirk of triumph playing on his lips.

Ezer swung his food tray at the jailer's bald head.

A glob of cold gruel slapped my face.

Isabelia disappeared.

The two men wrestled, but Ezer was much smaller than the meaty jailer.

We had to do something, so I sparked my gifting. A slow warmth crawled down my arms. I pushed and stretched my ability with all my strength, but my gifting crawled at the same pace, too slow to be helpful.

Now, the jailer turned Ezer over into a headlock.

Isabelia snatched the tray from the floor and banged it against the jailer's head.

More footfalls came racing from somewhere deeper in the jail.

My powers tingled in my fingertips, but didn't stretch too far out from my skin. If I continued at this speed, we'd all be jailed or dead by late morning.

I rocked on my toes, waiting for the perfect moment while Ezer continued to shift the jailer with his thrashing. The jailer turned so his backside faced me. I leapt onto his back and touched his neck.

A tray whacked my head, nearly toppling me.

"Sorry," Isabelia squeaked.

But I reached through his skin using my gift. The sensation of veins and soft tissue mapped out through my mind, and I found the right one and squeezed.

Footfalls thundered toward us, giving us only moments more to escape.

The jailer's arms slackened, and Ezer gasped for breath.

I tilted forward. The jailer was about to fall when I jumped off of him.

Ezer snatched my wrist, tugging us out of his passage and into the main corridor of the prison.

We fled.

"Hey, you!" A baritone voice shouted.

Isabelia grabbed my other arm and we formed a line with Isabelia leading the way and Ezer following like a tail. The buzz of energy encompassed my arm, chest, and head.

The jailer behind us swore.

We dodged away from the front door, keeping in step with Isabelia's guidance, unwilling to pull in another direction and risk losing our invisibility.

More jailers rushed through the main corridor.

Isabelia hid us in a nook and let go.

Ezer and I panted as we pressed up against the stone wall.

With a gentle tug, Isabelia pulled our arms to bring us closer to her mouth. "I'll keep the veil between us open so we can see each other. Don't let anyone touch you or they will see us. We are going to sneak around the guards. They won't notice us if we stay quiet and keep moving." She repositioned her grip on my arm, and I clung to Ezer's.

We tiptoed over the stone floors, winding through the corridors and dodging frazzled guards. The slow movement forward set my adrenaline running. All I wanted to do was sprint for the exit ahead, but none of us dared let go of the other. One guard swung the front door of the prison open and scanned the road with furrowed eyebrows. Though any gift might map out the bodies in this space, the dozens of forms would overload their senses. So long as we didn't make contact with a guard and stayed in a congested area, we'd be safe. A guard raced through the narrow stone passage, and we lined up against the wall.

Only five arm spans lay between us and the open doorway.

We continued moving and crossed to the other side of the passage to avoid another guard leaning against the wall.

But as we traversed the passage, another fellow ran toward us, and we swerved to the left side of the passage. Yet another man barreled from behind us. We dodged to the right, but my elbow rubbed against his side.

I flattened against the stone wall, hitting my chin with enough force to leave a wound. I hissed a sharp breath between my teeth.

Ancient One, help.

The young guard stopped mid-stride and reached to the side where Isabelia and I held hands. Ezer gripped harder on the other side as if his grasp could keep me from moving. When the guard's fingers met air, he wrinkled his eyebrows and got shoved forward by another comrade.

We remained still for a second. When I pulled away, a smudge of blood stained the stone where my chin had been.

Isabelia yanked me forward, and I tugged on Ezer's hand.

Every step pounded like a drumbeat. *Thank the Ancient One for the guards' stomping about to hide us.*

Isabelia got to the doorway where three men argued with sweeping hand motions. She ducked under an elbow, and I followed suit.

But when Ezer passed, the guard smacked his forearm over the top of Ezer's head.

A curse exploded from the man, breaking the calm I'd managed to maintain thus far. Ezer bit hard on his bottom lip, opening a cut on Ezer's skin, but we didn't stop moving. Isabelia dodged away from the palace toward the market road.

I tripped over an uneven cobblestone, breaking my connection to Ezer.

We blinked into view.

"Over there!" A guard pointed at us.

Ezer lifted me from the ground in one swift motion and set me on two wobbly legs that revived with unnatural energy. Isabelia grabbed our arms, shrouding us in her invisibility once more, but that didn't stop the guards from chasing us. A burly man tripped but a swarthier fellow took the lead.

I lifted my knees and pumped my arms faster, shrugging off Isabelia. Invisibility wasn't an option if we wanted to outrun them. Ahead, a crowd of people traded beneath tents and through a courtyard.

The market. We need to make it over there.

Now several men charged at us, and Isabelia swept right. We lost sight of our assailants and gained access to a plethora of market tents. Isabelia skipped the crowded jewelry stall and dragged us into the fourth stall to the left, sparking her invisibility. A single woman perused a table of fabric in front of the table, and a mom with four children worked behind the counter.

We scooted to a corner, unseen and catching our breath without being too loud. A stampede of guards rushed past us. The two ladies within the stall talked in hushed tones as if the king's men might arrest them for speaking too loudly.

A small girl with doll eyes peeked from under the fabric table with her attention focused on me. "You're pretty."

I clamped my mouth shut, unsure if she was speaking to me or just making a random statement. Were we still invisible? Flicking a glance in my direction, Isabelia mouthed a quick *sorry* and flipped her hood over her head.

The lady shopping spun and gasped. "Sorry, I didn't see when you all came in." She clutched at the ruffle around her neckline. "With the guards in chase, I'm just a mess. Forgive me."

I hedged around Ezer to get the others moving when a strong hand landed on my shoulder.

"Caught you!" a man said.

CHAPTER 51
COTTIA

A scream lodged in my throat. My heart threatened to hammer out of my chest.

The cloaked fellow before us smirked. His dark, round eyes, tan skin, and handsome features inspired a lip biting smile from Isabelia.

If I weren't still catching my breath, I would have rolled my eyes. Cristobal had that effect on every señorita back in Whyzer Patro's castillo, and my sister had fallen for his charms. I'd have to warn her about his reputation when we weren't breaking Ezer out of jail.

"You're welcome, Señorita Cottia," Cristobal whispered to me. "I thought you might need help after you tumbled."

"Yes, thank you for taking over my movement. It's a true gift." My sarcasm spread thick over each word. "Is the road clear?"

Ezer glared at Cristobal and turned away from me back to the weary ladies making a transaction. What must Ezer think has happened between the two of us after seeing Cristobal speaking so intimately with me? He had to remember that I'd lied about my betrothal to my assassin friend—in all honesty, he hadn't truly been a friend until Ezer's imprisonment.

Isabelia smiled and turned toward the woman working the stand. "Could we get this cloth?" My sister pointed to a plain, dark brown bundle and handed her several coins.

"Of course." The woman took the payment that more than covered the cost of the fabric.

"Thank you." Isabelia slid out of the stall.

Cristobal, Ezer, and I followed. As we made our way through the market, we didn't dare speak until we had walked several roads away from the palace. Isabelia unwound part of the cloth and ripped the fabric.

"I feel terrible." Isabelia passed Ezer a piece of fabric. "I can't make us invisible right now."

Ezer wrapped it over his head, and it draped down to his knees. "What's next in your escape plan?"

I hesitated to answer, knowing the next would be a blow. "If you're well enough, we'll sneak through the caves into the palace to save your parents."

He blanched. "What do you mean?"

Isabelia tore another portion of cloth and passed it to me.

"Thank you." I wrapped the rough fabric around my shoulders to conceal my clothes. "Do you think you will be rejuvenated enough to hide Ezer at the gate?"

My sister shook her head.

We had to get out of Giddel before the entire guard started marching the streets.

"*Caramba.*" I squared up to Ezer, now catching the dark smudge beneath his eyes, the thick stubble around his jaw, and his sunken cheeks. Guilt curled like a fire through my body. I had to make this right. "We could wait until Isabelia can hide us again or risk a long walk to the secret passages."

"Where are we going to hide?" Ezer pinched the bridge of his nose. "And what's wrong with my parents?"

Isabelia gnawed on a hangnail on her thumb. She'd be of no help with delivering the news.

I inhaled deeply, gathering the courage to explain. "We think they're being poisoned and don't have much time left."

"Time's up." Cristobal pushed Ezer and I through a narrow walkway between stone buildings.

Decisive footfalls marched behind us on the cobblestone road we'd just left. I risked a peek backward only to make eye contact with the bald guard who'd watched over Ezer's cell. Recognition twisted across his harsh face.

"Turn right." I prodded Isabelia.

"They're over here." The bald guard shouted.

The next road was busy and a place I'd traveled many times before when I'd meet with Whyzer Patro's associate. I ducked into a full bakery, pushing to get to the other side.

"How rude!"

"Don't you see the line?"

Customers snarled at us, but at this point, we hoped the prison guards would run past the shop and not notice the people inside.

A full-figured woman exited the back kitchen with a roller in her hands and flew at Ezer. "Don't think you can come into our store and do whatever you like."

He tugged the fabric over his head to shroud his features from being noticed. No one expected a prince to be so bedraggled, but if they continued to look, they'd recognize him.

Outside the window, guards in the dark garrison uniforms flew by the shop. One stopped to shout something at a companion across the road. At least Ezer's face wasn't in full view of the window. I continued to maneuver into the store and made it to the counter. Isabelia kept close to my elbow, and Cristobal waited at the back of the line as if he just happened to enter at the same time as us. His wanted posters for killing Señora Virginia had long since been covered by other notices which seemed to give him confidence in being out in the open, but I wasn't as sure of him being unrecognizable.

Female screeches whipped my attention back to Ezer who took a tongue lashing that looked like it might blow him over between her ferocity and his frailty.

The baker stopped packing an order and pointed toward the door. His voice cracked instead of the shout I expected. "It's you."

He'd known me as Whyzer Patro's assassin and always took my orders first.

I dropped my voice low. "Can I get a dozen bow ties and exit out the back door?"

"Anything, Señorita. I'm at your orders." The baker whistled to his wife and waved her to himself.

His wife stomped to her spot behind the counter where the baker leaned close to her ear. Her skin paled, and she stretched her mouth into a wavering smile.

If only she knew that she'd reprimanded the crown prince of Giddel. Would the reaction be as drastic?

Isabelia pitched her voice low. "They're starting to go into shops."

Ezer squeezed through the line and stood at my other side while the baker and his wife fulfilled my typical order. He smashed his lips together with a question present in the lift of his eyebrows, but he kept silent and surveyed what was happening outside the large window in the shop.

The baker passed me the basket of pastries when the bell to the shop rang.

"Come on," I hurried Isabelia and Ezer into the kitchen door.

"We're searching for an escaped convict," a baritone voice said.

Shuffling faster, we crossed into the kitchen and rushed to the back door. I leaned my head out of our exit. A guard stood at the front corner of the bakery some seven arm spans away, but then he spun his head around. Cristobal came into view with his dark cloak and clunky boots. He was a wanted criminal, though I suspected the fake prince didn't mind much who Cristobal had killed. Even so, Cristobal took big risks talking to the guard.

The young guard pointed off in the distance away from us, and I pursed my lips, pointing to a door across the narrow alley. This was our only chance. Instead of only Ezer being hanged, it would be Isabelia too. More blood would be on my head.

Ancient One, you can do miracles, and I need one, I prayed as I snuck out the back door.

Isabelia and Ezer followed close behind. Cristobal conversed with enthusiastic hand motions that had the guard tipping his head back in laughter.

I tapped on the door in the prescribed rhythm for an old associate who did clandestine jobs for Whyzer Patro.

Though a couple of months had passed since I was disassociated with the whyzer, my former contact might not know about what had transpired, and even if he did, he wasn't the type to attack openly.

The door cracked open, and I held the basket of pastries up for the man to see. He let out a deep laugh. "Desperation doesn't suit you. The whyzer will love to read about this in my letter to him." He slammed the door shut.

My fingers balled into fists. I spun to face Ezer and Isabelia, two out of three of the people I loved most. The only way out would be to walk past the guard. This small walkway was a dead end with not even another door to knock on. I flicked my eyes up to the blue sky above where the sun shot intense spears of light over the lines of clothes dangling between the buildings.

Ezer wrapped his arms around me; his warmth was the best consolation while we waited to be found. Isabelia joined in our hug and spread a blanket of her power over us. I let the warmth of my gift trickle. Ezer lit his gifting which made his tunic glow beneath his sleeves. An extra buzz of energy flowed, stronger than I would have imagined.

Isabelia and I shared a look.

"I thought you were weak and couldn't use your gifting." My voice came out accusing.

Ezer slid his hand down our arms. "I thought so too. It's been a while since I wielded this much power."

"Let's go." Isabelia tugged on Ezer's arm, and we snuck behind Cristobal. She stopped to pick up a rock and flung it at Cristobal's back.

Cristobal flinched. He glanced over his shoulder in response and continued his conversation.

We waited off to the side, invisible for now.

Cristobal combed his fingers through his hair and extricated himself from his new guard friend. "I'm late to the docks. I hope you find the criminals." He took the narrow route between the buildings that led directly to the docks.

Following proved easier than in the garrison, but the guards seemed to multiply on every road we traversed. We had to either cross onto the palace grounds or exit the city wall to walk around to the other side of the palace. The secret passage entrances all lay on the west side of the palace and we were on the east.

We intersected the last road, now clinging to each other's sweaty hands. Cristobal stepped onto the overlook and descended the stairs to the dock.

With the Assembly of Kings, these ships had been arriving all week. Judging by the blue flag and gold shields, a Pedrozian ship was being unloaded, and a man exited the ramp with guards ahead of him and a line of attendants behind. Wheat-blond hair shone in the morning sun, and the golden stitching on his doublet glistened more than the Agata Sea. He had a swagger to his step that bespoke that he was an arrogant fellow who had never been told "no" a day in his life.

Ezer let go of Isabelia. "We've got to get to King Rodulfo. He'll know me." He raced around Cristobal, striding along the dock.

The familiar buzz of power broke and left a vacant coolness beneath my skin, yet I still strode to try and catch up. Two sets of footfalls sounded behind me, reassuring me that I wasn't alone. I scanned our surroundings. Many people marched about like ants, doing their own business.

Just when I caught up to Ezer's side, King Rodulfo stated, "Who are you? Guards."

The king didn't recognize Ezer.

CHAPTER 52
GEMA

THE HEAT FROM THE kitchen welled up a layer of sweat over my forehead and under my arms, which didn't help the already boiling misery flowing through my veins.

"Grab the tray." Cook's loud voice had a biting edge to it that inspired a desire to slap her. If it weren't for the woman's ability to prepare the best churros I'd ever tasted, I might have done so.

I'd come back just in time for the mad rush that happened in the kitchen when another of the Agata Sea kings arrived. I closed the lid, still tasting the meaty flavor of Cook's stew over my tongue. It didn't make obeying easy, but I picked up the silver handles and carried the large platter up the exit steps. If Cottia ever got the real Prince Ezer back on the throne, I would give her an earful about this setup. She got to march around the kingdom in her cape making plans while I enjoyed the luxury of servanthood and espionage. I nudged the door open on the main floor and adjusted my hold on the platter. My foot slid the servant door behind me closed because, stars forbid, a royal should catch sight of how the servants worked.

I carried the large tray around the base of the grand staircase and through the front passage to the main dining room. Then I pushed open the entrance to drop the tray off on a back counter so I could gather my breath before heading back down the stairs to the kitchen, where I would smell and taste for poisons before repeating the cycle. The impostor allowed me to be a servant upon Ulyses's request, but that didn't mean he trusted me.

"You, there. Get out of that apron and serve at the table." The majordomo's shrill tone cut my planned route back down to the kitchen.

"At your orders." The snark in my voice couldn't be helped.

The majordomo held his nose high, wearing his superior position like a sword at all of our throats. "You can take the attitude off your face. The assembly will be more obliging with a pretty señorita laying food before them."

I contorted my expression into what I believed was a smile and untied my ratty apron to put on a frilly one.

"Much better." He shoved a wine jug into my grasp. "Prince Ezer requested you to serve him and King Rodulfo personally."

My heart smacked my breastbone like two claves in the middle of a vibrant dance. The impostor had to know I was once Whyzer Patro's ward which meant Whyzer Patro wasn't just after Cottia and Prince Ezer, he also wanted me to pay for leaving him.

Shaky but desperate to keep composed, I strutted from the servants' room and entered the gilded dining hall with polished wood and enormous windows. It was hard to say how the occupants—whose hubris only slightly outshone their inflated egos—fit on the upholstered seats. I snuck in between one of the imitator's new advisors and a courtier and refilled his goblet.

"This escape business has me unnerved," said the courtier. "If too many people believe the lie, then we might have an uprising in the streets of Giddel."

My ears perked, and I edged around the courtier to serve him and the next man over.

"The people don't believe such nonsense," said a man with a thick, curly mustache.

The courtier grabbed his goblet and gave his drink a slow twirl. "You underestimate the messiness when power transitions from one monarch to another."

"The monarchs are not dead yet," argued the curly-mustached courtier.

Tiptoeing, I continued around the guests while they debated the jailbreak. That must mean Ezer had gotten away, but they made no mention of who had freed him. Was Cottia safe? Of course she was. They spoke of the best assassin at Castillo Patro. The one who seemed to have nine lives even though she'd lost so much potency in her gifting.

I inhaled deeply to steady the nerves shaking all over my body. The drink landed in the goblets without spilling onto the tablecloth, which I'd call a win. I slunk around an empty chair and reached for the fake prince's goblet.

The impostor wrapped his lanky fingers around my wrist and pulsed with far too much power under his skin. I slowly twisted toward him but kept my head down, thankful for the protocol that mandated I not meet the dark coals for eyes in the fake prince's skull. I couldn't explain how this person could have the same features as the real prince but not look like Ezer.

Footfalls echoed from the main entrance, yet the impostor didn't let go.

"I know your friend had something to do with this."

"With what, Your Majesty?"

"Do you think I'm a dolt?"

"No, Señor."

Ulyses's voice echoed across the room. "Take your hands off her."

The fake prince let go. "I see my brother doesn't want anyone touching *his* girl."

Men chuckled at the insinuation.

My cheeks flushed. Flames licked beneath my skin's surface, ready to fry the fake prince.

"Where's Rodulfo?" The impostor asked impatiently.

Ulyses approached the empty seat to the impostor's left and brushed his sleeve against the bare skin on my lower arm. I kept my head down. An orange flame burned along my eyelashes, lighting the edges of my vision. Why did he have to be the one to defend me after breaking my heart? I couldn't let myself be weak. I corrected my posture and strode to the other side of the table.

The fake Ezer lifted his goblet. "You forgot something."

My fingers curled around the bottle as I swallowed the retort on my tongue.

I retrieved his goblet and filled it with magenta liquid.

"That wasn't so hard," the usurper said. "Now, I need you to get King Rodulfo from the blue room; I believe that's where he was settled. All this waiting doesn't suit me especially when Giddel needs to approve a sovereign." He snapped his fingers as if I were a trained animal. "And make sure someone more qualified takes your place."

I shook with barely contained rage and stormed out through the servants' door. I shoved the bottle into another maid's grip. "Here. Pour the east side of the table." I tore off the apron and flung it onto the counter.

The majordomo gaped and made an objecting noise in his throat. I didn't stick around to hear his reprimand. He hated that an outsider, with a non-matching dress, was allowed to serve on his staff from time to time and detested my closeness with Prince Ulyses. At the thought, tears welled in my eyes and evaporated as they hit my cheeks.

Wretched fire gifting. I couldn't even cry properly.

Taking the steps upward at a bouncing pace, I decided to head back down to the kitchen rather than the dining room after I retrieved King Rodulfo.

Cook could scream and complain all she wanted, but she'd still make me another batch of churros and love me again for making the request.

I strode to the blue room, aptly named for the wall color, and slammed my fist against the fancy wooden door. After a few seconds, I hammered the door again. And again. I should escape while I could, but the impostor wouldn't let me slip away if he thought I'd shirked my duty.

Ever since he noticed me serving, the fake prince did everything he could to exercise his dominance. Steam clouded my vision. The wretched tears wouldn't stop flowing. I simply couldn't go back to the dining hall to listen to the advisors suggest they should string up my friends. Most of all, I couldn't be near Ulyses. I might explode.

Where was the King of Pedroz?

On impulse, I turned the knob and entered the room.

"King Rodulfo?" I called.

Near the window, a muscular man slipped on his tunic and spun his head around. "Do you mind closing the door?"

A flush crept up my neck as I shut myself inside with a partially dressed king. Or at least that's who I believed him to be because, from this angle, he couldn't be much older than me.

He tousled his blond hair and laughed. "I'm sorry. I was so caught up in thought that I didn't hear you." He slipped on a doublet and pushed all the buttons into their holes with ease.

I remained pressed against the door, in too much shock to share my message.

Speak, Gema, just tell him to go to the dining hall.

He approached with a lopsided grin. "My name is Juan. Sorry I startled you."

My insides flipped like a tortilla, which only happened when handsome men were in my presence, and he was handsome, all right. What was wrong with me? I cleared my throat and asked, "You're not King Rodulfo?"

"No, I'm his personal guard." He stepped closer.

"Then where's the king?" The sassy tone I used with Cottia marked my every word, and I didn't bother to hide it. "He's needed in the dining hall."

"I'll make sure to let him know."

"You'd better." I turned the knob and bolted.

Every step onward and downward pounded the scene back through my head.

Did I really just tell the Pedrozian king's personal guard that he'd better fetch his sovereign?

Humiliation rose through each stride forward, and dread tumbled through my stomach. I didn't want to go back and serve. No one would know I was gone as long as the Juan fellow retrieved his king. I should return to the caves and find out if Cottia and the others had made it back from the jailbreak.

CHAPTER 53
COTTIA

"We have fifteen minutes at most." I checked the clock over the polished fireplace mantle in the king's bedroom and glanced back at Prince Ezer looming over his papá. The giant bed in the middle of the room seemed to swallow the emaciated king who slept under thick blankets.

Thank the Ancient One, King Rodulfo finally recognized Ezer with a code word between the sovereigns. I'm still not sure Rodulfo fully believes our story, but at least he helped get us into the palace with his gift of a small physical change.

Isabelia opened the king's door. "I'll keep a lookout."

"We'll be in the queen's room shortly," I said.

"The queen's maid arrives promptly at 8 am." My sister vanished in a blink, somewhat recovered from the strain of our escape as long as she didn't have to veil anyone but herself.

The door tapped shut, leaving me staring at the intricate wood paneling of the wall surrounding it. So much wealth, and yet nothing could be done to revive the monarchs.

Turning back to Ezer, I stepped to his side, almost touching his soiled tunic sleeve on his elbow.

The gold in Ezer's eyes had a sheen of tears as he leaned over his papá's body. Only a month ago, the king could command a room by getting to his feet, and now he lay prostate and gaunt.

Ezer placed his palm over his papá's hand. "Can you try to heal him?" A hint of desperation leaked into his voice. He hadn't seen my new limitations yet.

The warmth in my chest curled in on itself. Though I could heal, I wasn't very good at it, even when my gifting was at full power. He knew that every healing I'd ever done had been wounds from battle or injuries I'd caused myself. Yet the bitter lines bracketing Ezer's mouth, made harsher by his skeletal body, left me without the heart to reject his request.

I slipped my fingers into the king's tepid palm. His fingernail beds had a hint of blue, an indication of poisoning. Warmth crept from my chest, down my arms, and seeped out of my fingertips. Ezer's tears flowed down his cheeks, though his expression remained the same stoic one he'd worn since I'd told him about his parents.

Though my gift trembled up his arm, it did not spread. The king remained still with only shallow breaths rising and falling in his chest. Oh, how I felt my weakness. The discouragement shriveled the little energy I had to offer.

"Sorry, Ezer." I disconnected from the king and stood. "We should bring him to the caves so I can try again. I'm certain someone is still poisoning him."

A mournful shroud covered the three of us.

"Who's his caretaker?" he asked.

"Señora Myla."

Ezer grunted in understanding. "Then we shouldn't disturb him. Lugging him through the caves might cause more harm." He sniffled but hardened his jaw.

"We can't leave him here." My forceful tone earned me a glare I'd never received from Ezer before.

The chamber door creaked open and closed. I whipped my head over to find only the tap of boots drawing near.

Isabelia appeared. "We have to go. She's coming early."

"*Cielos!*" I sped to the false panel that led to a secret passage. "We didn't even get to visit the queen."

I released the latch and slid the panel open. Isabelia and I strode into the hidden corridor, but Ezer hesitated. He curled his fingers into fists, but in the end, he joined us. He must have known I was right about needing to do something. We had to figure out a way to steal his parents away where I would get another chance to try and heal them.

We sealed ourselves in, and Isabelia lifted the lamp we'd left on the floor. Ezer pinched the bridge of his nose while streams flowed to his prickly jaw. Isabelia eyed me with a question marked along her eyebrows. We should keep going, yet I couldn't push Ezer. Instead, I wrapped my arms around him, soaking in his warmth, and he leaned his head over mine.

His body trembled with the pent-up sobs he tried to tame. He leaned close to my ear. "I'm sorry for my reaction."

"You're more than forgiven." I meant every word.

In turn, I should be begging for forgiveness for allowing him to give the usurper control when I needed to save my sister. Because I'd made a deal to free Cristobal. Ezer's parents drifted from life because I'd brought Whyzer Patro's wrath on me and on Giddel. I had to make this right. Even if Ezer hated me for it.

After sneaking glances through a peephole in the notch on a portrait, we observed Señora Myla tending to the queen and confirmed that adequate care was given.

The queen awakened and limply waved Señora Myla close to her side.

Señora Myla leaned over the queen and nodded. "Of course." She sped out of the room, leaving a wake of silence in the space.

Ezer slid the panel open without consulting any of us. What if Señora Myla returned? What if his mother screamed? But he approached, and the queen turned her gaze toward him. Her lips parted, letting out a small gasp. Her once vibrant eyes, the same shape and shade as Ezer's, now appeared dull and vacant.

"*Hijo*, my son, it's you." The queen lifted a frail hand, and Ezer swooped in to collect it.

They spoke in hushed tones for what felt like an eternity. The door at the other side of the room remained a crack open as if Señora Myla meant to come back any moment. Isabelia remained near, ready to make us disappear. We both knew her attempt might be futile, but it was our only defense now.

I checked out the rest of the room, searching for signs of foul play. Both monarchs falling ill was improbable. Yet the taste testers had failed to detect poison, and the servants hadn't found anything unusual in their quarters. I meandered to a small stack of books on her clean desk. The smell of old tomes met my nose with no hint of anything other.

Isabelia waved me over with bulging eyes and pressed lips, so I obeyed though I didn't see what we could do if we were caught. I passed a tray of tea and soup on the side table.

Ezer and his mamá continued to murmur in a private conversation, so I dared to smell and taste the soup. A salty and savory flavor spread through my mouth. Then I tried the tea. The moment the warm liquid touched the inside of my mouth, I caught a whiff of something off. I spit out the tea, and the porcelain handle slipped from my grip. I tried to catch it, but the cup bounced off my hand and shattered on the wooden floor.

"Poison," I murmured.

It was as if the quarters took a collective breath. Footfalls rushed from somewhere off in the passageway outside the room. Isabelia grabbed my wrist and yanked me toward the gaping hidden panel now three arm spans too far.

Ezer fled behind us, "Are you sure?"

The queen nodded weakly.

A hinge squeaked, and we bolted.

CHAPTER 54
COTTIA

"WE CAN'T JUST LEAVE them there." I paced in the center of the fellow's cave bedroom. Though the space was large enough for Ezer, Gema, Cristobal, Isabelia, and me, it seemed too confined with the tempest building inside of me. I had to make my failures right.

At the four-person table against the cave wall, Ezer supped on the cod soup Gema had brought from the palace like she did every day. A lamp overhead cast shadows upon the set of cots against the opposing wall, and a lamp on the table illuminated four empty bowls.

Isabelia stood at the door, ready to bolt should our argument grow too wild just like when we were children when Mamá and Papá still lived. Gema remained seated with arms crossed and a hint of a smirk tugging up one cheek. I couldn't tell if she was amused at the way Ezer shook his head, or was lost in her own thoughts.

Cristobal sank into his cot and wove his fingers behind his head to lounge against the wall. His insufferable calmness fueled my rage. Why wouldn't Ezer try to save his parents when they were being poisoned? And why wouldn't anyone make him see reason?

"Let's go back." I slid into the chair beside Gema and pressed my hands around my empty bowl. The fish soup inside my stomach churned, threatening to erupt from its confines. I swallowed hard. *What did the Ancient Tome say about anger?* It didn't produce the righteousness of the Ancient One.

Ezer placed his spoon beside his bowl and leaned back in his seat. "No."

Arms trembling, I pitched my voice low. "They will die if we leave them."

A muscle in Ezer's jaw leapt. "And how do you propose transporting my parents all the way from their comfortable beds through the narrow passages and to this pit?"

"I tasted poison in her tea." I slammed my fists on the table, and the dishes rattled.

Ezer's eyes narrowed to slits, but I wouldn't relent on my position. Behind his marbled green and gold irises, pain burbled where there should be none.

Gema got up and collected the bowls. "*Caramba!* These dishes need to go back to the palace for cleaning, and I'm certain there is more information to collect."

"Yes." Ezer leaned in to meet Gema's furtive glances. "Can you go to Rodulfo? He's a bit of an illusionist, but I believe he will plead our case with the Agata Sea Assembly."

"An illusionist? For some reason, I imagined a different name for his smaller abilities." The gifting was known for bending the wielder to trickery and being more of a grand nature.

Ezer responded, "Yes, but he's harmless and uses it to conceal his imperfections."

Gema flicked a look in my direction as if to ask me permission. When I gave her a reassuring blink, she said, "And why would he help me? I'm no one to him."

"Tell him this"—Ezer massaged his chin—"I'll agree to the amendments he'd like to make to our trade agreement. He already knows my situation and has heard our password."

"I wasn't there." Gema stepped around me hugging the dishes to her chest. "How is he to know I speak for you?"

"Speak the truth-telling oath," Ezer said.

"Are you mad?" I couldn't help the indignation that leaked into my tone. Any of the words with power could kill a person if they weren't followed. In fact, an oath is what got us in this mess in the first place. Ezer had lost his identity because he didn't keep an oath.

Ezer shifted in his seat. "Fine. Tell him that you remember the ball in Aracibel. He'll mention something about the prince. You will fake a laugh and say if only he would have remembered the pudding."

For aching seconds, Gema and I locked eyes. She twitched her nose as if she had an itch or a question. We didn't have many other options, and I couldn't install myself as a palace servant with her after I'd fled the palace that vile day when Ezer had lost his identity, when Cristobal had murdered in his rage, when this cave had become my tomb. No, I had other plans.

She sighed. "Remember the pudding," she mumbled to herself and stepped back, heading out of the room.

Isabelia grunted as Gema knocked into her.

Gema regained her balance. "Sorry," she said and fled the room.

"We should let you rest." My terse voice revealed my sentiment.

Isabelia left, and I marched several paces behind her.

"Cottia," Ezer called. He drew near and stopped when he squared up right in front of me. "I'm sorry about suggesting an oath."

"Good. Let's not make that a habit." I spun on my boot heels.

Ezer caught my elbow and twisted me around. "You know that I love you and don't blame you for anything." A shadow covered his face, but I felt his warmth in every tender syllable he spoke.

My bottom lip quivered. It hurt even more to know that I'd destroyed Ezer's family, yet he still loved me.

"Promise me, *corazón*, that you won't do anything reckless."

I could feel, more than see, him looking down at me. He called me his heart, and he was mine. Yet I couldn't lie to him and say I'd be careful or passive.

"Please, Cottia."

"I promise I will never purposely hurt you." That had to be enough for him because anything more would be false. He needed rest. I pulled away from his hold, though it pained me to do so after weeks of wishing to be by his side. If it took being reckless to love him, I would.

CHAPTER 55
GEMA

THE LOAD OF DISHES I collected and dumped in the washbasin every day did nothing for my reputation in the kitchen. Hopefully they wouldn't send me home before I could find King Rodulfo to plead Ezer's case with him.

"Here she comes again, finding the scraps all the other maids missed." Cook's caustic tone cut across the large space. "It's almost like she hides them from us on purpose."

A tiny maid with reddened hands lifted her head from the washbasin. She placed the last pot on a counter from the darkened corner of the room. The fire from the open stove highlighted her ash brown hair and the sneer twisting her lips.

"Don't worry about it." I bumped the frail maid to the side with my hip. "I'll scrub these."

The washing maid sped to the worn dining table where Cook placed the leftover food before her. Footfalls rushed toward us from the passage just beyond the adjoining kitchen and servants' dining area.

The majordomo, with his prim doublet and tidy mustache, set his fiery gaze on me. "You decided to grace us again."

After I'd disappeared for hours, I understood his frustration.

"Gema is wanted upstairs in the *blue room*." The majordomo enunciated blue room with the strangest accent I'd ever heard, and I'd been around a lot of foreigners when I lived in Castillo Patro.

I wiped my hands on a towel when it struck me how odd the request was. "Are you sure he requested me? I've never even met the king."

The majordomo strode to the dining table, removed his overcoat, and placed his garment on a hook. He fixed a deep bowl of soup and a small plate of bread. "He specifically requested the pretty redhead. Oh, and Cook, could you brew some coffee?"

Heat flared up my neck. Had Juan told him about our little interlude? Even remembering how I'd caught the half-dressed man coiled a ball of nerves in the pit of my stomach.

Cook shifted her hips to the kettle and got straight to brewing. She then snatched my drying towel. "Your pretty little face should be up there giving the Pedrozian king his requested meal." She puckered her lips at the majordomo who bent over in that instant to grab a silver tray out of a cupboard. An unfortunate slip of his pants showed much more skin on his back end than either of us wanted to witness.

I guffawed, and Cook hid a real smile behind her fist—a once in a lifetime sight.

The majordomo straightened up and harrumphed while adjusting his pant slippage. He tried to play off his indiscretion by ignoring our reactions and preparing the food.

Cook threw the towel over one shoulder and swaggered back with the coffee cup in her hand. "Don't think we didn't notice, Señor Majordomo." She placed the coffee on the tray and chuckled.

The majordomo flushed a crimson color, and I tried to keep from letting my laughter bubble out when I took the tray from his grip. The heavy platter and sloshing liquids did more to steady my breath than I could have done on my own.

Up the service stairs to the second floor, I kept the soup from spilling and the coffee in the cup—a miracle if you asked me. My feet continued to shuffle forward over the hardwood floor and through the sconce-lit corridor. By the time I arrived in front of King Rodulfo's polished door, I felt heat spreading over my skin, making flames dance through my simple dress. Maybe the king saw me in the corridors, but this gown didn't suggest I was a maid. It was a special process to get me new clothes; I couldn't wear just anything, as new frocks risked being burnt off my skin.

I placed the tray on a side table set into the wall and knocked on the door.

Seconds passed, but I wouldn't barge in again. I pounded the polished wood and tried to recite Prince Ezer's coded conversation in my head.

Was it 'what did you bring to the ball?' or something about pudding? I should have written it down.

The hinge creaked, and the blond-haired servant from earlier peered at me through the crack in the door. "Come inside."

I collected the tray and strode into the chamber. The front portion had a small sofa and reception area with a table in the center of the space. "His Majesty requested me?" I set the food on the table and bowed my head in an exemplary submissive stance the majordomo would have praised if he were present.

"Actually, that was me." He closed us in the chamber and approached. "I just wanted to apologize for earlier today."

"No, I shouldn't have come in." I risked a glance at the tall fellow who carried himself with perfect posture.

His crystal blue eyes met mine, and I should have looked away, but something about him made me want to study every feature. His mouth lifted in one corner, showing off a smile that put Prince Ulyses's to shame. A prick of guilt attacked my chest at how quickly my eyes wandered.

"Could you get King Rodulfo?" I asked.

"I'm Juan, his personal attendant, remember?" He stepped even closer. Firelight reflected off his too-perfect sloped nose and flash of white teeth.

"It's a matter of great importance."

"Do you want me to interrupt the king's fellowship downstairs to retrieve him?"

"Unless you understand the joke about pudding from Aracibel, I need the king."

He stilled a moment and raked his fingers through his cropped hair. "I do know that one. It's Prince Ezer, isn't it?"

I nodded, but a wave of panic swept through me. *What if the impostor is impersonating King Rodulfo's servant?*

He pulled out a chair at the table and invited me to sit. "What does Prince Ezer need, and how can I keep my head in the process?"

"Prince Ezer said something about a new accord." I let my bottom touch the seat but remained on edge in case I had to run.

Juan sat across from me and gulped down the cup of coffee. "So, he's finally willing to acquiesce to the king's request."

It wasn't a question, but a bold statement of triumph. The steadiness of his countenance teased me to ask more questions about kingdom affairs, but I was acting the part of a mere servant. Even sitting across from Juan might prove the end of my spying position if I were caught.

I got to my feet. "What should I tell the prince?"

He slurped the fish soup, keeping his attention on me.

Crossing my arms to hide the nervous flames slipping from my fingertips, I asked, "Is that a yes, you'll help Prince Ezer?"

"It's an, I'll have to talk to the king." He scooted the chair backward, still watching me with his unnerving focus. "Why hasn't Prince Ulyses done anything? Certainly, he knows his brother better than anyone. Why haven't you gone to him?"

Hearing Prince Ulyses's name sent a shiver up my spine. I couldn't admit Ulyses's role in hiding us away nor his part in keeping me as a maid to spy on the palace from a different angle. I opened my mouth, and Juan leaned forward with a knowing smile shifting over his mouth.

"You can keep your secrets." Juan smoothed a hand over his chin. "Do I have to ask the majordomo for the pretty redhead again when I retrieve King Rodulfo's answer?"

"No, my name is Gema." I said a little too forcefully. "You see, the cook and maids will never let me live down your king asking for the pretty redhead. Could you meet me in the gardens in the gazebo on the cliffside?"

"Are you going to stand there waiting for me each night?"

I chuckled. "You can put a lamp by this window, and we'll meet when the moonlight touches the rose gardens."

He stood, now seeming like a giant, and walked me out the door. As I passed through the doorway, our hands brushed, and an electrical pulse shot between us. I inhaled sharply and met his gaze. The cerulean swirl of color staring back at me was beautiful.

And there I went again, moving on from Ulyses's heartbreak so quickly when I would have done anything to spend the rest of my days studying in the library with the reclusive prince.

Juan reached for me, but I fled backward. "Let me escort you downstairs."

"You really shouldn't." I had to go before I dreamed up a new life with someone beyond my station again.

"I think I might." He closed the door and got into step beside me. "I've been here many times and haven't seen you before."

"There are a lot of servants," I retorted.

"Your hair stands out."

Patting my braided curls, I wished to shrink to the floor and have a fresh batch of churros to keep my thoughts from exploding. Juan's attentions and Ezer's need for a miracle kept my midsection in a fiery ball of nerves. The impostor had an entire military to back him up, and we had us. My stomach growled even at the thought of those sweet morsels of goodness.

Juan glanced down at my hand over my abdomen. This is what pregnant women must feel like. We took the stairwell down and ran into the majordomo who lifted his trim eyebrow at me for walking with Juan.

"Oh, there's a servants' door ahead." I pointed.

The majordomo stopped mid-stride and turned around to meet us at the base of the staircase. "Señor, could you retrieve King Rodulfo for the assembly? Decisions can't be made without him."

Juan swept one of my hands into his and pressed a kiss to my knuckles. "It was my pleasure to meet you." He winked at me, and a hesitant quirk of his cheek had me guessing at his motives for requesting me to serve him.

The majordomo cleared his throat, and that sent me racing down the servants' stairwell to the kitchen.

What am I going to tell Ezer? I couldn't have called that interlude successful, since we didn't exactly gain an ally in reinstating the prince. Honestly, I think he had a mild infatuation with me, and I liked it a lot.

CHAPTER 56
COTTIA

"What's Prince Ezer going to say about this?" Cristobal dragged his hand along the rough wall, and a pinch of doubt wrinkled on his forehead. "We should have brought your sister."

The glow of our skin, created by our activated giftings, reflected off the old stones in the hidden passageways behind the palace walls. Not even the scurrying rodents could deter me from these necessary actions. Señora Myla and the palace guards could not be trusted.

"Isabelia needs to rest." I hauled a wooden cot but continued forward, crossing into the palace from the escape caves.

Cristobal grabbed at the frame corner of the cot dragging on the floor and yanked me back.

I jerked the frame from his grip. Heat flared through my blood, and I swung the makeshift bed at Cristobal.

He slammed against the stone wall and groaned. "Caramba! Cottia, are you trying to kill me?" He barked his question, slicing through a volatile layer in my soul, the one that still accused him of being a murderer.

My breath trembled. I had acted without thinking and without heeding the cost just like I would have in previous days. We had freed Ezer, yet we were watching the king and queen deteriorate without lifting a finger to help them. I couldn't stand to see the usurper crowned because of our actions. But if Ezer's parents recovered, they would rectify everything. It's not like Whyzer Patro had an army of impersonators.

With slow, jerky movements, Cristobal pushed from against the wall and adjusted his plain brown tunic. "I know you love the prince and can't stand to see him hurting, but you know his parents could die even if you carry them away." He risked touching my hand. His calloused fingers gently squeezed my palm, an attempt to bring me comfort.

"I can do this alone if you don't want to help." The lie almost seemed plausible with the overwrought emotions flowing through my blood.

He pinned me down with his dark saucers for eyes. "Your prince might behead me if anything goes wrong."

"And what if it goes right?" I jabbed my index finger at his chest, putting every bit of my frustration into that motion. "You're the same assassin you've always been, thinking about what you could get and what you could lose. Everything has to be about you. Have you thought about the two people dying because their fake son is poisoning them? How a whole kingdom of people will be under Whyzer Patro's thumb the moment the usurper attains full power? You don't care. You are the one who brought Pascual here, the one who allowed this to happen." I adjusted my hold on the cot, determined to use the rickety thing. One of the royals would have to be left behind to keep away from danger while we transported the other.

He caught my arm again. "Stop that. Saving these people isn't going to restore life to everyone we've ended. You know you're not this worked up just because of Giddel. You're in love with Prince Ezer."

I swallowed the walnut-sized truth I could never say out loud again, especially not when so much more was at stake than a broken heart or two.

"My chances were never good in the first place." He shrugged. "Don't worry, I won't tell him you love him after you save his parents. I'm sure he will already know." He let go of me and grabbed on to the edge of the cot, finally helping me carry the light but awkward thing.

"Fine, you left the whyzer, but are you even trying to change?"

He looked back over his shoulder. "I'm here, aren't I? I'm helping even though I could be across the Agata Sea starting a new life. I don't feel good about what happened with Señora Virginia. Come on." He tipped his head to the side and led the way while I carried the tail end.

His cocky gait and handsome face would surely grab the attention of a million other señoritas. Just not me.

We continued through the passages in silence and turned a corner to climb a flight of rough-hewn steps. My heart pounded. Cristobal was right that my motives for sneaking into the palace weren't purely altruistic, but he was wrong about everything else. I had to make things right. We finally arrived at the royal wing where the king also had a portrait with peepholes that gave us access to everything transpiring within the suite.

The cot I set up covered three-quarters of the width in the narrow passage. Muffled voices bled through the walls.

A male voice said, "If they die during the meetings, everyone will be here to witness your coronation. Even Prince Ulyses couldn't oppose you."

I positioned myself behind a low peephole. The man who had spoken was one of Whyzer Patro's implants. The lady sitting at the bedside wore a severe bun at the nape of her neck like Myla. When the lady swiveled to face the man, she had Myla's face yet wore a twisted smirk so conniving that goosebumps rolled over my flesh.

Myla stood. "I'm already working on it."

"Where'd you put the maid?" the man asked.

"She's locked in the palace hold." The fake Myla retrieved a vial from her pocket and dripped a liquid into the king's mouth. "I need the maid alive for inspiration and to take my place in the hanging she'll surely face when the healers examine the king's and queen's bodies. You get to be done hiding the evidence of poisoning by tomorrow. But no more slacking until then."

The man touched the king's fingers with a glowing touch. "That should be enough to keep them off our trail."

Myla examined the king's nail beds with clinical appraisal. "On the other hand, I heard the healers will be up here shortly."

The two exited the chamber and slammed the door in their wake. I counted three minutes in my head to assure myself that they'd exited the wing.

Cristobal kept his mouth locked shut. His flaring nose revealed his shared rage at how his old companion made light of the king's destruction. How could Cristobal object after witnessing his former associate in action?

I stuck my hand in the crevice on the wall to release the latch and pushed the door open. Cristobal freed the edges of the covers beneath the king, and I removed the blankets atop his body. We lugged the drugged monarch from the bed to the cot in painstaking silence.

Cristobal and I managed to lay the king on the canvas fabric held up by the small frame that left his bare feet hanging off the edge. I retrieved a blanket to place over the king to keep him warm while he waited for us to save the queen. We closed the wall panel and sidestepped around the king, grateful he was sleeping and not dead.

We made quick work of retrieving the queen. Cristobal scooped her out of bed with a small blanket to keep her warm in transfer. Unlike with the king, Cristobal didn't strain under her weight. She shifted to curl into Cristobal's chest, but didn't awaken, probably poisoned once more by Pascual who had taken Myla's form.

The darkened corridors proved long, but we marched at a quick clip so we could return and retrieve the king as quickly as possible. Cristobal remained sure-footed. A few times he readjusted his hold, showing signs of fatigue. How in all Agata were we going to carry the king through the passages and then through the hidden cave system?

After what seemed like an hour, Cristobal slid into the cave room where Isabelia, Gema, and I stayed.

Isabelia turned over on her cot and blinked awake. "Is that the queen?"

I nodded.

"Ezer is going to be upset." Isabelia rushed to the queen's side the moment Cristobal set her down on an extra cot. "What poison did they use?"

"I'm not exactly sure," I admitted. "Get some rest. You can't help us if you're spent."

She remained at the queen's side, and I was too exhausted to argue.

"We can't do it on our own." Cristobal wiped a sheen of sweat from his forehead. "It's too far to carry a sleeping man."

If Ezer were reasonable, we could ask him to help, but that wasn't the case. Let Ezer hate me for trying to save his parents. It was the right thing to do. An idea floated to my mind and tickled the part of me that believed all things were possible.

"Perhaps we could get someone else to help us." I tilted my head to the side and gestured for Cristobal to follow.

Cristobal grunted. "You better stick up for me if something goes wrong. Ezer made it clear that we shouldn't move his parents."

I marched into the darkness of the caves, ready to face the heat of Ezer's rage. The Ancient One knew I couldn't watch such evil befall the king and continue to do nothing.

CHAPTER 57
GEMA

Hard bread hit my lips as I hunched over a rough-hewn table in the servants' dining area. Piercing blue eyes winked through my mind and tempted me to draw a little closer. I dipped the hunk of bread in my fish soup. Cook had already escaped to her quarters beside the kitchen. Even the frail maid who washed the pots and pans had left me once I promised to clean off the table.

"Psst ... Gema." Cottia's voice whispered behind me.

I spun around to find an ember-lit kitchen with no shifting shadows and an empty passage. The sandstone walls were sprinkled with deep shadows from all the grooves and imperfections left on their surfaces. There wasn't a sign of another human. Even my subconscious was toying with me.

"Here, you dolt," Cottia said.

Now, I knew I wasn't hallucinating. I had been known for insulting myself from time to time with many words, but that wasn't one of them. Squinting into the corners of the dining area where tan stones, mouse traps, and heavy shadows lay, I couldn't find a hint of a person. Blood fired up through my veins with an aching force, but I reeled it back with a few deep breaths.

The cupboard behind me rattled with glass clinking against wood.

I yelped.

"Shhh!"

I slapped my hands over my mouth, trying to calm the sharp tang of fear that shocked more than a potent hot sauce.

Cook's door cracked open, revealing the grumpy old woman's bedraggled form. "Quiet down out there."

"Sorry, I saw a"—I glanced around the room—"a lizard."

Cook grunted and slammed her door shut, which was the best response I could hope for from the woman.

Cottia slid the cupboard over the slightest bit more to squeeze into the gap of space between the hidden door and the wall. "I need a favor."

My head tipped back. "Not another one."

"Please." Cottia slipped into the chair beside me. "Cristobal and I can't carry the king on our own. If you could get Prince Ulyses for us—"

"No."

"The king will die." Cottia clasped my upper arm with her too-big eyes rounded and picking up the sparkle of light from the single candle on the table. "Please."

The part of my heart ready to revolt, puke, and throw a tantrum threatened to explode, but she didn't know what she requested. I hadn't told her about Ulyses throwing away the possibility of our relationship. "Couldn't we ask another burly man to help us?"

She shook her head. "Who else do you trust in the hidden passages?"

Juan's name crept to my lips, but I bit it back. She didn't know about him.

"Where should we meet?" I asked.

"Behind the king's quarters." Cottia got up and tiptoed into the gap in the wall. She angled her chin high and pushed back her shoulders with confidence that I would get Ulyses to the meetup spot without any trouble. The cupboard slid shut with the subtle jingle of dishes.

I'd have to face the one person who could make my gift combust with his mere presence, yet I couldn't let Cottia down.

CHAPTER 58
GEMA

EVERY STEP FORWARD WRIGGLED doubt and fear into my legs. I pushed the servants' door open and entered the main atrium. Marble floors reflected flames from sconces on the opulent walls bedecked with panels chiseled to be masterpieces of their own. Baritone laughter echoed from somewhere deeper in the palace. The council must still be in session, or their gathering might have shifted into male camaraderie.

Sweet churro goodness, what am I doing? Cottia had no idea what she had requested of me. I turned right to enter the dim passage, ready to combust at the slightest provocation. Would I be admitted? Would I be able to talk to Ulyses without throwing up or being turned into a fireball?

The closer and closer I got, the more my nerves quivered through my limbs. I had marched into enemy castles and flirted with unscrupulous men when Whyzer Patro was my master. Yet, facing the fellow who broke my heart caused more trouble than any former mission.

The candlelight from the parlor spilled before the entrance. Running wasn't an option since the impostor's every decision would be dictated by a vengeful Whyzer Patro.

I marched into the room to find men at tables betting gold coins and others standing around holding goblets full of who knew what spirits. The room could fit a half dozen horses, spacious enough for all, yet the tension between the men made it feel as though they were a heap of cod in a barrel.

"Gema?" Ulyses clutched my elbow and dragged me out the door. "What are you doing here?"

Embers sparked in my belly, heating my insides to a dangerous temperature. "Don't grab me like that." I yanked myself out of his hold. "How else was I to reach you?"

He pitched his voice low and led me further from the party. "You could have entered the servants' room and come to attend us."

"Like that would have been allowed." I let my tone drop to a low rumble.

Ulyses looked over his shoulder and visibly swallowed. "I think I'm getting somewhere with King Rodulfo."

"But they're taking your fa—"

As if on cue, Juan exited the parlor with long strides. "Prince Ulyses, is everything in good order?"

An idea sparked in my mind. I snaked my arm around Juan's and gave my most compelling smile, the one that pressed into my cheeks and made me feel beautiful. "If it's not my favorite dignitary."

Juan wagged his eyebrows and slipped his hand into mine. He brought my knuckles to his lips, leaving a gentle warmth over my skin. I winked at him in a flirty mode I hadn't exercised in months.

Ulyses flinched, which fed the part of me that longed for the prince to beg me to forgive him. Instead, he turned to Juan with a deadpan expression. "And whom might you be?"

Juan bowed his head a fraction. "I am King Rodulfo's personal guard. You might not have noticed me standing among the men. The king would like to give his support about the matter of which we discussed."

I tipped my head to the side and whipped my braid from my back to over my shoulder, using the same tactics that always communicated my interest in a fellow. "Señor Juan, is it the matter we were chatting about earlier?"

"Precisely." Juan's chipper tone kindled the flames in my chest. "I very much enjoyed our last meeting."

"I see that I'm unnecessary in this conversation." Ulyses pressed his lips together and gave me a slight bow. "Work out the details with him instead."

"No, Ulyses, our friends have a message for you." I chased after him, but he didn't slow his pace until I caught a hold of his elbow.

Ulyses spun to face me and drew near enough to be heard at the softest of whispers. "I'm not here to play games." He clamped his mouth shut, and tears coated his eyes. With a few blinks and several deep breaths, he continued in a softer tone. "I think it's best if we keep some distance between us for a while."

"But your father needs you."

"Believe me, I know."

"No, you don't." I reached for him, but a look kept me from touching him.

He pitched his voice low. "We can't continue to act as if there aren't mountain-sized obstacles between us." He peered over my shoulder and tipped his head as if to point at Juan three arm spans behind me. "Juan seems enamored by you. Go ahead. You have my blessing to pursue him. I must get back to forming alliances that will back my claims." His forcefulness brought steam to my eyes. He spun on his heels and disappeared back into the parlor.

I trudged back toward Juan who cocked his head in question. Cottia still needed help and Ulyses's papá lay in a cot behind the wall of his own chamber. I clenched my fists as if that would make me strong enough to lug a limp man the ridiculous distance through the hidden passages and to our cave.

"Please, tell me what's wrong." Juan squeezed my shoulder and squared up to me with a heart-felt gleam that said he'd help with anything.

"I have a favor to ask of you."

He leaned his ear closer.

"But you have to promise me that this remains a secret." My jaw quivered. Though I had a sense of comfort with Juan, I didn't know him. Yet who else might help?

"Yes, if the secret remains between me, you, and my king."

"I understand." My limp voice betrayed my hesitation. "Follow me."

After the long trudge from the palace through the hidden passages to the caves, Cristobal and Juan laid the king on a cot near his sleeping son, who would be furious when he saw what Cottia had orchestrated.

I could go for churros.

Of course, I'd never say that aloud since it seemed insensitive and there was no way I would wake Cook in the middle of the night to make them for me. Though considering the long walk, it might actually be early morning when I returned to the palace.

Cristobal wiped his sweaty brow and crouched beside Cottia. Juan caught his breath beside me. His much too fancy doublet screamed *out of place*.

"So, who'd like me to make them hot chocolate?" I asked to lighten the mood. Hot chocolate was a much more practical treat to quell the riot inside of us.

"That's a hard pass for me." Cottia fled through the doorway on the opposite side of the passage into our cave room. "See you tomorrow."

"I should get some rest before Prince Ezer tries to slay me," Cristobal said.

"Don't be so dramatic." I dug my fingers into my biceps.

Cristobal crossed beside Juan and patted his shoulder. "Thank you. You know we'll have to kill you if you tell anyone." He chuckled as he entered the fellows' bedroom.

Juan lifted an eyebrow at me, but I couldn't reassure him in any way that Cristobal was joking.

"Let me walk you back to the palace." I let the dim warmth in my blood burn through my skin to light the way.

"Caramba!" Juan's eyes popped wide open, but his features twisted into delighted awe.

"I'm sorry we got you wrapped up in this mess." I led him to the cliff doorway and out to the beach path.

A cool breeze brushed against my skin from the peaceful waters. On the beach front, the moon lit our sandy path back to the palace. Each sinking step reminded me that I had nothing left to keep me here besides Cottia. If I knew she was well, I'd flee for good to start a new life.

Moonlight graced Juan who kept stealing glances at me.

"Just ask, I see you looking."

He chuckled with a light timbre. "You're very forward."

"You know my secrets. I think we're past the formalities."

"I highly doubt that."

Tilting my head in his direction, I appraised the cocky lift of his chin and his commanding stride. "You walk like a king and aptly carried a body through dark corridors without asking a question. I think we should focus on what this favor is going to cost us."

He shifted his lips into a pensive smile, almost too cute to drag my gaze away from.

"Cielos! That high? What will it be? A mortal oath to be your servant for life? Or should we come back to get Ezer in the morning? I'm sure your king would love a piece of Giddel."

"Nothing like that from me." He pointed to a peninsula of boulders up ahead, the same ones where my heart was torn to shards. "Why don't we sit?"

"So, now you plan on drowning me." I jabbed my finger at his chest.

The sweet melody of his laughter danced in the night air. "All right, you caught me. I'd love to have some of that hot chocolate you offered everyone."

I squinted, trying to play coy, but I already knew my answer. "If you insult my hot chocolate, whatever compensation you ask for will be off the table."

"Understood." He saluted, which tickled something desperate or slap-happy within my fiery insides.

"Good. Come this way." I marched him up to the palace and into a servants' entrance.

A dark stone corridor lined with closed doors lay before us. All the sleeping servants were stowed away for the night. I tapped my index finger over my lips to remind him to be quiet. Cook's snores carried from her room through the closed door, which promised some time alone. We still didn't want to push our luck.

"You sit at that table, and I'll whip up a coconut chocolate." I pointed to the dining room right next to the kitchen.

He quirked his eyebrow halfway up his forehead.

With the sconce dead and only embers from the stove giving off an orange glow, I had to admit, the table looked a little creepy. "Take it or leave it. I'm not having you breathing down my neck."

"Oh, but that's the whole reason I accepted your hot chocolate."

"To breathe down my neck?"

"To get to know the stunning señorita who caught me shirtless in my room."

I slapped his chest. "You don't have to keep reminding me about that. It was embarrassing enough." I poured coconut milk, cane sugar, and leftover cocoa powder into a small pot. A flame burst from my fingertip onto the stove, and I stirred the milky substance.

Though Juan leaned against the wall a couple of arm spans away, he emanated an enthralling energy through the room. I peeked over my shoulder, and the way his eyes caught the stove light had my heartbeat racing.

Forget Ulyses with his books and strange dream and inability to commit. I could have someone with a good position who wanted my company.

I grabbed a couple of glasses and poured the hot chocolate. "Sit. I'll turn on a candle for us."

He obeyed. I lit a single candle and slipped into the seat adjacent to him. We exchanged gazes with unspoken questions. I lifted my cup and sipped. The sweet chocolaty goodness warmed my tongue a little too much, but I wasn't about to spit it out. I swallowed and blew into my cup. Warm tendrils of steam raced up my face.

Say something.

Speaking had never been a problem for me but for some reason, him calling me stunning clamped my mouth shut.

"Here's the favor I'd like for my hard work. But I don't want you to think you must say yes. The exchange is that you allow me to make such a request on short acquaintance."

"Proceed." My heart throbbed. The dagger in my boot suddenly chafed. This request could either be ridiculously sweet or the most forward invitation I'd ever received.

Juan placed his cup in front of him and leaned his elbows on the tabletop. "Would you consider coming back to Pedroz with me?"

He remained still as if he held his breath for an answer. The expectation in those crystal blue eyes danced with something thrilling and forbidden.

"We only just met." I licked my bottom lip, trying to find the perfect words. "Are you asking for something more?"

The serious expression cracked into a gentle grin. "I've yet to find someone like you, and we don't have more than this week to get to know each other. I have connections in Pedroz and can find you a position in the palace so we can get to know each other. You can always return to Giddel since our kingdoms are very connected."

This was a very forward invitation, but it didn't seem indecent. Though a part of me flared to life, the other part saw Ulyses's anger when he'd told me Juan would be a good match.

"I'll think on it." I swept away our dishes and cleaned them with the little water left in the washbasin. So many questions stabbed through my thoughts, tugging me this way and that. I wanted to get away, but I also wasn't so mad to trust just anyone. I returned and pinched out the candlelight.

He sighed. "Let me walk you back."

"Look, I don't even know what you do for King Rodulfo that you have access to his chamber and that you stand by during nighttime meetings."

The seat shifted behind him, and the orange glow from the stove embers lit up the front of his face. "What if I told you that I am his body double?" His gaze remained fixed on me as if he meant to dissect my reaction.

From all my time with Whyzer Patro, I'd learned to keep my facial muscles still. It made sense that Prince Ezer wasn't the only one with a body double, though Yurde could never pass as Prince Ezer on closer inspection. I touched his prickly cheek. "Then, I see why you only have sword callouses on your fingers."

We both looked at his mostly unmarred hands.

"You noticed?"

I straightened my back and did a tiny shoulder shimmy. "It's my job to notice details."

"Tell me about your parents, about your life. You don't have to answer me now, but I am sincere in wanting to get to know you."

My lips pinched together. We'd chatted for far too long, and I allowed myself to daydream out loud. "My papá ... " I let him into an imaginary world where I got lost from two parents who loved me and still searched for me every day for the last five years. Though exhaustion tugged at my eyelids, this tale comforted me from reality.

It was then that I remembered why I had to return. Cottia. She couldn't be alone when Ezer woke up to find his father beside him. Why had I let myself get swept away by Juan?

"I lied to you. I'm sorry. Papá is dead." The truth poured out after so many half-truths. Heat filled my cheeks, and I fled, unable to meet his gaze.

Partway down the kitchen, Juan caught up to me, scooped me in his arms, and drew my body to his. He pressed his lips to mine. An unraveling of butterflies tumbled out of my belly and fluttered through my limbs. I couldn't have pictured a more romantic moment. Tears fogged my sight at how perfect this felt.

He whispered against my lips, "I want to see you again."

"Me too." I rocked up and kissed his cheek, hesitant to part, but I really did need to return to Cottia.

"King Rodulfo will support your cause, but try to gather your soldiers. Can we meet here tomorrow night? The accord has a couple more days."

It was impossible to think while captured in his arms with the cloying scent of sugar and chocolate on his breath. "I don't know if the soldiers will listen."

"We're going to restore the kingdom to its rightful heir." He traced my jawline and let go of my waist. "It was my pleasure to get to know you better. Consider my offer." He kissed my knuckles, looking up at me with a glint of mischief dancing along every line of his face.

I inhaled deeply, wanting to snatch him in my arms and kiss his cheek again, but I resisted the urge by fleeing out of the servants' corridor and down to the beach.

The cool darkness of twilight tousled my curls and refreshed my overheated body. I continued to stride along the path, cursing my thoughtlessness. I should have found a way to sneak into the hidden passages behind the walls rather than going out in the elements. I sped down a set of stairs and leapt onto the sandy beach where my boots sank down.

The remnant of moonlight reflected off the Agata Sea, giving a better view of where I needed to step or leap over a fallen log, but I also had to move faster if I wanted to make it by daybreak.

One check over my shoulder revealed an empty beach and lapping water on the shores. But when I spun my head back around, I crashed into a person.

Strong hands clasped my wrists. A large silhouette of a man hovered above me. "Whyzer Patro's been hunting you."

My heart punched against my breastbone. Not a moment to think. I flared with heat. An explosion of flames burst from my skin.

Burn, I thought. *Burn.*

CHAPTER 59
COTTIA

I squatted beside the queen's cot in my cave room and pressed my hand to her forearm, thankful to find it still warm with life. Her tall nose and the serious arch of her lips had the same shape as Prince Ezer's behind me. His expression was meant to show his displeasure, but the queen's breathing body solidified my resolve.

"Why did you disregard my wishes?" Ezer leaned against the rock wall of the cave and ran his fingers through his hair.

"They would have died up there. Señora Myla isn't the trusted servant you believed her to be." I let the warmth of my gifting slip from within my chest and pour through my arms. It searched again in the sinew of the queen's sluggish body. The few hours of sleep I'd gotten wouldn't help me perform miracles.

"Señora Myla is the most trustworthy of them all. She can be harsh, but she raised me—"

"It isn't her." I pushed the energy to touch on a different trajectory and prayed beneath my breath. *Ancient One, help me to understand what I need to fix. Mark my gifting on the path I need to find.*

Ezer continued to speak. "But Pascual can't be everyone." Though he continued to make a case for Señora Myla's innocence, I couldn't hear more than the cadence of his troubled words.

My gifting dove deeper and traveled along a path I'd never wandered before. I pressed my eyes shut, lost as to how I'd gotten there. The Ancient One had answered, yet I didn't understand. Whatever pressed against the tentacles of my reach pulsed with an angry rhythm and made the queen's core bulge. Another pressure deadened where it should have been alive.

What does this mean? I prayed again. Desperation worked its way into my soul. If it weren't for me and my decision to retrieve my sister, the usurper would have no hold over Giddel. To think of how I'd scrambled to collect poisonous flowers the moment Whyzer Patro had threatened my happiness. I was so selfish. Then it hit me.

If I recognized the poisonous flowers on the cliff, wouldn't another of Whyzer Patro's lackeys have done the same? The shape and color of the antidote flower traced through my mind, though the actual name for it remained just out of reach.

"Cottia, are you listening?" Ezer's hand touched my shoulder. "Did you find something?"

Like a whisper on the wind, the name of a prickly-looking flower echoed in the recesses of my mind.

I turned toward Ezer, whose expression slackened from the anger he had carried moments ago into worry lines arching in his gaze. "It's certainly poison. Her body is shutting down, but I think there's an antidote."

"Where can we find it?" He kneeled at the bedside. "I'll go get it; just tell me where to find it."

In that moment, a pink streak seemed to blur across the room.

"Isabelia?" I called. "Isa—"

She strode into view, wearing bright attire only she could pull off while trying to hide. "What do you need?"

I spilled my list in the matter-of-fact tone I used whenever doing a job. "Gema hasn't returned from the palace, or perhaps she slept there. Prince Ezer can't leave the caves with his parents so ill. Prince Ulyses is in those meetings. Could you stay here with Prince Ezer while I retrieve a flower with Cristobal?"

"Of course." Isabelia nodded.

"No." Ezer's vehemence startled me.

"You must understand that we haven't time ..." I stopped myself from finishing the sentence. We hadn't time for his jealousy, the seed I'd planted to push Ezer away. The fake courtship I'd flaunted before Ezer had been captured.

"Can't Isabelia retrieve the flower?" His chin trembled with hot emotion. "If anything is to happen, we need you. I need you here."

I cupped his stubbled cheek, and he turned his gaze toward me. The lamp caught the sheen of tears he didn't let fall. How could I argue with him when all I wanted was to stay near and wrap my arms around him to bring him comfort? The king lay in the next cave room over, suffering the same fate as his wife.

"I'll stay." I rubbed my thumb along his cheek. "I can draw Isabelia and Cristobal a picture and tell her where to find the flower. She'll slip past the guard much easier than I could, anyway."

Ezer exhaled a heavy breath. The smallest hint of a smile climbed his cheek before it faltered.

I tore from my spot beside Ezer and strode to the table with parchments atop the slick surface. Prince Ulyses continually replenished our stacks. I scratched out a quick sketch with the pencil and darkened its unique qualities.

"Where can I find it?" Isabelia's chin reached over my shoulder.

"Near the river at the first glen." I positioned my body to cut off her view. I still had to label the parts and write out directions.

"Is it the one south of the river or north, closer to Castillo Patro?"

A flash of annoyance tore through me, but I inhaled a long breath to steady my impatience. "Why don't you find Cristobal so I can say the directions once?"

She nabbed a candle and skipped from the room. Her humming echoed through the passageway, far more joyous than this situation deserved.

A minute later, she returned, holding onto Cristobal's forearm. Her lashes fluttered as she peeked over at the ex-assassin. Now, I understood why she'd skipped and hummed with joy.

Cristobal's dimples pressed hard into his cheeks with the most forced smile I'd ever seen. His shoulders slumped as if he took no joy in allowing himself to be dragged by my little sister. Who would have thought that the tall assassin could be captured so easily?

"What's this about a secret mission?" Cristobal asked.

I crossed my last letter and shoved the paper into his grasp. "Get this for me."

He caught my hand. "Anything for you." He leaned down and pressed his warm lips on my knuckles.

Heat crept up my neck, and I whipped my head around to meet Ezer's eye. Ezer stilled. The muscle on his cheek ticked as he watched. I yanked my hand free, and a smirk overtook Cristobal's features. He deserved a slap for that one, but I resisted the impulse.

For seconds, the calm of the cave sounds blanketed us. A drip of water somewhere in our dark space flowed into a pool. The hum of seawater crashing against the cliff intoned its constant melody, even through the thick wall of rock between us and the water. Then I heard something different: footfalls.

Sparking my gift, I pushed my sluggish powers out my chest and sparked my gifting to life. Isabelia vanished. A split-second later, Ezer's and Cristobal's forearms glowed with power.

"It's Gema," Cristobal suggested.

My reach didn't go far enough to feel beyond a few arm spans in front of me. I slipped past Cristobal and rammed into a body when trying to exit the ladies' bedroom.

Isabelia grunted, but I shoved her invisible form aside and continued around the rocky path to stare down the blackened passage. I sparked my gifting again, this time reaching into the blackness of the cave. My invisible touch grasped at air, thin and cool. I stretched the invisible thread of my gift, which floated like a transparent vine many arm spans away.

Sweat trickled along my temples with the exertion. Cristobal and Ezer stepped out of the room to my left, also straining to reach whoever or whatever might be out there.

A faint clicking echoed, and light flashed to my right.

The cave doorway opened from the outside, and the silhouette of a giant person stood on the other side. Shadows within the cave tangled into the darkness along the edges of my vision.

CHAPTER 60
COTTIA

THE FIGURE AT THE cave entrance was Gema, and a brawny man clutched a charred dagger at her neck. Had the Juan fellow tricked us, or had Whyzer Patro found her out?

I turned a fraction. "Guard them." I hoped Isabelia knew I meant the king and queen but couldn't explain more in front of our assailants.

A haze of pink color blurred in response, a sign of Isabelia speeding to follow my command. More men crept out from the secret passage system that connected to the palace, but I dared not take my focus too long off Gema. I had to trust the fellows to handle part of the fight.

Cristobal's skin illuminated his forearms and the nape of his neck. Ezer's skin flicked to life beneath his ratty shirt, showing off a dull light slowly brightening to what once had been radiant. They could both take control of an adversary's whole body.

The bulking figure grunted. His eyes widened.

Did they individually stop our attackers, or had they mastered the ability to blanket their gifting like Mamá's husband had taught them? I prayed for the latter.

Gema slipped from beneath her assailant's grip, answering my question. No, they were still pinpointing their targets, which took much more mental clarity to perform.

An arrow unleashed from somewhere to our left, and a pained look crumpled Gema's face. She collapsed a step away.

A band of five men rushed at us from the darkened cave to our left and two more emerged from behind the giant's stiff figure. Cristobal raced ahead with arms raised and powers flashing on his fingertips. Ezer joined the fray.

I dove for Gema. A long arrow stuck out of her chest just under her right collarbone.

"Go"—Gema inhaled—"help them."

Ezer and Cristobal now had swords in their grasp. Cristobal swung his sword, and his adversaries fell. I winced. So much death and destruction.

"Cottia!" Gema shrieked. The giant, who had held Gema earlier, lunged at us.

I reached into my boot and pulled out my trusty dagger.

The man stilled like a statue mid-reach and continued to fall with his previous momentum. From my crouched position, I whipped my dagger out and held it up as the man dropped atop Gema and me. The force knocked the air from my lungs, and the blade plunged deep into our adversary. I laid sprawled beneath his weight. Warmth slivered along my arm, and the man gurgled.

I pushed at his shoulder with all my might, but the giant was heavy.

Was he crushing Gema? What was the moisture on my arm? I wasn't willing to waste my energy when Gema surely needed healing.

Cristobal came into view. "Help me flip him off her."

Ezer joined Cristobal, and they heaved the man from atop us. Something cracked.

I filled my lungs and rolled from the ground. My dagger remained lodged in the giant's gut, and so did the wooden shaft of the arrow.

The stump of an arrow that remained in Gema's chest protruded at a different angle than before. Her wound gushed blood.

Without thinking, I yanked the arrow out from her chest and pressed my hands upon her wound. The energy in my chest tumbled along my arms and spread out through my fingertips. I prayed beneath my breath.

Please, Ancient One, heal her. The limp energy moved under my touch but not fast enough. Ezer clasped my shoulder, sharing his strength. A surge of power spilled into me and washed through my body.

The skin and sinew knit together more rapidly.

Tears trailed my cheeks. "You can't die."

The memory of a little curly-haired girl with happy eyes and a friendly smile swam before my vision. We were twelve years old and both small for our age. She offered me a candy she'd stolen from our captor's pocket. "Want to be friends?" she asked, and then held out half of the caramel treat to me. I knew then that we'd be the best of friends.

Cristobal leaned over Ezer and touched his shoulder. *He won't share power, especially since Whyzer Patro warned us to never do such a thing* I recalled, yet more energy flooded through me.

Gema gasped as she awoke.

"Are you all right?" I asked.

"Take her to the cot," Ezer directed.

Cristobal poked at our adversary, saying something about old Carlitos and how he never thought he'd see the man fall. Ezer responded, but I was too caught up watching the rise and fall of Gema's chest to follow their conversation. She was alive. Her eyes blinked open, and the fellows spoke a heap of words, one crossing over the other. I wrapped Gema in a hug and lifted her to a sitting position.

"I've got a headache," she complained. "Whyzer Patro's people have been following me."

If I thought streams had flowed before, now rivers poured from my eyes as her hair poked my face.

A scream pierced the caves.

My sister's scream.

Hadn't Cristobal and Ezer handled our attackers? Yet in my heart of hearts, I knew Whyzer Patro had collected unscrupulous individuals with the most sought-after abilities.

Ezer and Cristobal darted off.

CHAPTER 61
COTTIA

"What's happening?" Gema asked.

I held her close with one protective arm around her and another hand extended outward in case an enemy slipped past us. Though I didn't have enough power to do any damage, I had to try something.

"NO! No, no," Ezer yelled. Anguish marked his voice.

"Can you stand?" I got to my feet and helped Gema up.

Ezer wailed. The sound ricocheted off the cave walls, making it difficult to discern where he was located.

We crossed through the main portion of the cave at Gema's pace, but I couldn't take it anymore.

"Isabelia, Cristobal, where are you?"

A blur of a person strode toward me, and Isabelia appeared with a hard crease chiseled between her eyebrows. "I tried, Cottia, believe me I tried. It wasn't my fault." She shook like palm leaves in a storm.

I grabbed her hand to stop her from quaking. "What happened?"

"They're dead."

"Who's dead?" Gema and I asked together.

"The king and queen and the invisiblist." She clasped and unclasped her bloodied hands like she wanted to wipe away the stains. "He was like me. He snuck past the fellows. I caught him after he sliced her. I tried. I promise I tried to save her, but it was too late."

My heart dropped to my toes. The edges of my vision grew fuzzy. They couldn't be dead so soon. They were stable, and we were going to get the antidote. I flew as quickly as my legs would take me to the cave room. Cristobal stood at the foot of the cot.

Ezer hunched over his mamá. Heart-suffocating cries of lament poured from him.

All that work to bring them here had been futile.

I crossed several arm spans. When the queen's face came into view, I couldn't breathe. Her neck had been slashed open.

A short man stretched along the other side of the cot with an even more gruesome neck wound.

Before I could process the scene, I lifted my skirt and raced to the other cave room. Isabelia and Gema stared at the king's dead body. A pool of blood dripped from his cot.

My stupid decision had killed them. Perhaps they would have had more time if they'd stayed in their chambers. Perhaps we'd led Whyzer Patro's men here. I dropped to my knees and sank my face into my hands. How could I ever face Ezer again?

I killed his parents.

Nothing I did would ever bring them back.

CHAPTER 62
GEMA

Sleep came despite the shifty canvas beneath my side and the dead queen, king, and assassins in the cove across from us. My entire body ached from letting out the combustible explosion that had erupted when my attackers had first pounced on me. Add the arrow puncturing my chest, a giant scoundrel smothering me, and the bump on my head from hitting the cave floor, and I had the perfect recipe for exhaustion.

When my eyes blinked open, I wanted to clamp my eyelids shut. The living nightmare was worse than tossing and turning until I drifted to sleep again.

"Gema, are you awake?" Cottia asked.

I lifted the thin cover over my head but thought better of faking sleep. Cottia had saved my life. She'd also broken down weeping so badly that Cristobal had lifted her into a cot before someone tripped over her body.

"What time is it?" I dropped the covers from my face, giving in to my friend who needed me.

"It's half past noon." She wore a clean, rouge dress and had her hair pulled back to the nape of her neck. When did this girl sleep?

"Where are the others?" I pushed up to a sitting position. All the cots around us were empty. Across from me, the pool of the king's blood had been cleaned. Didn't these people need rest?

Cottia folded the clothes in our shared trunk as if our handful of frocks and towels needed to be reorganized. "Ezer went down the far exit away from the palace, and Cristobal went to check the palace side. They're making sure no one else sneaked into the caves. Isabelia has been cleaning all morning." Cottia's swollen eyes stared at nothing particular as she spoke.

This wasn't my friend. My friend wouldn't become a husk at witnessing death. She'd fight or claw her way back to normalcy.

"What are you going to do?" I stretched my neck to the one side and then to the other.

"I don't know what we can do. Prince Ulyses hasn't returned. You haven't shared what happened with King Rodulfo, and we don't know when a decision will be made about the regent."

"Stop talking like that." I twisted my legs off the side of the cot, wishing I could clap to life a piece of bread or anything to eat.

Think, Gema, think. The only thing I had to say might be harsh, but for Cottia, she, out of all of us, had to move on for the sake of a mission.

Cottia twisted her nose up at me. "Stop talking like what? Like I just murdered three people because I decided to be reckless?"

"Three? Don't you dare count the man who fell on your dagger. He tried to kill us." I took hold of her shoulders and flames licked my eyelashes. Yes, my flames had returned. "If you hadn't moved the king and queen, they would have been poisoned again today and would have died soon anyway. They didn't have a chance."

Hot blobs of emotion dripped along her nose. I grasped for an idea of how to continue with our plan. Juan had said to get the soldiers involved.

"Do you know how to reach Yurde?" I asked.

"Ezer's body double?" Cottia wrinkled her nose, showing some sign of personality—always a good thing.

"Yes, the man we've been buying information from. We're going to need some muscle when we march into the assembly." I tipped her chin up and stood. "You can cry all you like, but save it for after we kick Whyzer Patro's puppet off Ezer's throne."

She got to her feet and wiped her cheeks. "I can never make up for everything I've done to Ezer." Her fingers dug into one of my crisp crème gowns, reminding me that I should get out of the blood-encrusted one.

I snatched the dress from her grip. "You haven't done anything to him that he didn't choose for himself."

"That's not true." Cottia got to her feet, putting her hands on her hips and accentuating her thin frame. "Ezer would have been happier without me. He also would have had a wife by now—and his parents."

"Stop with the what-ifs." I ripped off my gross dress and slipped into the clean one. The bloody one lay in a rusty-red heap with frayed edges poking in every direction like a memorial to one of the worst days of my life.

Cottia retrieved the bundle and stretched on the fabric, examining the hole as if it were fixable. Why couldn't she just rip the thing to shreds and use it to make rags?

I worked my fingers through my hair, undoing the leather cord at the bottom and working the knots from my curls. Then I braided it down my back and rewrapped the leather at the end.

She dipped the dress in a washbasin.

Seriously, Cottia, you are being ridiculous, I thought, but I kept my exasperation from my lips and tried to pivot to a hopeful subject.

"Juan invited me to work in the palace of Pedroz." I slipped on a boot. "Come with me. We can start a new life and forget about all of our mistakes." I swallowed hard, leaving out the part about him kissing me and wanting to get to know me. The idea of leaving Giddel for a beau was even too wild for me.

"So, what's your plan?" The calm and calculated Cottia returned within a snap.

I jammed my foot into the next boot, feeling her response as a win. "First, we get breakfast."

She flashed me a deadpan stare that refused to give in to my stomach's needs.

"Fine. I get it. No time for food. Either way, we've got to get the military back to Ezer. Even the impostor is helpless without loyal subjects."

Cottia stretched out the stained fabric and set it on the edge of a cot. "Let's do it. Let's find Yurde."

I marched out of our new sleeping room which had been Cristobal's for the past month. We'd been installed in it after the dead were put into the ladies' cave room since the majority of the dead were already in it. The wooden door across the passage in the rocky wall now stared at us like a tomb face.

The main part of the cave remained all empty paths and one giant cavern with a boulder in the middle. The emptiness meant we'd have to leave without Isabelia and the fellows. I grunted with frustration. We didn't even have a week to put Ezer on the throne. I'd slept half the day already, losing precious time. For all we knew, the impostor could have been named regent, taking his father's place. Ezer had to forget his mourning for a day and make an appearance.

The telltale sound of boots scuffing stone echoed from afar.

"Someone's coming," I whispered over my shoulder.

Cottia sidled up.

Cristobal returned through the darkness with skin alight. He stopped in front of me and reached for Cottia's hand. She pulled away, leaving an awkward silence between them.

I spun him around to shake him from this sentimental state. "When Ezer comes back, make him ready for the meeting hall. He must be ready for an uprising."

"Yes, señorita." He saluted me in mock deference.

I pinched his shoulder. "None of that attitude, Señor Cristobal. You are going to get your revenge."

Cottia pulled my wrist. "No, we're out to make things right. Judgment is for the Ancient One to decide. Where's Isabelia?"

Cristobal adjusted his new doublet which I hadn't seen before. "She went off behind Ezer. She was worried about him."

"Well, when they get back, tell them we're at the garrison," I said.

Cottia tramped to the cave exit with the catlike gait she used when she meant business.

"Remember, get Ezer to the Assembly. We're gathering those who will back the true prince."

"Are you coming?" Cottia shouted from the other side of our cavern.

"She's back." Cristobal waggled his eyebrows in pleasure.

"I told you I could get the fight back in her." I winked at Cristobal.

"We'll see about that."

The cavern doorway clicked and scraped open. Cottia marched to the open-air side with hands on hips and impatience set in the stern angles of her face.

"Just get Ezer into the palace and let me worry about my friend."

He laced his fingers together and placed them over his head, unconvinced about our barely conceived plans. I'd told him about Juan and how our time had run thin last night. Our best chance to expose the fake prince was to have a royal audience who was not under the impostor's authority.

I jogged to catch up to Cottia and called out to Cristobal, "Either way, the impostor dies or we die. We can't wait any longer."

CHAPTER 63
COTTIA

Weariness tugged on each stride forward through the gardens. Deep sorrow wove its way throughout my entire body and didn't let me rest. We might be crossing palace grounds to the garrison to where the guards stayed, but I was calculating how to face Ezer again.

I'd failed him. I'd failed the Ancient One by killing three people in one fell swoop. *Perhaps starting afresh by embarking to Pedroz isn't so ludicrous.*

Gema called me over to a path and linked arms with me when I got to her side. She pitched her voice low. "It's midday. We might fit in better if we simply walk in."

"What of Whyzer Patro's people?"

"Our old master didn't send an army into the palace." Gema cocked her shoulders back at the sight of several guards exiting the garrison up ahead. "The impostor doesn't know how his plans turned out last night."

"He has to suspect something." I spoke through my teeth. "His people didn't return."

Several guards passed around us, but none of the faces were Yurde's. Though I didn't know if the schedule for the guards had changed much in the last few days, I suspected that Ezer's personal guard still had night duties and would be sleeping. The fake prince was wise to keep Yurde away from himself.

Gema looked over her shoulder and then trained her focus ahead, "They're gone. We've got only today to get Ezer some muscle. Thankfully, the impostor is missing many of his lackeys."

"Do you think they'll believe us?" I stopped at the entrance with the simple sandstone exterior chiseled to appear as a force in itself. The three-story building stretched across the barrier of the palace for a few stone's throws. I'd been here only with Ezer and mostly to watch him train with the guards. His personal visits must have given him some favor with his people.

Gema patted my bicep. "You should probably wipe that tear."

I rubbed my eyes. Emotion needed to wait until all was made right. "Come on."

We marched into the building.

"Excuse me." A male voice interrupted our trajectory. "Señorita Cottia."

My attention snapped to my right.

A tall man with a dimpled chin and curled mustache exited a small room. "You aren't sanctioned to be here. Prince Ezer has given us specific orders."

Gema and I exchanged a look, and we sprinted deeper into the building.

Dimple Chin swore.

But a zap of energy raced through me and stopped my forward motion. I willed my legs to move, but they remained still despite my best efforts. My head wouldn't turn.

"Señorita Cottia"—Dimple Chin marched in front of us with glowing fingers stretched toward us—"I was given specific instructions not to let you in and to put you in the keep if you resisted." He diminished his hold over us, but not enough for me to make any quick movements.

"Let me speak to Yurde." My words came out slurred from lazy lips still under his power's influence.

The man's dark eyes flashed, and a wicked grin cracked his face. "No, but I'll get a handsome reward for catching you."

Gema belted a furious scream. "You good for noth—"

The man's energy flowed through us once again. Like statues, we stood in the middle of a corridor, unable to shift our eyeballs a fraction. We had only a few more options.

I sparked my gift, and it trudged from its spot in my chest and crawled at a snail's pace down my arms.

The man lifted Gema and dropped her. He swore again. "She burnt my hand. Pedro," Dimple Chin called to the front guard's room at the entrance.

"Coming," a raspy voice called back. Footfalls approached. "You caught her."

"Help me carry them."

"Do I get a piece of the prize?"

"I get two parts, and you get one."

"Not if you want me to carry the girl."

Dimple Chin crossed in front of me and gave his comrade a nod.

Heat licked the side of my body, but I couldn't see what was happening. The heat grew farther until only an achy cold remained. The man hoisted me by my waist and tossed me over his shoulder.

He descended the stairs, and I continued the slow push along my arms. I should have slept more. Sleeping always charged my abilities beyond any other strategy. By the time my powers reached my fingertips, daylight had vanished, and the dim glow of firelight remained before my vision. Metal poles lined my peripheral with Gema in flames behind them.

Reaching with my gift, tentacles of power slid within Dimple Chin's veins in his chest. The pump of his heart pounded a little harder than a healthy man's.

Raspy Voice said, "That one's a feisty one." He continued up the stairs, giving me an unfortunate view of the backside of a thin man in a green uniform.

I had to make this quick but give myself a fighting chance of not being dropped on my head. My powers slithered along a line and constricted circulation slightly. A hinge shrieked, but I chose to remain focused. Dimple Chin hunched to drop me when I squeezed for dear life.

He gasped, but I didn't relent. My muscle movement returned. He let go of his grip on me, yet his body leaned against mine. The contact between us gave me greater strength on my hold. His mouth gaped open and let out a small grunt. I released my hold. He fell over, still breathing but unconscious.

I tore the hem of my dress and gagged him for when he awoke. An empty dark cell encircled us, so I patted his waist and was rewarded with a jingle of metal. I made quick work of unclasping the key ring from the chain at his waist. I dragged him to manacles chained to the wall, but they required a key.

Ancient One, what should I do?

Gema hissed at me. "Just get out of there."

With the keys in hand, I slammed the jail door shut. The metal clang was too loud, but only Gema watched me in this small holding section. There were six cells and a metal door to who knew what else.

"Give me the keys and go," Gema commanded.

"I can't leave you here." I lifted the dozen keys to the lock.

She snatched the ring through the iron bars. "You're sweet, but go before I forbid you from having a churro again."

Hesitation marked my steps.

"And this time, don't leave that Pedro scoundrel alive." Gema fitted a key in her lock, but it didn't turn.

I crept up the stairs, achy from the energy I'd exerted yesterday and even now. Sunlight shifted on the stone walls the closer I got to the main floor. I peeked my head out the doorway to find the backside of a thin soldier two arm spans away. I assumed he was Raspy Voice.

He rubbed his hands together while staring out the front door over the palace gardens. Deeper in the corridor, the building was drenched with sunlight from an open-air courtyard.

This was my one chance. I tiptoed along the wall, making sure not to drop the heel of my boot.

A scuttling noise sounded to his right. Raspy Voice reached out to the side of him, touching thin air, and stared at his fingers. Was he suspicious someone unseen had arrived? Either way, he hadn't seen me yet.

I moved faster, but he snapped his gaze over his shoulder, meeting my eye. I twisted to run. A hand caught my wrist, but it wasn't a guard.

It was my sister. "Hurry."

CHAPTER 64
GEMA

"Sweet churro goodness, get me out of here!" I plunged the next key into the keyhole and turned. The glorious sound of a click met my ears after so many failed key attempts. I pulled the metal door open.

Stairs beckoned me with light reflected off the top steps.

"Help me," a diminutive voice said.

The first fellow who had captured us groaned. Cottia had used her Ancient One card again. She had refused to murder for over three months now which would have been charming if it weren't for the fact that these men wanted to turn us in to the fake prince.

The impostor must know something is amiss if there's a bounty on us today.

"Please, help me," the small voice said again, and it wasn't the guard who spoke.

I tiptoed deeper into the keep and further from freedom. A chill spread over my skin which I couldn't abide. The tingle of fire burned beneath my skin, and I ignited the flames along my arms. It allowed the back corners of cells to reveal their secrets. Half-dead prisoners slunk in the corner.

Compassion burrowed its way through me, despite knowing that most of these prisoners might be criminals.

"Over here, Gema. I know you." The voice had to be a woman's. It was clearer. The jangle of chains shook somewhere farther ahead.

If she doesn't appear in two arm spans, I'm running out of here.

But when I peered over my left shoulder, a woman in manacles and a tight bun at the nape of her neck stared back at me.

It took a second for recognition to process through my mind. Señora Myla. I gasped. "No! How long have you been here?"

She sighed. "If you have the keys, release me now. We chat over coffee later and talk about the last couple of weeks."

My jaw dropped at her being alive and still full of the dagger-sharp attitude that remained intact.

"Tell me you have some intelligence in that skull of yours." Señora Myla's insults this whole time had come from the impostor and not the real lady. "Toss the keys and tell me you have a better plan than to just stand there."

So, I reached into the bars and tossed the keys at her. The metal clinked just beside her bare feet, and it occurred to me that the servants all respected Señora Myla. She could testify about the fake prince being a farce.

"Promise me you'll go to the staff and the majordomo and tell them your story." Desperation fueled the flames even more. "They'll believe you. The impostor was pretending to be you, and he poisoned the king and queen."

Señora Myla stuck several of the smaller keys into the manacle in quick succession until one responded and released its hold. "I'll help where I can. Now, can you tap down your flame before you roast my skin?"

I backed away, but kept a small fire in my palm to help her see the keys she was flipping through so she might release the main cell lock quicker. It only took her five tries before the door swung open—much better than me.

She ran toward the stairs, and I followed behind her. For such a frail looking thing, she maintained a rather brisk pace.

I overtook her on the stairs and froze at seeing a thin guard race past the doorway.

My blood grew hot. I crept up a couple more steps then paused and reached down into my boot to meet the hard edge of my dagger. The thoughtless guards hadn't removed my weapon. I wrapped my fingers around the soft leather of the hilt and kept it at my side, ready for the fellow to attack.

Señora Myla crept closer and whispered, "All clear?"

"Let me check." After a few seconds, I hopped out into the main corridor and turned right for the courtyard. Voices drifted from behind me.

"Where's Pedro?"

"Tell the commander. He's been leaving his post lately."

I slipped my dagger beneath the top layer of sleeve, leaving it resting over my underdress on my forearm.

"Señorita, are you in search of a strapping fellow?" A cocky guy with a chiseled jaw and somewhat pleasant features approached. He reminded me of a half-dozen bounty hunters who showed up at Castillo Patro with heads bigger than their good senses.

"Why hello there." I twirled a curl that had fallen from its braid. "I haven't seen a . . . friend lately, and he'd promised to meet me sometime in the rose garden."

The suggestive glances between the brash guard and his three giggling sidekicks almost had me vomiting in my mouth. Every servant and guard knew that an invitation to the rose garden meant something of a romantic nature.

I glanced at the garrison doorway. The faint echo of a groan met my ears. "Come along. Take me to him." I slid my arm through Smug Guard's.

He tensed with a chuckle. "Who are we looking for?"

Señora Myla slipped out of the stairwell and fled with only the lightest footfall meeting my ears.

I coughed to distract the guards.

"Do you need a drink of water?" Smug fellow snapped his fingers at his friends. "Give the señorita your canteen."

"I hear something coming from below," one of the sidekicks said. When he spun his head, he just missed Señora Myla exiting the garrison doorway.

Tugging Smug Guard deeper into the courtyard, I pressed the sleeve with the dagger to my stomach. "His name is Yurde."

"You go ahead. We'll meet you later," another sidekick shouted from behind us.

Smug Guard's carefree demeanor shed in an instant. "He's been confined in his room for days. I don't think—"

"Then you know where he is." I yanked at his arm, dragging him to the stairs on the other side of the courtyard.

We went up a level.

"Which is his room?" I asked.

Smug Guard's eyes now rounded into two dark orbs set into a haunted expression. "This isn't a good idea."

"Why?" I snapped at him. "Is it because you're not as brave as Yurde? Is Yurde being held in his room for a reason?"

Shouts came from below. Two of the sidekicks came out to the courtyard on the floor level and pointed at us. In the shadows, the man Cottia had knocked out was held aloft by another guard.

I flipped my dagger, ripping my dress sleeve, and held it to Smug Guard's side at the perfect angle to thrust into his heart. "You and I both know there is something wrong with Yurde being held. I don't want to hurt you."

A commotion on the floor above stirred. Heat raced along my arms and down my legs. It wasn't as powerful as the day before, but it would do damage.

"He's up there to the left." Smug Guard pointed to a room in the corner. "There's a staircase ahead."

A rumble of footfalls pounded the steps behind us. I darted without the guard. Flames licked my fingertips, ready to explode when necessary.

CHAPTER 65
COTTIA

Isabelia and I blinked into view on the third floor. Across the courtyard, our pursuer broke into a sprint to make his way around to us.

"I'm sorry, I'm too tired." Isabelia panted from our aimless run.

My gifting tingled in my chest but responded slower than a flower shifting to follow the sun. To make matters worse, we hadn't a clue where to find Yurde.

Flames streaked my peripheral, and Gema came racing from my left.

If we could just get to her . . . I couldn't finish that thought.

We weren't about to outrun the guards or come out of this unscathed. But we sprinted toward Gema anyway.

"He's here. He's here." Gema sped toward a corner door and slammed her fist against it. Guards chased her from the floor below.

Our pursuer turned the corner and was now in the same passageway as us. Isabelia and I joined Gema.

Why wasn't the door opening? What if Gema didn't know where Yurde was and this was a random room? Fear swam in my stomach.

"Yurde," I screamed.

The door cracked open and Isabelia, Gema, and I pushed our way into the narrow space with bunkbeds along the side and small trunks pressed against the wall.

"Close the door." Gema knocked into Yurde's side.

He hissed between his teeth and shook off his hand like he was burnt.

Isabelia aimed for the single window at the back of the room like that was an escape option—then again, perhaps it was our only possibility.

Gema slid a small latch on the door that wouldn't do a thing to stop the men from entering, but at this point, five minutes of relative peace might be exactly what we needed.

"Yurde." I yanked on his sleeve to get his attention. "We need you, and we need your influence. Ezer's going to approach the Kings Assembly today and he requires soldiers to back his claim. You know that man in there is a phony, so stop dawdling and gather those who will stand up for the truth."

The man rolled his shoulders back, his build a near match of Ezer's before his stay in prison. Yurde's mouth was wider than Ezer's, and his eyes had a golden touch like Ezer's, but lacked the spark that made the prince breathtaking. "Señorita, I'm not sure it will matter what I say."

Emotion swelled at the back of my throat, though Gema was right about needing to push past the feelings.

"Grow a backbone and try." I firmed my bottom lip to convey confidence. "Would you prefer taking orders from the evil man backing the fake monarch who will have no love for those close to the real prince? He will certainly have you executed."

The door rattled behind Yurde.

"You know they're going to break through in a minute." Yurde scratched at his stubbled chin.

Gema had her hands on her hips. "Can you help us or not?"

Yurde blew between his lips—never a good sign. "I haven't been able to leave this room all morning. I've already told the commanders that I think we have a usurper. The commander thinks Prince Ulyses is vying for the throne."

"He'd never!" Gema's offended tone bled with her love for Ulyses. Something must have happened for her to consider leaving him.

"Well, that's what everyone thinks." Yurde smoothed a hand over his hair at the next door rattle. "There's nothing I can do. The Ezer in the palace somehow knew the safe word."

A quiet filled the room at that knowledge. Every royal protected themselves from people with powers of disguise by enacting wards and keeping confidential safe words.

"Is there a way out of here?" Isabelia looked out the single window. "Guards are running into the building."

The quiet outside the door unnerved me.

"Do you have a rope?" I asked.

He shook his head.

"Fine, we climb." I threw the window open and tied up my skirts. If there was anything I knew, it was that we wouldn't be allowed to leave this building through the door.

"Are you insane?" Yurde slapped a hand to his face.

I double-checked my knots and helped Isabelia gird her skirt. Part of my dress puffed over my hips. "Do you prefer I be tortured or left in a cell to rot away?"

Gema sliced at her overdress with her dagger. I clicked my tongue, and Gema tossed the dagger at me. I chopped off the offending part of the dress.

"What's the plan?" Yurde's tone was deflated.

"Find the king's assembly and stand up for what's right." I leaned out the window. No new soldiers entered the building, which left the front perfect for our escape. I positioned myself on a ledge on the exterior of the building and shimmied across the narrow surface.

All my time climbing, hiding, and escaping as an assassin had taught me a few things about getting away.

Isabelia followed, and then Gema. They tracked every step I took. The focus required to climb had left me deaf to what transpired above. Once I touched the first floor, I leapt from the wall.

I craned my neck up to watch Gema and Isabelia slide their feet along the same path I'd taken. Would Yurde do what was right?

A body came flying out of the third-floor window. The sickening thud that resulted brought tears to my eyes. I risked a glance.

The unnatural position of Yurde's body confirmed that I hadn't a chance of saving him. I blinked back the tears.

Isabelia leapt from a couple of arm spans up, landed, and grunted.

Gema followed soon afterwards and popped up from the ground, ready to run. But Isabelia grimaced as she put weight on her right foot.

"Share your gift, Gema."

I dove to Isabelia's side.

A hot hand gripped my arm and Isabelia's power blanketed over us.

Isabelia remained on the grass, holding her ankle with a pinched expression. "I don't think it's broken."

"Can you walk?" I asked.

Gema inhaled slowly and exhaled through her mouth. Sharing her gift required controlling the flames so she wouldn't burn us or explode.

Isabelia got to her feet and winced as she stepped.

"We'll prop her up." I wiggled out of Gema's hot grasp and traced my hand along Isabelia's back to her arm so I wouldn't lose contact and invisibility.

I pulled Isabelia up, and we trudged to the wall to walk around the back of the building. Soldiers arrived, scouring the area as we continued to make our way.

The skinny guard, who had chased Isabelia and me, got close. We stilled to prevent any noise from jeopardizing our invisibility.

He sniffed the air with his bony nose and scanned the area behind the guard house. A stretch of grass lay between a tall wall and the garrison.

Gema's heat grazed my bare arm as she adjusted her hold on Isabelia. I bit my lip hard to keep from crying out.

"Pedro, come on! We'll keep watch at the palace," a man commanded from behind us.

Our pursuer flinched. "They're here, I tell you. I can smell the sea and salt from their skin."

A breeze whipped around us, catching our wayward hair, poking my eyes and cheeks, but I didn't dare move.

"Fine, stick it out, old man. They're probably long gone." The commanding man's footfalls fled, but our pursuer remained nearby.

If something didn't change soon, we'd be literal torches from Gema's heat or caught and imprisoned.

CHAPTER 66
GEMA

THE STING OF FLAMES threatened to burst from my skin. I tried to control it so I could share my power with Isabelia. Yet, even with all my settling breaths, Cottia pulled away from my touch and Isabelia winced.

I tugged them along the back of the garrison, but Isabelia struggled to put any pressure on her ankle. The stone building to our right was long, and Pedro continued to trail us despite our invisibility and careful movements. Whatever reward he'd been offered by the fake prince must have been good.

We could no longer go about among the grounds acting like welcome guests after killing Whyzer Patro's scum. They must have been following us and knew we were hiding Ezer.

A twig cracked behind us, and I stopped. Isabelia smashed her lips together like she was holding back a cry. Cottia, as usual, looked ever the regal queen-to-be. I reached into my boot and grabbed for my dagger. Cottia was going to hate this, but I couldn't keep my flames under control all the way to the palace, through the doors, and to the meeting hall. We had to make it to the Agata Kings' Assembly to expose the impostor even if our original plan had failed.

"What are you doing?" Cottia asked.

I let go of Isabelia and leapt at our pursuer. Skin aflame, I held the dagger at his neck. "Back off!"

He grabbed my wrist, and I let flames rage. His hand jerked away, but he caught sight of Isabelia and Cottia. "You'll all end up like Yurde once the day is through. Traitors, the whole lot of you." He reached for his side.

"Don't move," I said.

He flung a dagger, and I dove at him with my own.

My body collided with his, rattling my bones so much that it sent my thoughts spinning.

We crashed to the ground.

Pain laced my arm with bruises on my elbow that would be sure to show tomorrow.

Tepid blood soaked beneath me—a sure sign that it wasn't my blood, but that of someone who didn't run the same ridiculous temperatures as a furnace. I pushed up to find my dagger lodged in the man's neck. I gasped and pulled it out. Why couldn't he have let us go? Was the prize worth dying over?

Cottia got to her knees and slapped her hands over the bloody wound. "Gema, help me." Her skin had a slight glow that showed she was trying to heal him.

I shook my head. "He tried to hurt us."

"Are you going to help or not?" Her savage tone broke something inside of me.

"Why should we save him? We're going to need your power if things don't go right in the palace."

"I'm not his judge." Cottia flung her words like daggers. "He was just following his impostor prince's orders. Now help me."

Though I loathed wasting our depleting energy, I touched her shoulder. The tug and pull of my gift flowed into her as I struggled to keep flames from bursting out of my skin. Pedro's skin wove together and smoothed beneath her touch. Tiny inhalations gurgled and grew wispier with each passing second.

She let go of the man, and I released her. My hand had burned through her dress and left her skin red.

The man on the ground, drenched in his own blood, lay still and breathing.

"He'll survive." Cottia nudged my side and jogged to her sister.

I got close to Cottia. "What was that about?"

Her giant orbs for eyes flicked a look at me as if to say something I couldn't quite understand.

"Why save someone like him?" I demanded.

She placed her arm around her sister's back, and I did the same. Isabelia wrapped her arms over our shoulders while we limped over the grass toward a forest area behind the stables. It was the last obstacle before we reached the palace and gave us some sense of being hidden, though we could still see the palace garden and some commotion at the palace.

We threw ourselves behind some bushes beside the stables and fell to the ground, catching our breath. Pedro hadn't continued to pursue us, but we didn't bother to stick around and find out if his near-death experience had changed his mind.

"I say we go through the front door." Cottia peeked around the stables.

"That's asking to get caught, but whatever you think is best." A little sass bled into my voice, which earned me one of Cottia's deadpan stares. "What? I tried to defend us, and you revived a man out for our heads. I'm not sure I know who you are these days."

Cottia muttered something under her breath.

I crossed my arms, now all too aware of my blood-stained and torn sleeves. "Why couldn't you have saved your energy and let him go? Saving him isn't going to bring back all the people you've killed before."

"Because he was just doing his job. And if the Ancient One could give someone like me a second chance, then maybe that guard should get one too."

Heat percolated through my blood. "That's funny, coming from someone who doesn't act like she's gotten a second chance. You go around trying to make up for every mistake you've ever made. You know that you didn't kill Ezer's parents. You tried to save them, and when Ezer is done mourning, he's going to tell you that."

She closed her eyes and sighed.

"Promise me one thing."

Her eyes slitted open.

"If you get a chance like that to put an end to Whyzer Patro, you'll do it." I pointed off past the trees to where we'd left the skinny guard on the grass.

She mulled it over for a minute, rubbing her too-perfect nose like she always did when she didn't think I'd like her answer.

"Promise me." My voice grew weak. She had to know that Whyzer Patro had had his chance to do what was right and had chosen to become his own god and our living nightmare.

"If it's the Ancient One's will." She trained her eyes on mine, daring me to challenge her. When steam fogged my vision, she continued to speak, "We should see about going to Pedroz and starting afresh. Didn't we always say that we'd be washing maids?"

Some of my anger dissipated at our old dream revived. Juan's proposal now had new possibilities, ones where I didn't have to watch Ulyses fall in love with some other señorita or leave my best friend behind.

"Can you all try healing my ankle?" Isabelia piped in from the ground. "Just enough for us to walk into the palace. It's doesn't have to be perfect."

Cottia and I shared a look that said we were still friends and both idiots for not healing her sooner. Of course, we'd been on the run, and the only one with some semblance of energy was me. Cottia got straight to work, and I placed my hand on her unburnt back to share the little I had to offer.

CHAPTER 67
COTTIA

UNDER THE SHADOW OF the Giddelian palace, Isabelia, Gema, and I held hands, waiting at the side doorways nearest the ballroom for someone to let us in. Several more Giddelian guards than usual stood at attention in their green livery, perhaps waiting for us to attempt to gain entry. The palace that had once seemed so decadent and austere now felt so familiar, almost like a home.

A diplomat from one of the outer kingdoms arrived at the front gate with an army of servants carrying trunks. We had a choice in that moment: should we wait for these side doors to open for us with the changing of the guard, or should we risk the front entryway that would be propped open shortly? Isabelia winked at me, which was the signal for us to follow her. The decision was made. Our little caravan crept alongside the palace and around the grand ballroom to the front entrance.

The moment the entourage of servants crossed our path, Isabelia tiptoed behind them. My hand held Isabelia's on one side and Gema's on the other as we snaked into the palace. Our invisible bodies snuck behind the diplomat with enormous sleeves and a pompous hat and into the main hall. A table had been set up in the center of the decadent space normally used for balls and announcements. Now, twenty-three seats lined the long rectangular table with the fake prince at the head.

In that instant, I wanted to reach into the Ezer impersonator and choke the very life out of him. *Forgive me, Ancient One.*

We didn't stop until we reached Rodulfo's servants, bedecked in light blue garments, and slid behind them, crouching to hide even in our invisibility. I readjusted my handhold with Gema, keeping contact but allowing myself some relief from her burning grip. This was it. This was finally the moment when King Rodulfo's and Prince Ulyses's word would fly or drown.

Though our plan to give Ezer a military advantage had failed, we had to trust that the Ancient One would answer our prayers. Where was Prince Ulyses? I craned my neck checking the main entrance, the terrace doors, and hidden entries, but all of them remained still.

A man with a peppered beard, a golden tunic, and an angular face stood. "Now that we are all here at our annual meeting, there is the matter of recognizing the regent of Giddel while the king is indisposed. The obvious successor is Prince Ezer to take his father's place. Is anyone in opposition?" He peered at the fellow kings and high lords. The quiet left me wanting to scream my opposition.

Gema shifted to stand, but I yanked her back down. She scrunched her nose and lips at me, expressing every bit of my sentiment.

King Rodulfo peeked over his shoulder. His startling blue eyes scanned our area as if searching the marble floors for something. Though Isabelia cloaked us from sight, people could still hear our every rustle and tap as if through a muffled veil. Rodulfo turned his attention away from us and toward the main entrance into the grand hall where the Giddelian servants seemed like a chattering mob—very unusual. Giddelian guards closed the massive doors.

Cristobal and Ezer had to come. This meeting would solidify Pascual's claim that he was the real Prince Ezer in front of all the leaders around the Agata Sea.

"Good." Pascual spoke in Ezer's deep cadence. "Then it is settled. I will be taking my father's place until he recovers from his illness."

The pepper-bearded man lifted a parchment. "As the first matter of business, we'll have you all sign and stamp our accord as stipulated by the—"

"I have an objection." King Rodulfo pushed his chair from the table. This was the first time I had seen him from this close. He couldn't have been much older than Ezer, but where Ezer had tan skin, dark eyes, and brown hair like a milkless cup of coffee, Rodulfo was all the opposite. He continued, "I have heard objections to the authenticity of the man before us being Prince Ezer and know that a prisoner escaped but a day ago claiming to be the true prince."

Murmurs and grunts circled the table. Kings whispered to their queens. Some eyes popped wide open while others maintained the steady expression of those already informed on the matter.

"This is outrageous." Pascual slapped his palms on the wooden table. "I've already proved myself to my countrymen."

"Then, you should have no problem recalling the code words to your guards." King Rodulfo flipped out his jacket and returned to his seat as if he'd won a battle.

A rush of heat pressed against my skin as Gema leaned close to my ear. "I'm losing control. We've got to go."

The pepper-bearded man gestured to a servant at the door. "Call the guard."

Only a moment passed before the commander of the guard appeared. We used the noise of the open door to stand. He wore a tall hat that would have been laughable in any other situation and a pressed green suit with a golden hibiscus stitched on the fabric of his jacket. He strode into the hall with decisive steps. We shuffled forward in a line across the grand expanse of marble floor. Within the time it took us to cross halfway to the door, the commander had positioned himself at the end of the table.

"Has the prince been able to state the code word to verify his identity?" Peppered Beard asked the guard.

"Yes, señor." The guard answered.

A smug grin overtook Pascual's stolen face in a way that even made my Ezer look disgusting.

The pepper-bearded man nodded as if about to dismiss the guard.

I flung my hand from Gema's and Isabelia grip, allowing the kings and queens of the land to see me in all my rugged glory. I rolled my shoulders back and stood erect like I'd seen Ezer's mother do so many times before. "Ask him for last year's code word."

Queens gasped. King Rodulfo's hand covered his mouth like he meant to hide his smile. A vein bulged along Pascual's temple with barely kept rage.

"Excuse me, who are you?" the pepper-bearded man asked.

"She's a wanted criminal." Pascual stood and pointed. "They all are. Arrest them."

How badly I wanted my gifting to spring from my fingertips and hold Pascual captive, but I didn't have that power. I prayed under my breath. *Please give me the right words because I have none.*

The guard marched over to me but yelped in pain before reaching my side.

I strengthened my voice. "I am a friend of the true prince, and I know that every season he is given a new code word. He should know a year's worth of code words without having to look up his records."

The pepper-haired man worked his chin.

King Rodulfo said, "It's a reasonable request."

The guard beside me hissed again. Gema held a dagger to his throat with one hand and gripped his arm with torchlit fingers, burning through his jacket.

"Gema," I reprimanded.

She spoke between gritted teeth. "If he stops fighting, I'll stop burning him."

A droplet of blood trickled down the commander's throat.

"Fine," Pepper-Beard said, "we'll accept the request if only the señoritas let go of the guard."

More Giddelian soldiers burst through the entrance.

"What is this?" Pascual shouted.

The marching continued as lines of soldiers encircled the table. Footfalls pounded on the floors, the noise echoing so loudly that I couldn't hear myself laugh. Rodulfo stood, craning his neck. I spun around to find an austere Ezer with sunken cheeks and deep purple beneath his beautiful eyes.

He furrowed his eyebrows at meeting my gaze and crossed the room toward me. Once he reached me, he pitched his voice low. "I thought you promised me you wouldn't do anything reckless." But his playful tone, so unfitting for the moment, reminded me why I loved him.

Prince Ulyses and Cristobal trailed Ezer.

King Rodulfo now started again. "Have this man"—he pointed to the Pascual—"say the code words."

Pascual shouted, "Are we to allow disorder in our halls? Guards, arrest these men."

Even with so many soldiers in one place, not one of them moved at his command.

"Recite the code words for the past year." Prince Ulyses stepped to Ezer's side.

"Who can remember them all?" Pascual snapped his fingers to call one of the curious servants who'd trailed into the room with the guards. "Fetch me my records."

Ezer recited a series of words faster than I could understand their meaning.

"Are those correct?" Pepper-Beard addressed the commander who Gema had detained.

"Yes, señor."

Prince Ulyses gestured to the guards beside him.

As the soldiers strode to restrain Pascual, the false prince shifted into the same face as a man restraining him, and Ezer threw up his hands. A force of sheer power whipped through the room. My legs and arms became unmovable.

Murmurs erupted.

"What's happening to me?"

"I can't move."

The entire hall became human statues before Ezer. This was as Mamá's husband had said, that we must learn to stretch our gift like a blanket rather than trying to control the finer details.

In that moment, witnessing King Rodulfo, Ezer, and the lines of soldiers, I felt so silly for trying to do this all on my own. I glanced at Cristobal who also held out his hands as Ezer walked over to Pascual. Power dissipated in the room and tingled through my sleepy limbs, but Pascual didn't move. Cristobal must have been holding the usurper.

Ezer bent low and said something to Pascual before turning to the rest of us watching him. From this distance across the massive table, I could see his erect posture and a tailored doublet fit for a king.

"Get the gallows ready." Ezer commanded. "Impersonating a king is treason against the crown. Señor, Cristobal will escort him along with the guards to make sure mistakes aren't made."

Cristobal strode to Ezer's side with fingers lit from his gifting in use. He would maintain control of Pascual's movements until the execution.

"Will you excuse me." Ezer marched around the king's and queen's table and aimed directly for me.

"We need to talk." Ezer gestured for me to go first.

My heart just about sprung out of my chest. Of all the things to settle in this moment, I couldn't be the most important task.

Soldiers exited in lines, tension gone from their stances. Gema and Isabelia gathered together, ripped dresses with blood stains and wild hair poking out of each of their updos. I must have the same appearance, and now, I'd have to face Ezer and all the kings and queens of the Agata sea region.

"Cottia," Ezer called me again. He held out his hand as if he wanted me to take it, but I couldn't. I had meant what I'd said to Gema about starting a new life in Pedroz.

CHAPTER 68
COTTIA

EZER LED ME THROUGH the bustling main atrium where servants and guards flowed east and west, stomping and talking over the din.

A group of maids dropped into a curtsy, including a disheveled Señora Myla.

"So, Prince Ulyses was right? Señora Myla was right," the kitchen hand gasped.

The stern-faced cook grunted in response.

Another maid raced down the stairs. "The king and queen are still missing."

The majordomo approached Ezer and leaned close to him. With all the noise I caught but a few words. The older man pitched his voice higher. "What should I tell them?"

Ezer gazed at me and then back at the majordomo. "Gather everyone into the hall for an announcement."

The majordomo firmed his bottom lip and bowed in acquiescence.

"You may go. We can discuss things later." I blocked Ezer's way. "There's a lot to get done."

He shook his head and wove his fingers with mine. "No. This is most important."

We continued on to a parlor in the first corridor to the left. He leaned his head into the doorway, spying an empty space with windows overlooking Giddel and the sea docks. I continued to walk into the decadent space, now even more aware of the bloody, tattered skirt beneath my hands and the hairs that poked in every direction in my peripheral.

Ezer closed the door behind us and spun the lock. My boots echoed over the hardwood in the strange silence that vibrated within the four lavish walls. I patted my hair back and crossed in front of a mirror to find dark circles beneath my eyes that hadn't been there days ago.

"Why didn't you wait for me today?" Ezer asked.

Tears stung my eyes, and I rubbed them away. I had to tell him what I'd decided before he hurt me. My heart swelled in my chest, threatening to burst from its confines.

"Cottia, please look at me." Ezer touched one of my shoulders. "I'm sorry for getting upset at you about my parents." His voice cracked.

I closed my eyes, unable to meet his gaze. I'd killed them. They might have survived until today and the whole palace would have searched for the antidote to save them. I'd acted too rashly and would never be able to look Ezer in the face again.

Ezer spun me around. "Cottia, please speak to me. I would have been hung at the gallows today if it weren't for you." He slipped his warm hand down my cheek. "I wouldn't have gotten to see them one more time." His voice contained a warble like he was holding back a cry.

Yet I wouldn't be able to handle the guilt in my soul when I saw the pain I'd caused.

"My love, I don't blame you for all that happened." His voice contained a husky quality. "If I had to return back to the day I caught you pretending to be a courtier, I'd invite you to stay again. I'd also escort you to find your sister, and I'd be bolder to my parents about choosing you."

Dreaded tears flowed and dripped along my nose. I sniffed to keep the drainage from spilling down my face.

"Please, look at me." Ezer wiped my cheeks with his thumb, a trace of warmth lingering after his touch. "I beg you."

I allowed my eyes to slit open, but I cast my gaze downward. A blur of his body filled my vision.

"My feelings haven't changed. I love you and want you to be my wife." He dropped his hand and stepped back. "If you don't feel the same way, I will let you go. You're always invited to stay at the palace, but if that is too awkward, I can help you find a place here or in the country, wherever you like—"

"Stop." I touched my cheek with a trembling hand. How could he still declare his love for me after I'd ruined his life? I opened my mouth and snapped it back shut, unable to form the next statement without crying.

Ezer stood in front of me. His hazel eyes glistened with expectation. The hollows of his cheeks were still pronounced, and a cut I hadn't noticed from a distance ran along the side of his jaw. He smiled, one of those heartwarming ones that shifted all his features into the perfect place.

"I could never make up for everything that I've done." My voice warbled. "I'm scared you might resent me for it." Warm trails dripped off my chin with unrestrained emotion.

He closed in on me, swallowing me in a hug. "Why do you hold on to your past when the Ancient One forgives? You're not living your old life. You've given all that over to the Ancient One. You don't have to keep striving like that, trying to earn forgiveness."

And we both wept. So much had happened over the last several months. The Ancient One had freed me from the binds that had kept me a slave to Whyzer Patro. Ezer had asked me to be his chosen betrothed. I'd pushed him away, and he'd lost his identity and been imprisoned. I'd freed him but still clawed at every opportunity to fix the damage I'd done.

Someone knocked at the door. "Prince Ezer, a large gathering awaits you in the hall." The majordomo's voice called through the doorway. breaking us from our moment.

"I'll be out shortly. Have Prince Ulyses speak or King Rodulfo."

"They have, señor." The majordomo's muffled voice carried a pleading note. "Even a guard who says the señorita healed him from a mortal wound."

Ezer flicked a quizzical look at me. "Was that you?"

My heart rate ticked faster, and I nodded.

For a split second, we stood in each other's arms with eyes locked on one another. Would he ask more questions or believe me a fool like Gema for saving a pursuer?

Instead, Ezer visibly swallowed and said, "I love you. Would you do me the honor of being my queen?"

"Prince Ezer?" The majordomo knocked. "The crowd is growing restless."

Ezer pitched his voice louder. "We'll be right there."

The feel of being held in his arms and his lack of reproach stirred the greatest joy that even Gema's churros could never conjure. With Ezer, I'd been able to become a person who healed. Though my gifting had become a shadow of what it used to be, it didn't matter anymore when the Ancient One could turn a tide if He so chose.

"Yes, I want to live my life with you."

Ezer lifted me up and spun me around in his jubilation.

CHAPTER 69
GEMA

In my opinion, Prince Ulyses speaking in front of a crowd in his gold and black doublet with a newly trimmed beard and a sword at his waist had to be the most stunning sight I'd seen in my life. It beat drinking hot chocolate with a handsome stranger in the middle of the night. It beat eating churros with my best friend while laughing about our days.

Every person watched the prince explaining the circumstances that had proven the impostor was not Prince Ezer.

"But I thought there were wards and rules protecting the royal family," shouted a man in the crowd.

Murmurs ensued. How would Prince Ulyses explain Ezer's whirlwind romance with Cottia? Could he even explain the reckless oath that had allowed such a charade to take place?

Ulyses maintained his regal demeanor and said, "When Prince Ezer speaks, he will explain the circumstances and what transpired. I want you to be confident that we've done all we could to keep in line with the Ancient Script and to wield only the Ancient One's gifts. Thank you for your time and patience. King Rodulfo will speak again about the changes we've made to our alliance." He stepped off the podium.

Isabelia gnawed on her bottom lip and rocked on her toes. She could be Cottia's twin if it weren't for a few small differences. One being the birthmarks on her cheek and chin. Another being her softer edges, possibly due to youth or from a remnant of innocence that Cottia had lost while growing up in Castillo Patro.

A deep ache gnawed a hole through my chest which meant I needed a churro with chocolate to cope. King Rodulfo climbed the podium and scanned the crowd. His build and coloring reminded me of Juan, which was why Juan was his body double. But where the king had a pudgy nose and thin lips, Juan had the chiseled edges every señorita desired from a mate.

I searched the faces while the king spoke about who knew what. I didn't care much for political speeches since I had no control over the new rules. Where was Juan?

Last night, between his kiss and offer, I'd tasted my escape plan.

A commotion stirred at the door, but I couldn't see over the sea of courtiers, guards, servants, and townspeople.

King Rodulfo raised a hand. "Your prince." He clapped and scanned the crowd. For an electrifying second, our gazes met as if to confirm my next steps. But his attention drifted back to Prince Ezer, and he stepped off the podium to where I couldn't see what was happening. Bodies shuffled around like he was moving along the edges of the crowd toward the back of the hall.

The joys of being short.

"Who is that with Prince Ezer?" a señora asked with a snide tone.

I yanked at the puffy sleeve of the señora. "It's your new queen."

She twisted her painted red lips in an ugly snarl, but I didn't care. Prince Ezer climbed onto the podium, and so did Cottia.

The crowd erupted in applause and shouted questions.

Ezer held up his hands, silencing the masses. "We have an enemy in Giddel and abroad who would like nothing more than to usurp our giftings. I underestimated his power and the ways in which he would try to attain it. For that, I am sorry and have paid a great price."

A solemness settled over the listeners.

"With this, I bring you ill tidings. The usurper not only stole my face and throne, but he stole Lady Myla's face and poisoned the king and queen through her façade."

Gasps echoed up into the tall ceilings.

Ezer wiped his eyes and continued. "Here's all that transpired." He proceeded to explain the necessary details.

Isabelia yanked on my sleeve. I spun to see what she needed, but instead of Isabelia, Juan was there in a simple tunic and trousers. His blond hair kissed his temples in just the right way. Isabelia crossed in front of Juan to catch my attention, and she wriggled her eyebrows to make sure I knew that she knew how attractive Juan was.

Juan rubbed elbows with me. "Did you think about my offer last night?"

"I thought you forgot about it."

He lifted an eyebrow. "And what gave you that notion?"

"It was late, and my hot chocolate might have dulled your good senses."

He chuckled. "We leave tomorrow."

"Am I going to be a kitchen maid?" I held my breath, testing to make sure he understood that I wouldn't flee my comfortable circumstances to just be his conquest.

The people around us cried from whatever Ezer had been sharing. My eyes pricked from remembering the queen's and king's bodies after the attack.

Juan leaned closer. "Did you hear me?"

"I'm sorry. I was just remembering. What did you say?"

He pitched his voice low. "I got you a better position." A twinkle played in the blue of his eyes.

"Don't tease me."

"How would you like to be lady's maid to the queen?"

I smashed my lips together, unsure what to think.

"Then when the time comes, the king will bestow his favor on a señorita of your standing and offer his best guard in marriage—if I win your good opinion, that is. I know these things take time."

"We'll see about my good opinion in a few months." I flipped back a frizzy curl. "You'll have to earn it."

His lips curled up at the ends, and I giggled.

Reality finally struck like a bolt of lightning through my heart. Cottia wouldn't be coming with me to Pedroz anymore. Once all was settled, I'd have to talk with her and see where that left me.

CHAPTER 70
COTTIA

"DON'T GO." I SLAMMED the guest bedroom door behind me to find Gema holding a blue dress up to her body.

"It's the dresses Señora Myla found for me, isn't it? You want them?" Gema's tone had all the markings of sarcasm. She continued to model in front of the looking glass across the room.

"Stop joking." I traversed the two arm spans to a small desk and sat in the cushioned chair. "Before, we were going to travel together, and I have a bad feeling about this. You don't know Juan."

Gema folded the dress and shoved it into a sack. "I have to go. What's left for me here? There's you, but you're going to be busy with coronation stuff and being queen. I can't sit around pining after the king's brother."

"What happened between you two? You never said."

"He told me we couldn't be together and has made it very clear that he's not interested." She collapsed onto a trunk across from me and sunk her face into her hands.

The sight broke my heart. As a matter of principle, Gema didn't cry over boys. The sobs wracking her body proved she loved him, possibly like I loved Ezer.

"Even more reason to stay."

She lifted her head just enough to give me one of her fiery glares where a flame licked her eyeballs, and I lifted my hands in surrender. I couldn't argue when I hadn't a clue of Ulyses's sentiment and reasoning.

Instead, I took the spot beside her on the heavy trunk and patted her back. All night I'd tossed and turned, reliving the last two days in all the eerie quality of the moments. Though I'd thought the dead would come back to haunt me like they always had, I kept envisioning Gema's limp body on the cave floor. A pang had clenched my gut. If the dreams had stopped there, I wouldn't have come this morning to beg her to stay.

In some of the dreams, Gema had a baby in her arms, and in others, she kissed King Rodulfo and died at his feet. Though none of that had transpired, an unrelenting premonition that I couldn't explain crashed in waves over me.

"Why don't you stay until I get married?" I hedged, but beneath my touch she tensed.

"Cottia, I know this seems rash, but I can't stay." Gema snatched another gown on the bed and stormed to the mirror. The beautiful teal fabric and black lace proved lovelier against her red tones than the first. The stitching wove in curling patterns, giving it a refined appearance. It was much too fine for a simple servant.

"And what are you going to do with such attire in the kitchens?" I asked.

"Isn't Ezer mourning?" She waved a limp hand to the door. "You should go off with him."

"He'll be mourning for a while. You, my friend, are leaving today."

"Then you understand why I can't wait a month for mourning the sovereigns and a month for coronation and a month for your wedding. I might even return with King Rodulfo and the queen for the last one." She folded the beautiful dress over the bed and shoved it into her sack.

I swallowed the forceful words I wanted to lash out and tried a different tactic. "What position did Juan find for you in Pedroz?"

Gema's cold, green stare targeted me. "The queen's lady's maid."

"Aww, because positions like that are always readily available when the king's doppelgänger finds a pretty señorita." I got to my feet and walked to the door, ready for the two responses Gema might administer.

I turned the door handle, but she didn't stop me. I glanced over my shoulder, expecting her to be set aflame, but she cooly lifted a yellow gown and crossed in front of the looking glass.

The silky material held up to her body gave her a jovial appearance that matched her softer side. "Are you done conniving?"

Her question cut right through me. I grunted in frustration straight down the stairs and to the majordomo who commanded servants from the front atrium. Another servant scurried to him and darted away at his simple instruction. So much had to be done after the gathering the previous day and with all the royals readying to depart so quickly after the Agata Sea meeting. No other reunion could take place until the official mourning period had passed.

"Excuse me." I approached the majordomo who seemed to tower over me the closer I got. "Do you happen to know where Prince Ulyses or Prince Ezer is at the moment?"

"They're in the west parlor." He looked past me and shouted, "Where have you been? Go get King Miguel and Queen Irma's trunks."

I retreated down the dim front passage that contrasted with the sunny day outside the palace. An echo of guttural sobs drifted along the stone walls. Yet, I kept going into the parlor to find Ezer and Ulyses sitting in armchairs across from each other. Ulyses raked his fingers through his unruly hair.

Ezer had his full concentration on his brother. "And remember when Papá thought you were the one leaving rocks in his shoes?"

Ulyses slapped his knee, and Ezer cried or laughed—the sound could have been either. I tiptoed backwards out of the parlor, unable to beg for assistance to stop Gema from fleeing.

Ancient One, help. She's going to leave if no one intervenes. I prayed and prayed, wandering the passages until my soul settled from the storm within my skin. There was nothing to be done but allow what must transpire to occur.

Later that day, Ezer joined me on the docks to bid farewell to King Rodulfo.

But I remained several arm spans away in front of Gema who watched the brown trunk from her room being carried up the ramp into the lavish galleon.

"I see you are taking more than a couple dresses." I clutched at a shawl over my shoulders despite the savage heat pouring from the sun overhead. My fingers needed something to rub against and tear at while I watched my friend depart.

"They'll have to undergo a process before I wear them, but they're all so pretty, and Juan said it wasn't a problem if I brought a whole trunk with me." Gema crossed her arms like she was wearing a shield to guard from my attacks.

"Where is Juan?" I craned my neck toward the gold-trimmed galleon, much too ornate for my liking. Sailors raced around the deck and climbed the masts. "I have a word for him."

"He's already on board getting the king's rooms ready." Gema edged closer, blocking my view of the ship. "I'll see you in a few months. Promise you'll write to me. Correspondence gets sent between the kingdoms every week."

I pursed my lips, desperate for a last-ditch effort to hold her back. Tying her with ropes, causing her to faint, and begging didn't seem like the best plans. "What about Whyzer Patro? He's going to be out for revenge, and King Rodulfo might not put up wards against the whyzer—"

"Friend, Whyzer Patro infiltrated and almost gained sole control of the palace of Giddel. I don't think I'm in any more danger in Pedroz than here. A hug?" She wrapped her arms around me, giving a firm squeeze.

I couldn't return the favor or condone her fleeing. "You're an idiot." The words escaped my mouth before I thought better of them.

She pulled away, laughing. "It's come to that now? I'll miss you too."

Angry tears stung my eyes. My bottom lip quivered, but I couldn't find it in me to say goodbye.

Gema waved me a farewell and backed off until she had to turn around and stride up the ramp. All too soon, the galleon's ropes were undone and the ship floated away into the horizon. A blur of people and sailors stirred around me, but my feet remained fixed on the same spot of wood.

"Are you ready to go back to the palace?" Ezer bumped against my side.

I shook my head.

"It might do you some good to drink water or to eat supper." He blocked my view of the Agata Sea. "You can even write Gema your first letter."

"She's not coming back."

"No, but perhaps we should go into town and buy you a stamp and stationery."

"You don't have some in your palace?" I lifted my eyebrow.

"We do, but I don't think that proposition would get you off this dock." He shrugged in a boyish way that took years off the purple smudges beneath his eyes.

"Is that how it's going to be between us? Trickery and games?"

He smiled and kissed my forehead. His warmth awakened the joy that had died when Gema left. When he pulled away, he slipped his hand into mine. "I love you, Cottia Luzelena Jaime Pacheco, and I am not about to trick my queen unless it's during a game in my parlor."

I poked his side.

"All right, all right, you got me. I will only trick you during a game in my parlor if you're in the mood for some real competition." He tugged me along to the stairs, and I let my legs take me though my heart longed to wallow.

"That's much better. We can stop by a pastry shop to pick up churros and chocolate for old times' sake if you'd like."

We went up the stairs painted in the orange of the evening sun. Never had one stroll brought so much laughter and tears all wrapped into one beautiful moment.

EPILOGUE

COTTIA

FOUR YEARS HAD PASSED since I'd seen my best friend, and I couldn't stride fast enough out of the palace gates and to the docks along the shoreline road. Gema and I had been in touch through letters, but there was so much left unsaid and hidden between the lines on the page.

Ezer held our squirming two-year-old's hand. My little boy, Cosme, had pieces of both Ezer and me molded into his carefree smile and fiery stare.

I held a wiggly three-month-old Beatriz who had just discovered that the world was bigger than her family. Her head twisted around to spot where bells rang and horses snorted.

"Your Majesty, I can hold her for you," Señora Myla called from behind me. The woman was still trying to make up for her inability to protect the former queen by putting all her efforts into guarding the children.

"No, I'd like to hold her." I readjusted my grip, but Beatriz arched her back.

Señora Myla swooped in and took hold of Beatriz. "Señora Cottia, go see to your friend. Beatriz will be right here."

Ezer set Cosme over his shoulders. "Do you see the galleon, Cosme? The señora with the red hair is your mamá's dearest friend."

My heart pounded with overwhelming joy. I scanned the ship below to find Gema descending in a silky crème-colored dress that contrasted her pinned up curls.

I raced down the stone stairs, forgetting the queenly manner I tried to exude. Gema lifted her skirt and strode toward me; when we faced each other on the dock, we stopped short.

Gema somehow looked older. Was it the way she pinned her hair up and wore a mantilla flowing from the top of her head, or had her cheeks slimmed down? I couldn't tell.

"Forget decorum." She made the first move for a hug, and I squeezed her back.

Tears sprung to my eyelashes, and a thick well of emotions gathered at the back of my throat. I'd missed her so much. "You have to meet some people."

"Wait." Gema clung to me, keeping her mouth by my ear. "I have to tell you something."

I pulled away, feeling my eyebrows furrow. "What's wrong?"

She placed her hand over her stomach, and I knew.

"Congratu—"

"Shhh. Cottia, this is our secret." Her grave stare made the news seem much more ominous than the joy of a baby coming. "He doesn't know."

"Juan, your husband?"

A thin fog covered her gaze. "He's not who he says he is."

"What do you mean?"

Servants in red carried trunks onto the docks several arm spans behind us. King Rodulfo stepped off the ramp in a tunic lined with gold thread, his crown set over his golden hair, and a cocky smirk fitted in place as he watched Gema.

She lowered her chin in deference, but something more stirred in the air between them.

"King Rodulfo," Ezer shouted and marched up to the royal.

"A personal greeting on the dock and with the whole royal family? I am most honored." King Rodulfo patted Ezer's shoulder and Ezer returned the gesture.

The two kings went up the ramp that led to the palace grounds rather than the shoreline road. Myla carried Beatriz and turned in my direction. I waved her onward so she would follow the kings.

I flared my gifting and let a trickle of energy seep down my arms and into my fingertips. The powers vined into Gema's body which surged with a blood flow and a mixture of anxious energy.

Though sailors ran back and forth, I couldn't wait for the perfect place and moment for the answer to my question. "Why are you here?"

Gema blinked back steam and slid a mirthless smile over her lips. "Can we walk along the beach?"

I nodded, and we made our way up the ramp and hopped off the side onto the royal beach beside the palace. In silence, we continued under the perfect blue sky with the sun shining down like rain. Sand squished under my boots and water seeped between the seams, but I wouldn't stop until Gema was ready to share.

The moment the cliffs soared to our right she stopped and met my eye.

"Why are you here?" I asked again.

"Juan isn't the king's personal guard. He can't know about the baby."

"You didn't answer the question."

She sighed. "Can I stay here with you in Giddel?" A warble seeped into her voice. "I promise I didn't know for years. I assumed Juan was busy and working endless hours."

"What didn't you know?"

"She'll kill me if she finds out about the baby."

"Of course you can stay, but who?"

"The queen."

"Speak straight. I don't like all these hidden codes."

Gema pitched her voice low as if the sea might gossip about her secret. "Juan isn't real. I was tricked. This baby is an heir to the Pedrozian throne."

My heart sunk into my stomach. Our last conversation played through my mind with every insult and trepidation. None of it mattered any longer. *I warned you not to go* raced into my mind, but it would do nothing for Gema now.

I swept her in my arms and cried. "Our children will be the best of friends."

She wept with a chest-rattling shake. "I can stay in the caves. King Rodulfo will search for me."

"None of that." I squeezed her tight. "The Ancient One knows that we'll find a way."

ACKNOWLEDGEMENTS

I'd like to thank God for his provision while writing each part of this book. All the pieces were special in their own way and surprised me. *Ruthless* was the easiest to write. *Restless* was the most shocking for me. *Reckless* was a difficult write and was bittersweet. I knew how it must end, but I wanted something different to transpire all the same.

Thank you to my street team who have helped me get the word out for my books ever since my debut novel. I have to thank my editors Jessica Gwyn for her ability to see what I cannot and for her encouragement. Thank you, Sarah Everest and Claire Kohler, for smoothing out the rough patches. Charity, thank you for your eagle eyes.

Next, I'd like to thank my husband for his patience and encouragement through this writing process. I love you.

Thank you, Mom, for needing to see how the story ended.

Every author has author friends, and I have amazing author/writer friends. You keep me from quitting when I'm discouraged. Many of you are in my Christian Mommy Writers group.

Thank you to my amazing readers for your reviews, enthusiasm, and encouragement.

About the Author

CANDICE PEDRAZA YAMNITZ FELL in love with The Lord of the Rings and Pride and Prejudice in high school and hasn't stopped reading since. She taught in a dual-language elementary classroom for years until she decided to stay at home, teaching a crew of imaginative children. In between reading lessons and converting cardboard boxes into pirate ships, she writes YA novels with a Latin twist. She lives in her native Chicagoland.

Can you do me a favor? Your reviews make a huge difference in reaching more readers. Please leave your thoughts here:

If you enjoyed

ASSASSIN'S RISE

READ THE DAUGHTER'S STORY

AND A STEAMPUNK MURDER MYSTERY

www.ingramcontent.com/pod-product-compliance
Lightning Source LLC
Chambersburg PA
CBHW020237120726
47903CB00008B/2704